HAMMERHEAD

By the same author

Gunship
Lynx
Waterhole
Windshear

Julian Jay Savarin

HAMMERHEAD

St. Martin's Press
New York

Library of Congress Cataloging-in-Publication Data

Savarin, Julian Jay.
Hammerhead / by Julian Jay Savarin.
p.   cm.
ISBN 0-312-01770-7 : $16.95
I. Title.
PR6069.A937H3 1988
813—dc19   87-36706
CIP

First published in Great Britain by Martin Secker & Warburg Limited.

First U.S. Edition

10 9 8 7 6 5 4 3 2 1

CONTENTS

PROLOGUE

"I make it nine," Logan said, "two of them Europeans. Trouble, perhaps?"

She kept the binoculars fixed upon the tiny figures that moved along the thin slash of the trail on the far slope, thousands of feet below.

Lying on the harsh surface of the steep morainic incline, a metre or so away from her, Lal kept his own binoculars trained upon the slow-moving file, and did not answer immediately. In the clear air of the Himalayas, visibility was perfect on this particular day. There were clouds tufting among the far peaks; but where he and Logan lay at 12,000 feet, the sun beat warmly down, bouncing off the bleached boulders left by the passage of an ancient glacier. They were clad lightly, having left their heavier clothing in their tents 200 feet down in the high, narrow valley of the glacier's course.

At last Lal said, in Sandhurst-accented English, "I confirm nine bodies. Two Europeans and seven Chinese. Trouble."

"How do you know they're Chinese? We're twenty miles from the Tibetan border. They could be —"

"They walk differently," Lal interrupted; a rare occurrence. An ex-Ghurka officer, he had always been meticulously polite to Logan, and had scrupulously pitched his tent a short distance from hers throughout their three weeks in the mountains, as if to give not just Logan, but the tent itself, privacy.

She did not attempt to contradict him. His comment was based upon sound knowledge. That was the reason he'd been picked to accompany her in the first place. If Lal said that some of those

1

specks down there were Chinese, she was not about to argue the point with him.

As if to further confirm his observation, Lal went on, "They're not trekkers."

Logan decided she was not going to argue about that either. Trouble indeed. They had been watching the specks for an hour: at least.

She said, "Could they be after the same thing we are?"

Lal kept his eyes glued to the binoculars. He lay unmoving, as if spotting hits on a rifle range. If the jagged edges of the smaller chunks of debris left by the vanished ice mass caused him discomfort, he gave no indication.

"I think that most likely, ma'am," he replied in his correctly respectful voice. Logan was a superior officer as far as he was concerned, even if she seemed young enough to be his daughter.

"I was afraid you would," she said drily.

"Do we move on? Ah!" he continued sharply, before Logan could speak. "One of them has stopped and is sweeping in our direction. A European." He lowered the binoculars and flattened himself beneath the skyline.

"I saw him," Logan said. She had already done likewise.

Lal had turned his face towards her. A Gurung, his dark eyes studied her calmly. "I do not believe they have seen us, but they will come here eventually. They must search everywhere."

"How long before they make it to this ridge?" She hoped the distant person, who'd clearly been scrutinising their hiding-place through binoculars, had indeed not seen them. She had been warned to avoid contact at all costs.

As the crow flew, it was about five miles to the other slope, but the path was a good mile down and went on for several further miles before it crossed the valley. No track led to where they were.

Lal said, "Even if they knew we were here and could come directly across the valley, it would still take them a day. This is not a very steep slope, but it would be a climb through bad terrain. Some would not reach the top if they tried to do it too quickly. We could also pick off the remainder as they came closer. Going the long way round will take them many days."

"Allowing for variables, for how long would you suggest we continue to search in this area?"

"To avoid the possibility of a contact, we should remain no longer than four days."

2

"We'll make it three," Logan said, "and remove the possibility completely. I'm beginning to think we've drawn a blank here anyway. Still, let's see what the next few days bring us."

A large, dilapidated bag made of gunny lay next to her. Within it were the tools and spoils of her supposed profession. She was meant to be an alpine biologist, on the hunt for fossils. It was her cover, and in the firm belief that if you're going to tell a lie lace it with the truth, she had actually managed to find the remains of sea creatures that had lived on what had once been the seabed countless centuries before. Sharing the bag with her favourite weapon, a Ruger .357 magnum revolver, were three ammonites she'd painstakingly chipped from boulders and rock walls, during the time she'd been in the mountains.

"If anything goes wrong," she now said, "remember what we've agreed."

Lal looked unhappy. "I do not believe —"

"I don't want to make it an order."

Lal looked even more unhappy. "But Miss Logan, you should not ask me to run away."

"You won't be running away. One of us would have to warn London and as this is your neck of the woods, that makes you the right candidate. You know the villages, and the people. I think you'd agree," she went on drily, "it would be easier for you to melt into the background."

Lal was still unhappy, though he knew she was right. A Gurkha did not take kindly to turning away from combat; but this was more important than the possibility of doing battle.

He kept his thoughts to himself and nothing showed upon his face, though Logan could well appreciate what was going on in his mind.

She did not relish the idea of being caught on her own in this Himalayan wilderness, but London had to be informed.

She was about to say something when the sudden crunch of stone came sharply up from below and behind them. Neither reacted. It was as if the sound had never been, but their eyes were lively as they studied each other.

"Perhaps it's a wild yak," Lal suggested calmly.

"You don't believe that."

"No, Miss Logan. I do not."

"Another patrol, then. Perhaps one of many."

They had allowed themselves to be diverted by the distant group,

3

exactly as had — possibly — been planned. If so, the patrols could well have been studying their movements for days. Logan felt annoyed with herself. She continued to look at Lal, feeling a growing sense of frustration and anger. Imagine allowing herself to be caught out like that.

Lal said, "They fooled me too."

She smiled briefly at his attempt to make her feel better. "We'd better make our move before they get into position. Take the Ruger as arranged. Make it look as if we don't know they're down there."

Lal nodded, eyes showing how he hated to leave her alone and unarmed.

"We've no choice," she said.

He nodded once more and began rummaging in the gunny sack as if looking for an implement, while Logan busied herself with chipping away at a small boulder.

The Ruger moved surreptitiously from one sack to the other.

Lal said, "I've got it in with the rifle." In his own bag was a cut-down M16, with plenty of ammunition. "I hope to see you again soon, Miss Logan. If we're wrong and there *is* a yak below, I shall only be five minutes." He paused. "If we are right, I still hope to see you soon."

Then he was moving, without seeming to hasten; but in seconds, he had moved upwards and had disappeared over the edge. Soon she could no longer hear his movements. There were no shouts from below.

As she chipped away, Logan wondered if they had made a mistake about the noise after all. It was better to look foolish, she decided, than to be taken out here. She felt naked without the Ruger. She always did, and hoped Lal would be back soon; once he had checked out what had made the noise near the tents.

Forcing herself not to look back down the slope, she continued to work at the useless boulder.

Moments later, her worst fears were confirmed.

"Please stop what you are doing, and come down!" a voice called up commandingly. A European voice, with a Germanic edge to it.

Logan looked round and down suddenly, as if she had been startled. She remained where she was, perched uncertainly up the slope, giving a perfect impression of someone who was quickly becoming frightened. Fanned out by the tents were ten men — two Europeans and eight Chinese — who, though not attired in re-cognisable uniform, were dressed in a manner that was distinctly

4

military. Each held an AK-74 assault rifle across his body, ready for instant use.

Two hundred feet was hardly a range that would give them trouble. They would nail her long before she'd made it over the top.

Why hadn't they shot at Lal?

Playing her role, she called down querulously, "Who . . . who are you? What do you want?" She stared anxiously at them.

"My comrades are not noted for their patience," the one who had spoken said in a hard voice. "Please come down immediately. You would not like it if they came up for you. Bring your sack."

Deciding she had pushed it far enough, Logan complied, and began making her way down gingerly. When she reached the bottom, she stood irresolutely, regarding them with the wariness of a cornered but frightened animal. They all stared at her bare legs, but with expressions so devoid of lust she found that more disturbing. More than ever she wished she had not persuaded Lal to take the Ruger.

Not that it would have helped much, but she would have taken half their number with her. At least.

The frightened expression remained on her face. "Who are you?" she asked once more. "What do you want with me?"

The spokesman said, "Put on something more appropriate. You are going on a long walk. Leave your bag here. One of my comrades will be outside your tent. Hurry!"

"What about my guide? He's on the other —"

"We know where he is. He'll be attended to."

As if to confirm the words, there was a sudden burst of distant automatic fire. There was no answering burst.

Logan paused in horror. "You've killed him! You —"

"Move!" the man ordered harshly.

As she made for her tent, Logan felt a brief tightening in her stomach. She had seen the patrol leader before, somewhere a long way from here. She could only hope that he had not also recognised her.

It was the slimmest of chances; but it was the only one that might ensure her continuing survival.

5

BAIT

ONE

Cardiff Airport, Wales; four months earlier.

"She's here," Terry Webb said.

Pross had poked his head into the cockpit of the Jetranger. Now he straightened to look round at Webb. "The ADI seems alright to me. Who's 'she'?"

"That attitude indicator's on the blink," Webb said firmly.

A former RAF Chief Technician, he was an absolute martinet when it came to the servicing of aircraft. If something was on the blink, the chopper would be grounded. It was as simple as that; which was why Pross employed him in the first place. Terry Webb was responsible for keeping Prossair's two precious Jetrangers flying. If they flew safely, they made money. Customers had a habit of shying away if your aircraft tended to fall out of the sky.

"Alright," Pross said pacifyingly. "The ADI's on the blink."

"She's here," Webb repeated as if the matter of the ADI's serviceability had not been a subject for further discussion. A brief smirk had passed across features as square-cut as the rest of his body. His thinning grey hair looked as if it was still being cut by the same RAF barber. "*She* is the lady from Harrods."

Logan.

A mixture of emotions went through Pross. Webb always described Logan as the lady from Harrods, meaning she looked as if she bought her clothes there; expensively. But Logan was the most chameleon-like person Pross knew. She would look equally at home in attire that appeared to have come off the nearest backstreet barrow.

9

Logan was one of those people who would always be trouble for the discerning male. A tall young woman, there was more to her than the vacant sort of prettiness one could sometimes find on the pages of certain journals. Her attractiveness was startling in that it could sneak up on you when least expected. There was an air of strength about her, accentuated by the perfection of her shape. Naturally, as Pross now recalled with some amusement, she thought her body was all wrong: legs too big, bum too big, breasts too big. She was no emaciated clothes-horse; but she was no dumpling either. As far as Pross was concerned, everything about her looks was as it should be.

There were other qualities to Logan. There was an elfin air about her face that fooled you into thinking her vulnerable; an air that was helped considerably by her pale green eyes, and the strange pattern of freckles that curved from the corner of one eye, down one cheek to dot themselves across her face. They continued across the bridge of a nose that just stopped short of being too sharp and long. Their march went on until they again curved upwards, a mirror-image that ended at the corner of her other eye.

When she smiled, she could look like a mischievous child; when she spoke, it was with a soft voice with the barest hint of an Irish accent.

All these things, Pross knew, were effective aspects of her camouflage, for Logan was one of the deadliest killers he knew. Her favourite weapon, the .357 Ruger magnum, went everywhere with her. She even carried spare rounds in special garters fitted snugly about her upper thighs. He smiled as he remembered.

Looking at him, Webb said, "I don't know what you're looking so happy about. Every time she comes here, she brings trouble."

Which was certainly true. In Logan's wake, came Fowler and the Department; and in Fowler's wake, trouble inevitably followed.

For Pross.

"She's got her hooks into you," Webb continued, warming to his theme and refusing to let go. "She's grief, Boss."

"Give her a break, Terry. She's not that bad."

"Tell that to the marines, when you see them."

"You've been watching old American war movies again, Terry."

Pross glanced up at the swollen sky of the late November morning. The weather was not sure what it wanted to do. Brilliant early sunshine had given way to a threatening deluge. The Met Report had promised bright sunshine in the Lundy area. Great if you were going there.

Pross said, "Alright, Terry. Go to work on the ADI. Good thing Pete's away on a survey trip, otherwise how would we be able to afford our keep?"

Pete Dent, ex-Army chopper pilot, was, with David Pross, the full pilot complement of Prossair's two-ship fleet. Dent's position in the company was curious: more than an employee, but less than a partner. Pross liked it that way. Dent was an excellent pilot and worth paying well to keep out poachers.

Webb said, "My heart bleeds. We've almost got more work than we can handle."

Webb's words brought with them unwelcome thoughts that Pross had been trying to ignore ever since he'd been told of Logan's arrival. It wasn't Logan who had him hooked, but the Department. Its hooks were deep into Prossair. In the financially precarious world of commercial flying, Prossair was doing extremely well for such a tiny outfit. Some might even say inordinately so. In that, the Department's hand was writ large: for services rendered.

Pross was not certain how much Webb actually suspected. As if by unspoken agreement, neither had brought the subject up, except when once, Webb had professed a strong disinclination to know. In the true spirit of his personal air force maxim – treat volunteering with the greatest respect: never do it – he had chosen to remain aloof from Pross's "moonlighting".

"I suppose I'd better go and see what she wants."

"Send her packing," was what Webb said unrepentantly.

"You're all heart, Terry."

"That's what makes me so lovable. By the way, Cheryl's upstairs having a coffee. I suggested it. I thought you'd prefer the office to yourselves."

Cheryl Glyn was an RAF brat whose father was still at St Athan, just down the road from the airport and Webb's last station. She was Prossair's secretary-cum-everything else, was crazy about Pete Dent, to Webb's disgust – he felt she should have gone for someone with an air force background – and was very efficient.

"As I said, Terry. All heart."

Pross walked away from the helicopter, conflicting emotions vying for supremacy within him. It was always good to see Logan. He knew he was too fond of her. Not a smart move, all things considered. Together, they'd been under fire twice. The first time, she'd nearly lost her life and the second they'd barely managed to escape by the skin of their teeth.

For him, being involved with the Department was not merely irresponsible. As a married man with two small children, and a company to run, it was sheer lunacy, given the dodginess of Fowler's little jobs. Yet even as he entered the sprawl of the airport building from the flight pan, he found himself eager to see Logan again. He liked her a lot, and couldn't help it.

Pross walked along the polished surface of the terminal's reception area, turned right to pass through the line of red check-in desks. Gleaming proudly among the other company emblems, were the pale blue letters with their white borders announcing: PROSSAIR. And there she was, looking out at him from behind one of the large squares of glass. A beam of sheer pleasure was on her face.

The reddish hair was as he remembered it: spikily cut on top, shortish, and styled in a neat wedge. It shone with health. Today, she was not dressed in elegant Harrods gear, as Webb had led him to believe. Instead, tight stretch jeans hugged her thighs and legs. No room for bullet-studded garters here. A floppy black sweater that had seen long service completed her outfit. On her feet were plain, flat-heeled shoes; blue, with laces.

"Well," Pross said as he entered.

"Well yourself."

She gave him a tight hug, and kissed him softly beneath an ear. It was her customary way of greeting him. The warmth of her body gave him a quick jolt of pleasure, then they separated, each seeming to do so with some reluctance.

She gave him a sideways look, the tucked-in corners of her mouth teasing him. "Pross?"

"Behave yourself, Logan," he said. "And what brings you down here? As if I didn't know?"

It never ceased to amaze him how stunning she looked every time he saw her. To bring himself back to earth, he thought of something else about her that was equally stunning: her shooting. Thinking of the gun made him glance at the inevitable bag she had brought with her. She had placed it on one of the two armchairs in the cramped office. PROSSAIR was obviously considered safe territory.

"Brought your friend too?" he went on, nodding at the bag.

The impish smile came on. "Of course. Want to see?"

"I'll take your word for it. Well? You haven't answered me."

"Can't I visit you just because I want to?"

12

Pross said nothing.

"I've always wanted to come down," she told him, so seriously, he believed her, "but I stopped myself, several times. Well, it would have been pointless, wouldn't it?" she finished defensively.

They both understood what she meant.

He said, "Yes. I suppose so."

"There you are." The smile had gone momentarily, but now it was back. "But it's really good to see you. You look well."

"And you look . . . wonderful." It was out before he could stop himself.

The pale green eyes seem to widen, as if in surprise. "Thank you," she said, softly.

"Drink? Tea, coffee, or orange juice? Nothing stronger in here, I'm afraid. And you can stop looking at me like that."

"I never drink when I'm driving."

"Thought you were going to say 'on duty'."

"Now it's you who should behave, Pross. I'm not here to con you into a job. I'll have an orange juice, thanks."

He went to the tall fridge that stood in a corner between the two desks that nearly took up all the office space, poured the juice from a carton into a glass he'd taken from a cupboard above the fridge. Her eyes followed his movements minutely.

She took the glass, sat down, crossed her legs. He leaned against the larger of the two desks, his own, and watched her. Behind him on the wall was the large framed picture that told of his past, in part. It was the photograph of an RAF Phantom on the ground, fully armed, canopies open. Out of the navigator's seat, his younger face grinned cheerfully at the world. A young god.

Logan glanced round the office. "You must be doing well. Last time I was here, these armchairs were a little the worse for wear. New desks too, and a computer. You need more room."

"We're negotiating to take over some adjoining space. One of the other offices has become available."

"As I said. You're doing well. Talking of which . . . I saw a fancy-looking Jaguar XJS in the reserved car park when I arrived. Metallic green, beige hide upholstery. Yours?"

Pross nodded. "I sold my old XJ6C and bought this . . ."

"For a lot extra, I'll bet."

"For a lot extra, but it's a winner. Glenfrome in Bristol did the work. It's a complete rebuild, longer with a new roofline. Two adults are very comfortable in the back. It impresses prospective customers, and is great for taking the family on trips in something a bit exotic. The kids love it."

Logan smiled a little, perhaps wistfully. "Ah yes. The Dawn Patrol. How are they?"

"Still waking me up at five in the morning. They can't seem to realise I'm getting ancient."

"Ancient? How old are you, Pross, these days? All of thirty-three?"

"Thirty-four. I'd have thought your lot would have that sort of information nicely tucked into one of your many files."

"I'm sure you're right; but files are not my province."

"And you? Just how ancient are you?"

"My passport says I've just turned twenty-four."

"That's really old. You'll be collecting your pension soon."

She let the mild sarcasm pass and sipped thoughtfully at her drink. "Pension," she said, almost to herself.

Pross watched her, wondering what was going through her mind.

Suddenly she gave him one of her impish smiles. "You're not the only one with a new car."

"Oh? What have you got?"

"Why not come and have a look? Take a ride in it."

"Ah. Well . . ."

"Don't look so worried. I'm a good driver."

"I'll give you that. I only wish you wouldn't think you're on some kind of rally . . . at least, not while I'm in the passenger seat."

"I still think you ought to come. Besides, I've got to take you somewhere."

Pross stared at her as he moved slowly away from the desk. "And now it comes. I knew Fowler had sent you. I *knew* it! You know what you can tell him."

The pale green eyes seemed to flinch and grow less warm. "He didn't send me. I asked to come."

"That's nice. Pross is soft in the head when I'm about. I'll go, Mr Fowler. Let me go and collect. He'll think I came to see him. Should be a nice touch."

"That's not fair, Pross. It's not like that at all."

"Then tell me what it's like, Logan. I'm open to reason."

Logan tightened her lips briefly. "You know, sometimes I hate you when you go all sarcastic on me like this. You're jumping to conclusions, as usual."

"Oh no I'm not. I was just thinking as I came in how nice it was

14

to see you after . . . let me see . . . seven, eight months. But at the same time I was thinking where there's Logan, there's Fowler and where there's that scheming bastard, there's trouble. I was thinking I could do without Fowler's kind of trouble. I've got plenty of my own, thank you."

"David —"

"Oh I like it. Like it! *David*. The intimate touch —"

"Stop it!" Logan suddenly shouted at him.

At that moment, Cheryl Glyn appeared at the door, looking startled. Both Pross and Logan stared at her mutely. She backed away uncertainly, clearly unsure of her welcome.

They remained silent as she turned and made her way back through the line of check-in desks, and moved out of view.

Pross turned back to Logan. "Now you're terrorising my staff. Bloody hell, Logan."

Suddenly, she giggled.

"What's so funny?" he asked.

"I've been here just a few minutes, and we're already having a row. It must be love."

Pross found himself unable to resist her smile. He relaxed. "Logan . . . what am I going to do with you?"

"Agree to my every wish."

"Not as long as Fowler is behind it."

"It's not what you think."

"Pull the other one."

"Why don't you listen before you pass judgment?"

"Alright. I'm listening," Pross said in a voice full of scepticism.

"Fowler wants to see you —"

"Ah . . ."

"Listen!" The green eyes admonished him.

"Alright, alright."

"He wants you to take a look at something for him. He wants your opinion."

"That's a new one."

"Pross!" Warningly.

Pross raised a hand briefly in surrender.

Logan favoured him with another of her looks before continuing. "I'm serious. He really wants your opinion. He was going to send someone else down. Martins, I think. You'd have liked Martins."

"From the enthusiasm in your voice, he sounds a charmer."

"Martins is Security and a prize shit. He hauled me in once."

15

"You're joking. What for?"

"Remember our last little jaunt?" She gave him a fond smile, a secret shared.

"How can I forget?" He could still see in his mind the carnage he had wrought on the high Tibetan plateau, and taste the flavour of the final battle among the dangerous peaks of Nepal with the unmarked Russian gunship. "How can I forget?" he repeated softly. A thrill of excitement went through him as he relived it.

Logan was looking keenly at him. "Martins pulled me in," she said, eyes pondering upon something else, "after one of our people was killed. That happened before I joined you in Nepal. Martins accused me of killing him."

"Honour among thieves."

"I felt like killing the bastard, though."

"Which one?"

"Martins, of course. He was out of order."

"What I like about you, Logan, is the way you go straight for the throat. So having saved me from Martins," Pross went on, "you volunteered to run the errand instead."

"I like to keep in touch."

"What's six or seven months between friends?"

"Don't say it like that, Pross. I've got a job to do. Besides, as we've just agreed, it would have been pointless."

"Last time I heard, they sold things like cards in shops. You know, those little oblong things you write on, put stamps on, and slip through a passing letterbox."

"I'm not a great card-writer. In any case, I wouldn't have much to say . . ."

Her voice died off as if she wanted to stop more words from making themselves heard. An odd little silence slowly descended, seeming to physically place itself as a barrier against a possible crossing of the invisible frontier that lay between them.

Logan toyed absently with her glass, then said, "We'd better be going."

Pross looked at her in surprise. "Now?"

She finished the drink in one go, held the empty glass towards him. "Now."

He took the glass from her almost without realising it. "What do you mean 'now'?" He put the glass down on the desk. "Do you really expect me to walk out of my office and —"

"You'll like what you see."

16

"You've seen it then?"

"I know what it is, but I haven't seen it. If what Fowler's said is anything to go by, I'll lay any bet you'll like ... no, you'll *love* it. Come on, Pross. Don't stand there looking lost. You'll be back here tomorrow."

"Tomorrow! Logan, I've got a business to run. What are you talking about? Tomorrow! I can't just leave this place when Fowler feels like it, even if he tries to sugar the pill by sending you down to deliver the message."

"My being here is my own idea —"

"No!"

"Fowler doesn't give up. You ought to know that by now. He'll send Martins, or someone like that. I promise you it's not a job."

"I wonder why that sounds familiar?"

"I give you my word, Pross."

"It's not your word I doubt. It's Fowler's. Sometimes I think that man's got more scheming in his little finger than Machiavelli had in his entire body."

"Now you're looking angry."

"That's observant."

"You've got to understand, Pross. It isn't a job. All Fowler wants is your unbiased opinion ..."

"It smells. The whole thing smells of Fowler's scheming."

"Look, for what it's worth, I've already told Fowler I'd have nothing to do with anything that drags you into one of his operations."

"You've stood up to Fowler ... for me?"

She gave a little shrug. "It's not the first time. He knows exactly how I feel about pulling you into our affairs."

"That hasn't stopped him before."

"Oh I know, but I've checked on this one. As far as I can tell, he really does seem to want your opinion. I've also done a sort of sweep to check whether there's the slightest possibility of your getting involved in anything that's running at the moment. Nothing. Absolutely nothing. Not a squeak."

"Knowing Fowler as I do, little as that may be, perhaps that should make me suspicious. With your far greater knowledge of him, maybe even you should —"

"I've taken that into consideration. It's clean."

Pross still looked unconvinced.

"It's only a day, Pross," Logan reasoned. "Or is the thought of spending a day in my company so unattractive?"

"You'll be with us?"

"All the time." She favoured him with one of her most impish smiles.

He shook his head slowly. "Logan . . ." He responded to her smile with a brief one of his own. "I must be soft in the head. Alright. You've got your day. It so happens one of my choppers is temporarily grounded."

"There you are! It's Fate."

"Oh yes. Fate. I wouldn't put it past Fowler to screw up my ADI."

"Even Fowler wouldn't go so far. What's an ADI?"

"Attitude Direction Indicator. Terry won't let the chopper off the ground without it. Although if the thing goes potty in the air, you're already off the ground."

"Good for Terry, I say. Someone's got to look after you."

"I'm already well looked after."

Her eyes were conspiratorial. "In certain ways only."

"I think I'd better warn Terry," Pross said quickly. "He's bound to blow a fuse when he hears this."

He picked up the internal phone on his desk, and dialled the flight line.

"Terry," he began, "how long will the chopper be AOG?" He had slipped into service language: AOG meant aircraft on ground.

"Why?" Webb countered.

"Just tell me, Terry."

"Still with you, is she?"

"Yes."

"Thought so. And where does the little miss want you to take her?"

"She's taking me."

"Just as bad. Not in this chopper, she isn't."

"We're driving."

"Then why —"

"We'll be gone for a day."

"Oh. I see. It's a lot worse than I thought."

"I'll be back tomorrow for the flight test."

"You hope. Still, it's none of my business. You never learn, do you, Boss? I think you're soft in the head."

"Funny you should say that. I was thinking the same thing just a while ago."

"You ought to listen to yourself then. It might help. Still, as I said, it's none of my business."

18

"So you keep telling me," Pross said with a touch of asperity.

"Told Diane, have you?" Webb continued as if Pross had not spoken.

"I'll do that if you can possibly tear yourself away from this phone so that I can call her on the outside line."

"She should be pleased," Webb said unabashed. "I'd like to be a fly on the wall. On second thoughts, perhaps not."

"Terry . . ." Pross began warningly.

"Good luck," Webb said. "Soft on a bunch of freckles. At your age too." Webb hung up with a smirk in his voice.

Pross replaced the receiver slowly, then picked up the outside phone and began to dial.

Logan said, "Trouble?"

"With Terry? Oh no." His home number in the little village of Craig Penllyn near Cowbridge began to ring.

"Is he the man I saw when I arrived?" Pross nodded. "I don't think he likes me," Logan said.

"He says some very complimentary things about you. It's what you represent, or what he thinks you represent, he doesn't like."

She said nothing to that. The phone continued to ring in Pross's ear.

Logan said, "What are you going to tell her?"

"That I've been called away on business. She has no great love for your Department. She can still remember the very first meeting and all the dead bodies it left in the village."

"I suppose I'd feel the same way, in her place," Logan said quietly. "Will she believe you?"

"Who knows? She's got radar that can spot something fishy at a thousand miles, never mind on the phone. I'll just have to see how it goes."

Someone picked up the phone at the other end and gave the number. At times, when there were friends visiting and she was occupied, one of the visitors would answer. But the voice that had come on belonged to Dee.

Pross said, "Dee? Something's come up. I'll be away for the night."

Silence, then, "It's a bit sudden."

"It happens now and then. You know that." Gently.

"You're being evasive, David. I can feel it."

Bloody radar.

Pross said, "It's just a quick trip. And I'm not being evasive."

Absolute silence. The whole strategy was fast disintegrating. Situation hopeless.

"It's those bloody people again," Dee said with a quiet anger "They've been in touch. Why can't they leave us alone?"

Pross decided to drop all pretence. "It's not what you think, Dee I'll be back tomorrow."

"It's like supping with the devil," she said. "And this one keeps coming back to be paid. They seem to forget you've got a family.'

There was another long silence.

"Just be careful, David," she said at last. "I love you." Then she hung up.

Again, Pross replaced the receiver slowly.

Looking contrite, Logan said, "I'm sorry." The pattern of freckles seemed particularly prominent. "If I thought there was anything funny going on, I'd leave now, and let Fowler send someone else.' The pale green eyes stared up at him without guile.

"Now that I've told those who need to know, I might as well see what it is that Fowler thinks needs an opinion from me."

"Won't you have to collect some gear from home?"

"I always keep an overnight kit here, as does my other pilot. We always take them on flights in case there has to be an unscheduled stopover." He smiled briefly. "Company routine." He reached behind the desk to haul out a battered-looking flight bag. It had a military cut to it and was Air-Force blue.

"That looks like government issue," Logan said.

"Government surplus," Pross said with a straight face.

Logan stood up, smoothed her jeans down by stroking her hands down her thighs in an unconsciously sensual movement. "Of course," she said drily as she picked up her own bag.

Soft on a bunch of freckles. Pross recalled Webb's remark. Was that really why he was prepared to go on this mystery drive with Logan? He could not deny he found her company stimulating, but there were all sorts of reasons for that. They had been through the fire together and it had created a special bond. Each life had been laid on the line for the other. Yet while cancelling out the obligation, those same lives still appeared to be each other's custodian.

He could not further explain it to himself. That was simply how it felt.

"Besides," he said as he stood aside to let her pass out of the office, "it has a sentimental value, this knocked-about old bag of mine. It's been more places than you've had hot dinners."

20

"It looks it."

"Don't be cheeky."

She grinned at him, unrepentant, and obviously pleased to be in his company. As they went through the check-in line and into the reception area, Cheryl Glyn came past on her way back to the office. Pross paused briefly to speak to her.

"I'll be away for the day, Cheryl," he said to her. "Hold the fort. See you tomorrow."

"Alright, Mr Pross."

As they left the building, he said to Logan, "That's funny. When she first came to us, she began by calling me Mr Pross everytime she spoke a sentence; or it seemed like that to me. I told her to cut the formality. We were only interested in good work, not ceremony. She's been calling me David ever since . . . until just now."

"I can still feel her eyes lacerating my shoulder blades," she remarked drily. "You men. So blind sometimes. She hates my guts."

"Cheryl? Oh come on, Logan."

"Like Terry, she's very possessive about you, and anyone who threatens to take you away from them is to be viewed with the utmost hostility. You ought to be pleased. You've got a very loyal crew. But then, you sometimes have that effect on people," she finished enigmatically.

They had arrived at the car park reserved for airport staff and authorised visitors, just in front of the building. Her car was parked next to Pross's Jaguar. It was a brand new Ford RS Turbo in dark metallic blue. Everything was colour-coded, from the deep front air dam to the rear spoiler on the neatly chopped tail. On its chunky wheels, it looked quite aggressive.

Pross viewed it warily. "Nice," he said. "Tell you what. Let's take the XJS."

"Oh no you don't. In you get." Logan put the key in the lock and the central locking announced everything was open with a loud snap. "Come on, Pross." Her smile teased him. "No rallies today."

"I'll believe that when I see it," he said gloomily when he'd got in.

"Oh look," she said. "We're being watched."

The car was pointing towards the building. Pross looked up. From within, by the entrance, Cheryl Glyn was staring expressionlessly back at them. He waved to her briefly, a little guiltily.

There was a brief answering wave, then she turned and disappeared inside.

"Conscience?" Logan queried as she turned on the ignition. There was a muted whistle as the engine came to life. "That's the turbo," she went on. "I like the sound." She put the car into reverse and moved slowly out of the parking slot. "You haven't answered."

"There's no answer," Pross said.

When she'd reversed far enough, Logan went into first and began to drive out of the car park. The exit arrows pointed to the right. She turned left.

"Logan . . ." Pross began.

"It's alright, Pross. As you can see, there's no one coming and the exit road's only a few yards away. What's the point of going all round the shop?"

Pross shut his eyes briefly in resignation. "I knew it. I knew it!"

For reply, Logan gunned the RS. It leapt forward with a whistle and a roar as the turbo came on.

"I bloody knew it!" Pross muttered despairingly as the car seemed to snatch itself round a corner on the way out of the airport and headed for the main road.

Logan grinned at him. "Cheer up, Pross. Sooner you're there, sooner you'll be back."

"Thanks for telling me," he said gloomily as the passing scenery streamed in the opposite direction.

At the junction, the sign to Llantwit Major pointed left. Against his hope, Logan took it. He knew the road well, having often used it to and from the airport. The worst of his fears were confirmed when she turned right soon after and onto a narrow back road full of bends and switchbacks, heading north to cross the A48 and onwards to the M4.

"Why go into Cardiff when we can bypass it?" Logan said.

"Why indeed."

The RS snatched its way round a tight, narrow bend.

"Just like old times," she told him with a sideways glance.

"Whoopee. And keep your eyes on the road please, Logan. The tractor drivers around here move for no man or woman."

"Like tractor drivers everywhere." She didn't sound worried.

Pross stared balefully at hedges that appeared to be caressing the doors.

Bloody bunch of freckles, he thought.

TWO

London, the same day.

It was always like this, Fowler thought, his outward calm belying the irritation he felt. Winterbourne rated an emotion at no greater level. Despite well over a year and a half as Head of Department, Winterbourne had still not sorted himself out.

Fowler listened to Winterbourne's ramblings, his mind on other things. Most of all, he was wondering how Logan had fared.

Winterbourne was saying, "Are you listening to me, Fowler?"

"Most attentively, Sir John." You won't catch me out like that, Fowler did not say, with the contempt he felt.

Not sure what to make of it, Winterbourne said something that sounded like, "Hmmmpf!"

Rear-Admiral Sir John Winterbourne should never have been made Head after the suicide of his predecessor; but the inconsistencies of bureaucrats when making appointments held no further surprises for Fowler. With a bizarre sort of logic, given the nature of such things, Winterbourne was the perfect appointee.

He was incompetent, knew very little of the job he had to do, and had even less chance of understanding how to do it properly. He also, erroneously, saw himself as suited to higher things, and the Department as merely a stepping stone towards that shining goal. It did not help that he was quite aware that Fowler was looked upon by almost the entire staff as the man truly in command.

Besides, he was Navy, whereas most of the senior executives, if not all, were former or serving members of the Air Force; as was a good percentage of lower-ranking staff. Some were civilians, or

23

Army, but that didn't make things any sweeter. Winterbourne's way of getting back was sometimes to enlist outside help. Unfortunately, whenever he interfered matters usually went haywire, sometimes with serious consequences. Fowler would then be forced into pulling Winterbourne's chestnuts out of the fire. On one occasion, Winterbourne had come close to ruining an operation.

All these resentments showed in Winterbourne's face, enhancing the already strong impression that it belonged to a petulant cherub. When he wanted to make a point, Winterbourne tended to summon Fowler to the opulence of his vast office. He knew it would have been his subordinate's, had matters been different. He also knew Fowler did not care, and that was what rankled the most. Fowler was so good at his work, so fully in command, he hardly needed the promotion.

Winterbourne said, "I am not sure that I like these elaborate schemes of yours, Fowler."

"They get results, Sir John," Fowler said mildly. "Isn't that what this Department's about? Without results, we might as well pack up and go home."

Tall and lean, Fowler made Winterbourne look like a corpulent porker. Well into his late fifties, he seemed much younger. His hair, neatly cut, was as thick as it had been in his twenties, except that it was now distinguished by barely perceptible thin streaks of grey. His suit was well-made, but understated. His spectacles were perched upon the tip of an ascetic nose and somehow gave the impression he was looking down upon Winterbourne.

He was, and Winterbourne knew it.

Again, Winterbourne seemed uncertain of how to respond, then chose to ignore what had been said. Fowler had the grace not to smile at yet another victory.

"I suppose you're positive this operation will work?" Winterbourne began in a voice that was close to sulking. "That the risks involved are worth it?"

"With respect, Sir John, we are in the business of risk-taking. Not needless, or careless risks, but calculated ones with little or no exposure to our personnel. If we wanted safe jobs, we'd be at checkout desks in supermarkets. But I've been told even these are not so safe nowadays."

"Are you being flippant?"

"I'm never flippant, Sir John." Fowler's eyes appeared to gleam behind the glasses.

24

His mind changed gear, and went back to the matter of Logan's progress.

The rain slammed against the windscreen of the car as Logan drove through Aberdare and headed on the A4059 for Brecon.

Pross said, with as much calm as he could muster, "Shouldn't you slow down a bit? The wipers are having a rough time of it."

"Do I tell you how to fly helicopters?"

Pross kept his counsel, deciding on discretion. Earlier on, when she had crossed the M4 and had continued to head north instead of turning right onto the motorway as expected, he had voiced his concern.

"I thought we were going to London, or to that little manor house in the Cotswolds where you send your wounded warriors."

"As you can see," she had told him casually, "we're not."

She had seemed preoccupied, as if her thoughts were not engaged upon guiding the RS Turbo through the pouring rain.

Pross tried again. "Something wrong?"

"Should there be?" She glanced in the mirror.

"You tell me."

"Not as far as I know."

"For the last hour, you've virtually been silent. Not your usual gregarious self."

She flashed him a quick smile. "Just concentrating, Pross. I know how my driving worries you." She gave the mirror another glance.

"And you've been paying a lot of attention to that mirror, and the ones on the doors."

"Careful driving. That's all."

Pross stared at the streaming wet road, then glanced at the speedometer, and wished he hadn't.

She saw his glance. "Don't worry, Pross. You'll get there in one piece." The mirror got another quick scrutiny.

"You wouldn't be looking for someone who might be following us, would you?" he began with mild sarcasm. "After all, we're not really on one of Fowler's little jobs, are we?"

"I've told you. No."

"Then why so preoccupied? Why the mirror watch?"

"When you fly, don't you always keep a good lookout? In my kind of job, not keeping a good lookout could kill you . . . just as being careless in an aircraft can."

"Now she tells me."

"Relax, Pross, and enjoy the drive."

"Enjoy the drive, she says."

The RS hissed along the wet tarmac, and Logan smiled, guiding it with consummate skill.

They bypassed Brecon and took the A470 to Builth Wells. By now, the rain had ceased and in Builth Wells, it was as if no rain had fallen that day.

Logan decided they should stop for a quick snack. They found a small, unobtrusive place where a friendly woman served delicious ham sandwiches, allowed Logan to use her private phone, and would not accept payment for the call.

"Isn't she nice," Logan said after the call.

"Reporting to Fowler?" Pross suggested as he finished the last sandwich.

"Just letting him know we're on our way."

"Oh good. That makes me feel a lot happier."

"Pross." Warningly.

He gave her a fake smile. "Mind telling me now where we're going?" he went on. Throughout the time they had been at their table, he'd observed her constant scrutiny of the passing traffic, which he thought interesting, considering there was no need to study driving mirrors. He said nothing about that.

"I'm playing a little game," she said.

"Surprise me."

"And it's called," she carried on, unabashed, "'Wait and See'." She gave a soft little laugh, dangled the car key close to his nose. "Fit? Then let's move. We've got a lot of travelling to do."

"Ha, ha," Pross said as he stood up.

They bade their friendly lady farewell and went out. The day had brightened considerably and even felt warmer than normal for the time of year.

Logan gave the sparse traffic a sweeping glance before unlocking the car.

Bloody freckles, Pross thought as he got in.

"Did you say something?" she queried.

"I wouldn't dare," was what he replied.

She smiled to herself as she started the RS.

In his office, hutch-like and stark by comparison to Winterbourne's, Fowler stared at the phone he had just used.

Logan was doing alright with Pross and as yet, no one was following them. So far so good.

He gave one of his most enigmatic, brief smiles. Logan, Pross . . . Pross, Logan. A good combination, and of great value to the Department, even though Pross had to be dragged kicking and squealing. But Pross could be seduced in two ways: his quite obvious affection for Logan – considerably helped by her own feelings – and his love of helicopters.

Fowler did not normally approve of attachments, no matter how tenuous, between Department personnel. But then Pross was not truly on Department strength. At least, not officially. Besides, in the case of Pross and Logan, it helped.

In fact, as far as this particular operation was concerned, it was positively vital.

Fowler drummed a finger gently against the phone. Matters, he thought, were moving along smoothly.

They continued on the A470 out of Builth Wells and, thirty-five miles later, stopped for petrol in Caersws. The young man at the pumps gazed longingly at the RS, and even more longingly at Logan whenever he got the chance, which seemed to amuse her.

Pross noted, however, that her attention was really on the passing traffic; apparently she saw nothing to cause her worry.

After she had paid the attendant, she gave him one of her grins. He nearly fainted.

"What a nice young man," she said to Pross as she got in.

"Somebody ought to warn him that you bite."

"Now that isn't nice, Pross," she admonished, started the engine and sent the car rocketing off the forecourt in a manner that gained total approval from the attendant.

"Here we go again," Pross groaned.

"Shhsh, spoilsport. Lie back and enjoy it. It's a lovely day."

"As long as you don't sing as well."

Irrepressibly, she winked at him.

After a while, Pross found himself enjoying the greens and golds of autumn on the hillsides as the car sped deeper into North Wales, on a road that was dry and virtually empty of traffic.

At times they would come to a bend where he would expect her to slow down. But no. Down would go her foot, and when all his instincts were beginning to scream at him that his freckled tormentor was about to drive them into the surrounding scenery, the RS would seem to haul its nose tighter and negotiate the bend quite neatly without the slightest quiver.

He decided after that to keep his mouth shut and let her get on with it; but it didn't pacify the butterflies in his stomach when the next bend came up – and the next, and the next . . .

They parted company with the A470 at Llanelltyd and turned left onto the A496 for Barmouth. As they drove along the northern shore of the Mawddach estuary, a white Transit van appeared behind them in the distance.

Logan saw it immediately and at the first opportunity, passed a slow-moving car that was ahead of them. She kept an eye on the mirrors. The Transit made no move to catch up. She increased speed until it vanished from view.

She wondered where it had come from.

Pross said, "What's up?"

"Nothing."

"I see. That's why the mirror's become so important again, I suppose. More careful driving?"

"Something like that."

"Oh well. I'll feel really safe all the time now."

"Trust me, Pross, will you?"

"I wouldn't be here if part of me didn't . . . despite the man you work for."

She gave him a fleeting smile. "Well that's something, at least."

Soon they could see the Barmouth bridge spanning the estuary thinly in the distance, and on the approach to the seaside holiday town they came to some roadworks. Traffic was controlled by temporary lights. A sign warned there was a delay of twenty minutes each way.

The green was showing and had obviously been on for some time as no cars were ahead. The narrow lane left free by the roadworks curved sharply out of sight to the right. Logan pressed on.

Pross said, "I hate to mention this, but what if the lights change before we get to the bend?"

"That would be interesting. Do you want to wait back there for another twenty minutes? Besides, there's bound to be a time delay."

"We wouldn't be trying to lose somebody, would we?"

"Still on that tack?"

For reply, Pross turned his head round to have a look to see if anyone was following. There were no cars. Then just as the RS went round the corner, he thought he saw a flash of white, but wasn't sure.

He settled back in his seat to look out on a long line of patiently waiting cars, with their numbers continually growing. At least thirty, he judged.

As they drove past, the line began to move, slowly at first, like a many-jointed creature unsure of its initial steps after a long sleep.

Logan had a smug smile upon her face.

"What are you so happy about?" he asked.

"Do I look it?"

"It's either that or someone's just fed you some cream."

"It's the sea air."

"Ask a daft question," he said, and looked out to sea.

The light of the autumn day was fast going. In the distance, the descending sun was making a last show of defiance, burning its way palely through an elongated gap in an otherwise solid cover of dark clouds. A squall was on the horizon, heading landwards. Shafts of the weakening light created a starburst upon it.

Logan gave his knee a fleeting pat. "All will be well, Pross. Worry not."

"Who's worried?" he said, looking round at her as they drove through Barmouth. "I walked out of my office this morning, told my wife I wouldn't be home tonight without letting her know my destination − which incidentally *I* don't know − to go on a mystery drive on the say-so of a man I wouldn't turn my back on if we were both in a roomful of tigers. I'm not worried. I'm crazy, though."

"Fowler's not that bad. He just passionately believes in what he's doing; though to look at him you'd think passion is not a word he knows. He's the only one in there *I* trust . . . sometimes."

Back at the lights, by the roadworks, two men sat in the white Transit watching the traffic inch slowly by, and seethed helplessly. Then the one in the passenger seat picked up a two-way radio and began to speak into it.

The rain arrived quickly and caught the RS just under two miles later, at Llanaber. It had grown almost dark now, the weak sun so thoroughly blotted out it might never have been. A strong breeze came off the sea, now and then smashing the pellets of rain against the left side of the car.

Pross stared out of his window. The water was a dirty grey, and choppy. Strange, he thought, how swiftly it had all changed; but that was normal for the time of year. Besides, this was on the edge of Snowdonia. In the interior were the mountains, where sudden changes in weather was the rule. He had flown over them often enough, both in the Prossair choppers and in RAF Phantoms, to know the truth of that. Not particularly nice to be caught out if you're charging through a valley at 200 feet and 500 knots or thereabouts. A nasty splash on a mountainside could be the result. It had happened to others. He had actually seen it happen, once, and had been thankful to have been in the back seat. To this day he was not certain whether he could have landed his own aircraft safely, had he been the pilot. The crew of the other Phantom had been very good friends.

His pilot, and best friend, was thankfully the kind of person who had seemed to be fused into the aircraft. They had landed without drama and had reported the accident. And yet, searching his innermost feelings now, Pross could scarcely believe his own performance when flying for Fowler. A change seemed to come over him during those periods. He put it down to the sheer need for survival; but he also knew, deep down, there was something about combat that called to him. Fowler had somehow managed to tap its source and had hooked into it, like a leech gorging on the transfusion. Trouble was, what would happen when the leech had had its fill and eventually dropped off, fully sated? Would there be anything left of Pross?

"Good question," Pross said to himself.

"What's a good question?" Logan asked.

Pross roused himself. "Oh . . . ah . . . I was just thinking out loud."

"I did wonder about the bemused expression. You seemed miles away."

"I was. Years, too."

"Care to tell?"

"Just old memories. Nothing important. I was remembering what it was like in Phantoms. Big brutes, but I loved them." No need to tell her the entire truth.

"And that's all?"

"That's all."

"If you say so."

"Don't *you* play the radar game with me, Logan."

She gave him a quick teasing smile. She had turned on the lights and in the back-glare, the pale green eyes had become dark.

"I've got my own radar."

"Keep your eyes on the road . . . if you can see it in this clag."

The rain continued to lash at the car. Away to his left, among the dunes that abounded on this part of the coast, he could see a few twinkles of light. Holiday caravans. It was not a place he would choose to be for a long weekend. This being Thursday, he assumed that was what the people down there were here for. Perhaps the weather had fooled them, as it had countless others so many times before.

About seven miles later, they drove into Llanbedr. It was still raining, only much more heavily. Logan pulled off the road to the left and onto a filling-station forecourt. She didn't stop for petrol but instead drove slowly onto the attached open-ground parking area. A few other cars were already there, but she found a spot close to the garage wall. She reversed into it until the snout of the RS pointed towards the road. She stopped, switched off the lights. They were now hidden in the relative gloom, with a good view of the rest of the car park, the forecourt, and the road. In the shelter of the garage, the rain was unable to smear the windscreen.

"Waiting for someone, are we?" Pross suggested drily.

"Sort of."

He recognised the tone of her voice, and found it familiar. Logan was primed for action. He didn't like the idea one bit. This was not supposed to be what he had come on this crazy drive for.

Five minutes of silence passed. Logan showed no signs of moving from their parking spot. Another five minutes carried with them the same quiet. The rain had begun to ease. An uneven stream of traffic had passed, going in both directions; but nothing that had excited interest.

A couple with two small children ran to a parked car, crouching against the rain. They got in, and the car was started. It began to move towards the road, backwards.

Logan shook her head slowly, resignedly. "Can you believe some people? The kids are in the back too."

Suddenly, almost inevitably, there was the blaring of horns and the squeal of brakes.

"Whoever it is won't stop in time," Logan said tensely.

But the other vehicle did. It was the white van.

'Well, well," she said softly. "Thank you, Mr Bad Driver."

The car hastily drove back into the car park. The van revved its engine angrily and screeched off. The offending car described a full, sheepish circle, before easing itself cautiously back onto the road. It drove slowly away, giving a strong impression of having its tail between its legs.

"That should teach him," Pross said.

"It probably won't," Logan said, dismissing the unknown driver as a hopeless case.

"So what was all that about?" Pross queried.

"What was all what about?"

"Don't play games, Logan," Pross said with growing impatience. He could feel a tiny coil of anger beginning to writhe within him. "That idiot in the car forced the van to stop, which seemed to please you. I'd hate to think it was all planned. I wouldn't put anything past your lot."

"No, Pross," she said with heavy patience, "it wasn't planned. Fowler's not in the habit of employing children." But there was a defensiveness in her voice. A new tension too.

"That's nice to know ... although the safety of *my* kids didn't seem to worry him the first time he came into my life."

"That's not fair, Pross!" Logan was almost shouting as she turned to look at him. In the gloom, her eyes seemed to catch the back glare of the lights from the petrol station and become luminous. The tenseness in her was not that of coming action, but of something else entirely.

Pross wondered what it was.

He said, "He doesn't mind throwing you in at the deep end when it suits, it would also seem." It was a grudging, half-hearted apology.

Logan was staring at the road once more.

"It's my job," she said, voice cold. She started the car and drove off the parking area.

Pross said nothing further as she turned right onto the road to drive back a little way in the direction they had first come. She turned left up a narrow street soon after. Pross caught a fleeting glimpse of a sign, a simple strip of wood with an arrowed tip pointing. CWM BYCHAN, it said in unsteady letters. He heard the sound of rushing water. The wipers scraped across the windscreen intermittently. Logan switched them off, killing the annoying sound. There wasn't enough rain to lubricate them. The noise of rushing water was perceptibly louder.

"Is Fowler up there?" Pross asked.

"Do you know this place?" she countered, asking her own question.

"Which place? Llanbedr? Cwm Bychan?"

"Either."

"Never been."

"Well, there's a treat in store for you."

"Will I live to enjoy it?"

"You might."

"Oh goody."

The new silence that fell between them was not exactly friendly.

The road had begun to climb, and was becoming narrower. Houses became sparse. High stone walls began to encroach. There was now no room for another car to pass. There was barely enough for one. The lights of the RS bored into the darkness, illuminating the ghostliness of the place. To Pross, it felt as if they were leaving civilisation behind.

They came into a forested area, and the rushing sounds of water were now quite loud. A clearing appeared ahead. He saw wooden picnic tables, then they were past and the road was once again being encroached upon by the stone walls. One miscalculation, it seemed, and Logan would have a nice long gouge on her new car.

She said, "People come up here in the summer."

Pross wondered why. To him, the place held a strange air of menace.

After a dream-like time along the strangely forbidding road, with its seemingly continuous twists and bends, the wheels of the car rumbled over a cattle grid.

"That's for the sheep," Logan informed him, "but there'll be none here tonight."

"How convenient. So Fowler can even get the farmers to do his bidding."

The narrow track seemed to have suddenly disappeared, and instead of making comment Logan concentrated on not going off into what appeared to be a bog with plenty of surface water. The track had dipped out of sight and turned sharply to the right. For long moments, the lights of the car seemed to hang in the air before the front wheels found purchase once more.

"They were compensated," she said at last. She drove without worry, or error. "Fowler can be fair when he wants to . . . more than most people in his kind of work are inclined to be. I know. I've met some, and I've worked with others. Someone like Martins, for in-

33

stance, would have ordered them to move. Refusal would simply have met with forcible removal. Martins can be very rough. It's better to shoot Martins than reason with him."

"Love and honour among thieves. That's the second time you've expressed a desire to have him shot."

"I have a score to settle with that little shit."

"Who works for your Department."

"Unfortunately. Can't always choose the people you'd like to work with. Fowler seems to think we need his kind."

"What do *you* think?"

"Left to me . . ."

"You'd shoot him. So you've said, but —"

"But I have to accept that there are people out there who are even worse." She shrugged, having long since come to terms with that fact.

"How to meet a nice class of person," Pross said drily. "Join the Department."

"Oh I don't know," Logan said. "I'm not so bad." There was a hint of laughter in her voice. Peace was being declared.

He looked across at her. "No. You're not so bad."

A tiny smile, that he couldn't see, tugged briefly at her lips.

When he had looked round again, it was to see a huge boulder that disappeared upwards into the night passing within inches of the front of the car, then the track straightened out, undulating across open country. Away to his left, indistinct shapes of high ground rose into the darkness, while from the right came the roar of water.

Ahead, cliff-like forms, their edges marked out by the skyglow from Llanbedr, formed an impenetrable wall in the gloom. The track curved left, hugging the sides of the high ground. To Pross, it seemed more like a ledge that had been cut into a hill; but at least, it was tarred.

He was not prepared, however, for what the right side of the track showed him in the blaze of the car's headlights.

There was nothing. The ground had simply dropped away, and below he could see the sheen of water. He was looking down at a lake.

"Bloody hell, Logan!" he exclaimed. "We can't be more than two inches from the edge!"

"Don't exaggerate, Pross. Two inches, indeed. Who's driving this car?"

"Forgive me, Madam. I'll shut up."

"And so you should."

Nevertheless, he kept his attention warily upon the narrow strip of road. There would be nowhere to run, he thought gloomily, if the van had decided to follow them up here. No way off, except down into the water. Great.

"This," Logan was saying, "is Llyn Cwm Bychan. It's roughly three hundred yards across and perhaps half a mile long. The noise you've been hearing are waterfalls, and the Afon Artro . . . River to you."

"I know what Afon means. I live in Wales. Remember?"

"Ooh. Touchy." Her teasing was good-natured. "This lake is one of the river's sources, joining spillages from the mountains. There's a campsite further on, at the end of this track. It can really be quite beautiful up here. We'll be stopping soon, by the way."

The track was sloping gently downwards now, and Pross thought it seemed closer to the water's level. A quarter of a mile or so later, Logan stopped the car, and just on the edge of the lights Pross saw what looked like a pair of square columns forming a gateway through which the track continued.

"This will do for now," she said, turning off both engine and lights. The continued whirring of the cooling fan sounded loud in the abrupt silence.

Other sounds of the night began to intrude. Pross could still hear the rush of the water — though muted by the distance — above the cooling ticks of the engine. As his eyes adjusted themselves to the darkness, he noted that from his side of the car the ground rose in a steep incline until he could make out the faint outline of its summit. Perhaps three hundred feet. Hard to tell in the gloom. What looked like a footpath began near the car to work its way invisibly upwards.

He turned to look through the rear window. Across the lake, the cliff-like ramparts showed as sharper silhouettes against the background glow of an unseen Llanbedr, a good six miles away.

"Are we staying here?" he asked Logan, turning round once more to look at her.

"For the moment, yes."

"Can I ask why?"

"You can . . . and the answer is . . ."

"Wait and see," they said together.

Pross said, drily, "Of course. May I make a suggestion?"

"Make it."

"Why not turn the car round? There's probably enough room

35

further on. Just in case the van which you said was probably not following us was doing just that."

"If that van was following us, there'd be no point in turning round. They'd only be waiting back there. In case you hadn't noticed, this is the only way in, or out. By car."

"I had noticed, but I thought I was only frightening myself. Secretly, I fancy a walk across the Welsh mountains on a wet, cold night."

"Come on, Pross," she teased. "This is fun. It's beautiful up here. All we need is a bit of moonlight."

"You, Logan, have got the weirdest sense of fun."

Instead of making reply, she suddenly opened her door and paused, listening. The courtesy light was almost blinding.

"Shut that bloody door, Logan!" Pross said sharply. "It's freezing!"

"Shh!" she said, and her manner made him forget all about the cold. "I heard something." She shut the door, and the light went out.

"Maybe a sheep Fowler forgot," he told her sourly.

"It wasn't a sheep." She sounded quite certain.

Her whole manner warned him not to doubt that she had heard something to put her on the alert. It didn't make him feel any better. He felt even worse when she reached beneath her legs for her bag. He knew she was getting the magnum out.

"Just a precaution," she said lightly.

But she had not yet finished. She put the gun down on the floor, then took two other items out of the bag. She drew them on as if putting on a pair of stockings.

"What are you doing?" Pross asked, trying to see.

For answer, she took his right hand, and placed it on her thigh. "Feel. Don't flinch. What do you think I'm trying to do? Seduce you?" She gave a soft laugh. "I'd hope for a better reaction than that. Well? Now do you understand?"

"Er . . . yes."

The hand had settled on a bullet-studded garter. She had pulled it on over the leg of her jeans.

"Are you wearing both?"

"Of course." She released his hand slowly. "Six in each plus the full load gives me eighteen. Should be enough for the job."

The amazon, Pross thought with resignation, dressed to kill. Literally.

"You could be wrong," he said hopefully.

"I'm not. No one is supposed to be here, except the two of us."

"But you said we were waiting for . . . someone? Something?"

"We're waiting, yes, but not for whoever is out there."

"Now what do we do?"

"You stay here. I'm going after them."

"'Them'? What makes you so sure?"

"There's bound to be more than one. I'd take a bet on it. But first, a little diversion."

Logan took the key out of the ignition, handed it to Pross.

As he took it reluctantly, he had another go. "Perhaps it's a polecat. They're part of the wildlife of Snowdonia . . ."

"If they come down here, which I doubt, the noise of our arrival would have sent it scurrying. Nice try, Pross, but I've still got to get out there and find out." She took something else from the bag: a two-way radio. "Hold," she said into it, then clipped it to her belt.

No answering voice came back at her. Pross assumed that whoever was on the other end had found no need to acknowledge, but would act according to the terse instruction.

"There may be a polecat or polecats out there, Pross," Logan was saying, "but of the human kind. And we all know what happens to polecats. Right. Let's get on with our little diversion."

So saying, she leaned across suddenly and placed both arms about his neck, bringing her cheek against his.

Pross jerked back unconsciously, taken by surprise.

"Look as if you're enjoying it, damn you!" Logan said fiercely in a low voice. "I had a better reaction from you in your office!"

"I . . ." he began lamely, "I . . . was saying hello."

"Well say another hello. Put your arms about my waist," she commanded. "If someone's up there watching us through a night-scope, I want him to think he's got the wrong quarry; at least long enough for me to get up there to take him out."

Pross had been finding it quite difficult to cope with the soft warmth of her body without reacting; but the matter-of-fact way in which she had outlined her plan for neutralising whoever was secretly watching them effectively stifled any embarrassing response from his own body. Perhaps that had been her intention.

His arms went about her waist.

"That's better," she said approvingly. "Now look as if you mean it. We don't have to go through the whole kissing bit. Besides, I want to look over your shoulder."

"Very romantic, Logan."

"Isn't life hard?"

THREE

The watchers at the summit studied the car through night binoculars.

"Is this why we're waiting here, lying on this wet ground?" one said disgustedly. "To watch two people give way to their lust, in a car?"

"They're not at it yet," the other said.

They were not speaking English. Their words were uttered softly.

"They're squirming enough," the one who had first spoken rejoined. "They'll be at it soon. Are you sure we've got the correct information?" The manner of speech suggested a form of seniority. "Did you check?"

"I checked. A blue Ford with a man and a woman."

The other sighed. "How many cars do you think we've seen today, fitting that description?"

"It was described in detail. There can't be many like it."

"One other would be one too many. It will not go well for you if I've been brought here to watch two people copulating near a lake in the Welsh mountains."

"Isn't it odd they would choose this particular place?"

"Who knows what tastes some people may have? I have seen a couple do it in a swimming-pool, in broad daylight, with other swimmers around."

"These Westerners," the subordinate said contemptuously.

"I was not talking about Westerners."

Not sure how to respond, the junior man concentrated on the car beneath them. Suddenly, he stiffened.

"They're moving! They're leaving the car!"

"I can see as well as you," the other said testily. "Take another look. The man is carrying something. Does it remind you of anything?"

"Well . . ." Uncertainly. "It looks like . . . I don't believe it! A . . . a blanket?" Weakly.

"Now just imagine," the senior watcher began with heavy patience, "that you're hot for a piece of stuff, but the car is too restricting. You've got a blanket handy, nice and convenient. You've got perfect isolation . . ."

"But why *here?*"

"Why not?" The patience was dangerously benign. "Perhaps they're secret lovers. Perhaps they're nature lovers, mountain lovers, darkness lovers." There was no hint of humour in the voice.

"But the ground is wet!"

Another sigh. "People will do it anywhere, if the need is sufficiently great."

"Westerners!" The contempt was full of a sense of satisfaction, now that the junior man knew he'd got it right this time. "What if this is the place? We can't leave witnesses."

"Naturally not. They might as well enjoy themselves while they can."

Pross said, quietly, "Bloody hell, Logan! It's freezing out here."

"Keep your voice down."

"It is down!"

"And if you're cold, wrap the blanket about you when we're out of sight."

Pross shook his head in wonder. She'd pulled the blanket out from behind his seat, astonishing him with her suggestion.

They'd reached a bulge in the side of the slope, a few yards from the rear of the car. Judging they should now be out of the sight of whoever was up top, Logan squatted on her heels. Pross had no option but to follow suit.

"Whatever they're using, nightscope or night-vision binocs, we were not in sight long enough for them to make out the finer details. I hope."

Not wanting to take chances, she had made Pross put the blanket about her solicitously. It would be what any watcher would expect of a pair of lovers. More practically, it had hidden the radio, the gun, and the bullet-laden garters. Pross admired her thoroughness.

She had switched off the courtesy light so that the door would open without turning it on automatically.

"Here," she said. "You can have this." She passed him the blanket. She checked the garters to ensure that each group of six bullets was positioned on her outer thighs. "Now for the performance."

Pross hedged. "Do we really have to?"

"Yes we do, and loud enough to convince our friends up there."

"You're enjoying this."

"Not as much as the real thing, but it will have to do." A soft giggle accompanied her words.

"*Logan.*"

"I'm only teasing, Pross. Well ... half-teasing. Now come on. Let's hear you."

"For God's sake," Pross said in an anguished whisper. "I can't!"

"Don't be silly. It's quite easy. I'll go first then ... but you'd better back me up or it will sound very strange."

She began to whimper, working up slowly but with increasing urgency and volume; she gave an extremely good performance of someone in the throes of ecstasy.

"Oh. Oh. Oh. *Ooohh!*" her voice wailed while Pross watched her, amazed.

She let her wails end in a gasp.

"What are you *doing?*" she queried in a sharp whisper. "You're supposed to be part of this, you know. Grunt, or something."

"Logan, I —"

Without warning, stiffened fingers jabbed into his stomach. The air rushed out of him.

"*Aaahhh!*" he said, gasping.

"Very good," she said approvingly. "Very convincing. There. That wasn't so bad, was it? Shall I do the same thing again?"

"No, for God's sake! I can hardly breathe! Where'd you learn to do that? No, no. Silly me. One of Fowler's murderous schools for young ladies."

But Logan had started up again.

"I hope they're enjoying themselves," the junior of the two watchers said sourly.

"Obviously, they are."

"Animals. It must be as wet down there as it is up here."

"Perhaps she likes getting her bottom on hard, wet ground ... if they're doing it on the road."

"I hope her tits freeze."

"You're jealous," the senior watcher said dismissively. "Pity you won't be able to play with her before we kill them. There won't be time."

Another study of the car, wondering whether they had been given the wrong information, after all. Yet, an instinctive feeling said remain in position.

"What if they're finished before anything happens?" the subordinate asked, listening to the cries and grunts coming at them from below.

"Then they'll be fortunate. We'll let them go. We'll not kill them unless they become witnesses. The way they're going, I think they'll still be here. Like the lovers of Pompeii, they'll be caught with their pants down."

Neither of them laughed.

Logan gave a long shuddering wail, then let her voice fade to a whimper.

"Well, Logan," Pross said. "You never cease to surprise me. A beautiful piece of faking. Don't ever tell your boyfriends."

"That was not very nice." She sounded strangely hurt.

"A joke, Logan," Pross said, puzzled. What was she so upset about? "That's all it was. You tease me all the time. This is just a reaction against whatever is waiting up there."

"Well, I didn't find it funny."

"I'm sorry. Okay? It wasn't meant to be taken seriously."

She said nothing. He found her silence to be even worse.

"Look," he went on. "If you're not back in twenty minutes . . . half an hour at the most, I'm coming after you . . ."

"*No!*"

In the gloom, he saw her head move as she looked quickly upwards, as if anxious that her sharp whisper might have been heard.

"No," she repeated, quietly. "You'll be staying right here. In the air, you're the predator. Down here, you're a lamb. I don't want you complicating things further. This is my kind of job; a job for wolves. If I don't come back, you're to get out any way you can."

"I don't like the sound of that."

"Of what? Making your own way back?"

"No. Leaving you."

"You won't have the choice. If whoever's up there gets me, you'll be chewed for dessert."

"That's just great. I should have known better than to come on this crazy drive with you."

"It's a hard life, Pross."

He heard a soft click. She had checked the Ruger and was ready for action.

"I'd better be going," she said. "Give me a few grunts as a cover. Let them think we're at it again."

"What about the car?" he whispered at her urgently.

"Leave it if the worst happens. You'd never get it out. It's the walk across the mountains, I'm afraid."

"Great. Perfect."

"It's only six miles to Llanbedr, and even less to a track that leads to Trawsfynydd . . . about three. The problem is, you'll have to go in a wide circle from the campsite, to take you round these hills. Don't try going over them. You might not meet the right kind of people."

He could almost see the brief smile. "Cheer me up, won't you."

"I knew you'd understand. Besides, you'll be alright. You're a pilot, after all, and can find your way in the dark."

"They usually give us instruments."

"Think of our ancestors, Pross. They didn't have instruments."

"They didn't have nutters with guns waiting for them, either."

"Hardly nutters, Pross." A hand touched his cheek briefly. "See you later." Then she was gone.

He wrapped the blanket as he stared at the spot she'd last occupied, feeling at once angry, cold, and annoyed with her. He never liked it when she took off on her own. He always worried for her safety, though he knew this was irrational. She was quite correct in telling him to keep out of it.

Logan was a highly trained, highly skilled person. She clearly knew her way about the terrain. She probably went on jolly hikes in the mountains of Snowdonia with the SAS, he thought sourly, as a sort of lightweight recreational exercise.

He stared out at the darkened lake, listening to the sounds of the night. Behind and above him, tiny rivulets trickled down invisibly to drain away at the edge of the track.

"What the bloody hell am I doing here?" he muttered to himself.

The warmth of his bed, and the soft comfort of Dee, seemed a million miles away.

He stood up slowly, and decided he'd better give a groan or two.

*

42

"There they go again," the junior man said, half-disgusted with himself for his own anticipation. "I suppose she'll be screaming her head off soon." He moved, adjusting his position, and dislodged a stone that tumbled down the slope.

It made a soft, almost apologetic noise on the wet, scrub-covered ground.

"Idiot!" the one in command said with whispered annoyance. "That's the second time you've done that."

"They're not going to hear."

"Keep your mind on what's to be done," came the harsh rejoiner, "and forget about those two rutting down there." The hand reached into the waterproof anorak to take out a radio. A button was squeezed, and a yellow light blinked weakly for a brief moment. A satisfied grunt. Another button, and this time a green light performed the same way. The radio was returned to its hiding place. "The others are in position. It's nearly time. Something should be happening soon."

The junior man did not say something was already happening. He listened to the intermittent grunts coming from below and waited eagerly for the woman's moans and whimpers. It excited him to hear her, and he felt cheated when she continued to keep her enjoyment to herself.

It was a pity there would be no time. He would have liked to have played about with her for a while.

"What if we cannot capture it?" he asked his companion.

"We destroy it," was the cold reply.

Logan made her way carefully upwards. It would not do to slip. That would certainly seal her fate — and Pross's. The noise of her subsequent fall would give her unseen adversaries all the warning they would need.

She had picked a steeper route than she would have liked, given the time for choice. But this was the best way to arrive quickly and, with luck, quite unexpectedly.

She smiled grimly to herself. The Wolfe attack. She thought of Wolfe climbing up a virtual cliff with his troops to catch Montcalm with his pants down in Quebec. Strange, the things that came into your mind when under the stress of imminent combat. Her mind had done a back-flip down the years and into her childhood. Her father had been discussing military tactics in, of all places, a churchyard, with the local vicar. The vicar had once been an Army glider pilot during World War II.

Why, she now wondered, had she suddenly thought of her father? She put the distant churchyard out of her mind and concentrated on the task in hand; which was just as well.

Her right foot, resting precariously on the smooth protrusion of an almost fully buried boulder held in place by its bed on packed earth and roots, slid off suddenly and she felt herself falling.

In her right hand was the Ruger. She had been using her elbow to lever herself upwards while the left hand pulled, and the feet pushed. As she slid, her left hand clawed into the earth. The toes of her shoes pressed themselves into the yielding soil for purchase. She did not let go of the magnum. Nothing would make her do that.

Her slide lasted bare inches, but it had felt like hundreds of feet. The protruding boulder seemed to have raked across her leg. It felt numb from the knee down.

She had opened her mouth in a silent cry and felt the roughness of shrubbery on her lips. She did not remember biting into anything. She pressed herself against the ground, recharging herself, controlling the rate of her breathing as she listened for anything that would tell her her presence on the slope had been discovered.

But nothing seemed to have changed. The sounds about her were the same. A grunt from below told her Pross was still keeping up the subterfuge. She felt herself smiling fondly as she thought of him.

Feeling was returning to her leg. She flexed her muscles, wriggled her toes. Nothing damaged. She risked movement upwards. The leg was okay.

Stupid bitch, she chided herself in her mind, *that will teach you not to concentrate.*

She continued her climb. While the slope could not exactly pass for the Heights of Abraham, she tried not to remember that Wolfe had died in the battle.

"She's still keeping it quiet," the junior man said with a mixture of annoyance and curiosity.

"Why don't you go down there and ask her to give a few moans for your benefit?" his superior remarked nastily. "Perhaps she'll oblige. Then, after you've blown the mission, you can answer to me."

After that, the man wisely kept his counsel. But something worried him. He could not identify what it was, and only knew that it had to do with the lack of audible lovemaking from the woman. There was no reason why she should be yelling her head off, considering the bawling she'd recently done. Perhaps she was conserving her energy this time round for the serious business of the actual lovemaking.

All the same . . .

The man continued to consider all options and possibilities, but after the veiled threat from the mission leader, he did not give voice to his ruminations.

These, he thought, were obviously not the people their information had given them to expect. It was just one of those unforeseen things that could happen on any mission. Once, he had parachuted into a country at night, into a landing zone that had been made secure, only to find when he was thirty metres off the ground that a sudden powerful gust of wind was blowing him away from the zone. His steerable chute had taken too long to answer his frantic commands. He had landed on a deserted road . . . save for the car parked there on a jack, its owner replacing a wheel. The other had suffered a puncture. One of those things.

The unfortunate motorist had been killed, but the mission had of necessity been abandoned. The driver had been an off-duty policeman.

Remembering this, he took his superior's warning very seriously indeed; despite his unease, it never once entered his mind that the woman supposedly making love below might be climbing up the slope to kill them.

Had the male grunts and groans stopped for as long, he would have been instantly alerted. So he remained where he was, patiently awaiting the object of their ambush, completely unaware that he and his companion were being stalked.

Logan found that as she got nearer the top the ground sloped more gently. She no longer had to push-pull herself towards her objective. She could actually crawl without fear of sliding downwards. The incline, however, remained sufficiently steep to give enough cover for her purposes.

She smiled resignedly as she thought of the damage her upward trek might have done to her favourite sweater. The wet ground and shrubbery had soaked it, as well as her jeans, but wet and muddy clothes can be cleaned and dried. She was more worried about the havoc the stiff bristles of the scrub might have wrought. It was the first sweater she had ever knitted. She had been fifteen at the time, and had made it too big. She had grown into it.

She smiled again. What a thing to have on her mind at a time like this. When she had knitted the sweater, who would have believed it would one day see such service?

She stopped moving, and flattened herself against the soaked ground. The edge of the incline was inches from her nose.

She had reached the top.

She lay there, assessing the situation. She had arrived between two clumps of moor grass, which gave her good cover, while allowing her to sight through the opening.

Luck was with her. The quarry was little more than thirty feet away. Even in the gloom — which seemed lighter at this height — the two shapes were sufficiently distinguishable.

They had chosen their position well, she thought. There was no reason for them to expect an attack from where she herself now lay.

During her climb, she had heard the soft tumble of the accidentally dislodged stone and had altered her course accordingly. Now she brought her gun-hand forward, braced it with her right, and sighted carefully.

She would have to make every shot count. The two out there would be absolute professionals and would give her no margin for error. She needed a better target, however, and would have to get them to move; for despite the definition of their shapes, they had reduced their profiles efficiently.

She knew exactly what she had to do.

Down below, Pross was getting worried. He too had heard the soft fall of the stone and had wondered if Logan had been caught out, after all, and if that even as he crouched there trying to make himself invisible a pair of killers were stealthily making their way down towards him.

He strained to listen for any sound that might betray their approach. What the hell would he do? As Logan had so succinctly put it, in such circumstances he was a lamb.

He stared out at the lake. It seemed full of all sorts of malevolent secrets.

Logan was ready.

"Good evening," she called softly.

They were good, she had to admit; very good indeed. For even as the magnum was roaring out its first challenge into the night, they had moved.

They must have been startled out of their wits, but there had been no panic, no exclamation of surprise. Instead, they had gone swiftly into action with the fluidity of a well-rehearsed double-act. The one closest to her had rolled to face the direction her voice had come from, weapon tracking, she knew, with deadly accuracy. The other was in the act of standing, training his own weapon with the same deadliness. She also understood, in that same instance, what they were doing.

It was a classic manoeuvre to divide the attention; giving at least one of them a relatively unhurried shot with which to nail the opposition.

But she had already worked out her own routine. She was ready for them.

The one still on the ground would be the most dangerous. He would be the steadiest, needing the least time to centre on target. That was where her first shot had gone.

Certain she had scored and had thus delayed that threat, the second shot blasted into the roar of the first, it seemed. This one was for the man still rising to his feet.

He staggered as the heavy bullet struck him, but did not fall.

Logan's third shot went to the prone man, who had been effectively stopped by the first. It was intended to kill. This left the standing man exposed.

The fourth shot took him squarely. He gave a loud scream of what sounded like frustrated rage in a language that she recognised and understood. His silhouette moved indistinctly then toppled over the edge. She heard the body slam heavily as it hurtled downwards.

As she released her breath slowly and watched for movement from the other body, she thought puzzledly of what she had heard the screaming man say.

"You scheming bitch!" he had raged. In Russian.

Pross heard the sudden slamming of the four shots, and jumped involuntarily, startled by the combined roar. He knew it was the magnum. He had heard it at work on previous occasions, and knew its sound well enough. He would none the less never get accustomed to the fact that someone who looked so vulnerable could carry and use that massive cannon with such skill.

He waited anxiously for returning fire. Instead, he heard the scream reverberating into the night, seeming to travel round the lake. Then came the sickening thumpings of the crashing body. It rolled with an ever-gathering speed, dislodging a small avalanche in its wake.

Horrified, Pross realised the body was coming his way. He stood up, and took a couple of steps backwards. The body arrived at speed and slammed into the side of the car with the noise of a bag of coal crashing into an empty bin. It bounced off and back onto the ground, hitting a small pool of water with a flat, wet sound.

But it did not lie still.

Pross felt the hairs on the back of his neck spring to attention as the shapeless bundle tried to rise. Gurgling wheezings were coming from it. He remained rooted to the spot, staring with fascinated horror at what was happening. Every so often a strange, drawn-out moan would come from it.

If Pross could have understood Russian, he would have recognised the single word.

"Bitch . . . bitch . . . bitch . . ." the bundle was repeating, the voice weakening with each utterance.

At last, the moaning ceased. The struggles became weaker, until they too stopped.

Pross slowly let out the breath he'd been unaware of holding.

"Bloody hell," he said quietly.

Up at the top, quite oblivious of her part in Pross's recent traumatic experience, Logan continued to give the prone body her undivided attention. The magnum still pointed at the target. She did not intend to fall for any corny possum trick. If the man was not yet dead, she had certainly wounded him fatally. She was sure of it.

She gave it another estimated five minutes before taking her radio off her belt and speaking into it. Throughout, she kept her attention on the body.

"Two taken out," she said. "There's bound to be more, but they're probably running. Then again, perhaps not. Need assistance."

"On our way."

She replaced the radio, decided to check out the body. Very cautiously, she inched her way over the lip and towards the dark shape, ready to fire at the slightest move from it.

Nothing.

When she was a mere six feet or so away, she paused, lying still, on her stomach. Did he have an automatic booby-trap? she wondered.

Some pros she knew of carried a small frag or phosphorus grenade with them so that, if mortally wounded, they would use their last remaining strength to prime the little bomb and lie on it. Anyone turning them over would release the pin and – bingo. Revenge after death. A mercenary contractor had told her of it.

She didn't go in for that sort of thing, nor did she like contractors. Fowler never used them on principle, though other departments did.

She stared at the body. Was he one of those who killed after death? The rifle, with its nightscope still on, was lying loosely in his outflung hand, pointing away from her. She crawled forward to take it.

Then unbelievably, the hand tightened about the weapon and the body was suddenly *moving*.

Commendably, despite her shock, Logan did not pause to wonder how he had survived this long with two magnum rounds in him, without moving and without making a sound. All she knew was that she faced a formidable enemy and that survival was all.

Even as the man's hand had begun to tighten about the rifle, she was rolling away, knowing that despite his skills the two wounds he had received would slow him down.

Yet he was faster than she would have believed possible. He had somehow also managed to roll to track her and she saw the green disc of the glowing sight shifting towards her.

She was now on her back. No time to roll onto her stomach to form a bipod with her elbows and give the magnum a stable platform. She brought her feet back, raising her knees, and spread her thighs in a vee. Then she raised her head, as she held the Ruger in both hands, pointing along the centreline of her body. The glowing sight was coming round.

There were two bullets remaining. They'd have to count.

She fired, just above the disc. Two fast shots. Then she rolled away.

It was all over. The glow of the disc was gone; as was the body. She heard it tumbling its way down.

She sat up slowly, and heard herself give a nervous giggle as she began to reload. She wondered what Pross would say.

"Bloody hell!" was what he said for a second time when he heard the shots followed by the sounds of another falling body.

There was a brief, accompanying clatter which he assumed was a dropped weapon. The body came on alone to land heavily on the track, some distance from the car. He could not see it, but he had a feeling this one would not be moving again.

Then Pross heard a new sound upon the night. At first, he did not recognise the familiar noise, its signature being markedly different from any he'd heard before. But as soon as understanding had dawned, he felt a sudden lifting of his spirits. The sound pumped the adrenalin through him.

Without warning, a shape was above him. He was stunned. The sound he'd heard had led him to believe its source was still some distance away. Now his immediate world seemed filled with the whirr of an immense powerhouse as the downdraught from the blades caused the air to dance about him.

It was the quietest helicopter he had ever heard.

As it moved slowly past him, heading towards the pillars further down the road, he was able to study such details of its shape as the darkness allowed him to.

From underneath, it looked narrow and sleek, rather like an elongated peardrop, with a flat belly. There were stub outriggers positioned in line with the main rotor, on which were hung a varied weapon load. They seemed to have a shallow sweepback. There were twin stabilisers at the tail, with small fins at each tip. The tail rotor was enclosed. They had used a fenestron design.

Pross himself favoured such an arrangement. Apart from the fact that the enclosed fan was a major safety factor – people tended to walk into tail rotors – it was also quieter, and was a less voracious consumer of power; which in turn left more for the main rotor to do its job of keeping the chopper aloft.

Two thicker stubs protruded from each side of the nose. He assumed they would house all manner of electronic gear and weapon aiming systems. He could see no landing gear; which meant it was retractable.

Then the shape had whispered into the darkness.

"So that's what this is all about," he said to himself. His hands itched to get at the controls.

"Think it was worth coming?"

Pross jumped as he turned round. "Logan! For God's sake don't do that to me. I didn't even hear you." His pleasure at seeing her safe and well was tinged with the fright she'd just given him.

"As I said . . . a lamb. They would have got you."

He peered at her. "You look a mess. What I can see of you, that is."

"Thanks for the welcome. You'd look a mess too if you'd been crawling about on your belly up there." She seemed to shiver.

He took off the blanket, and put it about her. "Sorry," he said quietly. "I was worried about you, especially when I heard the last shots. Are you alright?"

He saw her head nod briefly. "The second one gave me a hard time. I almost fell for the oldest trick in the book."

"Be a little more careful, will you? I can't afford to lose you."

"That's a nice thing to say." She sounded pleased.

"Well . . . who's going to keep the big bad wolves away?"

She kicked him on the ankle.

His forced joking was as much an effort to soothe his own jumpy nerves as it was to help her. Did she feel as depressed as he did whenever he had killed?

True, his killing was always at one remove. When he blew another helicopter out of the sky it was the machine he was killing, he told himself. But it never helped, because he also knew someone else had been at the controls of the dying ship. Another person was burning to death, or falling like a stone; and his feelings at that instant were always those of thanks that he was not the one.

Logan was walking ahead of him, going towards the car. She reached it, stooped briefly by the untidy bundle near it. She straightened, continued walking.

Pross followed slowly, reluctantly. He didn't want to see the bodies at close quarters.

She became indistinct in the gloom as he edged between the shapeless bundle and the car, without looking down at it. He walked to the front of the RS and stopped.

From the darkness ahead, came a soft exclamation. "This one's a woman!"

"What?" Pross said, astonished. Then, without thinking, "Are you sure?"

She was coming back towards him. "She's got two breasts, Pross."

He could almost hear the inaudible sigh that had accompanied her words.

She stopped before him. "Which one came down last?" she asked. The blanket was tightly wrapped about her, as if for protection against something indefinable.

51

"The one you've just looked at."

She nodded slowly, confirming a point she had already made to herself. "She was good. Very good. She nearly got me." The words were quietly spoken, in a tone that was full of respect; and of wonder. "So that's what we're up against."

"What *are* we up against, Logan? And why are we still in this place? Shouldn't we be getting away from here as fast as possible? What about their friends?"

"Which question do you want answered first, Pross?"

"Only one for the moment. Do we go? Now?"

"We'll be going soon, but not together. Wait. Let me explain. The surprise Fowler had in store for you was the helicopter. You were going on a little joyride. According to Fowler, it can do wonderful things by day or night. He thought you'd be interested to try it out, especially at night. Unfortunately, someone else seems to be keen on it."

"That's what I call massive understatement."

"I can't work out how anyone found out about this," she went on, ignoring his words. "We're supposed to have a closed operation."

Pross remained pointedly silent.

"I know what you're thinking," she said.

"You don't know the half of it."

"Look, Pross. I'm sorry. I was caught out too. I thought it would be a nice surprise for you to have a flight in the new helicopter – especially as an old friend is flying it at the moment – and then I'd take you back tomorrow. That was all there was to it. It's all I know."

She was looking vulnerable again, and he could not sustain his anger for long. She had, after all, crawled up the slope and had laid her life on the line; and even if not totally for him, she had still placed herself between him and the danger. Yet again. And should another occasion present itself, he knew she would be there once more, without the slightest hesitation.

"Oh, Logan," he said. "I just don't know what to do with you. Tell me the rest of it."

"Not much more to tell. At least, from where I'm standing. You'll have to talk to Fowler."

"That's a pleasure worth looking forward to."

"You're getting sarcastic again."

"Blame it on my childhood." A friend was flying the helicopter, she had said. Who?

She reached beneath the blanket for the radio, and spoke into it. "Come in for the pickup." All the while, she seemed to be listening to the night, for sounds that broke pattern.

"Roger," the disembodied voice said.

She put the radio away. "Won't be long now, Pross."

Suddenly, a bright fire arced through the darkness, in a shallow trajectory. Pross felt his stomach freeze. He knew what it was. *Surface-to-air missile.*

"*My God!*" Logan said in a shocked whisper. "They're prepared to destroy it!"

Almost immediately, three sunbursts lit up the sky in a close group. They hung in the air, claiming a portion of the night for themselves.

A surreal scene greeted Pross's astonished eyes. Stark impressions were branded upon his mind: the ghostly portrait of Logan's face, staring upwards; the track, a gleaming slate-coloured ribbon disappearing through the open gateway; the surface of the lake suddenly turning into a galaxy of twinkling reflections; the sharply etched brooding ramparts of the surrounding hills.

But what stuck in his mind was the vivid tableau of the sleek shape that seemed to throw itself into a rolling, twisting series of manoeuvres as it darted away from the approaching threat.

Then the missile exploded into the fire of the flares with a roar that seemed to fill the world and a blaze of flame that bathed the area with the intensity of a giant flashbulb. Within this hellish photograph, Pross saw the helicopter, seemingly pasted against the fiery background, as if frozen in flight. Quite clearly, he saw each of its four main blades, spread in a black cross from whose centre it hung.

Then the noise of the explosion began to fade, rolling away like spent thunder; and the yellow-red illuminations vanished, leaving the night to reclaim its domain.

But now another, already familiar sound encroached upon the darkness. The powerful, throbbing whisper heralded the helicopter's approach.

"Your joyride's going to be a little hotter than expected, Pross," Logan said, voice still tense because of what she'd just witnessed. "We're going to have to find those people. Quickly. You can do your bit from the air."

"What about you?"

"Let me worry about that."

Pross was not so certain. "Look, Logan —"

"Come on, Pross. It's my territory down here. Up there, it's yours. How many times do I have to tell you?"

He was still unhappy. The soft thrumming had increased in volume. Just beyond the columns, a light blinked, once. The chopper was already there.

"Let's move it, Pross," she said briskly. "Your transport awaits."

"What about my gear in the car?"

"You'll be seeing me later," she promised. "Leave it for now. Come on. He can't wait out there forever."

She set off at a trot, and Pross followed.

As they drew closer, he began to see more details of the shape of the machine. From what he could judge, it looked like a blend of the Lynx and the A129 Mangusta. It was bigger than the A129, but much narrower than the Lynx from nose to main rotor. Yet the sleek resemblance to the Lynx was unmistakable.

It was a two-man ship, with cockpits arranged in stepped tandem. The canopies were side-opening. As he came up to the machine, Pross felt as if the power it generated had begun to claim his very soul. It seemed to be calling to him in the dark. Now he was closer, he saw that the faintest of glows, palest green in tint, came from the cockpits. A helmeted head, visor down, was turned towards him. The man in the seat raised the visor and grinned.

"Bloody hell," Pross said, raising his voice to be heard. "Cado Rees!"

It was doubtful whether Rees had in fact heard, but he had obviously gauged Pross's reaction correctly, for he grinned once more, and pointed to the front seat, indicating that Pross should climb aboard. There was a helmet waiting, held in place on the seat by the harness.

Crouching, Pross looked round to where Logan was standing, safely out of rotor range. He could barely see her. Her ghostly shape seemed forlorn. As if knowing what he was thinking, she motioned to him impatiently to get on with it.

He remembered something and ran at the crouch, back towards her.

"Time's not on your side, Pross," she began immediately. "We've got to find those people."

"It's alright. I'm not going to say look after yourself. After all, you're a big girl now. It's just that I heard the man yell as he fell," Pross went on quickly before she could say anything. "He was still mumbling when he reached the ground."

"He was still *alive?*"

"Unless bodies can speak these days, yes."

"My God."

"I just wondered if it was important. Couldn't understand what he was saying though. Thought you might. It was the same word over and over again. It sounded like this . . ." He gave an imitation of what he thought he'd heard.

Logan gave a short laugh. "You'll never make a linguist, Pross. But I did get the gist. It's what he shouted up there, more or less. 'Scheming bitch', or if it was just the one word, then it was 'bitch'."

"Anger with his girlfriend for getting him killed?"

"I think he meant me."

"*You?* But —"

"I'll tell you later. Now off you go, Pross, unless you want a missile down here."

"Alright, alright. I'm going." But as he turned to go, he asked, "What was that language, anyway?"

"I think you've already guessed."

"Not bloody Russian?" And when she'd said nothing, he went on, "Great. That's all I bloody need."

He turned away then, and went back to the aircraft.

He could now see on closer inspection that what he'd mistaken for weapons outriggers were in fact stub wings. In the darkness, there was no more detail to be seen. From where he now stood, slightly crouched at the right side of the machine, the protruding forward stub looked bulkier, full as it was of various electronic and sighting devices. He had no doubt the left-hand stub was similarly equipped.

There was a grab handle located centrally along the lower rim of the canopy. He reached for it, felt a long catch on the inside of the handle and squeezed. The canopy lock clicked open and the whole thing rose slowly upwards with a sigh. The front screen and the left side of the canopy remained fixed.

As he reached in to free the helmet, Pross glanced quickly at the interior fittings of the cockpit, and felt the old eagerness take him once more.

The cockpit looked a dream.

There was a looped step fixed to the fuselage just beneath it, about a foot or so off the ground. Pross climbed in, pulled the canopy down. It clicked home smoothly. Instantly, the already quiet sound of the rotors and the engines died to a mere background whisper, it seemed; but there was now a sense of awesome power, just waiting to be unleashed.

As he put on the helmet, quickly secured his harness and connected himself to the aircraft, Rees lifted it off the deck in a swift upward bank to the left. The power of the accelerating engines throbbed through the entire airframe, but in a way that was unlike anything he'd previously experienced when he had last flown the specially modified, high-powered Lynx for Fowler. This was almost like an afterburner take-off in the old Phantom, but quieter, and certainly smoother than any other chopper.

"Found the plug, have you?" Rees said.

The mournful voice Pross remembered came deeply on the helmet phones.

"It was about the only thing I recognised. My God, Cado. This looks a pilot's dream."

"It is, for now."

"You mean there's more?"

"Onwards and upwards, old son. Well, David? How are you? Fancy meeting you here."

"I could say the same to you. Last time we saw each other, you were acquainting me with the Lynx just before Fowler pressganged me into a cross-border operation from Hong Kong, and you were a Sergeant giving Sanders a bit of bother. Then I heard a nasty rumour that they made *you* into an officer. It's not true, is it?"

"Every word, I'm afraid." The voice sounded even more mournful.

"What have they made you?"

"Lieutenant, Acting Captain." Rees was almost apologetic.

"My God," Pross said again.

"Yes, I know. Makes you wonder, doesn't it? They give it to anyone these days."

Pross could sense Rees grinning. "Don't take it so hard."

"How about you? Don't you miss the old life a bit?"

"And have Squadron Leader Snotface Sanders call me Flight Lieutenant in that poncy tone of his? You must be joking. So you're still with Fowler's circus."

"Let's get out of the fire," was what Rees said, as if in reply, and took the Hammerhead smartly out of range. "We're not part of this little sideshow ... so they tell me." He didn't sound too sure. "Fowler's circus?" he went on. The mournful voice bore the barest hint of a chuckle. "They seem to think I'm a reasonable Development and Trials pilot."

Rees was being his usual modest self. Pross considered him to be one of the best chopper jockeys around; better, he was certain, than Pete Dent, who was himself no mean pilot.

"You're a fantastic pilot, Cado. You know that."

"Not as good as you are, David . . . which is why you're with Mr Fowler's merry band."

"I'm with *what*?"

"With the Department . . . which incidentally I know little about, a state of ignorance that pleases me in all sorts of ways."

"I'm not with *any* Department."

"Says you," Rees said ominously.

"Cado," Pross began with what he hoped was sweet reasonableness, "I'm only here for the ride. That's what I was told. Fowler wanted me to give the new ship a once-over." His eyes scanned the cockpit, noting the equipment fit. "If this handles half as good as it looks, he doesn't need my opinion."

"And you believed all you were told." It was not even a question.

Pross was silent for some moments. "I have a weak spot," he said, looking down at the unseen landscape. Logan was down there, with the two bodies.

Rees did not ask for clarification. "We may have some hunting to do," he said. "I'll leave you to familiarise yourself with the cockpit for a couple of minutes. Ask me anything when you feel like it."

"Okay. Thanks. By the way, that was a neat piece of avoidance."

Rees seemed to chuckle. "The SAM? Yes. I was lucky. Didn't expect that in sleepy Snowdonia."

"Lucky my foot. So what do you call this thing?"

"What does it look like to you? Remind you of anything?"

Pross recalled an impression that had come to him when he'd first seen the sleek shape with the protrusions at the nose, sliding through the gloom above him.

"A shark," he answered. "A hammerhead shark. Don't tell me that's what they decided to call it?"

"Give the man ten out of ten."

"It fits," Pross said, thinking of the menacing presence he had first seen. "It fits."

As he began to study the cockpit, he heard a sound from Rees that, this time, could have passed as a chuckle.

The equipment fit was so good that Pross was at a loss to decide what pleased him most. There was more room than his first look from the outside had led him to expect, with the up-front panel continuing along both sides of the cockpit, just like that of a fighter. Following the shape of the fuselage, the top of the panel was horizontal at the base of the steeply raked windscreen, dropped on either side at a shallow angle before becoming almost perpendicular after another shallow angle to end at the side consoles. Centrally, at the base of the panel between curving spaces for the co-pilot/weapons operator's legs, was a smaller console.

The standard helicopter flight controls had been done away with. At each side of the partially-reclined seat, and set into the side panels, were the collective and cyclic side-controllers. Each was about six inches tall with the expanded tops festooned with a seeming multitude of switches. They fell nicely to hand. Pross had no doubt the standard system had been retained, with the cyclic operated by the right hand and the collective by the left. The foot pedals for controlling yaw via the tail rotor had also been retained.

On the left side-console, ahead of the collective, was a multifunction data entry keyboard. Pride of place on the main panel was taken up by two multi-function displays flanking a full colour CRT attitude indicator. Various other switches and instruments covering all the needs of helicopter flying were ergonomically positioned about the rest of the panel. The small central console housed a CRT which displayed a silhouette of the Hammerhead, viewed from behind. Weapon positions were also displayed, as silhouettes of the individual weapon fit. The gun position, on the centreline, was represented by the muzzle of a rotary cannon. The whole display was a glowing green etching on a black background.

At the top edge of the main panel was a full-width rectangular annunciator board, with a multi-coloured series of warning signals and messages, from weapon arming through to fire warning. There were radar, laser, and infrared warning devices. There was even a schematic display which, in combat, would register hits taken by the aircraft, denoting their seriousness with a range of four colours: blue, green, yellow, and red.

Pross cast his mind back to the first time he'd become involved with Fowler, remembering a similar, though less sophisticated system; except that it had been for simulated exercises. Someone, somewhere, had obviously thought it a good idea to make the unit an integral part of the helicopter's survival kit. He was pleased to see that the all-important chaff and flare dispensers had also been catered for.

There was a head-up display too, with pitch lines and a central aiming reticle; but that was only part of it. The HUD was a wide-angle system, with a comprehensive display of immediately necessary information for flying and combat requirements. Pross was pleased to note that the Integrated Flight and Fire Control system that had been incorporated into the HUD on the Lynx he'd used in Nepal had found its way into this beautifully tooled-up machine. It didn't take a genius to work out that Fowler was carrying out a systematic development programme. Like most of the systems in the cockpit, the IFFC also glowed a soft green.

Who, Pross wondered, was *paying* for all this?

Down in the darkness Logan listened as the Hammerhead whispered out of earshot. Rees had taken it across the lake, keeping low. She assumed he would be going round the high cliff, remaining concealed as long as possible while curving back to find the SAM firers. She had no way of knowing.

She took out her radio, spoke softly into it. "They've gone."

"How many SAM teams do you think are out there?" the radio asked. Sanders' voice.

"Your guess is as good as mine. So you saw what happened."

"We did."

"How far are you from me?"

"A good couple of miles. We're on foot, Logan. It will take us some time to get to you. Can you drive out?"

"And make myself a target? No chance. Besides, they might have put a stopper on the bottle. The van could be out there, blocking the road, waiting. I'd rather take my chances here. I'll do some hunting of my own."

"What about the house?"

Logan turned to look briefly down the track beyond the columns. She could not see the building in question.

"Can't a see a thing," she answered. "No lights whatsoever. Nothing has come out of there."

"At least they didn't get that far. See you later, Logan. Good luck."

"Thanks for nothing," she said.

"Logan." Warningly. "Keep in touch. We may need to co-ordinate with the helicopter in order to sanitise the area. We must liaise, both on the ground and with Rees. Those are my instructions."

For reply, she switched off her radio.

"Sod you, Sanders," she said into the darkness.

In the gloom of the woods, Sanders swore beneath his breath and said exasperatedly, "That young woman will drive me insane one of these fine days. It's a source of constant amazement to me that Fowler keeps using her."

There were three other men in Sanders' team. One of them spoke *sotto voce* to a companion.

"Perhaps because she's bloody good."

Sanders heard the comment. "I may sometimes put up with Logan's impertinence, Browning," he snarled, "but don't make the mistake of thinking you can get away with it. Special Duties or no, you're still a Sergeant and I'm your superior officer. What's more, you haven't got Mr Fowler guarding your back. I can have you out of this mob and into some hell-hole like Belize in no time at all. Do I make myself clear?"

Browning muttered something.

"I didn't quite get that, *Sergeant* Browning," Sanders remarked, itching for trouble.

"Yes, sir," Browning said, choosing discretion.

Partially mollified, Sanders said, "Just so you remember it. Now let's get on with the job. We've wasted enough time as it is."

The others in the team wisely resisted an inclination to tell him who had actually wasted the time.

Logan now had the time to feel angry. How had something as simple as a demonstration flight managed to turn into this? The flight had been planned deliberately at night to avoid curious eyes — mainly those of the public. It was always surprising how accurate a picture could be constructed from low-level intelligence gathered from an unsuspecting and totally uninvolved member of the public. A stroller or holidaymaker who had seen something unusual, then mentioned it to a friend or relative in a bar or a café, could put into place the final piece of a puzzle that might have been mystifying a sharp agent for months. Logan herself knew people in the business who placed more value on such snippets than on anything stolen, or clandestinely leaked, as such items could quite easily have been carefully manufactured. Equally, an unaware citizen could be used to give credibility to a particular smokescreen. There were all sorts of permutations.

But as far as she could discern, tonight was not one of those occasions. There were no operations running that involved her.

Yet on a simple job that was meant to have no hostiles, she had killed two people. She had been looking in her mirrors merely as normal routine and had been surprised to see the van. From then on, despite the surprise, her training had taken over. She had gone into her personal alert mode and had acted accordingly.

She had not lied to Pross, but she knew he would not fully believe it, even though he would say otherwise. This, more than anything, angered her.

She did not like lying to Pross.

She glanced upwards at the inky sky. She'd make quite sure she found out exactly what was going on. Meanwhile, she had a job to do.

During the Hammerhead's lift-off, she had ensured that the magnum was ready for immediate use. Now, with the blanket still wrapped about her, she moved close into the side of the steep slope and flattened herself against the wet ground. She would not be going near the car. She wanted to see if anyone would approach it.

From her position, she could see enough of the track so that any vehicle or person approaching along it would give her plenty of warning. She did not allow the presence of the two bodies to distract her. It would be so easy, she thought, on this night in this particular place, to let the mind run riot. Here she was, all alone in the middle of nowhere, with those two things to keep her macabre company, and the nearest friendly help a good two miles away − if not further.

It would be so easy to imagine the bodies −

"Stop it, Logan!" she admonished herself in a fierce whisper. "Remember who you are."

She briefly wished she had one of the discarded nightscoped rifles; but she felt happier with the magnum, she decided. She went in for close-in work and for that, the Ruger was supreme as far as she was concerned. Besides, a rifle would have to be searched for, and she had no intention of doing that.

Bad enough being stuck in the middle of the mountains on this cold night. It would be sheer stupidity to go wandering around and eventually blunder into someone's waiting sights. How, she asked herself as she continued her lonely vigil, had the Russians found out about this?

She considered the possibility that the language had been deliberately used so as to sow confusion. They might not have been Russian at all. But could anyone be so highly trained that he would, in extremis, cry out in a foreign tongue?

She doubted it.

She waited, with her magnum, for further developments.

FOUR

"Any comments?" Rees asked.

The helicopter was beating its way quietly round Castell Carreg-y-saeth, the southernmost section of the Llyn Cwm Bychan rampart, a mile or so away. It now headed eastwards on a curving track that would eventually take it north.

Pross could not see the ground. No pinprick of light broke the velvety darkness. They were flying too low to see the light clusters of either Trawsfynydd to the northeast, or Harlech and Llanbedr to the west. He watched the glowing images of the figures showing the aircraft's course perform their digital dance on the HUD, as they changed in answer to the continuingly altered heading, while Rees unerringly threaded the Hammerhead between the unseen mounds of high ground.

"The problem," he began, "is where to start. This looks as if some really serious thought went into its design."

"And the rest."

"My first question then."

"Fire away."

"Where did the money come from? I thought there weren't any funds available for projects like this. We both know it takes years of hard graft to get anything off the ground."

"I'll have to duck that one. No see, no hear, no speak. Ask Fowler about it. He's the man with the answers, if he cares to give them. I'm just the D & T pilot around here."

"Somehow, I had a feeling you'd say that," Pross remarked drily.

"Sorry, David, but that one's outside my province."

"Don't worry about it, Cado. I've another feeling I'll be talking to

Fowler about a lot of things. This will be one of them."

"And the next question?" Rees prompted.

Pross lightly touched the concertinaed, gaitered boot of the collective side-stick.

"I'm itching to have a go," he said, "but I think I'll wait until I know her better. So I'll be the good little passenger while you give me a rundown."

Rees said, "Fair enough. Things might get a bit hairy later on, *if* we're asked to go after those people. If you feel like getting stuck in, just say the word."

"As I won't have much choice, I suppose I'd better."

"Fair enough," Rees said again. "You'll have recognised some old friends in the equipment fit," he went on, "and quite a few new ones. Let's start with the controllers. The system is a triplex fly-by-wire set-up *à la* F-16 —"

"A triple-redundant electrical system, with *no* back-up?" Pross was not happy with that idea. A total power failure would mean absolutely no control of the aircraft, if there were no mechanical back-up as a last resort. He'd have preferred the option to autorotate, at the very least. This system gave you one option: glide like a stone, all the way down. In the F-16, you could always eject.

Rees's mournful voice sounded even deeper as he continued. "It's actually a very clever system. You've in fact got the equivalent of five channels, *plus* a last resort. Channels Two and Three have each got a self-repairing capability. If Number One goes, followed by Two, Two is capable of patching itself into the serviceable part of One, to make a fully operational channel. This effectively gives you a new channel. Two and Three have a similar capability, to give you a second stand-by channel."

"And the last resort?"

"Ah. This is where it gets really clever. At the instant of failure of all five channels, the collective locks into autorotative mode and the stand-by generator comes on, driven by the rotation of the main blades. This gives you sufficient power to attempt an autorotative landing. The central computer's quite pilot-friendly, really."

"I hope it's read the same book that you have," Pross said, not entirely convinced.

"It works," Rees said. "I've done a simulated power failure three times, and one of those was onto the deck of a frigate ... at night."

"That must have been dicey," Pross remarked with admiration.

"It was . . . especially as that was not what I had intended." The mournful voice sounded as if it wanted to laugh at the memory.

"What happened?"

"We were carrying out night trials and I went into the simulation a little early. The brief was to land on a beach. Luckily, the frigate which was there as both nursemaid and minder was close enough; otherwise this piece of kit would have tried to walk on water."

"Can she float?"

"About long enough for you to get out, if you've managed to put her down correctly."

"You were lucky."

"I keep telling myself that every time I think I'm going to do something crazy. I can still feel the fright." This time, Rees gave an identifiable chuckle. "You'll have recognised," he went on, "all the usual stuff like tactical air nav, Doppler, IFF, IR jamming and so on. Outside, on the nose, are the target acquisition and night vision gear, but in addition to the TADS and PNVS, we've got a state-of-the-art forward-looking infrared system. The new Flir takes thermal imaging into the kind of realm a hard-working chopper stick-man like me always dreamed about. It will pick out a tank at five kilo-metres − just to give you an idea − and can zoom in on a selected target.

"The target radar can also be coupled so that you can light a target miles away and bring it into the imager. The designator box comes on and all you've got to do is keep it in the reticle and arm your weapon. If you've chosen a short-range self-seeking shoot, then you don't have to bother aiming after you've achieved lock-on."

"You make it sound so easy."

"It isn't, take it from me. You've still got to worry about hostile fire, as well as mother nature herself. Particularly at night."

Pross smiled at Rees's words, with their hint of admonishment. Rees could sometimes miss the joke.

"All immediately required information," Rees was saying, "comes up on the HUD. Zoom controls, some weapons selectors, comms switch, and boosters, are on the sticks . . . as, of course, is the all-important trigger. Not much use if you couldn't fire the wretched things after all that. For air-to-air, you will have recognised the IFFC, with which you're already familiar.

"Now let's see . . . oh yes, the multi-function displays. Each cockpit can be made autonomous, fully coupled, or partially coupled. In this last mode, some of the systems will work independently, while others will remain coupled. The required systems can be selected by either member. This feature was considered necessary in case one member becomes incapacitated, but is able to continue operating in a limited way. I think what they're trying to say in not so many words is that if one crew member has for example been blinded by a laser, and the other's lost his legs, but can still see and speak, then both crew can operate as one, if you get what I mean." Rees sounded at his most mournful.

"A sort of human duplex system," Pross said drily. "Two redundant bio-channels."

"That sort of thing, yes."

"That's bloody morbid, Cado."

"Practical though, when you think of it."

"Well, much as I like the looks of this piece of machinery, I'm glad I'm not going to be one of the redundant bio-channels when your lot are zapping tanks on the Eiffel Plain."

Rees said nothing to that. "Take a look at the left-hand MFD," he suggested mildly.

Pross obeyed. The display was a zig-zig of waypoints, with a pulse showing the Hammerhead's progress along it. This now changed to a navigation mode. Along each vertical border of the MFD was a series of buttons and near each one, on-screen, was a list of nav information that could be obtained by the press of the indicated button.

"You should now have one of the nav modes on-screen," Rees said. "Press a button."

Pross gave the one next to LAST WPT a gentle stab. Immediately, a display of the last waypoint came on.

"Last waypoint," Rees said with satisfaction. "You will see a row of six buttons on the lower border. Press the first."

Pross stabbed at the left-hand button. Nothing happened. The waypoint display was still there. Only the blue warning light in the button betrayed the fact that he'd done anything.

Rees said, "The warning light tells me you're now uncoupled. We've still got the same display, but if I change mine, yours will remain. I'll do that now, then cancel your command."

As Pross watched, the blue light winked out, and the original nav mode also returned.

"Magic," Pross said. "We could have used some of that on the old Phantom."

"From what I hear, they're updating them, but I don't think they'll come near this. The right-hand MFD, as well as giving you such goodies as a very comprehensive attitude and heading display, and hover control symbology, also gives you your main radar-coupled thermal imagery. This is of course repeated on the HUD during combat. Next, the life-support systems . . ."

Rees gave Pross a continuing rundown of the workings of the Hammerhead, until Pross began to marvel that he could still manage to fly the aircraft in the dark blanket of the night.

As if guessing Pross's thoughts, Rees said, "It's not as bad as you think. As long as you remember all this is here to make life less hazardous for you, you'll be on the right track. I'll couple the right-hand MFD to show you."

But before Rees could carry out his demonstration, three rapid bleeps sounded on the headphones. The group was repeated twice.

"Sounds as if we're in business," Rees said.

"Surprise, surprise," Pross heard himself say drily.

During his discourse, Rees had flown a pattern that had kept the aircraft well out of harm's way. Now he began curving back towards the hot area.

"We've got a little time," Rees went on, "so I'll continue introducing you to your new friend. I'm coupling the MFD . . . *now.*"

On the screen in Pross's cockpit, a thermal image of the passing landscape appeared. The definition was remarkable. The greenish, seemingly three-dimensional image was picked out in fine detail. Everything in the Hammerhead's track could be seen: shrubbery, boulders, rising ground on each side, a narrow stretch of meandering water, a small lake . . .

"That's Gloyw Lyn passing below," Rees said. "We'll soon be where those SAM firers were. Those trees coming up. There may be more than one team. Things might get really hairy. Still want a piece of the action?"

"If they're going to fire at me," Pross said, "I might as well discourage them." Despite himself, he could feel the pre-combat pulse beating perceptibly within him. The change was coming, and he was welcoming it.

Rees said, his mournful voice as pleased as it could ever be: "I was hoping you'd say that. I'll fly. You be the weapons man."

"My old job in Phantoms," Pross said with a sense of irony, "except my seat used to be at the back. Alright, Cado. We're going into combat."

He punched up the ground-attack mode on the HUD, and saw the more comprehensive version on the MFD. A small oblong window at the top centre of the frame gave the aircraft's current heading, with approaching and departing headings on either side of the marker. Directly beneath that was the true airspeed, indicated by digits that were rapidly decreasing from an original, sedate 100 knots. To its right, were two groups of figures. The top indicated height above mean sea level, the bottom figure was height above ground level. Further down, in the middle, but still within the top third of the frame, were the two dashes of the aircraft symbol, with a central point. Down to its right was a small window with the message ATTACK, indicating the current mode. To its left was a mobile guidance reticle, a small square quartered by crosshairs that did not quite meet at the centre.

Centrally placed beneath the aircraft symbol was a grid, looking like a squat runway drawn to perspective, indicating the helicopter's track. At bottom right-hand corner were two indicator boxes — a small square within an oblong — which showed current position and would show required optimum position when the target was designated, for the selected weapon to be fired.

Thus both pilot and gunner would be kept fully informed at all times. The whole was superimposed upon the thermal landscape beneath.

Pross said, "I've got this sudden, terrible thought, Cado."

"Yes?" Rees said cautiously.

"This was meant to be a joyride for my benefit, wasn't it?"

"Yes." Even more cautious now.

"I'm almost afraid to ask, but ... are those wicked-looking weapons we're carrying supposed to be armed? Or are they practice warheads or even worse ... dummies?"

"Ah," Rees began, and Pross knew the worst. "I had a feeling you'd ask that. Yes, this was a supposed joyride. Yes, most of the weapons are dummies —"

"Bloody hell!"

"— but, we've got four air-to-grounds with half-charges, more than enough to give those people down there a terminal headache. We've also got a pair of seven-tube rocket pods — with low charges, true, but still enough to make life very difficult down there. Our infrared jammer is on line, and as well as IR suppressors for the engines, we've still got a few flares left."

"How many?"

"About ... let me see ..."

Pross knew Rees was punching up the information. The annunciator panel told him what he didn't want to know: three flares remaining.

Knowing Pross had seen for himself, Rees said, "That's not such bad news." He added quickly, as soothingly as the mournful voice could allow, "Our ballistic tolerance is quite good. We can take small-arms hits anywhere, up to 12.7mm, even some 23mm without seriously affecting us, and we can take 30mm splinters."

"We the aircraft?" Pross asked grimly. "Or we our bodies?"

"Both. The seats are armoured."

"I'll remember that when one comes through the cockpit at head height. We're talking about SAMs, Cado. I've got an even better idea. Why don't we just forget it and return to wherever your base is?"

"Can't. We've got to take them out. As the hunt down there is on foot, they could get away, only to try again later. Fowler doesn't want the risk."

"I'll bet he doesn't. Alright, here's another thought. Go back, load up with some real weapons, and return to do business."

"Ah. Well ..."

"I don't think I want to hear this."

"All the weaponry is not yet fully cleared. We're only at the beginning of the weapons trials programme. There are a few glitches to sort out."

"You're beginning to spoil my fun, Cado," Pross said. "You know, I *am* crazy. I keep agreeing to things every time Logan turns up. She's like some Pied Piper and a bloody homing missile rolled into one, fired off at me by Fowler when he feels like it; and she hits the target every bloody time."

"Forget Logan for now, David," Rees said tensely. "Someone else has fired off at us!"

Pross knew even as Rees spoke. The infrared warning was beeping in his ear and on the panel its visual echo was winking balefully. A new sound had joined the beeping. Rees had activated the jammer.

Pross saw the missile warning box appear in the upper right corner of the HUD, moving fast. Rees kept the Hammerhead steady on its 010 heading. The small wood was right on the nose. The missile had come from there.

"Brace yourself!" Rees called, and the helicopter tilted over onto its left side sharply, only to reverse, within the same motion it seemed, before righting itself to drop vertically.

Pross watched as the altimeter told him the ground was now a stomach-freezing 50 feet beneath him. But the descent had already metamorphosed into ascent. The altimeter counted upwards. Something bright had lighted up the night. Rees had set off a flare.

"Eat your heart out on my sunburst," he heard Rees say.

If Rees talked to missiles, he decided, he was not the only crazy one. It didn't make him feel any better about the situation he found himself in.

A great blaze of light and a slamming explosion told him that Rees's avoidance had worked, but he had nearly left it too late. The Hammerhead danced in response to the shock-waves; then the night reclaimed its domain once more.

Pross was glad he had thought to lower his visor. His night vision had not been impaired by the proximity of the missile's dying flash. He saw that the heading was again 010. Rees intended to take out the SAM team once and for all.

Pross wondered if they were using the old SAM-7. If so, its effective range was 3000 metres – just under two miles. But the Hammerhead was well within range. It all depended on how many they were carrying, and how many teams were actually down there.

How had they transported the missiles? The answer was easy enough. Vans like the one he'd seen in Barmouth, and later just down the road in Llanbedr, would have solved that logistics problem.

All these thoughts charged through Pross's mind as he waited for a target to make itself known.

Then the infrared warning was going mad once more. The threat was from a different direction: 120, the indicator stated. From the rear quarter, to the south east.

"Now we know," Rees said, with a strange calm. "At least two teams then."

He had zoomed out the attack display, and Pross could now see a large patch of forest three kilometres away. Just within range . . . assuming, of course they *were* using SAM-7s and not something new with nearly twice the speed and twice the range.

Rees was saying, "Any suggestions?" He still seemed abnormally calm.

But something else had claimed Pross's attention.

"Target!" he said.

70

On the MFD, a red pinpoint was blinking. The scanner had found a sizeable heat source. A group of people? Not much fun killing a flock of sheep.

"I'll take the zoom right in," Rees said.

Even as Rees spoke, the attack MFD was zooming in on the target wood swiftly. The heat source grew into definable images. People running in different directions. The Hammerhead was still 800 metres away.

"They obviously realise we're on to them," Rees said. "I'll increase speed to shorten weapon flight time. Choose your poison. As for the other SAM, I've given it fifteen seconds from launch to impact. We're into four seconds of launch time. I'll let it cope with the jammer and a flare."

Pross could see all the relevant information on the HUD and the MFD. The urgent messages had pulsed five times before disappearing, then coming on again. Real attention-getters.

As the jammer started its song on the headphones, he selected rockets; a pair from each pod. No point using up the entire supply when there were more targets to account for. The system allowed staggered firings from each pod, simultaneous pairs, or full house as Rees had dubbed it, emptying the pods in less than a second.

Rees set the flare off at four seconds to impact, sent the aircraft into a swift lateral displacement and dropped almost simultaneously. He then increased forward speed and returned to 010.

Pross saw RKTS ARMED come up on the HUD and the MFD, while at the weapons CRT the rocket positions glowed red.

Rees began bringing the Hammerhead round on target. Pross watched as the reticle on the MFD shifted towards the IR source. When it had settled squarely, the reticle gave three rapid pulses before glowing a very bright red that almost eclipsed the IR source.

SHOOT, the cue said.

Pross squeezed the trigger and four rockets hurtled out of the pods at the instant that the SAM detonated itself on the flare Rees had conveniently left for it to feed upon.

Pross again felt the Hammerhead dance to the shockwaves as the flash starkly lit up the night for searing moments. Then the rockets were themselves tearing into the wood.

The subsequent explosions took him by surprise. Rees had said low charges, but had omitted to indicate in relation to what. The quadruple eruption of flame seemed to engulf the area of wood that the rockets had struck, billowing upwards in a vivid mixture of red, orange, yellow, and white.

The Hammerhead tilted sideways as Rees hauled it away to head once more across Llyn Cwm Bychan. At the far end of the lake he rotated the aircraft so that it was again pointing towards the flames. He held it at the hover a few feet above the surface, a nearly invisible beast of the night surveying its handiwork.

"The Forestry Commission are not going to be pleased with your act of vandalism," he said drily. "As for the people in there, I think their troubles are over. Good shooting."

"It was hardly good shooting. The Hammerhead did it all, with a lot of help from you."

"You're being modest again, David. I couldn't have had the same result with a novice in the front seat. Have you any idea how long it's been since I picked you up?"

"Ten ... fifteen minutes?" He'd been so engrossed from the moment he'd entered the aircraft, he had not taken account of the passage of time; an omission that could become fatal in combat.

"Six," Rees corrected.

"Six minutes?" Had that been all?

"Without realising it, David, you were working in your own combat mode." Rees seemed to be having a quiet laugh. "Did you like the rockets?"

"Some low charge! A joke at my expense, Cado?"

"No joke. They were low charges. Full ones would have taken out twice the area of woodland. The Commission would have been even less pleased. That's Fowler's little headache. So you see, we're not as defenceless as you at first believed. We've got enough for our purposes."

"In my day, low charges were never like that."

"They're exactly as they were, but this fit is specially for Hammerhead. We're working up to extra-powerful explosives for the full charge. There was a slight problem with them, but it's nice to see they work OK."

Pross digested this wonderful piece of intelligence for some moments, in silence.

"Cado, you're not trying to tell me this is the first time you've fired these things, are you?"

"You fired them, David." Rees sounded like someone trying very hard not to cough with embarrassment. "But to answer the question ... yes, this is the first time they've been fired on board,

72

so to speak. We weren't really expecting to, were we? But necessity —"

"What happened before?" Pross asked patiently.

"Oh . . . we've had rig firings . . . mounted on a raft, out to sea . . ."

"What happened, Cado?"

"Um . . . well . . . they tended to explode on release. Unstable, I was told. Or words to that effect."

"Those nice new pips have definitely made you crazy. You're happy to fly this thing as a test-bed while there's every chance of those rockets cooking off? Do you realise if it hadn't been for that other SAM team I might have let off the full salvo?"

"No you wouldn't. You like to leave some, just in case."

"Know me that well, do you?"

"I've heard snippets about your last two missions."

"Snippets," Pross grumbled. He sighed. "Alright, Cado. As we're both crazy and I, as a family man, seem to have no choice but to behave totally irresponsibly . . . where next?"

"The sensors plotted where that SAM came from and on my command, inserted the co-ordinates into the tacnav. For single-pilot capability — which this chopper has — it can be done automatically and called up or ignored as warranted by current battle conditions. Would you like to fly her?"

Pross hesitated. "I'd like to, but . . ."

"No time like the present, I always say," Rees interrupted briskly. "A couple of points. At the top of each side controller, just before it mushrooms out into the switch platform, you'll feel a serrated ring. Click that left or right to vary the feel. You can have a stick that hardly moves in response to pressure, or one that moves quite substantially. It's all very artificial, but feels like the real thing. Response is instant, so go careful at first.

"Next, the power. These engines are monsters. I've used sixty-five per cent available throughout. There's the usual auto-compensation for direction and attitude changes, but you've got additional settings on the collective. The sleeve moves vertically for power increase and decrease and laterally for engine matching . . . just like the old Lynx, but with some modifications. All movement is gradual, of course. Ready? You have control."

Pross wrapped his hands lightly about the controllers, felt the power of the Hammerhead thread its way through him. He gave the collective a gentle backward pressure. The Hammerhead leapt skywards, taking him by surprise.

73

"My God!" he said involuntarily. "This will need taming." Sheepishly, almost like a novice, he gingerly felt his way about the controls. "I see what you mean, Cado. Cado?"

"It's a good thing I know what you're capable of," came the mournful voice. "I'm trying to locate my spine."

"Sorry. It caught me . . . but it feels good. Really good."

"Thought you might come to that conclusion. We'll switch roles for the next strike. I'll punch up the target position."

Still treating the Hammerhead with respect, Pross took the same route away from the lake that Rees had originally flown; but instead of turning east to overfly Gloyw Lyn for a second time that night, he continued south. With each passing second, his confidence grew and he increased power to 80 per cent.

The Hammerhead thrummed southwards, slicing through the dark with a sound of whispered thunder.

Logan stared at the dying glow of the rocket attack.

She had kept her head down when the explosions had ripped the night apart, and had heard the Hammerhead scoot low across the lake. When she had again peered from her cover, the aircraft was nowhere to be seen, though she had still been able to faintly pick up its sibilance. She had judged it to be hovering close to the water, tucked well into the black screen of the rampart.

Then there had been a sudden surge of power, and a shape had leapt upwards. Moments later, it had again disappeared.

She wondered now if Pross had been flying it.

As she continued to study the site of the explosions, she considered the possibility that there might be survivors.

Would they come this way?

She decided to use her radio to find out how the others were doing. It seemed to blare at her as soon as she turned it on.

"Logan! *Logan!* Are you there?" Sanders, apparently yelling loud enough to wake the dead.

"I'm here," she replied, with heavy patience. "You're rather loud."

"We were worried in case that attack was too close to you."

"I'm worried in case your voice carries too far."

"That's not the right attitude, Logan." Pomposity returning.

"Forget my attitude," Logan said, keeping her own voice low as she thumbed the volume on the radio right down. Sanders could attract attention on his own patch if that was what he wanted. "I'm waiting to see if anyone comes out of that fire and heads my way. Do we take prisoners if the opportunity arises?"

"I doubt if they'd let you." Sanders's voice suggested it was really man's work.

Logan tightened her lips briefly, decided to let it pass. She had no intention of risking her own neck just to disprove his ridiculous bias.

"If they don't," she said coldly, "they're dead."

"That's what I like about you, Logan. Efficient to a fault, you and that field-gun of yours."

She refused to allow Sanders to needle her. "Have you seen any hostiles?"

"Nothing."

Well, she thought. You didn't expect them to be waiting, did you?

She said, "There was a second SAM from this location, and another from somewhere else."

"We saw the flashes, but couldn't ascertain the direction from our position."

"Ascertain," Logan thought. Sanders could sometimes sound just like a policeman making a report.

"So there are more teams," Sanders was saying.

"Looks like it. I think the chopper's gone after them." She continued to keep her eyes on the baleful glow of the rocket strike, and wished Sanders would sign off. He was of little use to her in the present circumstances.

But he was still there. "We've got some people coming up from Trawsfynydd to cut off any escape route."

Logan doubted that would be much use, but said nothing. There were countless escape routes to anyone as professional as the people she had recently come up against. They would not have planned their attacks without contingency arrangements. The one hopeful factor was that the Hammerhead had now turned their strategy from one of outright attack to one of a mixture of offence and defence while on the move. Their plan was going haywire on them; and that couldn't be good news.

It couldn't have helped either that those two on point duty had been eliminated.

"By my field gun," she said to herself, with some satisfaction.

Sanders was still talking. "What was that?"

"I'm having a conversation with myself," she told him.

75

"What are you going on about, Logan?" He sounded at once confused and annoyed.

She sighed. "I said —" Her eyes narrowed as she paused.

Movement . . . from the direction of the fire.

"Talk to you later." She switched off. Sanders's voice died in a soft squawk.

She replaced the radio beneath the makeshift coat of her blanket and crouched down to wait, the magnum held ready.

She had seen something move. She was sure of it.

The Hammerhead slid its way south.

"How does it feel now?" Rees asked.

"Better by the second," Pross replied.

It was no exaggeration. The feel of the aircraft was one of such high response, it was almost as if he merely had to think what he wanted and it would comply.

He had adjusted the sensitivity of the controllers to give him just the right amount of movement he felt comfortable with. This was a lot less than that of conventionally-rigged choppers like his own Jetrangers, or any other rotary machine for that matter. It was even less than Rees's own setting.

Rees had sampled it, and had pronounced, "Very finely tuned, David. Razor's edge. I could never handle it in this mode. I need a lot more movement; although I've had one of the project engineers say to me that my tuning was finer than *he* would personally have liked."

Pross had previously experimented a little and had gradually adjusted the controllers to maximum response, but had found the correspondingly large movement envelope too sloppy and excessive for his taste. The Hammerhead had seemed to wallow, though no doubt there would be heavy-handed chopper jockeys who would prefer it that way.

That was, he now thought, the beauty of this machine. It would tolerate a variety of skills, but certainly still needed to be treated with the greatest of respect. He was quite sure it could be very unforgiving if such respect were not forthcoming. It was powerful, it was agile, it was deadly.

And he loved it.

Almost immediately, he felt the guilt wash over him: as it always did at times like this.

What was he doing gallivanting across the darkened Welsh landscape in a machine worth several million quid of somebody's money (how *had* Fowler managed it?) daring the unseen waiting people to blow him out of the sky? There were other people dependent upon him: the tiny group of Prossair employees, his wife, his two children . . . And that was just the beginning.

Yet here he was, doing the bidding of a bespectacled Machiavelli who ran a Department no one seemed prepared to put name to. Pross was constantly aware of what Fowler had astutely latched on to from that very first meeting. There was that part of him that Fowler could exploit and use for his own devices. Knowing it didn't help. If anything, it made things far worse. It wasn't fair to Dee and the Dawn Patrol, nor to all those who helped run Prossair.

He decided he would have a strong talk with Fowler. It might not do him much good, but he had to try – if only as a sop to his conscience.

Fowler, bless his scheming specs, unfortunately held all the cards; and when one or more of his methods of entrapment failed, there was always his secret weapon.

Logan.

Down by the lake, Logan felt her ears burning.

She smiled ruefully to herself in the cold darkness. "Either someone's talking about me," she muttered, "or my ears are about to drop off with the cold."

She passed the magnum to her other hand briefly, and flexed the fingers of the now empty hand. They were alright. The cold had not yet got to them. As she returned the gun to its rightful place, she found herself wishing she had been more prepared. But she couldn't have foreseen these developments, she told herself.

Pick up Pross, deliver him here and wait until the end of the flight. After the helicopter had returned with him, take him to an already booked hotel in Llanbedr and early the next morning, drive him back to Cardiff. Simple.

Except it hadn't worked out quite like that.

She drew the blanket more tightly about her as she continued her vigil.

It hadn't worked out like that at all: especially as she had just seen *two* shapes coming towards her from the direction of the rocket strike.

Two survivors so far. Had those rockets missed after all, and had more of them escaped the blasts?

She huddled closer to the ground, trying to make herself as invisible as possible. From her position, if she looked towards Llanbedr, where the darkness appeared to be appreciably lighter, she could still see the car.

She turned her head, to concentrate on the shapes she had seen coming from the opposite direction. They were hurrying, and talking loudly enough for her to pick up their conversation, though their voices were not raised. They appeared to be arguing. One was a woman, and the language was neither Russian, nor English.

It was Polish.

Logan was one of those people who was not only good at languages, she could also detect regional accents quite accurately. She could even tell when a foreign language was being spoken by someone to whom it was not the mother tongue, no matter how adept that person was at disguising the fact.

Provided she knew the language in question.

She knew this one, and understood it well enough to be quite certain that neither of the two speakers was a Pole. One, the man, spoke with a soft German accent: Berlin. The woman, she was convinced, was English, or had lived in England from childhood.

She waited, all sorts of questions in her mind. She had already decided she was not going to take them; not yet, anyway. She wanted to see their reactions to the car, and the bodies.

"An easy job," the woman saying angrily. "Nobody said anything about getting killed."

"The trouble with you people," the man retorted contemptuously, "is that you like it easy. What are you complaining about? I pulled you away before the helicopter fired. You're alive."

"Yes. But all the others are dead." She sounded bitter.

Be thankful for small mercies, Logan said in her mind, pleased by the news. Only two to deal with in her immediate area.

"Next time your people want a helicopter stolen or destroyed, they can get someone else. I cannot take such risks for nothing." The woman had no intention of letting him off lightly. "I have other work that is more important."

"You were told to co-operate."

"Yes. And where did it get me? What about my other team? Will that wretched helicopter get them too?"

"If they're smart, they'll make their exit as fast as they can manage. The surprise is well over, and by now there'll be search parties hunting them down. It was stupid to betray their presence with that missile."

"They might have got it."

"They didn't, and that's what matters."

"I –"

"Quiet!" came the sharp interruption.

And Logan knew they had seen the car.

She remained so still she could herself have been a stone. The two speakers had halted, probably down on the ground by now, waiting and watching.

Long seconds passed. Nothing. She did not move, allowing her ears to test the sounds of the night.

At last, movement. One only. The barely perceptible noise paused, then continued, coming closer. Whoever it was was doing a crawl, stalking towards the car.

Logan breathed slowly, slowing the frequency right down. The noise was much closer now. She would let whoever it was go by. No point alerting the other one. The two would have to be taken when both were together.

The crawler paused once more, just out of sight, but mere feet away. Logan could actually hear soft breathing. She stilled her own.

Then the noise began once more: the slither of clothing on the wet ground at the edge of the track.

The crawler passed so close she could see the blobby shape as it moved past and towards the car. Soon, there came a soft exclamation. The first body had been found.

The crawler was the man, for now he swore softly: in German.

Logan allowed herself a fleeting smile of satisfaction at having identified his first language accurately.

The crawling noise continued until she could barely hear it. His body had now merged with the dark, but she knew it wouldn't be long before he discovered the other dead shape by the car.

Then she thought she heard his voice speaking softly. Soon after, his woman companion came up at a fast crouch. He must have used a radio.

The woman gasped when she reached the first body, but did not pause. She spoke, however, when she reached the car.

"Who are these people?" she asked in a sharp, stage-like whisper. She was again speaking Polish.

"I do not know . . . and please speak more quietly. Your voice must have carried for a kilometre."

79

"Do not exaggerate." She spoke as if she wanted to bite his head off. "Were they in this car, do you think?"

The man took his time. When he spoke again, he had obviously inspected the RS from outside.

"There are no bullet holes. *Don't* . . . do not try to open the door. I do not like this car being here. Keep away from it, but first . . ." He seemed to be doing something to the car, but Logan could not discern properly. "Now, let us go."

"And the bodies?"

"Are they your problem?"

"No."

"They are not mine. Now please let us get away from here."

Logan watched from her hiding-place as they made their way along the track until she could no longer see them.

Sod it, she thought. Let Sanders take care of them. She was more worried about what might have been done to her car.

Another long minute passed before she took her first cautious steps out of cover. No one shot at her. She moved past the body of the dead woman and on towards the RS. She stopped a foot or so away from it, surveying its dark shape for long moments. The magnum was still ready for action.

What had the man done to it? A bomb, perhaps? She would have to find out sooner or later. She wasn't going to leave it here for one of Sanders' boys — or even worse, Martins' — to blow it up in a "controlled" explosion. It would still leave her car blown to bits, whether it had been booby-trapped or not.

Still with the gun in one hand, she began feeling beneath the wings. There hadn't been time for anything more elaborate. As she moved round the vehicle, she had to step over the body of the man she had killed earlier. Counting in her mind, she spent the longest, most tense thirty seconds she could remember, probing cautiously beneath the car.

Then she found it, tucked into the rear nearside wing. It was not a bomb. They had left a tracer.

"Well," Logan said softly.

Flying nap-of-the-earth, Pross brought the Hammerhead about three miles south of Llyn Cwm Bychan, keeping high ground between the aircraft and the forest from which the last SAM had been fired.

He changed course near Maes-y-garnedd and went northeast, scooting low along Bwlch Drws Ardudwy, a deep pass between the

700-metre peaks of Rhinog Fawr and Rhinog Fach. He kept the Hammerhead at a mean height of 50 feet above ground level. The end of the pass would bring them directly on to the forest, but too low to warn the SAM team until too late.

He hoped.

The aircraft was handling beautifully. Everything about it felt right. Pross felt relaxed in the reclined seat as the pulse of the helicopter flowed through him. It was as if the sidesticks were terminals to which his hands were attached. On reflection, he decided that was precisely what they were.

As the Hammerhead slid, like its deadly namesake, through the depths of the night, Pross heard an astonishing sound on the headphones. The rousing opening measures of the sixth movement of Handel's *Water Music* seemed to fill his mind.

"Where the hell did that come from?" he asked of Rees. The reception was crystal-clear, the stereo transmission perfect.

It sounded as if Rees was laughing as he spoke, "Radio Hammerhead, at your service." The music had faded into the background.

"What are you talking about, Cado?"

"There's a special cassette loader in the pilot's cockpit, with direct input to the central computer. This is meant to be for highly classified instructions to the pilot, in time of war. These instructions can be linked to the co-pilot/gunner's phones if this becomes necessary. The pilot decides."

"So what's Handel doing on my phones?"

"Stirring the blood."

"Cado, you're not telling me you've stuck a music cassette into the loader?"

"Music can be quite soothing, or stirring, or whatever, when you're flying."

Pross shook his head slowly. "They haven't really changed you, have they? What about normal flying communications, and threat warnings? How are you going to hear them?"

"Ah, but you see, that's the beauty of it. For threats, the system cuts out, so nothing is impaired. If the radar or the IR warning wanted to tell us we were being tracked, the music would stop immediately and the warning would sound. As a matter of fact, the sequence is even more of an attention-getter. If I wanted to communicate or were receiving communications, the same thing would happen. None of the warning systems are affected. This way, the pilot receives his instructions while continuing to operate his aircraft normally."

"Sounds dodgy to me. You could get carried away by the music – literally, if you hit the ground."

"Not if you pick the right time. If you're cruising along, it's a nice effect."

Pross knew that, as a first-class pilot, Rees would never take risks with his flying.

I've done more dodgy things in choppers than he'd dream of, Pross thought drily.

Even so.

"Does Fowler know of your little concerts in the air?"

"If he does, he's never said or done anything about it. To tell you the truth, I've only seen him once since I got this posting. Sanders tends to pop over a bit more often."

"What would *he* say if he knew?"

Rees chuckled. "Probably lay an egg on the spot."

They laughed.

Then Rees said, "Want me to turn it off?"

"No ... no, leave it on. It's ... an interesting idea. I can see it now. Crews going into battle with *Onward Christian Soldiers*, or *Pomp and Circumstance* ringing in their ears." He smiled at the incredible thought.

"More like a Madonna record, or the theme from *Miami Vice*, or whoever's fashionable at the time," Rees said mournfully.

Pross could believe it. Give a soldier, airman, or sailor anything and he'll find a use for which it had never been designed. The ingenuity of servicemen everywhere would continue to defeat the efforts of the most rulebook-minded supply officer. The makers of the condom certainly never imagined that their product would one day do sterling service as waterproof protectors for small-arms muzzles.

The sixth movement had come on once more, from the beginning. Rees had rewound while they'd been talking.

"My favourite movement," Rees said, and turned up the volume.

With Handel pounding in his ears, Pross took the Hammerhead towards the dark forest.

Beneath him, the hidden landscape, betrayed by the imager, fled as if pursued. The helicopter seemed to float upon the strains of the music, as if it were itself powered by the sounds on his headphones.

The Flir had begun hunting and the reticle on the thermal image was getting excited. Pross reduced power as the forest drew closer. No warning screamed at him. Had the SAM team moved? Most likely. But where to? They were still in the forest. The Flir would not have been sniffing round otherwise. But where? Come on, come on. Find them.

At the mouth of the pass, the path that had been running through it had now forked, and Pross brought the Hammerhead to the hover a few feet above it. The aircraft's nose pointed at the forest, 600 metres away. Slowly, he began to slew it round with delicate touches of the rudder pedals.

Then a red glow appeared on the thermal image. The source was just under a mile into the forest.

Rees zoomed in on it. Plenty of trees came up, but eventually there was a broken shape among the trunks.

Rees said, "Vehicle of some kind."

"Ours, or theirs?"

"Theirs. None of our vehicles will go in. That's to give us a clear run. Can't blow away our own people, can we?"

"How about Sanders?"

"Now, David, that wasn't nice. Besides, he's too far away. You realise," Rees went on, "we'll have to go in, don't you? This one's not going to be like the first. The trees will block our fire."

"The same unpleasant thought had crossed my mind."

"Theirs too, looks like. They want to draw us out. *They* can shoot through the trees. However, I've got a trick they don't know about. I know this forest well ... both from the air, and on the ground. There are many tracks suitable for vehicular use, and one in particular describes a rough square. The location of the IR source tells me it's on that square; on a corner, in fact. There's just enough of a break in the trees near that corner for us to get a clear shot. We'll have to risk overflying though."

Pross said, "Is there room to set this thing down?"

"*What?*"

"You just gave me an idea."

"Are you sure I'm responsible?"

Pross smiled to himself. "Now who's getting worried?"

"Imagine what Fowler would do to us if we bent his expensive toy."

"Imagine what will *happen* to us if we take a hit from a SAM. Fowler will have his wondrous machine bent. Permanently."

"You're the pilot," Rees said gloomily.

HOOK

FIVE

Pross took the Hammerhead to treetop level. It rose, a ghostly dragonfly on muted wings.

"Alright, Cado," he said. Handel had died on the headphones. "Give me a thermal image of the square."

The MFD switched displays as Rees went to work. In an instant, the target area filled the screen. The heat trace of the vehicle was prominent.

"Give me a zoom," Pross said.

Now the vehicle itself was prominent on-screen, more clearly defined than before.

"A six-wheeled Range Rover," Rees said. "More than enough traction to get them up here, and plenty of room for their portable SAMs. Now what? They must be out in the woods, waiting."

"Hunt for heat traces."

Rees zoomed out and soon found them. "Three. Two together, one a short distance away."

"I see them. What do you think?"

"The trees are an effective screen. Any one could have the SAM."

Pross considered his options. "Alright, Cado. We'll hit them quickly and hard."

"You're really going to try for a let-down?"

"Don't sound so enthusiastic. Yes. I'm *going* for a let-down. We'll fire at ground level. I'll move away from here, come in low, pop over the trees, down to the track, we fire, and off again."

"This I've got to see."

"As you're coming along for the ride, you will."

"It's getting to you."

"What is?" Pross asked as he took the Hammerhead in a swooping dive away from the forest.

"This piece of kit. This chopper. It's got to you already. Perhaps that's what they were hoping for."

"Who?"

"Who, the man says. As if you don't already know. The bait was set, the line thrown, the fish hooked. Now you're being reeled in."

"And you were part of it."

"Me? Sorry, David, I'm the hired help. Whatever's going on is way above my head. I'm —"

"Just the D & T pilot around here," they said together.

"Yes," Pross continued drily. "So you've said."

"Well? What weapons would sir like?"

Pross grinned briefly at the droll voice in his helmet.

"An AGM for the Range Rover, and a spread of six rockets for our friends with the SAM. We'll take out their transport first."

"Your wish is my command."

"You sound so happy, Cado."

"Oh I am, I am," came the mournful voice, reminding Pross of Droopy.

He took the Hammerhead south, skirting the rising eastern flank of Rhinog Fach; then he turned and headed back towards the forest, staying low. On the MFD, the reticle began shifting towards the target and on both the MFD and the HUD, the message AGM ARMED came on. On the weapons CRT, the missile station on the port stub wing gave its warning glow.

"Mind if I take Handel in with us?" Rees asked.

Pross was not sure whether the droll man in the rear cockpit was feeling amused. It certainly sounded like it.

"By all means, Cado. This is not the Royal barge, and we're not over the Thames, but let us have George Frederick serenade us on our way."

"No sooner said than done."

And for the third time, the strains of the sixth movement poured through the headphones.

Pross brought the Hammerhead leaping over the trees to find the gap that led down to the track. The aircraft plunged swiftly down.

"The wheels!" Rees was shouting. *"You forgot to lower the gear!"*

"Leave the gear!" Pross shouted back, fearing Rees might choose to lower them from his position. "I don't intend to land."

There was something like a gasp from the back as Pross went into hover. The helicopter seemed to have suspended itself inches from the ground, its main blades apparently whirling within a hair's breath of disaster. Pross tried not to think of eager branches waiting out there in the dark.

The missile had achieved its lock-on, the reticle pulsed, and there was a sharp explosion, audible even above the sound of the music, as Rees launched. Its flight was short, its termination awesome.

Rees had not exaggerated about the force of the new explosive. The practice missile tore into the Range Rover, ripping it apart with a roar that echoed through the forest and lighting up the night with a malevolent flame that belched in all directions like searing tongues from a giant furnace.

Launch had taken place from 400 metres and Pross lifted the Hammerhead, turning at the same time to bring the other targets to bear.

"*Rockets, Cado!*" he bawled.

But Rees was already thinking with him and the six rockets were on their way even before he'd finished speaking. As their fire scorched about their targets, Pross was hauling the aircraft up, laying on the power, increasing pitch with the collective.

The Hammerhead seemed to throw itself upwards as the blast from the missile that had destroyed the Range Rover tried to snatch at it, as if to hurl it into the waiting trees.

Pross glanced down during the soaring climb. Two beacons lit the forest. He sent the aircraft skimming across the treetops.

"We seemed to have managed that alright, Cado."

Silence. Handel was taking a break too.

"Cado?"

A monologue was coming from the back seat. "I can hear the sound of engines. If I look up, I can just about see something whirling above my head. That must be the main blades, and they're still working. If I look out, I can persuade myself we're moving. Yes . . . it really looks as if I'm still alive."

"That bad, was it?" Pross queried mildly.

"It wasn't bad. It was good. It was bloody brilliant, but that doesn't mean it didn't terrify me. I'd forgotten what you could be like."

"You didn't freeze with the rockets. They went off at exactly the right time."

"I was just in a hurry to get well away."

Pross smiled, knowing differently. Rees might have been scared, but he was also an absolute professional.

Pross said, "And what do you think was happening to the heart that was trying to jump out of my mouth?"

"Marvellous. Two terrified people carrying out a stunt like that. We need our heads examined."

Logan heard the rumble of the multiple explosions and hoped Pross was alright. From her position, she could see nothing of what had happened, although she thought she had detected a faint glow to the south-east that had appeared briefly above the dark rim of the mountains. It had been so fleeting she decided that perhaps she had been mistaken.

She was still standing by the RS, and having made up her mind to drive it back, unlocked the driver's door carefully, pulled it gently open. The edge of the track was close to the water and she momentarily wondered if she'd have the time to throw herself into the lake should the car be booby-trapped. On the heels of that thought came the realisation there wouldn't be time anyway.

Nothing happened.

She removed the blanket and dropped it behind the front seats. Then she eased herself behind the wheel and shut the door just as carefully. Still nothing.

She placed the magnum on the passenger seat, then rummaged in her bag to take out a wig which she pulled on over her short hair. In the light, she would appear to have long black hair, transforming her appearance entirely. From the glove compartment, she took out a pair of thick-rimmed glasses and put them on. They were quite useless as spectacles, but served to enhance the image she was creating; which was the sole purpose of their existence. They had proved invaluable on previous occasions. Next she removed her garters, re-stocked the one she had used for the reload, and placed them in the bag.

Satisfied, she called Sanders on the radio to warn him of the two survivors. She made no mention of the tracer — if it were indeed one and not a cleverly disguised trembler device that would blow her to pieces as soon as she started the car.

"Wait for us," Sanders told her. "We're nearly with you."

"Forget about me. I'm driving out. If I were you —"

"You're not me, Logan!" Sanders interrupted testily.

"Don't I know it," she muttered to herself.

90

"What was that?"

"Nothing. I was talking to myself ... again. That's the trouble with women. If I were you," Logan went on quickly before he could think of a suitable retort, "I'd concentrate on those two. They're big fish."

"Why didn't you get them?" He sounded annoyed.

"I thought you didn't think I could," she said sweetly and cut transmission. She smiled as she thought of him fuming. He'd be feeling even worse if any of his companions had heard.

She put Sanders out of her mind as she put the key in the ignition.

"Here goes," she said. And turned.

The engine came smoothly to life with a muted whistle of its turbo. That was all.

"Ah well," she said, clipping on her belt. "So it's a tracer."

It didn't have to be, of course. A trembler could easily ignore the starting of the engine, waiting to go off at the first bump. It all depended upon how sensitively it had been primed.

She drove forward slowly on sidelights and managed to turn the car round by reversing partially up a path that went up the slope. There was just enough room for the manoeuvre. She avoided running over the bodies lying by the track. She drove slowly back towards Llanbedr, conscious of the stowaway beneath the rear wing.

She had deliberately not removed the magnetically attached bug. She wanted to know who had thought it a good idea to put a trace on the RS, and she intended to haul them out into the open.

If she got out of here alive.

Pross said, "Is this as agile as the Lynx?"

He was still piloting the Hammerhead and they were flying out to sea. The wind appeared to have died down considerably and the aircraft flew steadily.

"More so," Rees answered.

Which was something. The Lynx was the most incredibly aerobatic helicopter of its class and size, by virtue of its rigid rotor head which, if Pross remembered correctly, was the only one of that type in the world. It could thus be looped and rolled where other choppers would head for mother earth alarmingly quickly if their pilots were insane enough to try the same manoeuvres.

91

"It's got the same rotor system," Rees continued. "Imagine what that means."

Pross could well imagine it. Sleekness of fuselage, less all-up weight, and more powerful engines.

"I'd like to find out."

"*Tonight?*" Rees sounded more than a little worried.

"You're not worried, Cado, are you? After what we've just been through?" And when Rees had remained pointedly silent, Pross went on, "I didn't mean tonight. I'm not that eager to go into the sea." He smiled at the glow from the instruments.

"Thank God for that. We'd better take her in. They'll be wondering what happened, considering we haven't communicated with them since I picked you up."

They would be landing at the experimental airfield on the sands near Llanbedr, which Pross knew well from his Air-Force days.

"You take over," he told Rees. "You know the procedure. There may be someone down there ready to blow us out of the sky if they hear a different voice. You have control."

Rees gave a deep chuckle and said, "I have control."

Pross took his hands off the sidesticks and relaxed. He felt a strange sense of loss, as if the Hammerhead had parted company with him, releasing him from its embrace.

As he listened to Rees communicate with the airfield in preparation for the landing, he wondered how Logan was getting on, and hoped she was alright.

Logan made it safely to Llanbedr. She turned left towards Barmouth, but was not going that far. She was looking for a public phonebox, deciding to ignore any in Llanbedr itself. She wanted to see who would be following her.

She drove quickly until some two miles later, at Coed Ystumgwern, she saw one. She went on past it for a short distance, turned, and parked pointing the way she had come. She put the magnum in the bag, which she grabbed, got out, and ran towards the box, which was not only unoccupied, but actually worked.

Positioning herself so that she could see the traffic clearly, she called Fowler in London. She had parked the RS between two other cars. It had been deliberately done. Anyone following would miss it on the first pass while going for a visual. The darkness would not help, neither would the two cars which might even temporarily screen the bug. Whoever was chasing would have to brake when the signal appeared to be coming from behind.

She wanted to see who did the braking.

"Fowler," came his voice in her ear.

"Change of pick-up." She did not elaborate, and he did not ask her to. Fowler trusted her instincts.

"Where?" he asked.

"Maentwrog."

"I'll get on to it. Check with them by radio. Different hotel?"

"Yes."

"Do they need to know?"

"No."

"Do I?"

"Not unless you order me to and then I'm not sure."

"I'll save both of us the embarrassment," Fowler said drily. "Are you alright?"

"Yes."

"Very well. Keep in touch."

"I will." She hung up.

As she was about to leave the phonebox, a car went past, going much too fast. It braked suddenly and began to reverse.

Logan slipped quickly out of the box and hid in the shadows near it. The car had stopped opposite the RS. A man climbed out, briefly pinned by the lights of a passing minibus. She did not see his face, but his walk would be remembered. It was a brisk military gait, the broad shoulders swinging slightly. The man had appeared indifferent to the lights. It spoke of supreme confidence.

A man to be very careful of; a dangerous man.

She watched as he went up to the RS and peered in. Instinct told her it was the same man she had seen by the lake. This was confirmed when he went round to the back of the car to reach beneath the wing. He was obviously checking that the bug had not been moved. A different position would have betrayed knowledge of its presence.

If this really was the same man from Cwm Bychan, then somehow, he and his companion had managed to elude Sanders.

So much for Sanders, she thought wryly.

Logan peered at the car they had come in. There seemed to be someone in the passenger seat. It could have been anyone.

A car approaching from Barmouth gave an angry blare of horns as another car going the opposite way pulled out to pass the stopped vehicle. There was a squeal of brakes and more honking of horns. Their lights framed the pursuit car long enough for Logan to positively identify it. One of the big Mercedes coupés.

"We'll see how you perform where I'm going to take you," she said to it quietly.

The man returned to the Mercedes as the angry pair of motorists decided to call it a day with parting honks on their horns. He paused by the car and looked about him, clearly trying to decide whether the RS had been deliberately dumped, or had merely been parked to await the driver's return. Once, he turned to look at the telephone box.

Although Logan was certain he could not see her, she nevertheless pressed herself deeper into the shadows.

The man looked up and down the road once more, then climbed in. The Mercedes shot off with a squeal of tyres. There were no other cars on the road at that moment and Logan seized the chance to dart back across in the relative darkness.

It was just as well that she did, for the brake lights of the Mercedes came on. He was going to turn round, having apparently decided to wait further down the road.

Logan opened the door, flung the bag inside, climbed in and was starting the engine even before she'd hauled the door shut behind her. She left her lights off and did not use her seatbelt as she pulled away from her space and sent the RS hurtling down the road, back towards Llanbedr. She clipped on the belt one-handedly on the move, while she held the car steady with the other. Only then did she switch on the lights. In her mirrors, the tiny pinpricks of red told her the Mercedes had not yet turned; but it soon would.

She had achieved what she'd wanted. They did not know who was driving, while she had at least seen one of them. She wanted to keep it that way, because she knew exactly how she was going to get them to show their faces.

She drove fast and competently, the RS eagerly rushing on, its turbo whistling happily.

She picked up the radio, selected a frequency, then switched it on, wondering if that would affect the tracer.

"Martins," she said.

He came on immediately. "Here."

There was no love lost between them. Martins had once made the serious mistake of hauling Logan in on suspicion of having killed a Department agent, and so enamoured was he of his reputation as a hard man, he'd been eager to believe the allegation. He had been looking forward to getting very rough with her when Fowler had stepped in.

She had given Martins warning that she would shoot him the next time he tried that on her. He believed her and for that reason, she knew she would never turn her back on him, metaphorically or literally.

"You've got the change of arrangements," she now said.

"Yes. They've just come in."

"The change of arrangements, or the parcels?"

Martins knew she meant Pross and Rees. "Both. We'll deliver yours as per new directions."

"Right. Meet me by the bridge."

"Got it. Shouldn't we be accompanying you to the new destination? Considering what has happened recently?"

"No. I can manage."

There was a silence that clearly showed Martins did not agree. "I feel I should know —"

"I have a totally opposite feeling. Meet me. Start now. Out." She terminated transmission before Martins could argue.

She glanced in her mirrors. No one coming up fast; but they'd be following. It was what she wanted.

Llanbedr was about a mile away, approaching rapidly. She hoped Martins had not hung around and had bundled Pross into the Department Rover, and was even now speeding towards the rendezvous. She didn't want to meet them on the road.

She took the RS into the sweeping right-hand bend that led into Llanbedr, and a glance in her mirror showed nothing was following. Had she been mistaken? She found that difficult to believe. The Mercedes *had* braked sharply, and the man *had* got out to inspect the RS. She had seen him stoop to check the wing. All his actions had aroused suspicion. She was certain she had not been mistaken. The lack of pursuing headlights could only mean she was succeeding in her strategy. The more she gained on them, the better for her purposes.

She slowed briefly for Llanbedr, increasing speed again the moment she was free of it. A short straight came up and she gave the RS its head. There was no sign of Martins' Rover, which would have left the airfield at Llanbedr. She hoped he was already up ahead.

There was still no sign of it when she went through Llanfair and on to Harlech. After Harlech the A496 opened out into a two-and-a-half mile stretch that was virtually free of traffic. Far up ahead, a pair of tail lights were moving away very swiftly.

It must be Martins, she decided, and increased her own speed, though not intending to catch up. She kept a wary eye on the mirrors. Her lead still seemed safe.

The sudden flare of brakelights told her the driver had been caught out by the sharp righthander at Llanfihangel-y-traethau; but it was negotiated safely.

Logan smiled. If the car ahead was indeed the Department's Rover, Pross would have shut his eyes on that bend. Poor Pross.

She changed down and took the RS nicely into the bend, keeping the power on. She never used the brakes. There had been little need. She changed up and the car leapt forward, then she was setting up for the sweeping left-hander.

She drove thus along the Vale of Ffestiniog, keeping the tail lights in sight, while checking her mirrors constantly to ensure she was still well ahead of her pursuers. A few cars and a couple of lorries was all the traffic that passed going the other way, while on her side of the road she had to overtake only twice. One of those was a big truck that gave her a flare of a battery of lights as she tucked in ahead, just before a bend.

Then it was into Maentwrog where she slowed right down. The route through the tree-hidden little town was a one-way system that formed a triangle. The road forked left over the bridge that crossed the Afon Dwyryd to join the A487 from Portmadoc, on a bend. The A487 re-crossed the river, on its way east and south. Logan would be turning right to follow the A496 towards Blaenau Ffestiniog, to then join the A470 to Betws-y-Coed, her eventual destination for the night.

Waiting by the bridge was the white Rover.

She pulled up behind it, got quickly out of the car and went up to the Rover just as the doors opened. Martins, his driver, and Pross climbed out.

"Logan!" Pross began, both pleased and surprised to see her. He stared at her wig and glasses. "Going to a fancy-dress party, are we? What —"

"No time," she interrupted. "Into my car. Come on, Pross! Move."

"Alright, alright. I'm going. This night might as well continue the way it began."

'Sorry," she said. "No time to explain."

"I can hardly wait."

"Pross!"

"I've just gone." And he hurried to the RS.

Logan was about to join him when Martins, small and weasel-like, said, "That's it?"

"That's it, Martins," she said quickly. "Thanks. Now we must be going. Move your car, please."

"Logan," Martins began, annoyed. His driver stared at Logan expressionlessly. A large man, clumsy looking. Logan knew this to be a dangerously false impression. This was one of the men who had brought her in for Martins's session.

"Logan," Martins was repeating. "I —"

"Right," she cut into his words. "Want to argue? Stay here and argue with yourself." In the glare of the RS headlights, she saw his face begin to darken. "I've got to be going." She went back to her car, and climbed in.

As she started the engine, Pross said, "What now?"

"Later, Pross. Later."

"Promises, promises." He stared pointedly at her disguise.

She smiled, put the car into reverse.

"Logan, for God's sake! What are you doing?"

"That little shit won't move his bloody car and we've got to get out of here." She turned the RS, taking the wrong way out.

"The sign says 'No Entry'," Pross remarked with heavy sarcasm.

"I can actually read signs, Pross." She drove on, taking the forbidden route to the main road.

Unfortunately, Sod's Law went to work. Another car chose that very moment to enter the town.

"I don't believe it," she said. "The only car, and it manages to turn up at exactly the wrong time."

The car flashed its lights fretfully.

"Tough," Logan said, and kept going.

The other car stopped, and the flashing became frantic. Pross closed his eyes and sank lower in his seat.

Logan pressed the switch to lower her window as she inched past the outraged car. "Sorry!" she called. "I'm a stranger here myself."

Then she raised the window as she finally drove past and onto the main road.

But Sod's Law had not yet finished with them.

The biggest truck Pross had ever seen since one never-to-be-forgotten night in Italy, or wanted to see again, was bearing down upon them just as Logan was driving across the road to turn right.

He stared at the blaze of powerful headlights disbelievingly.

"Oh my God!" he heard a voice say in a whimpering prayer, then realised it was his.

The night was suddenly filled with the thunder of the truck's engines and the fanfare of its airhorns. He heard the hissing of its powerful brakes. He saw Logan turn the wheel sharply, felt the surge of the RS as it seemed to leap away; felt the tail swing out, halt in its slide as if stopped by an invisible wall; then blissfully, the car was hurling itself into the welcoming darkness of the now empty road. Why, he asked himself, was he always being driven by women who liked mixing it with trucks?

The whole incident had taken a fleeting instant, but every stage was imprinted upon his mind.

"They're certainly coming out tonight," Logan said calmly.

Martins had watched in a suffused rage as Logan reversed to take the right fork out of the town, smarting under what he perceived to be her insult.

"Get after them!" he commanded his driver, as he prepared to re-enter the Rover.

"I don't think –" the driver began uncertainly.

"Exactly!" Martins yelled. "Don't bloody think! Do as I tell you! Get after that bloody woman, Chalcott!" He slammed the door as Chalcott climbed in behind the wheel. "Well? What are you waiting for? Get *moving*. Do you want to sit here and twiddle your thumbs all night?"

Whatever Chalcott's thoughts on the matter would have been were relegated to a very low priority, because something far more urgent was about to concentrate his mind wonderfully.

The truck driver, having only just recovered from the shock of seeing the RS pass seemingly beneath his front wheels, was doubly alarmed when the snout of the white Rover appeared bent on doing the same thing.

He flashed his lights, and sent the raucous music of his airhorns blaring into the night once more.

Sleepy Maentwrog was having a rough evening of it.

*

"What do you think you're doing, Chalcott!" Martins screamed as the great mass of the truck bore down upon them.

They both heard the hiss of the truck's brakes, even as Chalcott stamped on the Rover's. The reactions of both drivers were commendably swift, but they were still too late to avoid a collision.

The Rover took a glancing blow on the right side of its nose from a massive front wheel. The impact slammed it against the bridge, doing as much damage to the left side. The truck travelled on for a few yards and stopped. It had itself suffered nothing.

Martins and Chalcott were unhurt, but Martins's temper was about to explode in a fury of recrimination.

"You boneheaded idiot!" he bellowed. "Get out! I can't open my door! Who taught you to bloody drive, anyway?"

Chalcott contained his own anger, and climbed out slowly. Martins crabbed his way across the car to follow. When they had found themselves out in the cold once more, they saw a man who made Chalcott look like a pygmy, striding up purposefully.

The man planted himself before them, ready for battle. "Which of you is the wally who was driving? What's the matter with you people around here? First a woman tries to commit suicide under my truck, then you pull the same fucking trick." The man had a London accent, and his manner indicated he wanted explanations, fast.

Martins, at his most supercilious, said, "If you have suffered no damage, leave it alone, and go on your way. We work for the Government."

"I don't care if you work for the bloody Kremlin. You are bloody dangerous on the road and I'm going to report you. Let's have your insurance, your name, and address — and your licence."

Martins squared up to the giant. "Listen, sonny. I'm running out of patience. Leave it, and get on with your job like a good little boy. Alright?"

The thought that a weasel like Martins would instil fear into the giant before him at first seemed like a bizarre fantasy, but the truck driver appeared to pause, as if thinking things out. He was, however, reluctant to back down.

"Or what?" he sneered.

"Or," Martins began with poisonous pleasure, "I'll have you covered in patrol cars so fast you'll wish you'd taken my advice. I've got a radio in the car. They could inspect your entire load, and keep you at it all night. That's for starters. How many smashes are truck drivers allowed before they lose their jobs and their licences?"

Martins let the question hang in the cold night air.

Discretion took over. "You bastards," the big man said with contempt, and spat at Martins's feet; then he turned away and walked back to his truck.

There was the slam of its door and the revving of its idling engine. A hiss of released brakes, and it was off, trundling away on its interrupted journey.

Martins turned to the Rover and kicked it hard on the door. The metal resounded like an untuned drum.

"Bloody woman!" he snarled.

A sound made him turn to look. Some of the good citizens of Maentwrog had come out, curious to know what had so disturbed their peace.

"Have you never seen a smashed car before?" he said to them harshly. "Go back to your homes! There's no bodies to look at."

He wrenched the door open and picked up the radiophone.

"Bloody woman!" he muttered to himself as he began to speak into it.

Logan had been glancing into her mirror when she had safely negotiated her way past the truck.

"I think Martins has just had himself a little accident," she said with glee. She wondered what would happen when the Mercedes eventually got there. Anything that held them up was good news.

Pross said, "You know, Logan . . . I've come to the conclusion that you're certifiable."

She flashed him a grin and said, "I know, but I'm nice, warm, and exciting with it."

Pross shook his head slowly and stared at the dark, speeding ribbon of the road. "Oh God," he groaned. "I commend myself to thee."

"Oh come on, Pross. I'm a very good driver. You know it. You're just a bad passenger."

"That's a novel way of putting it."

"How did you like your new toy?" she asked, changing the subject entirely.

"Fowler's new toy, you mean."

"I know what I mean."

"It's a pretty good machine," Pross said, trying to keep the excitement out of his voice and failing.

"A pretty good machine," Logan mocked. "Admit you enjoyed flying it, and fighting with it."

"Alright. I give up. I admit it. Now that point's been made . . . how come?" He was staring again at her wig.

"The wig, or the helicopter?"

"Both. Answer in any order you like."

"Let's start with the helicopter. What do you want to know?"

"More than you'll be prepared to tell me, for a start. But I'll be content with morsels for the time being. The world and its mum-in-law is agog about choppers for all sorts of reasons at the moment. What I want to know is this . . . where has the money come from for a machine like that? It didn't just happen. Plans were laid a long time ago. I asked Rees and he became the good Army man. Need-to-know basis, and of course, he didn't know anything. Just a poor chopper jockey, he said. How about you, poor little misunderstood waif?"

"I'm going to disappoint you."

"Ah. Now why did I have a feeling you'd be saying that?"

"Not because I don't want to tell you, but because I genuinely don't know enough. Fowler will tell you. I know he will."

"Fowler will tell me what he *thinks* I should know. There's a very big difference. I was counting on you."

Logan seemed to go into a thinking session. "Look," she said. "Tell you what. I'll see if I can snoop around and find out. I didn't even know it was flying until I came down to get you. I knew one was being built, but I saw it for the first time tonight; and that wasn't much. Performs well, does it?"

"Let's put it this way. I think it's a world-beater, if it ever gets into production. It feels alive, much more so than the modded Lynx I flew in Nepal. You can tell the pedigree, of course. No question there, but it's still a very powerful new generation by comparison. A pilot's dream. Somebody's managed to get it right."

"I think that's what Fowler wanted you up here for . . . to give that kind of opinion. I know he's been involved, but not by how much."

"If the idea weren't so bizarre," Pross said, "I wouldn't have put it past him to organise our little reception committee, just to see how the thing would perform under fire."

Logan glanced at him quickly. "You're not that cynical."

"No," Pross said with resignation. "I'm not that cynical; which is why I keep getting caught up in his schemes. Now let's hear about that unbelievable wig and those glasses. I'd never have recognised you. You're pretty good at changing your persona. What does it all mean, Logan?" he added theatrically.

"What it means, dear Pross, is that we're having a change of hotels, and we're going to spend the night as Mr and Mrs Plumstead . . ."

"I don't believe it. Mr and Mrs Smith's better than that. *Plumstead?*"

"That's where you're wrong, Pross. Smith arouses instant suspicion, or a sort of nudge-nudge-wink-know-what-I-mean syndrome in some people. A name like Plumstead has got to be for real. Besides, I've got a cheque book in the name of Plumstead to pay for the room."

"I should have known. Next question."

"Yes?"

"Why are we driving along like maniacs? Running away from anyone I'd like to know about?"

"No. No, we're not. I just want to get there quickly."

"Now why didn't I think of that?"

"Besides," Logan went on, "I want a long, hot bath. I've got mud and God knows what else all over me. This car will need a good clean soon . . . especially my seat. Now relax and enjoy the drive, Pross. You're in safe hands."

Pross watched as a bend seemed to be approaching at alarming speed, and thought it best not to comment.

SIX

The Mercedes was approaching Maentwrog.

"The signal's fading again," the woman said. She was still speaking Polish.

"We'll soon catch up," the man said unworriedly. "That little transmitter is one of the most powerful for its size." There was laughter in his voice as he added, "We stole the design from the Americans. They make very good stuff, sometimes."

They entered the town and followed the route out. Soon, they came upon the white Rover. He stopped the car before getting too close.

"Why are you stopping?" she demanded. "They'll get away!"

"Don't be so eager to get caught," he said quietly.

The big engine idled powerfully and almost silently in the cold of the night.

"What do you mean?" she stared at him.

"That car up ahead, with the two men."

"It's had an accident."

"But there's no one around. The noise would have brought people running to look. There are always spectators. Why not now?"

"I still don't understand."

The man sighed with exasperation. "I have been to many places around the world. I can spot a security man almost before I see him. And those two are security men, or I am the Director of the CIA."

He smiled at his joke. The woman looked at him stonily.

"Don't you people ever laugh?" he went on.

"You'd better drive on," she said coldly. "They're looking at us."

Instead of doing so, he reached into a door pocket to pull out a map; then he turned on an interior light and began to study it.

"Lower your head and look as if you're trying to see where we are!" he said urgently. "Do it!"

Reluctantly, she complied.

Surreptitiously, he glanced up to where Martins and Chalcott were standing, looking disgruntled.

"They don't seem very happy," he said. "Perhaps they were chasing the same car. I wonder how they came to crash. Alright. Time to go. They have lost interest in us." He put the map away, and turned off the light. "They must have radioed for assistance. Note that they did not come over to ask for help. In a normal accident, it would have been a natural thing to do. I shall ask them if they need our help."

"*What?* Are you mad!"

"It would look very suspicious if we did not. It is what an innocent motorist would do."

"I can't allow myself to be seen! I may be recognised later! I am not as disguised as you are."

"I shall do it from here. There is no need to worry."

Without waiting for her reaction, he lowered his window, poked out his head and shouted, in perfect English, "Need any help?"

"No!" It was Martins who answered.

The man waved a hand in acknowledgment, brought his head back in, and raised the window.

"An unpleasant man," he commented, reverting to Polish.

"I didn't realise you spoke English," she said.

"We shall continue in Polish." His tone brooked no argument.

The Rover had been pushed to one side, and there was room to pass. He drove the Mercedes slowly forward, as if worried about his paintwork. He saw the two men watching his progress without interest and gave a friendly wave. It was not returned.

"Miserable," he said, and took the direction in which Logan had gone.

The RS was passing Rhyd-y-sarn on the A496 when Logan said, "You must know it quite well around here, Pross. Don't you fly up here a lot in your helicopters?"

"Much of our work keeps us down south. I've done a few surveys up here, but only in a very small area. Mainly near the coast. Used to do low-flying practice in the mountains, of course, when I was in the RAF. I wouldn't say I know them, though. You need years on the ground before you can come near to thinking you know any mountain. Ask the rescue boys and they'll tell you every day on the same peak will be different. Just like flying, in fact. You never know where the surprise may be coming from."

Logan was glancing into her mirrors. "Just like this job too."

"Want to tell me what surprise is waiting for us?"

"No surprise, Pross." She took a bend at speed.

"Except perhaps what might come round one of these corners," he remarked drily. He'd forced himself to accept the speed with which she drove. There was little else he could do.

"Are you still going on about that? Really, Pross. If I didn't know you better, I'd be quite hurt."

"Logan, nothing I could possibly say about your driving would hurt you. You'd just ignore me."

She laughed briefly. "That's true enough. So take my previous advice. Enjoy being driven in style."

The A496 joined the A470 to Betws-y-Coed at Blaenau Ffestiniog. She turned onto it and kept up her speed. The road had begun to descend and in some places, quite steeply, with bends at the bottom of the inclines. She took these in ferocious fashion, handling the car with precise, unhurried movements, steering wheel turned just so, hand dropping to gear lever, feet tap-dancing on the pedals, gear swiftly changed, power on . . .

And so it went, until Pross found himself mesmerised. Despite his outward belief that he'd again been kidnapped by a maniac at the wheel, he had a sneaking admiration for the way she drove. Her finely-tuned control of the machine was something he could appreciate. She was as good with the car as she was deadly with her magnum. She could, he thought, when he allowed his fear of imminent departure off the road to recede, give an accomplished rally driver a hard time of it.

He still wished she wouldn't drive so fast.

"My God!" the woman in the Mercedes exclaimed. "We nearly came off the road! Don't drive so fast."

The man said, "Whoever he is, he knows this place well. We've got to keep up. I thought that was what you wanted."

"If he wants to kill himself, let him. We've got the signal. We don't need to be right on his tail. I would not enjoy being driven off one of these mountain roads."

105

"There is no need to worry," the man said. But he eased off the speed a little.

The police car pulled up behind the Rover, still waiting at the side of the road in Maentwrog. Its engine had not been affected by the shunt, and Chalcott had turned it on to get the heater going.

A patrolman got out of the police car, leaving his partner inside. He walked up to the Rover, tapped on the driver's window.

Chalcott wound it down.

The policeman peered in. "Mr Martins?"

Chalcott pointed a thumb towards Martins in the passenger seat, and said nothing.

The policeman lowered his head a little and peered further in. "Mr Martins?" he repeated.

Martins stared at him. "Yes."

"We were told to offer you assistance, sir."

Martins appeared to be thinking something out. He let the policeman stand in the cold while he thought out his reply.

At last, he said, "Take us back to Llanbedr."

"Tow you, sir?"

Martins almost sighed. "No. We do not want you to tow us there. A truck is supposed to be coming to do that. We want you to *drive* us there. Did you see the truck on your way?"

"We know nothing about the breakdown lorry, sir. We were on patrol when the message came in to assist you."

This time, Martins did sigh. "Alright. Leave your partner here with the car and drive us to our destination. He can wait for the truck. You can return for him, or meet him in Llanbedr. Alright?"

"If you say so, sir."

"I do say so. Come on, Chalcott. Let's see if we can find you another car to smash."

The road was wet on the gentle curves that bisected Dolwyddelan, but that did not deter Logan. The RS swept through with a muted whistle of its turbo.

"Not far to go now," she said to Pross.

He watched apprehensively as a low stone wall flashed past in the headlights. "Oh good."

"Pross, oh Pross. What am I going to do with you?"

"Get me to a phone box, for a start. I've got to ring Dee."

"No! No phone calls tonight, Pross."

106

He turned to stare at her. The patterns thrown up by the passing scenery in the backglow of the lights made it seem as if her profile was swimming against a background of mottled shapes.

"Why not?"

"It would be better not to at this stage. Trust me, Pross. You've seen what has happened tonight. A short flight in the new helicopter turned into a small war. That was not on the agenda. Until I know what's going on, it's best that we make contact with no one."

Pross said nothing about the wars that were supposed to be on the agenda. "Not even Fowler?"

"No one . . . *including* Fowler. We've gone incommunicado before, Pross. That's not new to you."

"Never in this country. I don't know about you, but *that's* new to *me*."

She patted his knee briefly. "Trust me," she repeated.

The thing was, he did trust her; and with the exception of one lapse when he'd found himself in Nepal, always had. That didn't necessarily mean he was going to admit it to her whenever she wanted him to. So he stayed silent, and tried not to think of what Dee would say to him when he returned the next day.

"You are taking me back tomorrow, I hope? I know it's Saturday, but Prossair works on Saturdays. I've got a test flight. Remember?"

"I remember and yes, I will take you back."

They came to a junction. The A470 had reached the A5. Logan turned left onto it and staying with the A5, took the RS into a tight lefthander. The road took them across a bridge.

"And here we are," she began in the perfectly cadenced, fake voice of airport announcers, aircraft cabin crews and tour guides everywhere, "being taken across the Conway, courtesy of Thomas Telford's Waterloo Bridge . . . Smile, Pross," she added in her normal voice. "We've arrived."

"Look at my grin," he said. "I'm smiling. See? I'm smiling."

She gave his knee another brief pat as they came off the bridge and began to slow down. "Poor Pross. That's what happens when people think you're a top-class helicopter pilot."

The road curved to the right, then straightened.

"I don't mind being a good chopper pilot. It's the kind of people that sometimes attracts that's a constant worry to me." That and the fact that I also enjoy flying Fowler's machines, he didn't say.

She glanced in her mirrors.

107

'Well?" he continued. "Have we shaken them off? We burned enough rubber getting here."

In the gloom of the car she smiled, but said nothing.

She turned left off the road and into an unpaved drive. The car rocked slowly over the undulations. The drive went on for about a hundred yards or so through woodland before opening out into a paved car park. There were a few cars there, but plenty of space was still available. She pulled up before what looked like a long, multiple garage, and switched off.

"And here we are," she said as the engine died. She stretched like a great cat. "Ah! I needed that. Right, Pross. Out we get."

They climbed out and she went round the back of the car to open the boot. She took out his overnight bag and handed it to him; then she took out a long, dark coat and put it on.

"I look a mess with all the mud on my clothes," she explained. "Imagine what the hotel staff would say."

"They expect muddy people around here. This is walkers' paradise."

"I'd rather hide mine."

Her real reason was to avoid the possibility of being identified as having come in muddied, should their pursuers choose to enquire of the hotel staff. There were all sorts of ways of finding out information like that without arousing suspicion. Any reasonably competent questioner would not find that particularly difficult. She was quite certain that the man she had seen was a most competent operative.

She took out her own overnight bag, shut the boot, then went back for her smaller bag containing the magnum. She then shut the car, and locked it.

As they walked towards the large rambling hotel, Pross heard the sound of rushing water, more powerful than that he'd heard on the way to Cwm Bychan.

"The Conway's in full flow," he said. "It sounds very close."

"The hotel overlooks it. They've got a long stretch of river."

"So you know this place well? Been here before?"

She took some time to reply and Pross wondered at the reason.

"Some years ago," she answered at last. "I was in my teens. Don't worry. It was all a very long time ago, and I looked quite different. I don't mean just this." She shook her head to indicate the wig. "I mean generally. I was a little tubby as well. No one will recognise me, even if the same staff are here, which I very much doubt."

She wouldn't say more, and Pross did not push it further. There had been something in her voice that had warned him against doing so.

As they walked on, Logan thought of the bug beneath the car's rear wing. It was a beacon that would bring the Mercedes in like a homing pigeon.

The Mercedes was taking it slowly, a mile out of Blaenau Ffestiniog.

"Fifteen minutes," the woman was saying. "It's fifteen minutes since we lost the signal. He could be on his way to Scotland by now."

"Possibly, but I very much doubt it." The man was quite unperturbed. "It is my judgment that he was trying to get away from the security people ... hence his speed. Since he has no idea we are also following him, I believe he has stopped for the night. The transmitter is temporarily screened. These are mountain roads now. We are bound to lose it from time to time. We are on the correct route."

"Is it really necessary to follow him? What can we learn that will be of use to us?"

"Consider what has happened. You have been instructed to co-operate with me on a particular assignment whose objectives were quite clear. We find two dead unknown bodies, after disaster has struck your own teams. We also find a car which, if it had belonged to the dead people, should still be where we left it. Instead, it has led us a merry chase through the Welsh countryside, apparently being pursued by British security. A colleague of the dead ones? Or their killer? Either of these questions poses problems for us. Who engaged the second group to do the same job? Or were they there for another purpose? The questions mount. There are several more that I could raise, none of which make me feel easier.

"Perhaps he's an independent. I might recognise him. I have had to deal with independents before. If we have met, he is unlikely to recognise me with this beard. Besides, my manner will be quite different if I do recognise him as someone I know."

"It blinked!" the woman exclaimed sharply. "For a second, as we went round the corner."

"I was right," the man said with satisfaction. "We must have passed through a weak screen. He's down there. We'll find him."

*

109

Logan watched with amusement as Pross signed Plumstead in the hotel register. In the address column, he put London.

They collected their key from the young woman in the small office and made their way up to their room.

The hotel was reminiscent of a hunting lodge and was all oak panels and trophies on the walls. They found they'd been given a large room with bath, overlooking the river. Pross could hear it thundering away beyond the closed windows. There were separate beds.

"That solves that little problem," Logan said meaningfully.

"Stop it, Logan," Pross said. "You realise I won't be able to come here again, particularly with my family?"

"You weren't going to, anyway."

"True."

"And besides, I have special memories . . ." Her voice faded as she looked round the room, keeping her thoughts to herself.

"Don't tell me this is the room you were in."

"What? Oh. No. No. Not this room." She removed her coat slowly and put it on the bed she had chosen. "I'm going to have a bath then perhaps we can try and get something to eat. We're too late for normal service, but we may be able to plead for a few sandwiches and coffee. I'm sorry, Pross. You must be starving."

Upon her face was the expression against which he had no defence: the vulnerable one, with the green eyes seeming extra-large above the pattern of freckles. She had done plenty this night. It was a wonder that she still managed to keep in control, but every now and then something slipped through. It was this quality about her, he knew, that kept him hooked. The tough Logan . . . the soft Logan; both the same person. His weakness.

"Don't worry about me," he said. "Sandwiches will be fine."

"Right. I'll have that bath, then."

He nodded as she removed the fake glasses and the wig, and placed them on the bed next to the coat.

"It's amazing," he said, looking at the wig. "I thought your wig wouldn't stand up to scrutiny in proper lighting, but it looks so natural it would be very difficult to tell the difference."

"It is natural. You're looking at real hair. It cost a few hundred pounds at a top people's store."

"For a *wig?*"

"If you're going to do it, do it properly, I say. In my line of work, it can be the difference between life and death." The green eyes

110

were serious now; then just as suddenly, the impish look came into them. "Anyway, it's Department funds doing the paying. You don't seriously think *I'd* pay a small fortune for a wig, do you? Why should I want to hide my hair when I'm not working?"

Why indeed, he thought. It was rich hair. The trouble was, it would always be difficult to know when Logan was not working.

She picked up her overnight bag. "Bath time. You can come in and talk to me if you'd like, Pross." She smiled, teasing him. "Alright, Mr Plumstead. Stay and listen to the river. Better take this, I suppose." She reached into the smaller bag, and pulled out the magnum.

Pross said, "Surely, you don't expect anyone to come barging in?"

"I always expect everything, and nothing, Pross." She gave him another quick smile and left him to his thoughts.

He shook his head slowly, smiled to himself. Keeping up with Logan was no easy task. He went over to a window, to stare out at the dark. Far up a hillside, he saw a speck of light. A house, perhaps. The muted roar of the Conway came to him clearly. He opened the window slightly and the roar, accompanied by the night's chill, invaded the room. He listened to it for a while, then shut the window once more.

Well, he thought. *What now?* He worried about Dee and the children.

The Mercedes had reached Dolwyddelan and the signal from the bug was transmitting strongly.

"Scotland, did you say?" the man remarked with a faint degree of smugness.

"Alright. I was wrong." It was not said with good grace. "And if we find he has stopped for the night?"

"We use the same hotel."

"Are you mad? That will warn him!"

"I want to see who he is," the man said firmly. "If we spend the night somewhere else, it means waiting up to catch his moment of departure. Once I have identified him, the chase will be over. However, if you would prefer to wait up all night, you can do so by yourself."

"And what will you do when you have identified him?" the woman asked sourly.

"That depends on many things."

*

Logan came out of the bath looking fresh and gleaming. She had put on a simple pale blue dress and low-heeled shoes. Her bare legs were lightly tanned. They were legs that commanded admiration.

Pross said, "Been somewhere hot recently?" He noted a slight hesitation in her eyes and went on. "It's alright. You don't have to tell me, but it would cause me no surprise to know that Fowler might have had something to do with it."

"You know how it is, Pross," she said apologetically. "Besides, it had nothing to do with you. I never keep anything from you if you're involved. You know that."

He believed her; but that didn't mean Fowler would not keep things from her, especially if they concerned Pross.

He said, "Of course I know that."

She took the wig off the bed and put it back on. "Well? What do you think?"

"A complete transformation, but it does not do you justice. I prefer the genuine Logan."

"Thank you," she said, pleased by his words. "And how about this?" She put on the glasses.

"Definitely not you. A new person entirely." He marvelled at the way she could alter her persona. "You remind me of someone on the telly, but we won't say more about that."

"I've a horrible idea I know who you mean. I suppose I should feel pleased. After all, this makes me positively unrecognisable . . . at least to someone who's never met me before, and who sees me again as the real Logan, if you see what I mean."

"In a convoluted way, yes."

She picked up her magnum bag. "Come on, Mr Plumstead."

"You're taking the gun down with you?" Pross raised his hands briefly in a gesture of surrender. "Oh alright, alright. I know. Don't say it."

She pulled the door shut after them as they left the room and put the key with its heavy plastic tag into her bag. Then she tucked her arm in his as they made their way down.

"Might as well look the part," she said.

They found a cosy lounge on the ground floor. There was a well-stocked small bar at one end, and a cheerful fire roaring in the hearth at the other. Its décor gave an even stronger impression of a hunting lodge. There were no other guests around.

They went up to the bar and the woman behind it said, in a

112

friendly voice, "Good evening. I heard you'd come in. Can I help you with anything?"

Logan said, "We know it's past dinner, but we've been on the road all day and don't really feel like going out to a restaurant. We wondered if we could trouble you for some sandwiches and coffee?"

"It's no trouble at all. Coffee's available till quite late, and there's a bar menu." The woman reached beneath the counter for a pair of wine-coloured, stiff-backed booklets, and handed them out. "Everything's available."

"Thank you," Pross said.

"Pleasure."

He smiled at her, then turned to Logan, who was poring over the menu uncertainly, playing the hesitant wife to the hilt.

"What do you think, darling?" she asked, looking demurely at him.

He pinched a part of her body that was out of the woman's sight, and she kicked his ankle for his pains.

"Take your pick," he told her evenly.

"I think I'll go for the ham. Two rounds, please."

"I'll have chicken," Pross said to the woman.

"Two rounds as well?"

"Yes please."

"Any drinks?"

Logan gave Pross a look as if for inspiration, then said, "A pot of coffee?"

He nodded, remaining silent.

"A pot of coffee," she told the woman. "We'll have it now, if that's okay."

"That's quite alright, my dear." The woman had a kindly manner, and was obviously coming to certain conclusions about Pross and Logan. Young wife, new husband, her eyes said. "Please take your seats and I'll attend to it."

Logan gave Pross a smile full of mischief as they found comfortable chairs round a table near the fire. The woman had gone out.

"That's two of the staff I don't recognise," Logan said. "So far so good."

Pross said, "You were over-acting a bit back there, weren't you?"

"Was I?" Innocently.

"You know you were."

"Fun, Pross. Having fun. The thing about subterfuge is that it must look the part."

113

"Subterfuge. I see. Is that what it is?"

His ankle got another kick. "Stop it."

"I'll do that coffee now," the woman called to them. "Your sandwiches won't be long."

"Thank you," Pross said.

She made them a fresh pot of filter coffee and brought it over.

Logan said, "Where's everybody?"

"Oh, most of them are in town. Gone for a walk and then to a restaurant. They should be coming back soon, to round off the evening in here. Your first time in Wales?"

Pross decided to let Logan carry the ball.

"No," Logan answered. "We actually live in the south, but we don't get to come this way often."

"Ah. I see. But you're not Welsh." It sounded like an accusation.

"Well, I'm actually quarter Welsh, from my paternal grandmother."

Pross kept a straight face, not daring to contemplate the veracity of the wonderful tale Logan was spinning. He wondered what she would say about him. He soon found out.

"David's not, of course. Despite his name."

Well at least she had not called him Damien, which was what she had once bestowed upon him during another of her "subterfuges".

"I come from Shrewsbury myself," the woman was saying, when voices from outside interrupted her. "Ah," she continued. "The first of the returning revellers. I'd better get back to the bar. Sandwiches should be along any minute now."

She left them with a smile and returned to the bar just as a youngish couple entered. They both wore jeans and short jackets. The man was not the one Logan had seen.

"Hello," the woman at the bar greeted them. "Enjoyed your walk?"

"Went for a drive instead," the man answered. His accent was Scottish. "Up to Capel Curig."

"I see. Have you eaten?"

"Yes thanks. I think we're just about ready for a spot of drinking now that I'm finished with the car for the night." He gave a nervous laugh.

Pross said to Logan, in a low voice, "I saw you give him the quick scrutiny. Did you expect him to be someone else?"

"Getting a bit quick, are you?"

"It's the company I keep."

A young girl brought in their sandwiches after that.

"She's too young to have known you," Pross said when the girl had left.

"She's about the age I was," Logan said, and went quiet.

Pross wondered what had taken place all those years ago. He would not ask her to tell him. It was her own private affair.

The Mercedes pulled into the car park. The man stopped it well away from the RS. He got out, walked over to the smaller car quickly, and felt its bonnet. It was cold. He did a swift check of the other cars, and found two that were still warm.

"We know where he is now," he said to his companion as he re-entered the Mercedes. "He arrived some time ago. The car is cold."

"We shall have separate rooms," the woman said.

"Do not worry," the man told her drily. "I had no intention of sharing a room, or a bed, with you."

"Good," she said stiffly.

The man smiled in the gloom of the car. "Let's get our things and pretend we are studious people. With my beard, I look like a professor, I think, and I have a passport to prove it."

Still smiling, he climbed out, and waited for her to get organised; then he locked the car and in frigid silence they walked to the hotel.

The lounge had become almost full and the noise of conversation was quite loud. Pross looked up to see the kindly woman from behind the bar approaching them.

"More coffee?" she suggested.

Pross looked at Logan. "You?"

She nodded. "Yes, and I think I'd like a brandy."

"Fine. I'll get that for you," the woman said.

Pross stood up. "No need to bring it out. I'll come and collect it."

"Will you? Oh thanks." The woman seemed pleased. "As you can see, it's getting a little hectic." She began collecting the empty glasses from the tables.

"Here. Let me help you with those." Before she could demur, Pross took the glasses she had already picked up, and went up to the bar.

She followed soon after with some more.

"That was kind," she told him.

"Not at all."

115

Perhaps it was that act of kindness that made her say, "Another latecomer tonight."

"Oh?"

She turned to search the bottles before replying. "What kind of brandy does your wife like?"

Pross thought of Dee's favourite tipple and announced with a private glee, "Napoleon. Five-star."

"Ooh. Expensive wife, is she?"

This time he thought of Logan, with the same sense of glee. "She can be."

The woman smiled. "I wouldn't let her hear you say that."

"Be more than my life's worth," he said ruefully; which was probably true . . . in both cases. "I think I'll join her." After all, the Department was paying.

"Another brandy coming up. Yes . . . as I was saying, we've just had two latecomers. A professor somebody and his assistant. One of those interested in rocks, probably. We get a few of those around here. Foreign. They sound American. Well, the man did."

"Who?"

"Those two that just came in."

"Ah. I see."

"They won't be coming in here."

"Why not?"

"Didn't look the type. It's straight to bed for them and up with the dawn to go digging for what they call samples, in the hills."

"I can see you've had plenty of experience with that kind of guest."

"Oh, we get all kinds here. Here are your brandies. The coffee won't be long. I'll make you a fresh pot. What room number are you? That's for the drinks. Coffee's on the house."

Pross gave her the room number and rejoined Logan.

"She's insisted she'll bring the coffee," he said as he sat down. "She also said," he continued, watching her for a reaction, "that they'd had two latecomers. Foreign. American. The man."

Behind the fake glasses, the eyes seemed to grow keen. "So there's a woman as well?"

"I expect so. That's the impression she gave me."

"I see." Logan was definitely on guard.

"Care to tell me?"

"Nothing to tell." She cupped the brandy glass in her hands.

"I see," Pross said quietly, then leaned across to whisper in her ear, "Warn me before the shooting starts, won't you?"

"It won't be like that at all," she said sweetly, and smiled at him as if he'd said something wonderful to her.

At the bar, the woman saw them and smiled knowingly.

SEVEN

Ten minutes later, Logan had a shock.

A voice said in her ear, "Don't pray to that brandy. Drink it!"

Pross had seen the ebullient man with the expression of a benign uncle approaching. The newcomer had worn a friendly, pleased smile and Pross had not judged him to be a potential threat. Accordingly, he had been slow to react in time to warn Logan who had been deep in thought, still nursing her brandy. He was therefore quite surprised by her reaction.

She jumped, and nearly spilled her drink.

"John!" There was evident pleasure in her voice, but something else too; as if she wished the man she'd addressed as John had chosen any other time but this to make his appearance. "I didn't expect to see you here. I thought you'd moved to Cornwall years ago."

"Cornwall didn't agree with me, my dear. Or I didn't agree with Cornwall. The result was the same. I returned a year ago." He smiled again, like someone who had just solved a puzzle. "I didn't recognise you at first, although I thought there was something familiar when I came in. You're so changed. But essentially, still the same Sian. It was the brandy, of course."

"The brandy?"

"Yes. The way you held the glass. The way you're still holding it. The very first time I saw you, that was exactly how you were holding it, and I greeted you with the same words."

"Oh." Still quite at a loss for words, Logan put the glass down carefully.

Pross was intrigued. He'd never seen her so unsure of herself. He also thought, drily, that even the very best-laid plans could come

118

unstuck, usually in a spectacular manner like this. He waited with interest to see how Logan would introduce him. She was, he could see, already regaining control of herself.

"John," she began, "this is David. David, John McNeil, a very good and old friend."

McNeil grinned. "Less of the old, please. I'm not a day over sixty." He held out his hand. "A pleasure, David. You're a very lucky man, if you will excuse my presumption. She's an extraordinary lady."

"I know," Pross said truthfully, knowing McNeil's interpretation of his words would be quite different. "I find that out every day." He moved his ankles out of reach, but did not escape her quick glance of promised revenge. He shook McNeil's hand.

McNeil said, "Well, Mrs Plumstead, what brings you to my humble hotel?"

"How did you —"

"What does a hotel proprietor do when he sees new names in the register and thinks he recognises a guest? He asks a member of the staff to identify the particular guest. Elementary, as a certain great detective would say. May I join you?"

"Of course you may, John."

McNeil sat down at their table. He was a man of medium height, with a flowing mane of hair that had more white in it than black; but his open, wide-eyed face had a tan to it that owed more to the weather of the hillsides than to a couple of sybaritic weeks on a far, sun-drenched beach. He was stocky in build, and wore a dark pinstripe three-piece suit. Out of the waistcoat, the thick loop of a watch-chain gleamed.

"Why didn't you let me know you were getting married? I've been saving a beautiful present for you, in anticipation of that day. Can you guess what it could be?"

Logan's smile was one of genuine pleasure. "I think I can. But I couldn't warn you," she went on. "For a start, it was very sudden." She did not give Pross a warning glance, but he still kept his ankles well out of danger. "And I didn't even know you were still here."

McNeil said, with gentle reproof: "You have been somewhat infrequent with your correspondence . . . Ah, but I shall stop there. I see I am embarrassing you. Forgive me. More brandy, I think. David?"

"Er . . . yes, please."

"Sian? The Napoleon, is it?"

"Yes, but I'll pass for now, John. I've still got most of the original."

"Very well. So it's just you and I for the moment, David."

When McNeil had left to get the drinks, Pross said, "Logan, I'm sorry. He was here before I could warn you."

"It's alright, Pross. Nothing you could have done. If it hadn't been now, it would have been later. I had no idea —"

"You don't have to explain things to me. It's your private business."

The green eyes stared at him. "It's not what you imagine, you know."

"I'm not imagining anything. It's nothing to do with me. I'm more worried about the people who are not supposed to be following us, and who may be in this very hotel."

"I didn't have an affair with him."

"Logan, didn't you just hear me? I don't want to know."

"I want you to know. It's important. To me."

"Alright, but if you want to stop . . . just do so."

She nodded. "I was eighteen, and I thought I was in love. It didn't work out. He was much older, but that was not the reason. He was just looking for a diversion . . . only, I didn't realise it until much too late." She smiled sheepishly. "The old cliché. I thought I was above that sort of thing. It could never happen to *me*. Well, it did . . . in a quite devastating way."

"Oh Logan, I am sorry."

She patted his knee gently. "Anyway, he married someone else . . ."

"He needed his bloody head examined," Pross heard himself say before he could stop himself.

Her smile was one of real affection. "Keep saying nice things to me, and I promise not to kick your ankle . . . for now. So I came here," she continued, "to nurse my feelings. A friend had come to this place once with her parents and thought I might like it. I wanted to be well away from anyone I knew. I came without telling anyone, except my friend who was sworn to secrecy. John's family virtually adopted me for that week. They kept me occupied, and John, especially, refused to let me feed on my pain. He really was quite wonderful. I think he saved me."

Pross thought he could begin to understand a little of that strangely attractive quality of her vulnerability, but knew it to be of far greater complexity.

120

"There are sometimes periods in your life," she was saying, "when a single act by someone else can mark you for years, perhaps forever. John McNeil's act of kindness is one of those. It's a little difficult now, all things considered, to know exactly how to handle this. I need you, Pross. I don't like lying to him, yet I can't tell him anything. Will you play this through for me?"

"Of course I will."

She smiled at him. "Thank you."

In a room well away from the one occupied by Pross and Logan, the couple from the Mercedes were in the man's room.

"There are many people in the lounge bar," the woman was saying. "It would be too risky."

"I am not asking you to accompany me."

"Our rooms overlook the car park. We shall see who uses it in the morning."

The man said: "One of the reasons I'm still alive is because I make no assumptions. All I know is that we have been chasing a car which was where it shouldn't have been. I need a better picture, another piece to the puzzle. I am going downstairs to see if I can find it. When we came in, our names were the first at the top of a new page. I want to see who came in before us."

"You said yourself his car was cold. There were two warmer ones. Their occupants would have arrived after him."

He smiled at her without friendliness. "Humour me," he said, and went out.

McNeil returned with the drinks, but did not sit down.

"Look," he said. "You're not just guests. You're friends. This place is too crowded and noisy now for a decent chat. Let's go to my office. We'll be able to talk in peace there."

Pross and Logan looked at each other, and nodded.

"Alright," she said.

"Good," McNeil said as they stood up. "I'll lead the way, shall I?" And he set off, threading his way skilfully between the tables and standing drinkers, the brandies barely shifting as he moved.

Pross and Logan followed him out of the lounge and across the entrance hall, past Reception then through another room to the door of his office.

He handed Pross one of the glasses. "Yours, I think, David. Need a free hand for the keys." He reached into a trouser pocket as Pross took the glass, and pulled out the bunch of jingling metal. That too was secured by a heavy chain, linked to his belt. He inserted a large key, and turned. "There we are. After you, my children."

They entered, followed by McNeil, who shut the door and locked it from the inside. Pross noted that the inner panel was sumptiously upholstered in dark red padded leather.

Certainly, he thought, it would prevent eavesdropping.

The room had about it the same cosy sense of comfort felt in the lounge, only more so. Four high-backed and equally well-upholstered armchairs formed a crescent before a large inlaid pedestal desk, behind which was a black high-backed swivel chair. McNeil took one of the armchairs and indicated that they should sit.

When they had done so, he said, "Well, children. What tales have you for uncle John?"

The man arrived at the reception counter just as McNeil was turning the key to lock the door to his office, with Pross and Logan inside.

The man was pleased to see that the reception office was temporarily unoccupied. Swiftly, he flipped back the page of the registration book to check the names that had been written in before the ones he had given.

"Mr and Mrs Plumstead," he read softly, and promptly ignored them. Directly above that name were two others. "P. Johnson, Charles Scott," he murmured.

Both of them had given their nationalities as British, addresses in London. He noted their room numbers. Possibilities, he thought.

He heard footsteps, flicked back the page to its original position and waited. He smiled at the receptionist.

"Sorry to have kept you waiting," she said. "Can I help you, sir?"

"Ah . . . yes," he began in his best professorial manner. "That is . . . er . . . I hope so. Would it be possible to serve my colleague breakfast in her room? She has had a rather hard day and I don't think she feels she will make it in time. Would you do that for me, please?"

"Of course, sir."

"Thank you."

"My pleasure."

With another smile, he left her to enter the lounge.

"Tales, John?" Logan said.

"Well you know . . . the usual. How you met this lucky man and

122

what happened to you after you left us. I can still see the bruised eighteen-year-old, but much has changed." McNeil paused, looked at Pross. "Do you know the story, David?"

"Some of it."

"Well, let me tell you about this wonderful young lady. She came here out of the blue all those years ago, a wounded young fledgling, looking for shelter. Forgive my poetic licence, but that is exactly how I saw her. She would give us no clues to her background, only that she wanted to be left to herself. She would go for walks along the river, and I must admit there were times when I feared for her safety. No need to be, of course. Sian is made of sterner stuff."

"Oh I don't know, John," Logan said. "There were times . . . But your persistence dragged me out."

"Rubbish. You did it all by yourself. I could not have done anything either for a weak person, or for someone determined to give in. You were neither of those. But to continue . . . I persuaded her, David, to accompany us on a rough shoot. Well . . . ha . . . that day, I got the surprise of my life. Would you believe it if I told you, your Sian is a magnificent shot? No. No. Not magnificent. She's brilliant. An absolute natural. She put many of the men to shame that day."

If only you knew, Pross thought drily.

"Well, I thought," McNeil continued. "Let's see just how good this young woman is. So I took her on a target shoot, with a *rifle*. Astounding results. Eye like a hawk. I told her she could wipe the field at Bisley. I don't suppose you ever took that up, Sian."

"I'm afraid not, John."

"Pity. You would have been a champion several times over. Do you still hunt?"

"No."

"Pity," McNeil repeated. "You never did tell me who taught you."

"My father," Logan said.

"He must have been good."

"The best, in his day."

"Then I would have heard of him, surely. I would not have missed a name like Logan."

"I don't carry his name. I never did."

There was a long silence.

"Oh," McNeil said at last, softly. "Ah." He cleared his throat. "I'm sorry, Sian. I didn't mean to pry."

"There's nothing to be sorry about, John. I know who he is, and we have a good relationship. We always did. I didn't have to tell you. So you see, there's nothing to feel awkward about, Alright?"

"Yes. Yes," McNeil went on briskly. "Tell you what, children. I've got something that I think we should all enjoy at this moment." He stood up and went to a cabinet placed in a corner near the desk.

Pross was looking at Logan with a bemused expression on his face.

McNeil opened the cabinet, took out two bottles with some reverence, and put them on the desk. He then got out three glasses, and shut the cabinet.

"I'm about to introduce you," he announced, "to a royal drink." He raised one of the bottles briefly. "Behold, one bottle of ancient malt, not obtainable outside a particular vault in Scotland, unless one has extremely good connections to same. And here, Bonnie Prince Charlie's own, the golden Drambuie. Now, I am about to commit what some might think a heinous sacrilege: the adulteration of two of the finest liquids to grace a man's throat. But, I argue, when excellence meets excellence, what do you have? A sense of true wonder. And after all that," he finished with a wry smile, "if you hate it, I shall throttle you both."

Very carefully, he proceeded to pour equal measures of each drink into each glass. Then he handed them round.

"Your health, my children."

Pross took a cautious mouthful. It seemed to explode smoothly within him.

"My God!" he said in a wheezing whisper.

"Don't you like it?" McNeil looked anxious.

"Like it? I love it! Great. Great. Just let me call my breath back. It doesn't know what hit it yet."

McNeil grinned. "Take a look at Sian. You're not going to be shamed by a wee woman?"

Pross looked. Logan seemed serene.

"Don't be fooled," she said hoarsely. "I . . . I can't speak!"

McNeil looked pleased with himself. "Wait till it warns the stomach with its silky strength. And so, my children," he went on, "to matters of serious import." He looked at each in turn. "I will not pretend I understand what's going on. All I know . . . all I feel . . . is that you're here for a purpose other than that which meets the eye. No, Sian. Please let me have my say.

"I have always prided myself on the fact that I am able to take

124

the measure of someone quite accurately when I have set my mind to it. I do not believe I have made a mistake about you. You were a young woman of strength and character when I first met you. You are that same young woman today. It is possible that you are here for your own very private reasons. It is also possible that this dear old place having once been a haven for you, you chose to return a second time, perhaps to again use it as a reasonably safe port in a storm. I don't know. You do not look as if you're in trouble . . . at least, not the normal kind of trouble.

"Which, of course, sets me wondering. Earlier, I said you had the eye of a hawk. I believe you still have. Unless something quite sudden has happened to your vision over the years, the glasses are unexplainable except for the purposes of disguise. I also remember your hair; a rich mane of fire it seemed at the time. Even though it appears you have chosen to dye it in a somewhat lacklustre colour, it does not seem quite right. So I've asked myself, if Sian wants to hide herself so completely . . . why? I feel there are new mysteries about you that perhaps you will not wish to tell me, but if I can help in any way . . ."

McNeil left the words hanging, his meaning plain.

Logan was at a loss. She did not want him involved, yet she knew she could no longer hide part of the truth from him.

"If it's any consolation," McNeil was saying, "it's a good disguise. It was only the brandy and the way you held it that gave you away to me and excited my curiosity. Only someone who knows that about you would have reacted the way I have. It's a point to remember in the future."

"Why in the future?"

Instead of replying, McNeil turned to Pross. "David, I think I'm old enough, and experienced enough in observing people, to note certain things about Sian and yourself. Again, if I did not already know her, I might have been taken in. Perhaps, against all my instincts, you really are married; but somehow, I doubt it. However, I don't think Sian would really pretend to be married just to satisfy some whim. If she wanted to spend a weekend away with a man, that is precisely what she would do and hang anyone else's opinion. Having come to my conclusions by this circuitous route, I am left with even more questions. I do not require answers, save for one. I must have it, though this will not alter my offer of help. Are you two in trouble with the law?"

Both Pross and Logan smiled at the question.

McNeil looked at them puzzledly. "I have obviously said something very funny."

Logan said, "You couldn't be more wrong about the law, John."

"Is this some kind of code? You *are* the law?"

Logan said, "John, I never imagined you would be here and in a way, I wish you weren't. Oh dear. I don't know how best to put this. There's not much that I can tell you. We're not the law, but . . ."

"Something official?" McNeil had obviously been considering that option.

"In a way . . . yes."

"Well. So Bisley's loss is the nation's gain."

"I wouldn't put it quite like that."

McNeil was studying her with narrowed eyes. "I do hope you're careful, whatever it is you do."

"I am, John. I'm very careful."

"And you, David. I do hope you look after her."

"We look after each other," Pross said.

"She's very special."

"I know."

McNeil took a generous mouthful of his drink and swallowed it with relish. "Are you at my hotel for a specific reason?"

Logan said, "It's only fair to give you a peripheral . . ."

McNeil smiled, almost mischievously. "'Peripheral'. That's a fine word. Peri — boundaries of . . . or evil spirit, if you're Persian; although I believe it now means good. Which is it?"

She went straight to the point. "Among your guests are two people who came in after us. They are extremely dangerous. Nothing is going to happen here, and I am not going to tell you who they are. As for David and me, we are simply guests you've chosen to entertain privately. Not even your staff — particularly not your staff, as a matter of fact — must think differently. In short, you have not recognised me."

McNeil nodded slowly, a tiny smile on his lips. "Yes," he said, almost to himself. "I can see the steel in you. Very well, my children. I have never seen you before, I do not know there are, or may be guests of dubious character in my hotel, and we never spoke of this. Alright?"

Logan smiled at him. "That will do, John. And I'm sorry."

"What for? I'm very happy to see you, and impressed too. Just as long as you don't take chances with your life, whatever your job is."

"I won't. I promise."

"And now, may an old friend receive a welcoming hug?"

"Of course he may."

Logan stood up and McNeil embraced her. He winked at Pross.

"Not jealous, are you, David?"

"Perish the thought," Pross said.

Back in his own room, the man from the Mercedes was saying, "There are two likely possibilities. Johnson, and Scott. Perhaps together, perhaps only one of them. A husband-and-wife couple is registered after them. Theirs was probably one of the warm cars. I also went into the bar. Barmaids are always good for a slice of gossip."

"Well?" his woman companion began. "Did your trip make you any the wiser? Was your gossipy barmaid helpful?"

The man smiled at the tension in her voice. "There's a time to question, and a time to listen. I listened. Scott was at the bar, talking to her. Before you ask, I knew he was Scott because she called him Mr Scott. Outdoor type, very tough-looking, in an unobtrusive way. A man in control of himself. There were no others in there worth my interest.

"She was also in conversation with a young couple – not the Plumsteads – but they were talking about them; the Plumsteads, I mean. It would seem that the manager of the hotel has taken to them and is entertaining them privately. It is an apparent habit of his when he likes a guest. It appears he is a genuinely friendly man. Not like some hotel managers I've seen in my travels," the man concluded wryly.

"Well? What shall we do about Scott?"

"Nothing."

"*Nothing?*"

"For the moment. Be patient. I have no intention of drawing attention to myself by doing anything here. We shall follow when he leaves. There is more to this. I am certain of it. Oh by the way, you're having breakfast in your room."

"I am?"

"Yes. I was inspecting the register when the receptionist returned. I had to tell her something credible to explain my presence there. So I ordered breakfast for you."

"I do not want breakfast in my room."

"Then cancel it," the man said tightly. He had clearly had

enough of her. He went to the door and held it open. "Goodnight."

She glared at him as she walked stiffly out.

He closed the door softly and leaned against it, shutting his eyes wearily. He sighed, went to the bathroom and began washing his face with thoughtful care. There was a mirror above the sink and he stared into it.

"Sometimes," he said to the image, "I wonder why you do this job. It is dangerous enough without having to cope with unstable people who are a danger to themselves, and therefore to you."

He spoke in German.

"Time for coffee, I think," McNeil said. "Shall I have it brought here? Or do we retire to the lounge?"

"I think we'll go up," Logan said. "We'll make some in our room. Poor David looks almost out."

"Almost is right," Pross said. "I've had two brandies and three of your concoctions, John. Good thing I'm not driving. That stuff will still be sloshing about in me tomorrow morning."

McNeil grinned. "I am pleased to see such evidence of the potency of a supreme hundred-year-old Highland malt. As for you, Sian, it's only because you've pleaded tomorrow's drive as a reason that I've let you off with the wee one you've nursed all evening."

"That was more than enough." She stood up. "Coming, David?" She gave him a sweet smile, and he wondered what was up.

"I could sleep right here," Pross said, but he rose to his feet.

At the door, McNeil said quietly to Logan, "Don't leave it so long next time. Come up and see us, preferably when you're not working. And I was quite serious about the present."

"You can't give those to me," she protested.

"Of course I can. Who will appreciate them as much?"

She said to Pross, "He's got two beautiful Purdeys. I think he's crazy. I can't take them," she added to McNeil.

"Make her, David," McNeil said.

"What are you trying to do to me? I'm keeping well out of it."

"Coward."

"It's alright for you. I've got to put up with her. Oow!"

"What's up?"

"She kicks as well."

McNeil gave his infectious grin. "You two sound like a married couple. I'll be getting rid of those shotguns yet."

Logan put her arm in Pross's. "Come on, David, dear, you drunken wretch," she said in her sweetest voice. "Bedtime."

"Sweet night, my children," McNeil said expansively, and let them out.

Logan gave him a kiss on the cheek before they left, calling goodnight back to him.

On their way up the stairs, Logan said, "Are you really as drunk as you look?"

"I really am as drunk as I look. That was powerful stuff."

She giggled suddenly. Her arm was still linked to his.

"What's so funny?" he queried.

"You."

A thin blonde woman passed, going down. The expression on her face made her look as if she was doomed to suck on a lemon permanently.

"She looks happy," Pross said in a loud whisper.

"Shhh!" Logan cautioned. "She'll hear you." She giggled again. "My God. You really are drunk."

The woman continued her way down the stairs with a tightening of her lips. She had heard the comment. She went to the reception counter and got there just as McNeil arrived from his office.

"Can I be of assistance, madam?" For all he had drunk, he was steady on his feet, his eyes keen, missing nothing.

"Who are you?"

"For my sins, the manager of this hotel, madam," McNeil replied patiently.

"Ah. My colleague the Professor ordered breakfast for me in my room. I wish to change it. I shall have breakfast as normal."

"Very well, madam. But you could have used the telephone and saved yourself the trouble."

"I wanted a walk before going to bed."

"I see. And your room number?" McNeil turned a small notepad lying on the counter towards him and waited.

"Number 23," she said.

McNeil wrote it down. "Number 23 it is." He added instructions on the pad. "I'll see that it's cancelled. Thank you, madam. Be careful if you walk along the river. It's quite fast at the moment."

"I won't be going near the river," she said.

McNeil watched her leave, and thought of the conversation he'd had in his office. Could this woman be one of those people? She certainly looked hard enough. She was a recent guest too.

"Don't get involved, Sian said," he told himself quietly. "And that is precisely what I shall do. I don't want to know." He glanced up at the ceiling. "I do not know by which route you came to be what you are, although perhaps I did see the beginning. But be careful, child."

Logan watched with amusement as Pross got his bed ready.

"Can you manage?" she asked.

"Perfectly."

"I've never seen you so drunk."

"You've never seen me drunk . . . though after a day like today, I think I needed to be."

She stifled a laugh. "Those three drinks you had with John must have been something."

"Let me tell you, my lass . . . that friend of yours Mr John McNeil was loading me with the equivalent of four drinks each time he recharged my glass. Work it out. But it was beautiful, though. Bloody beautiful." He'd drunk some coffee on their return, but that hadn't seemed to help.

Logan shook her head slowly, smiling at his efforts.

"I'm going to get undressed now," Pross said. "Don't scream."

"I promise not to," she said with a straight face.

He stripped down to his underpants, went to the bathroom, and climbed into bed when he returned.

"Chicken," she accused. "You cheated."

"I'm not that drunk. Let's see you do better."

"I'm not drunk at all," she countered.

She turned off the lights before she got undressed, and climbed into her own bed.

"Now who's cheating?" he said.

"My strip was complete," she said.

Pross listened to the river in the dark of the room. It seemed very loud, despite the closed windows.

He said, "Logan?"

"Yes."

"I'm sorry."

"About what?"

"Well . . . your father . . ."

"Why should you be? It doesn't worry me."

"What I'm trying to say is —"

"I know what you're trying to say, Pross," she said gently. "Thank you."

"I'd really hate it if anything happened to you."

There was a long silence, then, "It must be the drink talking."

"Do you believe that?"

"No."

"Well then."

There was another silence and this time, it was Pross who broke it. "Do you have that cannon of yours handy?"

"Yes."

"I might get up in the middle of the night, given the stuff that's been poured into me. Don't shoot me by mistake, will you?"

"I think I'll know it's you, Pross." She sounded as if she was about to giggle again.

A longer silence followed.

"Pross?"

"Umm."

"Weren't you just a little bit jealous when John hugged me, all things considered?"

"No," he said.

"Liar," she said, and smiled in the darkness.

"Go to sleep, Logan."

EIGHT

Pross opened his eyes to find Logan, fully dressed in clean jeans and sweater, sitting on his bed. The wig and glasses were also back on, and the green eyes were dark with mischief. Daylight streamed through the windows.

"And what are you looking so bright and bushy-tailed about?" he queried groggily.

"Well," she said, "I could say it was because you woke up in your drunken stupor last night and had your filthy way with me; but as you slept like a great log and didn't stir till this moment, I can hardly say that."

Pross groaned. "Behave yourself, Logan. It's too early in the morning."

"Sorry to disappoint you. It's not too early, and if you stay in there much longer, you'll miss breakfast. I don't intend to miss breakfast. While you've been happily in the land of nod, I've been out for a walk."

"You've been *what*? My God, it's obscene!"

"Come on, Pross. You're the man who gets up early and works late to keep his firm running. Remember? And what about the Dawn Patrol?"

"I don't usually have mad Scotsmen trying to turn my blood into alcohol."

"Don't exaggerate. Come on. Up! Or I'll pull the bedclothes off."

Pross groaned once more. "You bloody well would, wouldn't you."

"Oh yes."

"Logan, I think I hate you this morning."

"Dear oh dear. And after last night too."

"What about last night?" Suspiciously.

"A woman's got to keep a few secrets," she said with theatrical coyness.

"I don't believe a word of it."

She smiled at him. "Suit yourself." She stood up, and went to a window to stand, legs slightly apart, as she looked out at the river.

Pross found himself looking at her with quiet pleasure.

"Don't stare at my bum," she said. "It's too big."

He didn't think so at all, but said nothing.

"I give you three seconds to get up, Pross, or I will rip those bedclothes off.' She sounded as if she would enjoy herself. "One, two —"

"Alright! I don't like the sound of anticipation in your voice."

He got up hurriedly, grabbed his clothes and went to the bathroom. She turned to survey his departing form with an amused expression on her face. Her own things were already packed and ready, so she turned to the window once more while she waited for him.

Their room overlooked a long stretch of the river bank. The Conway rushed on in swollen majesty. She cast her mind back to the time when she had walked along that route every day, trying to forget; trying to rebuild her shattered belief in herself . . .

How different things were now. It was almost as if she had more than enough confidence for one person . . . sometimes. She thought of Pross, and smiled. Funny how he, of all people, always managed to bring her own uncertainty back, despite her valiant efforts to hide it.

"Logan," she said to herself softly. "You like looking for trouble."

"What was that?" Pross had returned, partially dressed.

Without turning round, she said, "Just thinking aloud. Do you . . ." She stopped suddenly, then, "Pross! Come here. Come and have a look at this."

"Hang on. Just let me tuck my shirt in."

"Forget your shirt! No one's going to see you."

He went up to the window and looked down. A bearded man and a blonde woman were walking by the river.

"So?" he said.

"Don't you recognise her?"

"Sorry. Not guilty."

"Oh dear. You were drunk last night, weren't you. She's the one you insulted on the stairs."

He was horrified, "*I* did? Nonsense!"

Logan gave a low chuckle. "She came down as we were going up, looking as if someone had put vinegar in her coffee, and you said in a whisper loud enough to wake the dead, how happy she looked."

"Now who's exaggerating?"

"You did," she insisted. "And she heard you."

"Blame it on McNeil, the old reprobate."

Logan ignored the comment. "When I went for my walk earlier on, I met her along the bank. 'Good morning,' I said."

"That's one way to start a conversation . . ."

"She said 'good morning' . . ." Logan stared at Pross warningly. "Don't."

"Not a word. Promise."

"I wanted to hear her speak," Logan continued. "And of course, it was the same voice."

"Hang on. You've just lost me. What voice are you talking about?"

She gave him one of her sweet smiles, which warned him he was not going to like what came next.

"While you were sitting cosily in your warm helicopter," she said, "I was freezing my bottom off by the lake . . . and who should come wandering out of the dark?"

"I'm going to be really bright this morning. The woman out there?"

"Don't sound so sceptical. The woman, *and* the man with her."

"Oh Logan. Come on."

"I know," she said firmly, "because they passed a mere foot from me . . ."

"And you didn't shoot them? That was restrained."

"Pross!" Warningly. Her eyes were becoming hard.

"Alright," he said quietly. "No more jokes."

"They were talking, in Polish. But I could tell it was not their mother tongue. Then I saw the man stop by the car and do something to it. I later found out it was a tracer, which I decided to leave in place. I also thought Sanders' people would pick them up. But of course they bloody well weren't able to."

Pross was staring at her. "Are you trying to tell me you deliberately led them here? Are they some of the people who were setting off those SAMs?"

134

"Yes to both questions."

"Bloody hell, Logan! You should have shot them!"

"Now who's getting bloodthirsty?"

Pross groaned. "Oh sod it! And just when I thought things were going to get better today . . ."

"I wanted to know what the hell was going on. I wanted to know how the hell Sanders managed to miss them."

"And how do you intend to find out? Barge into their rooms and rip out their fingernails?"

She actually giggled. "Don't be silly, Pross."

"You could be wrong," he said hopefully.

"Sorry. I wasn't wrong. I wanted to hear the woman talk some more so I apologised to her for your quite shocking behaviour last night." An impish grin. "She gave me a po-faced look and said it was quite alright, and she wasn't offended anyway. The lying bitch. Of course she was offended. I walked on. I'd heard enough to confirm my suspicions. Then just as I was about to enter the hotel I saw the man in the car park. He had just straightened up from feeling under the wing of the RS."

"Did he see you looking at him?"

"Of course he didn't, Pross. What do you take me for?"

"Sometimes, an enigma, Logan. Well, I'm ready. Let's go down to breakfast and face the day."

"Cheer up, Pross. You might enjoy it."

"If I live that long."

"If they're real pros, and I think they are, nothing will happen here."

"But if they're unprofessional loonies?"

"We'll cross that bridge when we come to it."

"Better take your cannon, then."

"But of course."

The breakfast room was only half full when they got there. They found a table in a secluded corner, with a fine view of the river.

There was barely a wait, and Logan was soon tucking into a vast plate of bacon and eggs.

Pross stared at her in disbelief.

"Making up for last night," she explained. "We were too late for dinner, remember?"

"You must make your boyfriends cringe when they take you out."

"Don't have boyfriends as such."

"Rubbish. I don't believe you."

"Jealous?" The green eyes held mischief.

"Behave, Logan. But seriously, what do they say?"

"They get so worried about the dent in their wallets that I insist on paying my way. I don't see why I should starve just because some man is worried about being able to pay. Besides, it wouldn't be fair on him. No, I didn't sleep with them."

"Logan, for God's sake!" Pross whispered to her. "I don't want to know."

"Now you do." She smiled sweetly at him.

Pross was saved further embarrassment by the entry of the couple from the river bank. The man, looking round for a suitable place to sit, glanced fleetingly in their direction. The man's eyes rested upon Pross's for the barest of instants, but it was enough to make his stomach freeze.

Logan, whose own attention was upon the woman, glanced quickly at Pross.

"Are you alright? You look as if you've seen a ghost."

The newcomers had found themselves a table and had sat down, a good distance away. The man had his back to Pross. The woman saw Logan, and smiled tightly in recognition.

Logan nodded at her, then turned to Pross again. "You're looking a bit better now, but you're still green about the gills. It's not the food, is it?"

"No, Logan. Not the food. You're not going to believe what I'm about to say."

"Try me."

"I think I recognise that man."

She stared at him. "Oh come on, Pross . . ."

"Don't ask me to explain, because I can't. All I know is that he seems familiar and I can't even begin to understand why. I don't know where I could have seen him."

Logan said, "I don't believe it. A while ago you were sceptical about my certainty that those two are the people I saw by the lake, now you're telling me that you *know* one of them. That's not possible, Pross. Those two are part of a group that tried to shoot you down last night."

"I know. I know! It sounds crazy, but there it is. I even feel he recognised me. In that one blink, there was something in his eyes that said he knew exactly who I was."

"This is baffling me, and worrying me at the same time," Logan said. "Couldn't you be mistaken? Perhaps he reminds you of someone else."

"Perhaps ... but how about his own sign of recognition?"

"Are you sure it was recognition? Everybody at one time or another sees someone who looks familiar, only to find they've made a mistake. The other person also gets caught in the whole thing and thinks, 'Do I know that person?' It happens all the time. What you thought was recognition was probably just that. He's wondering why you think you know him. It's still not good news, of course, given the present circumstances, but it makes more sense."

"It probably does; but though I'm not a professional at this kind of work the way you are, I know when someone looks at me with recognition."

"And you still can't imagine why."

"No."

"Let's assume you're right. It makes things really tricky. They won't know me, but they'll begin to wonder."

"Just what I was thinking."

"Perhaps he's someone you met through Prossair."

"That still doesn't make me feel any better."

"No, I suppose not."

"Because if he knows me through my company, he might know of my family; and if he knows of them ..."

"Hold on, Pross. You're beginning to let this run away with you. You don't know all these things. Take a deep breath and *think*. Work it out, before you make the wrong decisions. Imagine you're flying. Apply the same kind of thought processes. We'll work something out."

"I'll have to call home."

"Not from here. We'll find a box on the road."

"Alright. Now what?"

"We finish our breakfast, without hurrying."

At the far table, the man said to his companion, "Do you know that woman? I saw you give her one of your non-existent smiles."

"Why?" came a counter-challenge. "Do you find her attractive?"

The man smiled. "If she took care of herself a bit better, she could be very much so."

"You like other men's wives? Do you find that exciting?"

"Spare me the lecture. I asked you a simple question."

"She was out for a walk this morning and I met her on the

river bank. She apologised to me for her husband's boorish behaviour."

The man was interested. "Oh? What did he do? Make a pass at you?"

"Why should I pander to your warped sense of humour?"

"So he didn't make a pass at you. What really happened?"

"It is not important. She apologised, and that is enough. If what you're trying to do is find out more about her for your own ... private purposes, they are the Plumsteads. But let me remind you we have work to do ..."

"Spare me the lecture."

Their breakfast was continued in hostile silence.

"Finished?" Logan asked. "Still no ideas about where you might have seen our bearded friend?"

"No further than I was before."

"We'll have to play it by ear then. We'll leave the table as relaxed as possible and walk out as if we haven't a care in the world."

"That should be easy enough."

She tucked her arm in his, and they left the breakfast room unhurriedly. Once safely in the hall, Logan became brisk, She dug into her bag and took out the key to their room.

"Get our things. I'll see to the bill. Meet me back here as soon as you can. Hurry!"

He did not waste time arguing, and hurried up the stairs.

Logan did not hang around either. She went quickly out to the car park, felt beneath the wing of the RS, and tugged at the tracer. It came away after her third try: its magnet was necessarily a strong one. She threw the bug far into the bushes beyond the parking area, then went swiftly back into the hotel, without apparent haste. The whole thing had taken so little time no one had seen her, and no one was in the hall when she returned.

She next went to McNeil's office and knocked.

"It's open!" came his voice mutedly from behind the upholstered door. "Ah!" he greeted as she entered. "You look as fresh as a daisy, my dear. Enjoyed your breakfast? And how's your young man?"

"Made a pig of myself, and he'll survive your malt."

McNeil smiled. "I remember your breakfasts ... when you had finally persuaded yourself you could eat again. And as for David, tell him I'm happy to share a wee dram with him whenever he chooses. And now, my dear ..."

"There isn't time to explain, John, but I need a favour from you."

"Ask, and it shall be given." But his eyes had become serious.

"I hate involving you . . ."

"You can save even more time, lassie, if you stop telling me how much you hate involving me."

"First, the bill." She pulled out her chequebook.

"Put that away. There's no bill."

"But John . . ."

"Time, my dear. *Time.*"

She returned the chequebook to her bag. "I want to borrow your car."

He immediately put his hand into a pocket and brought out a small bunch of keys. "The red Volvo with the personalised number plate."

"Don't you want to know why?"

"I'll know soon enough and time's precious. Next?"

She got out the key to the RS. "I want you to drive my car. It's quite powerful, and can be fierce if you don't watch it."

McNeil's smile came on briefly. "Like a certain young woman I'm not sure I know."

She put the key on the desk, and picked up those for the Volvo. "Drive across the bridge and turn right, then take the road to Dolwyddelan. Stop somewhere convenient, and we'll change back to our own cars."

"Sounds exciting."

"John, you're a dear . . . but it's not a game."

"Never imagined it to be. Is this all to do with my . . . er . . . dubious guests?"

She nodded. "And it's still best that I don't tell you. We'll be drawing them away from here."

"Do you want this done immediately?"

She nodded. "I'm afraid so."

"Don't be afraid, my dear. I needed some air, come to think of it."

McNeil stood up, and walked to the door with her. In the hall they found Pross, who had brought the bags down with him.

"Feeling fragile, David?" McNeil asked with a grin.

"You should have seen me earlier."

"Good Highland malt," McNeil said. "Can't beat it. Well, I'd better be going. See you later."

Pross watched as McNeil departed through the main doors. He turned to Logan.

139

"He seemed in a hurry to leave. What's up?"

She placed a finger on his lips briefly. "Wait." Her eyes were on the door to the breakfast room.

Soon there was the sound of an engine coming to life.

"That sounds like a familiar noise," Pross said.

"It is. Wait."

There was the slight crunch of gears, and Logan shut her eyes for a moment. "Gently, *gently*," she pleaded.

"He's never driving your car," Pross said.

"Shh! Don't make it worse."

Outside, the car whined in the wrong gear as it crept away.

Logan let out a long sigh. "I hope it's still in one piece when we get to him. John is a wonderful person, but he's one of the most terrible drivers I know. I'd forgotten just how bad he can be. My poor car."

"You can always get the Department to buy you a new one."

"*I* paid for that car."

"Oops. Sorry."

"I should think so too. Okay, Pross. Time for us to do our bit. Someone's coming out."

But it wasn't the expected people.

Almost immediately after that, however, the door was again being pushed open.

Logan said quickly, "Here. Keys to a red Volvo with fancy plates. On your right, nearest the hotel. Put our bags in and wait for me."

Pross was walking out of the main doors just as the blonde woman entered from the breakfast room, followed by her male companion. Even the briefest of conversations was unavoidable.

"You are leaving?" the blonde woman said. She seemed pleased about something.

"Er yes," Logan said, putting on the slightly vacuous voice she'd used at their first encounter. "We're having a sort of driving weekend and we've decided to go off to Anglesey for the day, and perhaps spend the night there."

"I see. Enjoy yourselves."

"Thank you. 'Bye," she said to them both.

"Goodbye," the woman said. The man merely nodded, though pleasantly enough.

Outside, she found Pross waiting by the Volvo.

"Have you seen the state of this car?" was the first thing he said.

"It's a Volvo, Pross. It can cope with John. Get in. You drive."

"You're sure it's safe?"

But she was already climbing into the passenger seat. "Any time now, we should have a couple of well-wishers to see us off. I can't wait to see their expressions when they find out the RS has gone."

"And where is it?"

"Waiting for us. We'll be giving John's car back to him."

"Thank God for that. I was afraid we were going to drive all the way back to Cardiff in this."

"Start up, Pross. By the way, you'll be pleased to know I've chucked the bug away." She gave him her impish grin. "That should really make them nervous."

Pross started the engine. It sounded very smooth.

"That's a surprise," he said.

"I told you. Even John can't do much to one of these cars. He knew what he was doing when he bought it. It was either that, or a Centurion ... and I wouldn't have given a Centurion much of a chance."

Pross put the car into gear, and began to manoeuvre out of the car park.

"What did I tell you? Don't look! They're at the hotel entrance, watching." Logan turned to look back. "I'll give them a little wave." She did.

"Wasn't that a bit excessive?"

"Oh no. It's perfectly in keeping with the character I chose to lay on for their benefit." She laughed. "You should have seen their faces ..."

"Difficult, considering you told me not to look."

She gave his knee an admonishing smack. "You know what I mean. They're trying to work out what's happened. If that man really is someone you've seen before, he's bound to be wondering what your presence here means. Or he may be thinking it's just one of those things. If he suspects us in any way, he'll still not be able to work out what could have happened. He'll wonder where the RS has got to, and as soon as it's decently possible, they'll be checking their receiver, only to find that the bug is still around. Then it will hit them that they've been conned." She laughed again.

"So what will they do? You know, this car is not so bad."

"I told you it could cope with John. What they'll do is try to get out as fast as possible. I have a feeling John's going to have two unpaid bills today."

"Why two?"

"He wouldn't take money from me."

*

141

In the hotel, the man and the blonde woman were hurriedly clearing their rooms. They had rushed to the Mercedes to check the receiver, and knew the worst when the bug had registered strongly. Now, they made sure nothing incriminating was left in their respective rooms, and hurried out. They met on the stairs.

"What about the bill?" the woman whispered.

"That hardly matters," he said coldly. He seethed deep within himself, hating the fact that he had been so completely led by the nose, still without knowing who had been responsible. "This place may well be crawling with their agents. We shall know all about that, when we try for the car."

The grimness in his voice made her ask, "Have you a weapon ready?"

"Of course. If they want a fight, they'll get it."

They went down the stairs quickly. No one stopped them. There was no one in the hall. They moved without apparent haste towards the entrance. A glance at the reception counter showed someone was behind it.

They stopped. The man went up to it.

"We are going for a walk into the hills," he said to the receptionist pleasantly. "Do we keep our keys? Or shall we leave them with you?"

"As you please, Professor. We can get in to make the beds."

"In that case, we shall keep them."

"Will you be back for dinner?"

"I think not. We shall be eating out."

The receptionist gave her neutral smile. "That's alright then. Enjoy your walk."

"Thank you. We shall."

They went out to the car, and still no one attempted to stop them.

"Would you have shot her?" the woman asked as they got in.

"If that had been necessary, certainly."

"I would have shot her anyway."

The man started the Mercedes, glanced at her with unmistakable contempt. "Would you? What would that have achieved . . . apart from unnecessary complications?"

"She can identify us."

He sent the big car scurrying out of the car park. "Typical. Concentrate your mind on a simple fact. We were *led* here. They already

142

know who we are. It is time for us to go our separate ways and disappear. They clearly did not want to take us at the hotel, and could now be waiting anywhere. We must dump this car soon."

The woman said nothing as the Mercedes bucked and rocketed down the unpaved drive.

"There he is!" Logan said.

The RS was parked at the side of the road, near the driveway of another hotel. McNeil was waiting, leaning against the boot.

Pross stopped the Volvo just behind and both he and Logan got out quickly.

She went up to McNeil, gave him a quick hug. "Thank you, John."

McNeil's eyes twinkled. "Be my guest."

"And now we must hurry," she continued, watching as Pross opened the passenger door to fling their bags inside. "Don't go back to the hotel just yet . . ."

"My staff . . ."

"They'll be alright. I know how these people react. They'll have left by now, trying to get as far away as possible. Another bill unpaid, I'm afraid."

"I'm just pleased they're gone."

"I can get the . . . er . . . I can get reimbursement to you."

"You can actually do that?"

"Yes."

McNeil looked at her with increased respect. "Well, well, my dear. You have come up in the world."

"That depends on how you look at it."

"Well, I won't debate the point. You're clearly anxious to get on, so I won't delay you further. Just look after yourself. Forget about reimbursement; but don't forget the Purdeys. I'm still hoping to present them one day."

Pross, who had been standing by the door, said, "Sort of shotgun wedding."

They both looked at him with pity.

"Pross!" Logan said admonishingly. "That was a terrible joke."

"Wasn't so hot, was it?" he admitted sheepishly. "My brain's still affected by your malt, John."

"Come up and sample some more anytime."

"I'll take you up on that."

"Alright, my children. Off you go." McNeil gave Logan a quick kiss, held a hand out to Pross across the car. "Take care of her, David, or you'll have me to account to."

Pross said, "She's the one who usually takes care of me."

Logan said, "Don't forget, John. Leave your car out of sight. Give it about an hour. That's allowing a decent margin. I don't want them to make the slightest connection to you."

"You will note where I've parked," McNeil said. "Conveniently, I have some friends here. I think I'll pay them a visit. The Volvo can be kept well out of sight."

She smiled with relief. "Good. And I promise not to make *my* next visit so hectic, now that I know you're back."

"I'll hold you to that. Go now, and God bless."

Logan climbed in behind the wheel, and sent the RS howling up the road.

Pross said, staring pointedly at the speedometer. "All go, isn't it? Nice damp road too."

"Shh, Pross. Time to spring the trap."

The RS tore on without a slackening of speed, and Pross resigned himself to his unfavourite pastime of watching the racing scenery with stifled alarm. The five miles to Dolwyddelan was covered in less than five minutes.

Logan saw a telephone box and brought the car to a quick halt. She was out of her seat and running towards the box before Pross had time to say anything. Thirty seconds later, she was out of the booth and returning to the car.

"That should sort them out," she said as she entered and secured her belt. "I've given Fowler a full description, car and everything. My orders now, sir, are to take you back to hearth and home. No more excitements for you."

The RS shot away with a scream.

"No excitements, she says. Why don't you have a phone in your car, anyway?" Pross continued, keeping his eyes firmly averted from a bend he could see coming up with manic speed. "It would make life easier for you. No hunting for elusive phoneboxes."

"Phone in *my* car? No thanks. That would only make me more accessible to idiots like Martins and Sanders. I don't even like carrying a radio. At times, it can be a positive disadvantage if you're pretending to be a normal citizen. On some jobs I've got to compromise with Fowler and take a radio, but that's as far as it goes. Reporting to him direct also keeps those farts out of my hair. They hate it, of course, but that's their worry. I only hope

144

they manage to get those two after I've laid it out so nicely for them."

"I can't see them being grateful. You've shown them up."

"Again, that's their hassle. On these roads, even in the Mercedes, the greatest distance I'd expect our friends from the hotel to cover is about sixty miles. They might not even make that. Martins and Sanders can call on sufficient forces to saturate the area. They'd have to be really incompetent to miss them."

"They could stop somewhere and hide."

"They could. But it would still mean they're locked tight within the area. I have a feeling they wouldn't like that. Now relax, Pross, and enjoy the ride home."

"Do I have a choice?"

She grinned impishly at him. "No. It's a pity," she went on, almost to herself, "that I won't find out about those two until later, perhaps. I'd have liked to know what their roles were. But Fowler insisted I take you back. Perhaps I can do my own digging later."

"If you're allowed to."

"I have my own ways of finding things out."

The return to Cardiff was uneventful, save for the rally-style driving that Logan employed to achieve it. She pulled into the airport carpark early in the afternoon, looking as fresh as when they had left Betws-y-Coed.

She stopped the engine, and looked at Pross. "Delivered, safe and sound."

"Safe, perhaps. I'm not so sure about the other."

"Come on, Pross. It wasn't so bad."

"Logan, I have to say this. Being with you is —"

"Exciting."

"I was going to say 'different'."

She leaned across suddenly, and kissed him full on the lips. "Mmm," she said, then pulled away, green eyes enigmatic. "Now I've got to be going."

Pross got his bag, and climbed out of the car. He shut the door, hunched forward to look down at her. "Be careful, Logan."

The impish grin flashed on. "I'm always careful."

Then he had straightened, and the blue car was tearing its way out of the parking area.

He shook his head slowly, and walked towards the airport

buildings. Logan would always be Logan. He really would take it badly, he thought, if anything ever happened to her.

"Thanks for calling," Terry Webb said accusingly in the office.

They were alone. Cheryl Glyn was given as many Saturdays off as possible, though she tended to take them reluctantly.

"Don't have a go at me, Terry," Pross said. "I was not able to. And I'm here for the air test as I promised."

"Well," Webb began, "as I wasn't sure how long the ... er ... young lady was going to keep you away for, I asked Pete to do it. The ship's okay."

Pross trusted Pete Dent's flying capabilities absolutely, but he still felt a bit put out that Webb had not waited. He also knew that Webb had done the right thing. It still didn't make him feel any less guilty for being absent.

"That's alright, then," he said. "I'd better go home."

"I think you'd better," Webb said ominously.

"What's that supposed to mean, Terry?"

"Better not let Dee see that kind of thing, either."

Pross stared at him. "Alright, Terry. Give it to me slowly in words of one syllable so that I can really understand. What isn't Dee supposed to see?"

"Far be it from me to ..."

"Out with it, Terry. I suppose you saw us arrive, saw her give me a goodbye kiss —"

"A goodbye kiss! Is that what you call it ..."

"And put two and two together and came up with seven."

Webb said, "What's it to me anyway? I only work around here."

"You sound like someone I know."

"Anyone I know?"

"Oh Terry, Terry. Come on. No harm's been done. The air test went off okay, and now I'll go home and make my peace with Dee."

Webb looked at him steadily. "Look, Boss. I don't want to know what goes on between you and that young lady's people. What I do know and what I can guess already gives me the shivers. But try not to get too close to her. God knows I've already warned you about that. Won't do you any good, you know."

Pross said, "There's nothing like that to worry about. She's very good at her job, believe me. She's too professional to cross any boundaries."

"Oh yes? Then I'd hate to see what happens when she does cross over."

Webb left the office, shaking his head as if in despair.

Bloody hell, Pross thought. *That's all I need. A grumpy Terry Webb.* He shut the office, and went out to his car.

NINE

It was two months later, towards the end of January, before Pross heard from Logan again. During that time, there had been an absolute silence from the Department. It was as if the entire episode with the Hammerhead, and all that had transpired, had never occurred. Terry Webb had long since made his peace, and Prossair was running smoothly. And after initial fears, Dee had managed to persuade herself that perhaps she had been too hasty in her reactions about Fowler's motives.

Then, one cold Friday afternoon, the phone rang in the office.

Pross was checking out insurance papers with Cheryl Glyn. She picked the phone up after the third ring.

"Prossair," she said, and listened. Her expression froze over. "Yes. He's here." Her voice too had cooled several degrees. She handed the instrument over wordlessly.

Pross raised questioning eyebrows at her. She tightened her lips and looked away.

Puzzled, Pross said in the phone, "David Pross."

"I really don't think she likes me at all. I've got icicles coming out of the phone at this end." The voice was instantly recognisable.

"Logan!" The pleasure in his voice made Cheryl Glyn look at him censoriously. "This is a surprise. By the way, thanks for the Christmas card I didn't get."

"Oh Pross, I'm so sorry. But I couldn't. It wasn't ... er ... practical. I promise to send you a card next time I'm away ... wherever I may be. How's that for a promise?"

"I'll hold you to it."

She laughed. "Alright. It's nice talking to you, Pross."

"It's nice to hear from you," Pross said truthfully. Cheryl Glyn gave him a disappointed stare which he chose to ignore. "Even after two months," he added.

"What's a couple of months between good mates?"

"What indeed. So how have you been?"

"Oh . . . I've been . . . alright. Keeping well. The usual."

"And being careful?"

"Always."

"Good."

"And how have *you* been?"

"Plodding along."

"You never plod along, Pross."

He smiled at the phone. Cheryl Glyn gave him a disgusted look. "Is she still in there with you?" Logan asked.

He knew what she meant. "Yes."

"Being quite disapproving I'll bet."

"Your bet is right on the nose."

Another laugh came down the line. "Oh dear. Good thing she can't see me. Her eyes would probably have turned into daggers by now."

"Forget probably. They are. Incidentally, how did that little affair with our two friends turn out?"

"Oh that. A fifty-fifty resolution, I'm afraid. The blonde lady was caught, but she put up a fight. She . . . er . . . lost. She came up against the weasel."

That meant Martins.

"Bad luck," Pross said.

"For her, yes. It ran out."

"And the other?"

"That's the second fifty. No sign."

Which, Pross thought, must have left a lot of egg on both Martins' and Sanders' faces.

"I'm sorry," he said. "After all your work too."

"Not my hassle."

Indeed it wasn't, and neither Sanders nor Martins would love her for it.

"Watch out for the weasel and friends," he said.

"I'm watching," she assured him, knowing exactly what he was driving at. "Worry about me, do you?"

"Now and then," he said off-handedly.

"Every little helps, I suppose." The voice was teasing now.

He could almost see the impish smile, the freckles, and the mischief in the green eyes.

"Now tell me what the message is," he said.

"You don't want to talk to me any more. Is that it?" She sounded as if she'd been hurt by the tone of his voice.

"I'm not falling for that one, Logan. I know there's a message."

"I could have called because I wanted to have a chat."

"Ha!"

"You can go off some people."

He grinned at the phone. "Tell me."

She made a big deal out of sighing. "Oh alright. Someone's coming to pick you up tomorrow."

"Just like that?"

"Saturday was picked to make it easier for you."

"I've told you before, we work on Saturdays in this firm."

"At eleven hundred," Logan said, as if he had not spoken.

"Didn't you hear me?"

"Of course I did. I'm just not taking any notice." She was laughing again.

"It's not funny. We've also got a dinner tomorrow night. A few friends."

"You'll be back in time. No nasty surprises either."

"I remember what happened the last time you said that," he remarked drily.

"There won't be a repeat. I promise."

"Trouble about that is . . . other people don't keep to the same promise. I'm not missing that dinner. Dee would strangle me, for a start and secondly, I'm not going to leave her in the lurch."

"I wouldn't expect you to. I'd strangle you myself, in her place, if you did."

"It's nice to know you're on my side."

She giggled. "Come on, Pross. All that's happening is that you'll be getting to play with the new toy all by yourself, to put it through its paces. The man himself will be there. He'd like to discuss it with you."

Fowler.

Pross's reluctance to meet Fowler vied with his own eagerness to fly the Hammerhead unrestrictedly. He wanted to feel his hands on the controls once more. He could not pretend to himself that it did not call to him. Fowler knew, and Logan knew, and Fowler used Logan to get to him.

As bloody usual.

"I'll be there too," Logan said into his ear as if already detecting, by her own long-range radar, the wavering of his resolve.

He sighed in his mind. Fowler always seemed to have the best cards every time. Fowler had all his weak spots covered. First, there was his taste for flying, then there was Logan; and if that didn't work, there was the biggest weak spot of all. His family. All Fowler had to do was say there was a threat to Dee and the children from an unknown source. Fowler had not been loth to use that little ploy on occasion.

And of course it had worked, even though Pross had known what was being done because, once, the threat had been very real. He didn't have to try too hard to re-live that particular nightmare. Then there was Prossair itself, whose rising fortunes had been invisibly guided by Fowler, for services rendered.

Face it, Pross, he now thought pragmatically, you can wriggle, but you can't get off the hook. Even if you did, he'd find some other way.

"Pross?" Logan was saying. "Are you there?"

"I'm still here. I'm thinking."

"I'd like to see you, anyway," she said. "I'm off on a little trip. It would be nice to see you before."

She hung up before he could say anything to that.

Neat. Now she'd really made it impossible for him to refuse Fowler's invitation.

He put the phone down slowly.

"Don't frown like that, Cheryl," he said, "or you'll get wrinkles all over your lovely young face before you're much older."

"She's got a nerve," Cheryl Glyn said, "calling you up like that."

"Don't give me a hard time. Please."

"It's Dee I feel sorry for."

"Cheryl," warningly. "Don't get cheeky with the boss."

"Well," she said, running out of words with which to express her profound disapproval.

Oh wonderful, he thought.

At precisely 11.00 the next morning, Pross was out on the flight line with Terry Webb. The sky was grey and looked heavy with promised snow. That didn't mean anything. During the week, snow had come and gone twice. The Met report for the day

151

expected rain in the area. For the moment, however, the day was dry, if cold.

Pross had decided if Fowler was sending someone to pick him up, he was not going to make it easy by waiting meekly in the office. They could come and find him.

But Fowler knew how to spring surprises.

Right on time, a powerfully thrumming noise made itself heard on the morning air. Pross knew it instantly for what it was. Fowler was picking him up in style.

From over the 30 runway, a small shape grew swiftly in size to become the sleek form of a late-production Army multi-rôle Lynx. In gleaming camouflage warpaint, it looked somehow neater with skids instead of the wheels of the naval version. It swept along the runway in a crescendo of its singing twin Gems, pulled up to go smoothly into a complete roll before banking steeply right to come tightly round towards where Pross and Webb were standing. It carried civilian, and not military markings.

Watching it swoop towards them, Webb said, drily, "I did wonder about their long silence. Two months, they left you alone. Must be a record."

"They've left us alone for much longer before, Terry," Pross said.

"Well they're making up for it now." Webb was unrepentant.

"You don't know it's for me."

Webb gave him a look of pure scepticism. "Oh I forgot. It's me they're after. Cheryl told me about your phone call yesterday."

"Cheryl should keep the boss's confidence."

"Like the rest of us, she's worried about you," Webb said. "She doesn't want to see you killed."

Pross stared at him. "What? That's rubbish, Terry. Who's talking about getting killed. Have you gone mad?"

"Grief. That's what that young lady and her boss are going to bring you one day. You wait."

Webb began walking away.

"Terry!" Pross called after him; but Webb continued walking. "Oh bloody hell. They're all going bonkers around me."

The Lynx was coming down, nose high, bleeding off speed. It was going to be one of those fancy, inclined descents, instead of the more staid, vertical landing. The fly-on landing, he knew, was favoured by the Army. It made for getting your troops in swiftly. Less exposure too. Can't hang about in the air waiting for someone to take a potshot.

Pross knew instinctively that Cado Rees was at the controls.

The Lynx began to level off when it seemed inches from the ground and had virtually bled off all forward motion. It settled with feather-light smoothness. The left-hand seat was empty.

Pross walked round the nose to the right side as the rotors wound down to idle. Rees was indeed grinning at him from beneath a dark green helmet.

"Morning," Rees said. "Your taxi, sir. We can swop seats if you'd like to fly her. There's a helmet for you."

"So I see. Where are we off to?"

"Llanbedr. You've got a solo with the Hammerhead. I'm to play watchdog in this while you enjoy yourself."

"In that case, I'll save the flying for later. I'll be the passenger for now if that's alright with you."

Rees shrugged. "That's alright with me."

"Give a minute to have a word with Terry Webb, and we'll be off."

Rees nodded, and Pross hurried away to find Webb. He found him tinkering with one of the Jetrangers. Webb was always fussing over them.

Pross said, "Well, I'll be off, Terry. Be back later this afternoon. No need to hang around. You can pack in for the day if you'd like."

"I've got a few things to do then I'll shut up shop." Webb did not turn round.

"Look," Pross began reasonably. "I –"

But Webb was turning round and interrupting him. "I know what you're going to say, David. I know that lot out there have been responsible for putting some nice jobs our way. I know they make it difficult for you to say no to them, and I know you're not going to do anything daft and break your neck or something silly like that. But when all's said and done, it still means they're always going to keep coming back for more from you. I'm just worried about the price they may ask you to pay one of these fine days. We all are."

Moved by the longest speech he'd heard from this normally taciturn man for a long time, Pross said gently, "I understand, Terry, and I'm grateful." Webb was looked upon more as a friend than an employee. "But this is not anything dangerous. I'll be back in time for the dinner. We've been planning this for some time. You don't seriously think I'm going to let Dee and all of you down, do you? The firm and a few friends. It's our annual pre-Spring bash, Terry. I'd never miss that."

"If they let you."

"They'll let me," Pross said firmly. "They'd better." The sound of the waiting Lynx intruded upon their conversation.

"Sounds a bit souped up," Webb commented. His ear for engines was as finely tuned as that of any conductor able to pick out the slightest deviation from a fiddle, in an orchestra in full chorus. "Impatient too," he added.

"Yes," Pross agreed. "I'd better go. Sooner I'm gone, sooner I'll be back. And by the way, perhaps we'd better not tell Dee about this one."

"My feelings exactly." Webb grinned suddenly. "And yes, I'll sit on Cheryl to make sure she keeps her little mouth shut."

"You're a mate, Terry," Pross said with a brief pat to Webb's shoulder as he hurried out to the waiting Lynx.

"A fool more likely," Webb called after him.

Pross climbed into the aircraft, secured his straps and put on his helmet. "Alright, Cado. Off we go."

Rees lifted the Lynx up smoothly, tilted it through ninety degrees, rolled upright and headed inland, gaining height at the same time. The machine sounded and felt very powerful; almost as powerful in fact, Pross thought, as the one he had used in Nepal.

"Terry's right," he said.

"About what?" Rees asked.

"This. It feels almost supercharged."

"It's been modded," Rees confirmed. "We've got a few over at the airfield undergoing special fits. We're trying something out."

"Anything I should know?"

"You'll soon see," the mournful voice said. "Fowler will be there."

"So I've been told."

"You'll be able to ask him all sorts of questions."

"Most of which he'll probably choose not to answer."

"You know how it is," Rees said.

"Don't I just."

Rees glanced in his direction to give one of his rare smiles. "Forget Fowler. Think about the Hammerhead."

"I'm thinking. I'm thinking." He did not try to keep the excitement out of his voice.

The flight took an hour, during which Rees had put the Lynx through its paces for Pross's benefit. The performance had been most impressive, and Pross was in no doubt that a lot had been learned

154

from the modifications on the aircraft he himself had used, some of which had been incorporated into the version that Rees had said was being up-rated.

Rees did his fancy landing in front of a neat row of similar machines, gleaming and lined up as if for inspection. There were seven of them, glinting in the cold sun. The Hammerhead was nowhere to be seen. Pross assumed it was still under cover.

As the rotors wound down and he climbed out, a white Rover approached. It stopped, and Fowler and Sanders stepped out from the back seat. The driver, whom Pross had never seen before, remained where he was.

Fowler came forward while Sanders remained by the car. Rees was still in the aircraft, apparently doing post-flight checks.

Fowler said, "Good to see you, David. Glad you could come . . . doubly so, given your performance with the Hammerhead last November." Fowler put out his hand.

Pross shook it. "The Hammerhead's a pretty good machine."

Fowler's smile was ghostly. The sun flashed briefly off his spectacles. "Captain Rees was less modest about your capabilities. You took to it like a duck to water. His words."

They began walking back towards the car.

"We'll have a spot of lunch," Fowler said, "talk a few things over, then you can enjoy yourself in the air. Rees will accompany you in the Lynx, to observe. There'll be one or two people with him." They had reached the Rover. "You remember Squadron Leader Sanders, of course."

"Of course," Pross said.

They nodded at each other. Fowler did not introduce the driver. Sanders went round to the front, while Pross and Fowler got into the back. The Rover took off down the apron, gathering speed swiftly. A couple of minutes later, it pulled up before a cluster of buildings that overlooked the dunes and the sea.

Pross and Fowler got out, but Sanders remained in the car which soon sped off again. Pross was relieved. He had decided he would never take to Sanders.

The building to which Fowler led him reminded Pross of many others he had seen during his RAF service. He could almost see in his mind the exact location of each room.

They entered and Fowler took him along a familiar-looking corridor past doors with various numbers and acronyms identifying unknown departments and sections. The building was oddly quiet,

155

though Pross thought he could hear distant evidence of its occupation. Some of that noise grew in volume as they walked.

Then Fowler had stopped at a door with no identification and was opening it. The faint smell of cooking came to Pross's nostrils. Fowler stood back for Pross to enter.

The room was warm, surprisingly comfortably furnished. It was long and narrow, with a table set for two at one end. There was another door close by.

"Hardly the Mess," Fowler said, "but it will serve. Do take a seat, David."

That was twice Fowler had called him David. It felt ominous.

Pross looked about him. Three large windows gave a fine view of the dunes and the sea. He heard the faint thrum of an aircraft and something moved across his vision. A Lynx. Rees? He wondered.

He sat down, and Fowler joined him.

"I do hope you're hungry," Fowler said. "I've had a particularly fine joint flown up for the purpose."

"I'd rather not have too much of a full stomach if I'm going to put the Hammerhead through its paces soon after."

"I shan't force you, but I think you'll eat rather more than you at first intend."

A middle-aged woman put her head through the door nearest the table. "Are you ready now, Mr Fowler?"

"I think we are, thank you. David?"

Pross nodded. "Er . . . yes." The woman withdrew, and Pross continued, "I still won't be eating much. I've got a dinner on this evening. I must get back," he finished with emphasis.

Fowler was good-natured about it. "You'll be back in plenty of time. Special dinner?"

"Yes. It's our annual bash. We call it our pre-Spring. It's a little thing we do to mark off a very special anniversary."

"The founding of Prossair," Fowler said calmly.

Pross stared at him.

Fowler said, "You shouldn't be so surprised. After all, we did study your company carefully. The first day of its operation would hardly escape our notice."

"I keep forgetting how wide your net is."

Fowler let that pass, and said, "There's a question you haven't asked me."

"There are several questions I haven't asked you, all of which I intend to."

"Possibly. But above all that, there is still one. As I see you will not bring yourself to ask it, I shall answer instead. She's delayed . . . but she will be here. Does that not answer it?" Fowler was smiling, eyes seeming to have a life of their own behind his glasses.

Pross said nothing.

Fowler's smile appeared to widen. "Do you know, if it were not for the fact that I know Logan to be an utter professional, and that you, in your own way, are also thoroughly professional with a strong sense of honour, I would be most reluctant to put you two together. Things could . . . emotionally . . . get quite out of hand."

Pross did not fall for that for one minute, but chose to let Fowler believe he was not aware of Fowler's quite calculated use of the very strong and perhaps dangerous feelings that came into play when Logan was around.

"In that case," Pross began, heading into tricky waters, "it might be a good thing if we did blot our copybook. You might decide to let me off the hook."

Fowler's smile was at its most benign. "You know you enjoy flying too much. Where would you get the chance to fly something like the Hammerhead?"

"Less chance of getting my head blown off."

"Besides," Fowler continued, as if in the same sentence, "you have qualities that we find very useful. It would possibly merely mean you would no longer be allowed to work together."

The threat, delivered mildly, still carried a formidable punch. Working for Fowler without Logan, despite knowing she was one of the levers used to obtain his services, would be intolerable. Pross accepted defeat graciously.

"What's more," Fowler was saying, "Prossair does quite well out of it."

The woman returned just then with a laden trolley.

"Thank you, Mrs Blake," Fowler said to her. "Leave the trolley just there . . . yes, yes . . . that's it. We'll help ourselves."

"Drinks and sweet are on the bottom," she said.

"Ah yes. I see. Thank you. You've been very kind. The joint is quite magnificent."

Mrs Blake was pleased by the compliment and almost curtsied as she went out.

"A treasure," Fowler said.

Such fulsome behaviour seemed at odds with the normally ascetic Fowler Pross had come to know. True, Fowler owned a very comfortable, small mansion in the Cotswolds that Pross had found himself visiting on occasion, if unwillingly. It could therefore be said that, privately, Fowler lived very well indeed.

Yet, despite the mansion — which he had once been told sometimes doubled as a safe house and as a recuperation centre for wounded Department personnel — something did not feel right. The appetising smell of the roast did not help either.

"I'll do the serving, shall I?" Fowler said, and promptly began to do so.

"Why do I feel like a goose that's being fattened?" Pross asked rhetorically.

Fowler glanced up from his work. "Oh really, Pross. What an idea."

It was back to Pross, now. No more David.

Perhaps that was a good omen, Pross thought. Unfortunately, that did not make him feel better.

"You haven't eaten much," Fowler said.

"I've had plenty," Pross assured him.

Fowler had chosen to conduct the meal in near silence, apparently preferring to get through the serious activity of eating before tackling the real reason for Pross's presence on the airfield. There was still no sign of Logan.

Then Fowler decided to get down to business during the coffee.

"As I said when we came in," he began, "Rees passed on his observations of your first go at the Hammerhead, so we know how you handled it during the attacks on the SAM teams. You will by now have come to the correct conclusion that we're working on a series of aircraft with which we expect to keep control of the air over the battlefield. The aircraft you have already flown, and now the Hammerhead, are stages in that programme.

"Should we ever be forced, God forbid, to fight the AirLand battle, I intend to ensure that the men who will be required to fight it do so in the best helicopter for the job, with the best in quality and capability for the inevitable disparity in numbers."

The AirLand battle, Pross knew, was the military euphemism for Battlefield Europe, Western Germany in particular. That was where everyone expected the bloodiest clash to take place; but things, as the sage said, had a habit of not working out as expected.

"There can't be many people in this business above the mental age of three," Fowler was saying, "who do not recognise that the

Mil Mi-24 Hind can chew to pieces almost anything we've got. Not only is it fast, it is agile, *and* it can carry a useful number of assault troops to the front and behind the lines. Nothing in the West can come near to such performance, and nothing I can see for a long time will come near in the same category.

"True, we've got our transport and utility helos, but they're limited, and none would last against something like the Hind. It's a machine that carries its own war with it. It can put forces to your rear, fight its way out, and come back with more. It's a flying tank that can take out your tanks. It's a fighter-helicopter that can take out your helicopters; and that's not counting the new Mil Mi-28 Havoc, plus of course, the Hellhound − if we ever allow them to get it going properly." Here, Fowler gave one of his more benign smiles.

"With such formidable capabilities in their favour," Fowler went on, "one would be forgiven for believing them invulnerable; which they're not, as you have so admirably shown on two separate occasions. The right pilot, in the right aircraft, will chew *them* to pieces. Hence the programme.

"The Russians were very quick to latch on to the potential of the chopper, and we were lamentably slow. Despite the lessons of Vietnam, we still are. On this side of the pond, I intend to make up that shortfall. For that very reason, the programme must be proved feasible. There are an enormous number of what I call the cavalry-versus-tanks types: the same kind of people who once thought pilots would no longer be needed, and who virtually killed our fighter industry for good. Thank God, there were a few people who refused to roll over with their legs in the air. I'm trying to ensure it doesn't happen to what's left of our helicopter industry.

"We have our tank-buster. The standard Lynx is excellent in that rôle, and the ones we're modifying will be quite formidable. I happen to believe it has years of modification left inherent in the design but . . . we need something extra. We need advanced tank-busters, something to take out the assault choppers and *their* tank-busters, plus something else again to take care of the escorts that will inevitably accompany the assault and tank-busting gunships. The helicopter theatre is not going to be as simple as some would have us believe. I am not interested in utilities and transports. My specific field of interest is in offensive helos. Those are the ones that are going to command the lower levels of future air battles.

"It cannot have escaped your notice that the Hammerhead is a blend of the Mangusta and the Lynx. It combines the best of both designs, plus a lot more, as you've already experienced. Since your last flight, we have added a few more refinements. We have a very fluid programme, and improvement is continuous. Any questions?"

Pross had been so attentive to Fowler's words that his coffee had grown quite cold. Seeming to rouse himself, he asked, "Who's paying for all this? I wouldn't have thought your Department could . . ."

"You know very little about my Department, Pross. What it can and cannot do hardly matters to you. I think, however, you've had ample evidence of its capabilities."

Which was certainly true, Pross found himself thinking drily, after the mild put-down.

"Sorry I spoke."

"There's no need to sound like that. I was not being offensive; merely pointing out a fact."

It was still a put-down, no matter how polite.

Pross said, "What about that little fracas the night Logan brought me up here? SAM teams, assassins . . ."

Fowler was unperturbed. "We steal from them, or more correctly, we ruin their programmes, and they try to do the same to us. Par for the course."

"With yours truly in the middle."

"You're hardly in the middle, Pross. I have personnel who are permanently in that uncomfortable spot."

"Yes, but they work for you. They know what they're getting into. I don't. On both counts."

Fowler gave a fleeting smile, taking no offence from Pross' words. "You'll have nothing to worry about today. You're merely being turned loose in a very expensive aircraft, which you can't deny you'll enjoy flying. You are here because I happen to think you're an excellent pilot.'

And the rest, Pross didn't say.

The Hammerhead had been wheeled out at last. It stood in the cold sunshine, its gleaming coat of dark camouflage making it seem almost black. It looked even more lethal in the brightness of the day.

Now that he could see it properly, Pross found himself again drawn to it, as if it were indeed calling to him; as if the feelings he had first sensed that night by the lake now grew in strength. He did a slow walk-round of the aircraft, implanting upon his mind all his perceptions of it.

Its retractable landing gear was arranged differently from that of the Lynx he'd last flown. Instead of the tricycle set-up with a nosewheel, the reverse had been employed. The main wheels protruded out of their housings from beneath the wing roots, while the tailwheel was actually positioned just aft of where the fuselage began to taper into the longish tail. This gave the Hammerhead a slightly nose-up stance on the ground, making it effectively aggressive to look at.

There were flaps, he noted, on the stub wings, which could be lowered even with weapons fitted. On their upper surfaces were panels which could be raised in flight to serve as airbrakes. He wondered how much of an off-load to the main rotor the wings gave. Remembering the 20–25 per cent off-load for the Hind, and the massive 30 per cent for the Hellhound, he knew how useful that little extra could be. More power with which to manoeuvre.

He'd half-expected the arrangement to affect the hovering capabilities, but that had not happened. Remembering the night by the lake, he had found the Hammerhead to be rock steady at the hover, though there had been the insistent feeling that the aircraft had barely been able to contain itself, wanting to leap away like the high-spirited mount it really was. No stolid transport, it was an inherently unstable, superb fighting machine; which was as it should be.

He continued his walk-round, coming to the tail. The fin, projecting upwards from the circular shroud of the fenestron rotor, was steeply raked backwards. At its top were housed the blisters containing the rear navigation light, as well as the tail radar and infrared warning units, and ECM and ECCM jammers. Beneath the tail was a rearward curving skid.

Pross stroked the aircraft as he moved around it, not unlike the manner of someone calming a skittish horse. Just behind the main rotor housing and between the shrouded exhausts of the twin Gems, was the infrared pulse jammer which would confuse the guidance systems of enemy heat-seeking missiles. The four blades of the main rotor seemed like great broad-tipped swords, itching to slice through the air. The canopies of the tandem cockpits, he saw, had been designed to keep reflections to a minimum. No point in concealing your chopper nicely if some sharp-eyed ground observer or crew is going to catch a bright reflection from your canopy.

Pross eventually came back to the nose of the aircraft and stood before it, looking at the side stubs that housed its all-weather eyes and sensors. There was no doubt about it, he thought. It really looked like a bloody shark. Then there was the massive six-barrelled 30-millimetre rotary cannon recessed into its belly, looking hungry for a bite.

There were no identification markings.

During the hangar inspection, Pross had renewed an old acquaintance. He had not really been surprised to meet the tall angular woman whom everyone called Mabel, and who spoke in a voice that reminded him of Lady Bracknell. Every time she did so, he kept expecting her to cry out, "A *handbag?*"

He smiled to himself. Mabel, in her long white coat, with a permanently unlit expensive cigar in one pocket which she tended to sniff when someone made her nervous, or caused her to become agitated. That was her story. Pilots tended to cause her agitation.

Mabel, a truly brilliant aerospace engineer, was about as nervous as a cliff face and liked wearing pearl necklaces, worth small fortunes, to work. Few people with all their mental faculties intact would dream of upsetting her. As a result, she had a team that looked after Fowler's special aircraft with all the care lavished upon very privileged newborn babies. Mabel had been in Nepal with Pross. He still did not know where she came from, or who she really worked for: he also knew no one would tell him.

"Well," he said to the aircraft, "I think I'm just about ready for you." He tugged at the diagonal zip of the olive-green flightsuit that went from left to right from waist to the right side of his neck, checking that it was secure. Beneath the suit was another, the close-fitting G-suit that would be standard wear for flying the Hammerhead.

The measurements were perfect. No reason why they shouldn't have got it right by now, he thought drily, considering the amount of flying he'd already done for Fowler.

He opened the rear canopy, and climbed in. He put on his helmet and was doing up his straps when Mabel appeared.

"Satisfied, are you?" Her glasses were hanging from her neck by a gold chain. She looked less severe, but no less formidable.

"It will do," Pross said, teasing her.

"If you bend it —".

"I know. Don't bother coming back."

"That's the spirit. And don't forget what I said about the

manoeuvring thrusters. They're exactly the same as the one you had in Nepal, except you're now dealing with a far more powerful machine. Remember airframe stresses." She put on her glasses, and the eyes behind them seemed to twinkle. "Someone's arrived."

Pross looked beyond her and saw Logan standing some distance away, still in jeans and sweater, with the inevitable bag slung from her shoulder. She waved to him, and he briefly raised his hand in reply.

Mabel said, "She'll be here when you return . . . and Fowler's gone off."

"I don't know what you mean, Mabel."

"Ha! Alright, David. Let's see if you can master Hammerhead. Off you go." She backed away, put her hand in a pocket and pulled out the cigar. She began to sniff at it as she turned to walk towards where Logan was standing. Pross had never seen her smoke.

He pulled down the canopy, heard it click home. He made a final check to ensure he was fully connected to the aircraft, then turned on the master switch with a firm stab of a gloved finger.

All instruments glowed as the central computer came on-line. The analogues showed faint green behind their faces while the digitals and the MFDs flickered before swiftly stabilising to pre-flight settings. Pross moved the twin power levers on the left-hand console, partially forward, then squeezed the bright red button on the top of each. He was going for a simultaneous start, although standard Lynx procedure was one at a time.

The powerful, modded Rolls-Royce Gems sprang into immediate and aggressive life, matching themselves automatically, so that there was not a single instant of asymmetric power. Within the cockpit, Pross felt the muted thunder translate itself into a well-damped low-level vibration that was more a pulse of the aircraft's life-blood than a mechanical shudder.

He took the rotor brake off and, automatically engaging, the blades began to rotate. He increased power, watching the temperature leap upwards then stabilise. It was a fast warm-up. He held the Hammerhead down against its will: it wanted to fly.

Then gently, he eased back on the collective side-stick. The ground vanished. One moment it was there; the next, he seemed to be flinging himself upwards into the sky.

"Bloody hell!" he said softly. "Oh God. This is beautiful!"

"I heard that," a voice said on his headphones.

"Cado! Where are you?"

"Still on the ground where you left me. Mabel's nearly having a baby from what I can see from here."

"Why? I barely touched it."

"Simultaneous start, a fast yank off the deck to shoot upwards like a homesick angel. Naughty, naughty. Impressive, though." Rees sounded amused. "I'd never have dared. Wait for us lesser gods, won't you? I've got you on radar."

"Then catch me if you can."

"Unfair!" Rees said at his most mournful. "Don't forget to pull up your gear, will you?" he added gleefully.

"Oh very nasty," Pross said as he retracted the wheels sheepishly. He'd have to watch out for that in the future.

"Had to get my own back somehow."

For the next half hour, Pross played with the electrifyingly responsive machine as he took the Hammerhead through every manoeuvre he could think of, nudging the boundaries of its flight envelope. It performed magnificently. Loops and rolls were only the basics of what he did. The Hammerhead was a killing machine of extraordinary agility. He went through dogfight sequences with Rees, and despite the other's own outstanding capabilities as a pilot and the well-known agility of his machine, the Hammerhead came out on top each time. Fowler's people had certainly got it right.

Pross wondered whether it was intended for production. It would be a form of madness not to do so.

He brought the Hammerhead down for a rolling landing, coming to a stop in a matter of feet.

"I remembered the wheels," he said to Rees who was still in the air.

"And here I was, hoping you'd at least mess that up," came the mournful voice in return.

Pross smiled to himself, feeling quite pleased as the Lynx came hurtling in to pull up into Rees' familiar neat roll before winging over to come in for the landing. The Lynx alighted with great aplomb, next to the Hammerhead.

As Pross climbed out, he saw Rees come out of the other aircraft with a strange look on his face. It was meant to be a smile.

"What's giving you so much pain?" Pross asked him.

"I think I just ruined a few lunches."

They both turned to look as two men crawled out of the Lynx, looking very much the worse for wear.

164

"Damn it, Rees!" one of the men called, "that was uncalled for!" It turned out to be Sanders.

Rees grinned at Pross who said, "Oh well, if he's the one."

Sanders came up to them, looking furious and ill at the same time. Quite a feat.

"I suppose you two think that was very funny."

"No we didn't," Rees said with a straight face. "Very serious business, flying."

Sanders looked at him balefully. "Remember, Rees. You're still in the Army and a *Lieutenant*, despite the three pips you're supposed to be wearing when you're properly dressed. Acting ranks can be revoked. As an equivalent Major, I therefore outrank you quite substantially. You would do well to remember that. And as for you, Pross . . ."

"Yes . . .?" Pross said dangerously, and waited.

Sanders stared at him for some moments before stomping away, saying nothing further.

Rees sighed. "What it is to be a civilian."

"You can always leave," Pross suggested.

Rees looked at him aghast. "With unemployment the way it is? How many vacancies do you know of for ex-Lynx chopper pilots? Outside banana republics, that is."

"I see your point. Still, working with Sanders can't be much fun if you can't bite back."

"I can live with it. We don't meet very often. Besides, he can only go so far. He wouldn't like me to report him to Fowler." Rees gave one of his less-mournful smiles. "So you see, I'm not totally helpless."

"I ought to have known." Pross gave the Hammerhead a pat. "A top piece of kit, Cado. They ought to put it into production."

"Such decisions depend on other people . . ."

"Who may have all sorts of other fish they may want to fry."

"Fowler has a vast armoury of persuasive ways. You of all people ought to know that."

"You can say that again," Pross said drily.

"Company," Rees said, staring at something behind Pross's back.

Pross turned and saw Mabel, accompanied by Logan, approaching.

Rees said, "I'll leave you to it. Got to do some checks on the Lynx. I'll be ready to take you back whenever you want."

"Alright, Cado. Thanks."

Rees waved a hand and returned to his Lynx.

"And what do you think you were trying to do?" Mabel said as soon as she arrived.

Logan watched Pross amusedly. "Hello, Pross."

"Hello, yourself." To Mabel, he went on, "I didn't try to do anything, Mabel. I behaved."

She peered at the Hammerhead, as if looking for scratches. "Go away, you two," she ordered. "I've got to see how this ship has coped with the trauma at this man's hands." Then she smiled suddenly. "Not bad, Pross." The cigar came out, and she began to sniff at it as she walked round the aircraft.

Other people were coming out to join her.

Pross said to Logan, "I think we should leave."

She smiled at him. "I think we should."

"Let me get out of these things, then we can go somewhere to talk before Cado takes me back."

"Alright."

"You were very impressive up there," Logan said. "But then, it was no surprise to me. I've seen you at work."

"You say that to all the boys."

The green eyes seemed to tease. "Only one. I don't give my compliments lightly."

They were in the room where Fowler and Pross had previously sat down to eat, and had chosen two deep armchairs, facing each other, near one of the windows.

Pross said, "You're terrible at keeping in contact, Logan."

"As I explained on the phone, I was a bit . . . busy."

"Which, of course, I mustn't ask about."

"No."

"Okay, I won't. Can I ask about what happened to the mad professor and Lemon-Face?"

Logan smiled. "No harm in asking. As I said, she put up a fight."

"What happened?"

"They had split up, of course. Sensible thing to do. She stayed with the car, although the licence plates had been switched. She changed her clothes and had combed her hair out. Apparently she had a fine head of hair, and looked quite different — attractive even, according to one of the blokes on the scene. She'd have got away with it too, but for Martins." Logan made a wry face as she mentioned Martins.

166

"I don't understand."

"Martins has a thing about getting heavy with women. I'll never forget how he was with me when he thought he'd really caught me out. There are times when I think Fowler ought to let the Department shrink have a few sessions with him. I'll bet they would find all kinds of nasties crawling around in that little mind."

"They've probably already done so," Pross said, "and have discovered he's got just the right mind for the job."

"Oh you cynical man." But she was smiling at the thought. "Well, Martins leaned on her. She'd been stopped by a roadblock, you see. In the end, her hatred for the little weasel made her snap. It's very easy to hate someone like Martins. For a woman like that, it must have been intolerable to put up with his bullying. She was still in the car, so she went for her gun. Silly thing to do, I'd have thought. Unprofessional. Unstable.

"She was very fast. She got one of the blokes − not a killing shot − and Martins got her. I think the bastard enjoyed it too."

"Sounds as if you almost wish she'd got him."

"If I'd been there I'd probably have shot her too, but I wouldn't have shed tears if she'd got Martins first."

"What happened to the man?"

"Would you believe Sanders was supposed to take care of that?" Pross said, "I think I can guess the rest."

"Sanders couldn't fart his way out of a wet paper bag."

"Logan, where'd you learn to talk like that? Sometimes the things you say . . ."

She grinned at him, freckles seeming to dance on her face. "My father. Very colourful turns of phrase, my father has. Remind me to take you through them one day."

"He ought to be ashamed of himself."

"I'm not a little girl, Pross. I know what the big bad world is like."

"I know it, you know it, we both know it. Even so . . ."

She suppressed a giggle with difficulty. "Oh Pross. Sometimes, you're very sweet . . ."

"*Sweet?* My God! Don't ever call me that, Logan. What about identification?" he went on. "Who were they?"

"No real IDs on any of them. The Department got no live ones, it appears. They found some weapons, and what was left of their vehicles. It was a fairly determined operation."

"But how did they get so close?"

"Bad analysis of the intelligence gathered," Logan said. "It was apparently thought they were after the nuclear power station at Trawsfynydd, and the knowledge that the real target was the Hammerhead almost came too late."

Pross suppressed a shiver. "Tell me about it."

"I'd still like to know how the devil that could have happened." Logan's eyes had grown momentarily hard. "I don't like being left open by the incompetence of others. I won't give up till I find out."

"Don't get into trouble."

"I won't be the one in trouble if I find out who screwed up."

"Sanders, or Martins?" Pross suggested hopefully.

"No. That would be too easy. It's deeper than that." She seemed to pause to think, then added, "Did you ever remember where you could have seen the man at the hotel?"

Pross shook his head. "I'm no wiser, even now."

"Oh well, perhaps it will come to you eventually. If it does, will you let me know? Just me."

"I will, if you keep in touch. I'm not likely to talk to any one else from your Department, anyway, not if I can possibly help it. Just keep in touch."

"I will. That's an absolute promise. Well . . ." Logan stood up.

"You'll have to be leaving soon, won't you?"

"Yes." He got up from the comfortable chair. There was something about her manner that didn't seem quite right. It had nagged at him ever since they'd entered the room: but he could not identify the cause of his unease. She could switch moods so easily at times.

She came up to him. "Take care of yourself, Pross."

"You're going now?"

"I must. I'm late already as it is. I always stay too long with you."

"We can walk back to the Lynx together."

She shook her head. "No. I hate goodbyes. Bad for the system."

"Who's saying anything about goodbye?"

"Shh," she said, and kissed him fully and gently, on the lips.

To Pross, it was one of the most unbearably sad kisses he'd ever had.

Then she was walking towards the door, the inevitable bag slung from her shoulder; her magnum bag. She was looking vulnerable again.

"Logan!" he called. "Wait!"

She turned at the door to give him a quick smile. " 'Bye, Pross." Then she was gone.

He ran to the door, pulled it open. "Logan!" But he was looking into an empty corridor. He went slowly back into the room and walked to the window. He stared out across the dunes.

Why had this sadness within him come so suddenly with her departure? Something was very wrong and he felt certain she was going into some kind of danger. A shiver passed through him, making him fear the worst; making him feel helpless too, because he knew there was nothing he could do about it.

Later, as he climbed into the Lynx for the flight back to Cardiff, he said to Rees, "Cado, I'm worried about Logan."

"What do you mean?"

"I have this feeling I'm not going to see her again. Don't ask me to explain it, because I can't."

"Aah no, David. I don't think that will happen. You're worrying over nothing. She'll be alright, and you will be seeing her again. Mark my words."

"I'd like to believe that, Cado. I really wish I could."

Rees lifted the Lynx into the cold of the late afternoon, and headed south.

LINE

TEN

On a Wednesday morning, towards the end of March, Terry Webb entered the Prossair office before going on to the flightline. Pross was alone, at his desk. Cheryl Glyn had not yet arrived.

Pross looked up. "'Morning, Terry." His eyes searched for someone else, expected with Webb. "No Cheryl this morning? Isn't she travelling in with you these days?"

"Cheryl's here. I sent her upstairs for a coffee."

Pross cocked his head to one side. "Alright. I'm waiting."

"I don't know anyone in Lhasa, and I wouldn't go on Mastermind with my knowledge of alpine biology. Besides, I'm the kind of person who thinks Lhasa is a fever."

"Alright," Pross said. "I give up. What's the question?"

Webb handed him a postcard.

It was the portrait of an Oriental clay figure, clearly an image of a woman of some rank. The figure was seated in the lotus position, hands hidden within brocaded sleeves.

Pross turned it over. There were two stamps in the top right-hand corner. One was the postage stamp itself, depicting a train crossing a gorge on a high railway bridge. The train was coming out of a tunnel. Next to this stamp was a smaller one which simply looked like an oblong of blue recycled paper that had been rubber-stamped with a smaller black oblong, within which were two groups of Chinese characters. It was AIR MAIL in any language.

The circular postal stamp, with a bar bisecting an inner circle that reminded Pross of the London Transport logo, said LHASA at the bottom, with the corresponding Chinese characters at the top. Within the central bar was the date of posting, beneath which was the figure 3. Pross assumed that to be the postal district number. The message made interesting reading. It had been addressed to Mr Terry Webb, Alpine Biology Research Centre, and went on to give Webb's full address.

In the top centre of the card was written TIBET, followed by the date of writing. The address had been written in capitals, the short message in shaky-looking script, as if the writer had either been ill, old, or had simply not been able to find a steady surface upon which to put the card while writing.

The message said: "Having a wonderful time. Most interesting fauna. Wish *you* were here. Much love, Freckles XX"

He didn't have to guess who it was from. The message made him feel very cold.

"I don't know anyone called Freckles, either," Webb was saying. "Thought perhaps you might."

"You thought correctly, Terry."

What was Logan doing in *Tibet*, of all places, for God's sake?

"So it's from her then."

Pross nodded.

"By the look on your face," Webb said, "it's not a card you like the idea of receiving. I nearly caught a packet from Maureen this morning. She wanted to know who the devil this Freckles was. Could have been funny if it wasn't serious."

"What makes you think it's so serious?"

"Well, your face for a start ... and if she writes to me, with that daft address, there's a good reason: like she doesn't want people to know it's really you she's sent the message to. She knew I'd bring it to you. If she doesn't want anyone to know she's written to you, then it has to mean she's in pretty bad trouble and can't get through to her own people. Am I right so far?"

"More than I want you to be."

"That bad?"

"Worse. This card has taken a month to get here. I dread to think what state she's in."

"You think she's in prison or something over there?"

"It's the 'or something' that scares the hell out of me."

Webb said, "You hear of people being slung inside in all sorts of places for God knows what. It must be even worse when it happens to a woman ... and in the kind of job she's in ..."

"Cheer me up, won't you, Terry?"

"Sorry, David. I really am. I know I've told you she was bad news and would bring you grief, and I think this is the real stuff. You've got to try and help her."

"Change of heart, Terry?"

"No change of heart. You've got a bad one on your hands; just what I've always worried myself witless about. But she's called to you for help and as you've said, it's been a month. Perhaps I'm soft in the head, but she's young enough to be my own daughter. I know how I'd feel . . . She's still bad news for you, but you've got to help."

"I'm going to."

"That's alright then. I think she wanted you to get in touch with her people. They can take over. David . . ."

"Yes?"

"Don't do what I think you might be thinking."

"And what might that be, Terry?"

Webb's eyes were very steady as they looked at Pross. "Don't even think of going there yourself. They've got their own people to do whatever is necessary. Just pass the message on, and let them take care of it. You've got Dee and the kids to think about. Remember that. You owe it to them."

I owe it to Logan too, Pross said in his mind. *Christ. Where do I start?*

"Boss," Webb was saying. "David! Are you listening to me?"

"I'm listening, Terry."

"No. You're *not* listening. You're hearing, but you're not bloody listening. This is not a job you have to do for them. Let them handle it."

Pross stared at Webb calmly. "If I were in trouble, Terry, she'd be coming in like the bloody cavalry to my rescue, and more than once, she's put herself between killers' guns and my body. Have you any idea what that means, Terry? There are things that I've never told anyone, not even Dee, about Logan. She's got the kind of guts that frighten me sometimes. I can't leave her to rot. I'd never forgive myself. You don't believe this now, but neither would you when you've had time to think it through. She's a mate, Terry. You know what that means. I'd do it for you, I'd do it for Pete, I'd do it for Cheryl. I'd do it for Dee and the kids. I've got to do it for Logan. More than anything, I've got to do it for her. In my place, you'd be saying the same thing to me. You know that, don't you?"

Webb gave a long sigh, and nodded. "That's what makes it so hard. Reason tells me to try and stop you. The rest . . ." He moved his hands in a gesture of defeat. "How are you going to explain it to Dee?"

"God knows. I don't as yet." Pross picked up the phone. "Here goes the first step." He dialled the airfield at Llanbedr.

Three hours later, waiting alone in the office, Pross watched as Fowler, trailed by Sanders, came through the main entrance. They crossed over to the check-in desks and as they began to make their way past, they were stopped by one of the stewardesses who worked for one of the other companies. One of the airport's uniformed security men was coming up behind.

Fowler said something to the stewardess who turned to look up at Pross. Pross nodded, and she allowed Fowler and Sanders to pass through. Fowler took the slight delay calmly, while Sanders looked annoyed. Pross noted it with a wry smile. Trust Sanders to make more of it than was necessary. The security man had gone back to his pacing.

"Hullo, Pross," Fowler said as he entered. "Is that fresh coffee that I smell? Yes, please . . . and I think Sanders would like one too."

Fowler took a seat while Sanders chose to stand by the door.

Pre-empting the possible demand, Pross had asked Cheryl Glyn to replenish supplies, then had sent her on a spurious errand to Terry Webb. He knew Webb would keep her there. If Pete Dent had already returned from a trip to Tenby, Webb would have no trouble wondering how to keep her occupied.

Pross handed the coffees round, then sat on the edge of his desk.

"We were hoping you'd call," Fowler said as opening gambit.

Pross frowned at him. "Hoping? I don't follow."

"You soon will. We've known of Logan's whereabouts for some time."

"You've *known*? Then why didn't you tell me?"

Fowler's eyebrows appeared to do a lift-off behind his glasses. "Tell you, Pross? Logan is a member of the Department. Why should we need to inform you of her location, under any circumstance?"

"Well . . ." Pross stopped, unsure what to say next.

"I think I can follow your drift. You have, shall we say, a special feeling for Logan which makes you want to go to her aid if she happens to be in some difficulty. Understandable, because she has herself kept you from harm's way, so to speak, on occasion. However, had we been in touch and asked for your help, saying she

176

was in trouble, would you have believed us?"

Remembering past experience, Pross said, "No."

"There you are. So we had to wait for her to make contact."

Pross said, "So she did get in touch with you."

"And compromise herself? Oh do come on, Pross."

"Then how . . ." Pross stopped. "Oh alright. You've got people there."

"Naturally."

"Is there anywhere on this planet where you haven't got someone in place?"

"Now that would be telling, wouldn't it?"

"Ask a silly question."

"Quite."

"Did you know she'd got in touch with me before I contacted you?"

Fowler's eyes seemed to gleam behind the lenses. "Yes."

"You read my bloody mail, Fowler?" Pross said with a quiet anger.

"When matters of the security of the State —" Sanders began.

"Belt up, Sanders!" Pross snapped at him. "I'm talking to your boss."

Sanders flushed a bright purple.

Fowler gave him a look that appeared to turn Pross's words into an order. Sanders looked even worse.

Fowler said to Pross with his usual calm, "We don't read your mail, Pross. We monitor it. That simply means we check to see where it comes from. This is not a habit of ours, and now that we've discovered what we were hoping for, the monitoring has ceased."

"Till the next time, you mean."

"Don't be so distrustful, Pross."

"Ha bloody ha!"

Fowler smiled. Sanders looked at Pross with venom.

Fowler said, "Once we had located Logan, we began making arrangements for her release. Well . . . perhaps not a release as such; more of a rescue."

Pross nodded slowly. "Rescue," he said drily. "In the middle of Tibet? How many squadrons and how many battalions are you going to need?"

"No squadrons," Fowler replied mildly. "No battalions. Good planning, a good aircraft, and a good pilot." He smiled fleetingly.

"I'll say one thing for you, Fowler. You've got enough gall to supply the bloody world."

"Such flattery, Pross. The Hammerhead will be ready and waiting for you in Nepal," Fowler continued smoothly, "at the same site from where you carried out the last operation: appropriately so, as you'll later understand."

Pross stared at him. "You were ready for this, weren't you? You were ready for it all along."

"I am ready for everything. Pross, and for nothing. It is the basis of good Intelligence work. It is also the basis for successful combat, as you should know. I do not presume, but base my actions upon judgments made from forward planning and preparedness. In two days, a civilian executive jet will land here at 0800 Zulu. It's a BAe 125-800, and will take you to Kathmandu non-stop. Sanders will be on it. He'll be accompanying you."

"How cheering," Pross said.

Sanders, with a face like thunder, said harshly, "You don't believe for one moment, Pross, that I'm looking forward to this?"

"If I thought you were, I'd die."

"You'll arrive in darkness," Fowler continued as if neither had spoken, "which is precisely what we want, and will be taken directly to your hotel where you'll sleep off any effects of time-zone skipping you may feel you have suffered. You'll have been well catered for on the aircraft, and should need nothing to eat before going to sleep. Sanders can organise a drink if you should want one.

"Sanders will also organise an early breakfast and by 0800 local time the next day, you will leave the hotel and, accompanied by Sanders, return to the airport. A helicopter will then take the both of you to the site. At the site, you'll be kitted up, then you'll take the Hammerhead to the pick-up point. You'll naturally be travelling alone, as the front seat is reserved for Logan."

"Will it be armed?" Pross asked quietly.

"To the teeth," was Fowler's mild reply. "You will, after all, be invading someone else's airspace and may need to defend yourself. Note I use the word *defend*. You are to enter into combat only if threatened."

"Oh I see. You believe I'll be allowed to land, pick Logan up, and fly away nicely while they wish me bon voyage?"

"It may not be quite like that."

"I didn't think it would."

"But you get the gist."

"I get the gist alright. If I were a very cynical person, I'd say there's nothing you'd like more than to see the Hammerhead in real combat, with yours truly as the suckered pilot. But I'm not a cynic. Not really."

Sanders decided to make another of his contributions. "There is no reason why I can't do the pick-up. We don't need Pross." He spoke as if Pross had gone out of the office.

Pross stared at him, said nothing, turned to look at Fowler. "Is he serious? Or was that just for effect?"

"He's serious. Aren't you, Sanders?"

"I'm quite serious," Sanders replied stonily.

"He's serious," Fowler said.

"And Logan would probably wind up getting killed," Pross said with cold dismissiveness.

Sanders' eyes blazed at Pross. *"How dare you!"*

"That will be enough, Sanders," Fowler said, still calm, but an edge of hard authority had come into his voice. "Let's leave it there, shall we? Pross is going. Aren't you, Pross?"

"I thought that was what you were here for."

"Exactly. To continue . . . your route to the target area has been plotted and loaded onto its cassette. Insert it when you're already in the air, and the Nav MFD will display the course, giving the best track for . . . er . . . optimum lack of interference by possibly hostile forces. It means you'll be avoiding SAM sites and/or troop concentrations. The Intelligence is as up-to-date as is possible, but you know as well as I do that some staff officer may suddenly decide he wants an exercise precisely where we would not like him to hold one. It's a very slight risk, given our information, but it's one that must be put into your calculations . . . Your route out . . . I leave that to you. If it all goes smoothly . . ."

"We all know what happens if it all goes smoothly. I'm more worried about what happens if the shit hits the fan."

"An almighty pong all round."

"As if I didn't know."

"You shouldn't have any trouble. Your course will take you over the most lonely and desolate of landscapes. You should see no one on the way in, and no one on the way out."

"Which is why I'll be taking in enough weaponry to sink a few battleships."

"Such cynicism, Pross."

"I know. Isn't it terrible?"

Fowler stood up. "Any further questions?"

Looking steadily at Fowler, Pross said, "Last time I saw Logan, a strange feeling came over me. I knew she was going into trouble. Why did she go out there? Why Tibet?"

"As a matter of fact, she did *not* go to Tibet ... at least, not of her own free will. She was in Nepal, travelling under cover as an alpine biologist. It was a good cover, since she does actually know her way around that particular science. As far as I know, it's still holding, though that state of affairs may not last for much longer ..."

"It still doesn't tell me why she was there, and how she wound up in Tibet."

"I don't have to tell you anything, Pross, but I'll satisfy your curiosity. She was there because of your little run-in with the Hellhound. You may or may not have destroyed the last of the flying prototypes. It does not necessarily mean, however, that even now, newer, modified versions are not being prepared for future flight. In the area where the Hellhound met its demise, bits of wreckage were found by some of my people, and some of theirs. The search has been going on for some time.

"Unfortunately, there has been no sign of the flight recorders. We know of at least four, though other sources put the figure as high as seven, each monitoring different aspects of its performance, particularly, of course, in combat. You can appreciate that both sides put a high value on those innocuous little boxes. We want them to determine the weaknesses of the aircraft, so that methods to accentuate those in combat can be devised; while knowledge of its strengths will enable us to find ways of neutralising them. Our adversaries need that information just as eagerly, for exactly the opposite reasons.

"We pulled some of our people out because they were becoming part of the furniture, so to speak. One can only trek for so long or pretend to be a hippie in Durbar Square for a limited length of time before being rumbled by those people keen on your movements. Nepal can seem very crowded at times.

"Logan went in once, as a hippie, to keep her ear to the ground. She was not actively involved in the search ..."

"But you decided to send her back, this time to go on the search."

"Yes," Fowler said. "But it now appears that was a fundamental error."

"Fat lot of good it's done her, admitting it now. Bloody hell

Fowler! You risked her. How could you *do* that? It was her third time out there, if you count the time with me. You must have known you were pushing it."

Fowler's eyes were hard behind the glasses. "Do not presume to lecture me on Logan's worth, Pross. I am far more aware of it than you could possibly imagine. Bear that in mind. If you want to get her out as much as you indicate, the best way is to follow instructions. If you do not wish to, ignore the card she sent you, and we'll consider other options."

"Pull the other one, Fowler. You want *me* to go. *Me!* So don't bleed all over the carpet."

"Save your anger, Pross. You may just need it for others." Then Fowler became conciliatory. "Look, I understand how you feel. Let's have done with the recriminations. Get in there, pull her out, and we'll all heave a great sigh of relief. The people who took her in think they've caught one of our searchers, but they're not sure. They're holding on to her in the hope that she'll break. We must get her out before that happens."

Pross felt the chill descend upon his spine. He couldn't bear to think of Logan being tortured.

Fowler, correctly reading the expression on his face, said with some degree of gentleness, "The news we have is that, so far, she's been reasonably well treated."

After a while, Pross said, "Thank you for telling me."

"I'm not a complete ogre, Pross," Fowler remarked with a smile that was so quick, it appeared to have vanished before existing.

Tell that one to the judge, Pross thought.

"Come on, Sanders," Fowler said briskly. "We must be getting along. Plenty still to do."

Sanders went out, after nodding a distant goodbye to Pross.

Fowler paused. "Good luck, Pross." He held out his hand.

Pross shook it, with a touch of resignation. "One thing still bothers me."

"Oh yes?"

"The man with that woman Martins shot."

Fowler waited, eyes guarded.

"On two occasions," Pross went on, "Logan set it up so that both of them could be taken. The first time, Sanders screwed up and on the second, with Sanders set to take him, somehow he managed to escape. I'm worried about Sanders. I don't know if I'll feel comfortable going out there with him."

181

"No need to worry about Sanders. He's so straight and true you could crease your trousers with him. But I agree with you he has been somewhat remiss. That's why we're sending him out with you. It's his punishment."

"Thanks a lot."

"Knew you'd see the humour of it. Have a good flight. And don't worry about what to say to your wife. Some very kind people have been to see her to let her know Queen and country need your services for a very brief few days. No mention of your destination, of course, and I'd appreciate it if you saw it our way. Oh yes. Leave your passport at home. You won't be needing it. Well . . . that seems to be that. See you when you get back." Then Fowler was out of the door and threading his way between the check-in desks.

Pross watched until he was out of sight, before going back to sit behind the desk. He rubbed his face in his hands, as if trying to wipe away the effects of a deep sleep. Then he sat still for long moments.

He was not looking forward to explaining things to Dee.

That evening, Dee went about her household affairs in silence. Dinner was had in silence. The Dawn Patrol were put to bed in silence, and she did not play with them as she normally did. At those times, Pross would sometimes be hard put to decide who was the adult. It was one of the things about her that he loved.

They went to bed in silence and lay unmoving in the dark of their bedroom.

At last, she spoke the only words she would speak that night.

"I hate the bastards!" she said. Her voice was on the edge of an angry scream.

She wouldn't let him touch her when he tried to hold her, seeking comfort for the both of them.

ELEVEN

The all-white BAe 125 with its civilian registration waited, twin engines idling, their combined whine seemingly pitched at just below aural level. The fumes from its burnt fuel came strongly to Pross as he walked slowly towards it. He had always liked the smell of jet efflux. It was all part of the spirit of flying that had hooked itself securely into his blood. He could never leave it.

Knowing Terry Webb was watching him from the spectator terrace, he turned to give him a brief parting wave. Webb raised an arm equally briefly in farewell. Cheryl Glyn, who had maintained a stony face until the time had come for Pross to leave, had thrown her arms impulsively about him, asking him not to do anything silly. She had remained in the office, preferring not to come to the terrace to see him off.

Dee had mellowed during the hours leading up to his departure from the house and had sent him off with a warm, though worried, smile, and a long kiss. He could still sense the taste of her mouth, and the pressure of her lips on his. She had stayed at home.

He walked up the lowered steps of the aircraft, his mind full of visions of Dee and the children; but superimposed upon their images was one of Logan. The green eyes seemed to haunt him.

A young woman in a cream outfit that looked very much like a stewardess's uniform smiled at him from within the aircraft as he reached the top step.

"Good morning, sir," she said brightly. "Welcome aboard."

The smile cheered him up. "Glad to be aboard," he told her as he entered the aircraft, wondering whether he might not live to regret that statement — or, far worse, die regretting it.

183

The combined stair and door was being raised as he made his way along the eight-seater cabin. Sanders was the only other occupant, already belted into his seat.

"'Morning," Pross said.

Sanders nodded, almost curtly. "Good morning. Sit across from me, Pross. It will be easier to talk."

"We don't have to talk throughout the flight, Sanders," Pross said, not relishing the idea of having to sit next to Fowler's man for the duration. "Anything comes up, you'll know just where to find me."

He ignored Sanders' stiffening lips and walked along the central aisle to take a seat on the left, two rows down, The door had sealed itself and the stewardess was coming towards him as he sat down and fastened his seatbelt. She picked up the small case he'd brought with him.

"I'll stow that for you, sir," she said, "until you require it. We've got a good selection of books, magazines, and papers. Just let me know what you'd like whenever you wish. We've also got personal stereos and a selection of tapes, if you'd prefer. My name is Wendy."

Pross looked at her wonderingly. Fowler certainly knew how to lay it on.

"You've got quite a system, Wendy," he said to her.

"We try to do our best, sir," she said, smiled at him once more, then went to put the case away.

The jets had begun to spool up and the 125 was starting to taxi. Wendy returned, took her seat across the aisle from him and secured her belt for the take-off.

Pross wondered if she'd given her real name. Probably not, he decided, and she was no doubt as skilled with a gun as Logan. No, Logan was in a class all by herself, and could out-shoot anyone in the Department with ease. Pross was certain of it. Bloody marvellous Logan. He hoped he could get her out. There was no "hoping" about it, he told himself admonishingly. He *had* to get her out.

The sleek executive jet did not pause at any of the stopbars but rolled straight onto the runway and began winding swiftly up to take-off thrust. The power came on with an accelerative force that gradually pushed Pross into his seat and in a remarkably short space of time the 125 was leaping off the ground and into a steep climb. The wheels clunked into their wells and upwards speed increased.

Pross smiled to himself. If the crew up front were not ex-fighter

184

pilots, he'd be very surprised. The 125 had come as close as an executive jet could to performing an afterburner take-off. He glanced at Wendy. She was staring out of her window, taking it all in her stride. It was quite obviously all in a day's work for her.

He closed his eyes as the aircraft continued to gain height. He could relax. Those two up front knew what they were doing.

The two pilots, blissfully unaware of the supreme accolade that had been bestowed upon them, took their aircraft into a high climbing turn, eastwards.

Exactly thirty minutes after the 125 had taken off, a swift burst of code shattered the ether for precisely 0.50 of a second. It was sent in clear, as if the senders couldn't care less who eavesdropped, and it had no apparent destination.

Intelligence-gathering stations all over the globe picked it up; some immediately, others had it relayed to them. Decoding experts from both power blocs bent their minds to it. The clever ones broke it in five minutes. Others took nearly an hour. The real duffers would still be working on it a day later, unless entitled to a mutual transfer of information from their allies.

But the problem didn't end there. Having picked up and decoded the message, no one could understand what it meant. To anyone but those involved in Intelligence-gathering, it would seem as if someone had decided to play a joke — some teenager perhaps, who had managed to hack his way into a computer somewhere.

At Pine Gap in Australia, an American duty officer stared at the message and said, "What the hell's this?"

"You're asking me?" said the one who had showed it to him.

"Yeah. I am."

"How the hell should I know?"

"You decoded it."

"I still don't know what it means."

"Where did it originate?"

"England."

The duty officer stared at the message again. "What the hell do you think the Brits are up to?"

"Who knows, with them?"

From Langley to Moscow, Buenos Aires to Tokyo, Berlin West to Berlin East, Rome to Pretoria, Tel Aviv to Tripoli, Thule to Khabarovsk, and so on, similar conversations were taking place, with the same results. But in some quarters, strenuous efforts were being made to find out what was going on. Copies of the message, perhaps in their hundreds, would eventually reach even the smallest of surveillance units. Individual agents would be quizzed; suspected hostile elements, perhaps after months of covert surveillance, would suddenly find themselves being hauled in for questioning.

While all this activity was taking place, the one person who was meant to receive the message and who knew what it meant, saw a copy of it, and gave no outward sign of the relief felt.

The signal had been scattered like leaves in autumn and many people had picked up a leaf: but only one could read it.

He looked at the message in his colleague's hand. The ridiculously simple code, with its translation first in English, then in the language of officialdom in the territory appended beneath, made amusing reading:

zkkovh ziv tildrmt rm gsv tziwvm zq ml vo
apples are growing in the garden at No 45

The only important word was "apples". The rest was nonsense.

His colleague said, "It came in an hour ago. What do you make of it?"

"Absolutely nothing. Why did they send that to us?"

They were not speaking either in English, nor the language of the territory.

A shrug. "They're desperate. It came from Central Command HQ, who sent it to all Regional and District HQs, who sent it to us, among others." A grin. "Perhaps they think our prisoner knows something."

"Do you, Comrade?"

"Of course not. For all we know, this concerns someone in Tokyo, or Tashkent, or Togo."

"Ignore it, then."

"I wish we could." A sigh of resignation. "We'll have to go through the motions. How stupid can the brass get?" Another sigh, this time of annoyance. "Do they think we have nothing better to do? Look. I'm sorry, but would you mind carrying out the interrogation?"

"Is there a hurry?"

"Do it when you feel like it. I dare say there must be others like us all over the country feeling as we do. I don't even think they really expect an answer at Central Command. One thing is certain, whoever sent that message is having a good laugh at the expense of every Intelligence service that has decided to act on it. Think of the waste of time! And here we are playing his silly game, because no one wants to be caught out, just in case they may be the target."

"It may even be a false trail, while the real message has gone out without anyone noticing."

"My feelings exactly. Anyway, I'd be grateful if you'd go through the motions of trying." A grin. "Besides, you might find it diverting, Comrade."

They both knew what he meant.

Yangpachen, Tibet, late afternoon.
Logan stared out of the tiny square of the wooden window at the massive pink slopes of sandstone across the valley, and wondered if she'd ever get the smell of rancid yak butter out of her hair and from her body. True, she had been given daily rations of water in a bowl with which to maintain a semblance of cleanliness and once, during yet another move, she'd been allowed a glorious bath in a natural hot spring.

But that had been two weeks ago.

After she had been taken off the mountain in Nepal, there had followed an eleven-day march to a rendezvous point deep into Tibet from where she had then been taken in an open truck on a gruelling, dust-filled ride across the high plateau to Lhasa. *That* journey had taken three days. Sore in limb and spirit, it had taken her more days to regain her resources.

Throughout that journey, she had barely been spoken to: but she had not been maltreated. The members of the patrol had suffered the same discomforts as she had. The blow to her spirit was the certain knowledge that Lal had been killed in his attempt to get away. She blamed herself for it still, all these weeks later.

The European she had recognised as the man from the hotel in Betws-y-Coed had to this day given no indication that he'd seen her somewhere before, a factor she held to be in her favour, no matter how small. He had been correct in his manner towards her during interrogations, if cold and forbidding.

Though she had seen no evidence of a Russian presence, she had come to the conclusion that he was some sort of a go-between; a liaison man for the Russians in dealing with the Chinese. Despite outward noises of possible renewed ideological friendship, the mutual suspicions were still there. The search for the downed Hellhound prototype would therefore need to be handled with skill

187

and sensitivity. Whether some of the other search teams were being led by Russians was debatable; but she was certain that the man who had led the team that had captured her was East German ... and despite the fact that his beard was gone and his longish grey—white hair was now cropped militarily and blond, he was none the less the same man from the hotel.

Whom Sanders had missed twice.

That thought, too, had exercised her mind over the past weeks. Was Sanders bent, then? Or merely a raving incompetent?

She shook her head slowly, walked away from the single window which was all the lighting she had in the small room, and went to sit in a darkened corner. The sole furnishings were a woven carpet upon which she slept, and a pile of rough blankets given to her to keep out the severe chill of the nights.

Each day she was interrogated. The questions were the same, the answers the same.

What were you doing on that mountain?

I'm a biologist. I am on a field search for fossils.

Who was the man with you?

My guide.

Why was he carrying a rifle?

To protect me from bandits, he said. It was his country and I trusted his judgment.

Why did he fire at the patrol?

How could he know it was a patrol? He thought they were bandits.

It took some time to overcome him. By then, he had killed three of our Comrade's men and wounded three more, two very badly. How do you explain that?

I'm certain you know that many Nepalese serve with Gurkha regiments. My guide was an ex-Gurkha. (*Poor Lal*, Logan had thought at the time of the first interrogation, as she did even now.)

Do you still insist you are a biologist?

It is not a question of insisting. I am.

Your name?

You know my name.

Answer the question, please.

Janet Stewart.

A Scottish name. I know the Scottish accent. You do not have it.

And I know people with Italian names who do not sound Italian.

No impertinence, please. We have not mistreated you. It would not do to cause offence.

I was born in Scotland, but grew up in England. I went to school there, then on to Oxford. It tends to blur accents.

Your . . . guide took a bag with him. We have not found it. What was in it?

The usual. Samples, plus his own personal belongings, and a few tools.

We shall be back, Miss Stewart. We shall be back.

It had always ended like that. The East German — Schuler, he had introduced himself — usually did all the talking, while a senior Chinese officer, a Colonel Wu, would merely watch her in unnerving silence.

In Lhasa, they had put her in the Tibetan Quarter, a move she had found rather strange at the time. A group of dwellings near the Bazaar had been commandeered, and she had been installed in one room, introducing her to the all-pervading smell of rancid yak butter, tea, and fat, and to *tsampa*, which by now she had got accustomed to; if very reluctantly.

Logan was not a food snob. She was not one of those people who expected bacon and eggs and cornflakes in every corner of the globe. She normally delighted in sampling all kinds of cuisine; but the current diet was proving too difficult for her. Perhaps, she decided, wanting to be fair, the conditions under which she was forced to eat it had much to do with her lack of enthusiasm.

At infrequent intervals, Chinese dishes were brought to her. Those times were looked forward to with eagerness. She was well aware that this was a deliberate method, aimed at weakening her resolve, in the hope that she would change her story to the one they believed she should be telling. So far it hadn't worked; but the treat of the Chinese meals had not been stopped: yet.

In Lhasa, she had thought it incongruous that while she sat trapped in a dark little room, there were probably people from the outside world — tourists, or even mountaineers wanting a crack at Everest from the north side — walking about marvelling at the Forbidden City and the Potala, rubber-necking, clicking away with cameras. She had found herself hoping that Fowler had somehow managed to know of her whereabouts and had sent in his own "tourists" to get her out.

The days had become weeks, and then the weeks were threatening to become a month, and she had begun to wonder whether she would ever get out.

Then had come a surprise. Schuler had come on his own, with a postcard.

Miss Stewart, we feel that as you have been with us for some time, perhaps you should write to your colleagues. Tell them you are well.

Aren't you afraid they may start making enquiries?

Why should they? No one knows you are here.

They will, if they get my card. If you're really going to send it.

Why should we not do so? There should be no trouble if you are careful about what you say.

This may just be a trick to see if I really have colleagues to write to. Well, give me the card and a pen, and see for yourself.

Wordlessly, Schuler had done so, and she had written the card. He had stared at the brief message, and at the address.

Why do you sign yourself Freckles?

Because I've got them. See? That's what they call me. If I signed it any other way, they would wonder ... and that's not what you want, is it?

No, Miss Stewart. That's not what we want.

Well? Are you going to send it?

I think it may be passed.

Bully for you.

Schuler had gone out, and she had heard nothing further. She doubted strongly that they had in fact sent it.

After Lhasa, she had been moved to another town. It had been done at night, and she'd had no idea where she'd been taken. A third move had brought her to this place. She'd been here for four days now. She wondered where they'd be moving her to next, and why they were doing it.

She thought again about Schuler and Wu, and the combined search for the Hellhound's remains, wondering what price the Chinese would exact from the Russians for the co-operation. A slice of the Hellhound's technology, perhaps? The People's Republic was badly in need of some up-to-date technology for its army; but she had a strong idea the Russians would not play ball with their latest helicopter prototype. As a pacifier, however, they would probably offer a few other titbits in the hope of keeping the sleeping giant, if not exactly friendly, then not hostile; with an outside chance, perhaps, of becoming jolly Comrades again.

Was there, maybe, out on the vast desolate plateau somewhere, a Russian contingent staying well out of sight, waiting for the results of the search?

190

Forget it, Logan, she said in her mind. *You've considered all aspects of this, and you're still in the dark.* She smiled wryly as she looked about the little room. "Literally," she said aloud.

She heard voices, stood up to go back to the window. A short distance away, two Chinese soldiers were walking unhurriedly. They did not look in the direction of her prison, although they would have known she was there. Her four-day stay had shown her that this was a garrison town.

From her vantage-point, she had seen no Tibetans; although that did not necessarily mean there were none in the area.

She went back to her corner. Spotting soldiers could pall after four days.

Still, it was a pleasure to wake up to the view of the pink sandstone slopes each morning, even if she could not go freely to them.

Schuler and Wu were walking along a narrow, dusty alleyway; Wu in uniform, Schuler in olive greens with a padded combat jacket. Schuler wore high boots, but there were no insignia on his clothing to denote either rank or service. He might quite easily have been a civilian traveller or mountaineer who favoured military-style attire.

Schuler said, "I think perhaps you should come with me to see Miss Stewart, Comrade Colonel."

Wu, a small, thin man, looked up at Schuler with mild amusement. "Does she frighten you? She has spirit. These British women can sometimes be formidable; the kind that take to the Himalayas on the backs of donkeys long after they should have become great-grandmothers. Or is it because you find her . . . attractive?"

They were conversing in German, which Wu spoke excellently.

"I do not find her attractive," Schuler said good-naturedly. "Although I will admit that despite her lack of comfort over the past weeks, she has the appearance of a reasonably attractive young woman."

"Not what one would expect of an academic?"

Schuler smiled briefly. "The bookish academic is a thing of the past, Comrade, or so it would appear, particularly in the capitalist countries."

Wu said, "I have sometimes accompanied trade missions to the West, and some of my Comrades have shown passing interest in Western women. For my taste, they are far too graceless and big. They cannot surpass the elegance of a Han lady."

"'Lady', Comrade?"

"I can describe her as 'Comrade' if you prefer, but I think we understand each other."

"I happen to agree with you. Your Republic is vast and has women of breathtaking beauty throughout its provinces."

"Now, Comrade, you are being diplomatic."

"There is no need to be diplomatic when the truth is being spoken."

Wu gave him a quick glance. "You do mean it, it would seem. I will admit to you, Comrade Major, that I am pleased that you are the one sent to liaise with us. Over the weeks, I have had the time to study your attitudes. You are unusually sensitive for a . . ."

"Barbarian?" It was said without rancour.

"I was about to say Westerner, but of course, you are not."

"Ideologically, no. Geographically, yes."

They smiled, amused by the apparent conundrum.

Then Wu said, "I do not think I could have coped with a boorish Ivan, if you do not mind the heresy."

"I didn't hear a word," Schuler said.

"Diplomatically spoken," Wu said approvingly. "They are nicely out of the way where they are," he continued, "but I wish this business to be settled and to have them out of our country. You, of course, my dear Comrade, are welcome to stay as long as you wish. Come back to Beijing with me when it is done. Stay for a while. I would be pleased to introduce a respected Comrade from the SSD. Our peoples should liaise more closely. You would also meet some Han ladies. I am quite sure your manner would be correct."

"I am flattered," Schuler said. "If my superiors give permission, I shall be happy to accept."

"Good. It is settled. Now what was it you wanted me to do?"

"I would like you to watch Miss Stewart's face when I show her the transcript. See if she reacts. She'll be watching me, but her body may make unconscious movements, which you'll see. If she does not react, then we'll know she has nothing to do with it, and we can pass the problem of solving it to some other unfortunate."

"Very well. Let us return."

On their way back, they passed a Tibetan woman, brightly dressed in cheerful colours.

Wu's mouth turned down. "We'll never civilise these people."

Schuler diplomatically kept his mouth shut.

*

When the single bulb hanging nakedly from the low ceiling came on, Logan knew she was about to have another visit.

A short while later, Schuler and Wu entered.

"Come closer to the light, Miss Stewart," Schuler commanded.

Logan noted that, as was his custom, Wu had retreated into one of the corners of the room. Better to observe her unguarded reactions, she was certain. She prepared herself for a shock, but not as big as the one she got.

"Take a look at this," Schuler said and without warning, thrust the transcript into her hand.

Logan would never understand how she was able to contain the reaction she felt; the relief, the excitement, the total surprise. She put it down to her training and her self-control.

Even so.

She stared at the message puzzledly. "Am I supposed to know what this means?"

Schuler was staring at her intently. She was also quite certain that the silent Colonel Wu was studying her with all the attention of a hawk about to pounce upon an unsuspecting prey.

Schuler retrieved the piece of paper. "Obviously our mistake, Miss Stewart. We shall leave you for now. Enjoy your afternoon."

"Thank you. I'm off to the supermarket in a minute."

Schuler smiled thinly. "You have a very British sense of humour, Miss Stewart."

"Yes. Strange, isn't it?"

Schuler and Wu left without further conversation, and soon after, the light went out.

Schuler said, "Any reaction?"

Wu shook his head. "Nothing at all. She's either who she says she is, or she's very, very good. But I'm inclined to believe the former. We have had her with us for weeks now, and nothing has changed in the pattern. Of course, we have treated her relatively gently . . ." Wu let the words hang.

Schuler said, "Physical abuse will get us nowhere. If she is an agent, we'd probably kill her before we got anything . . ."

"Not necessarily. As a woman, she is vulnerable to any number of interesting forms of encouragement . . ."

Schuler was as hard as they come, but even he felt a shiver go through him when he heard the anticipation in Wu's voice.

"I can also call on a number of lusty men who would find the

193

exercise interesting, to say the least –'

"No," Schuler interrupted calmly. "That would get us nowhere, except perhaps a few thrills. Intelligence work is not about cheap excitements. I leave that to some of the people in the KGB." He crumpled the message, put it in his pocket. "At least we know we can leave someone else to worry about that little missive. We have other things to do, Comrade Colonel."

"Indeed we do," Wu said with a tiny smile on his small face. "You realise, of course, that she cannot come out of this alive. Innocent or not, she has seen armed men from across the border, in Nepal. We have an agreement with Nepal. We should have asked their permission; but of course, with the Ivans, it would be rather difficult, given the reason for our presence in the first place. We expect handsome rewards for our reticence, and our forbearance. Perhaps some knowledge of the machine that went down? Although, it would make more sense from our point of view, perhaps, to show more interest in the one that shot it down." Wu smiled once more.

"It was not my helicopter, Comrade," Schuler said evenly. "It matters little to me. They never give *us* the most up-to-date weaponry, except when it suits their purposes. So? What should be done with our guest?"

"People are always falling off mountains," Wu began reasonably. "This world knows that; and in the Himalayas, foolhardy young foreigners are the biggest casualties. The mountains kill. Their beauty is fatal. Bodies are not found for years. How many people have so far fallen foul of the search units?"

"Twenty, at the last count."

"There is the reason why she cannot live. She would return to Nepal with tales of armed patrols terrorising the locals. Think of the diplomatic embarrassment for all concerned; your government, mine, the Ivans'. We need the time to smooth it all out through proper channels. Our young guest would have it in all the world's news media within hours of her return. Do you see our dilemma, Comrade?"

"Perfectly," Schuler said.

"I knew you would understand. Sensitivity is the key. Take her back across the border, and find her a suitable perch from which to fall." Wu sighed. "A pity. She has spirit. But it is no disgrace for such a spirit to be taken by the magnificent mountains. It will be fitting." He looked up at Schuler, and smiled beatifically. "I shall give you some men as escort. Take her anywhere, as long as it's across the border. Pity she could not help us."

"When should we leave?"

"This evening would be a good time."

While Wu and Schuler were discussing Logan's immediate future, Fowler was standing in Winterbourne's opulent office, listening to his superior with the kind of benign patience that always drove Winterbourne crazy. It was 11.00, British Summer Time. Outside, the March day was bright and appreciably warm for the time of year.

Fowler stared dreamily through the vast areas of glass that were the windows to Winterbourne's office and thought, not for the first time, how easy it would be for an enterprising sniper to succeed in taking out the Head of Department. The thought was merely for his recurring amusement whenever Winterbourne became tedious, which was often. If Winterbourne got taken out like that, it would be his own stupid fault.

Fowler himself would never expose his back like that, as his own virtually windowless and relatively spartan little office proved. Incongruously, outside the Department premises he moved about quite openly, on several occasions without a minder. Winterbourne, by contrast, never went anywhere without one – even to his club.

Fowler permitted himself a fleeting smile as he considered this double incongruity.

"I am obviously very amusing today," Winterbourne was saying testily. "You have not listened to a single word I've said, Fowler."

"On the contrary, Sir John. Every word is firmly printed upon my mind. I can give you a résumé, if you wish."

"I do not wish, as you put it. You most probably could. Any word on Logan?"

"None at all. But we're expecting something within the near future."

"Have I ever expressed the opinion, Fowler, that I think you sail pretty close to the wind? Too close, in fact?"

"On several occasions, Sir John."

"Yet you seem not to take a blind bit of notice."

"But I do, Sir John. Constantly."

"Then why did you not inform me that you were using that civilian pilot ... what's his name ...?"

Fowler, having no intention of helping Winterbourne out of this spurious display of forgetfulness, remained stubbornly silent.

Winterbourne floundered for a few moments, then said biliously, with a glare at Fowler, ". . . ah yes, Pross. Why was I not told?"

"There was as yet no need, Sir John. I was concentrating on the most important matter on hand: getting Logan out. She has been in captivity for weeks, and we have no indications as to her state of health. We are naturally anxious to pull her out before much longer."

"But why a civilian pilot? I grant you Pross has done well by us in the past, but why can't we do this thing through proper channels? A few diplomatic words in the right places . . ."

Good Lord, Fowler thought with some exasperation, mentally despatching those who had appointed Winterbourne as Head of Department to unnamed hells. What does he think we're engaged in? Proper channels indeed! Does he really think the other side are worried about proper channels unless it happens to suit their own purposes?

Patiently, he told Winterbourne. "Logan's cover is still intact, Sir John." He let the words rest there. Let Winterbourne ponder upon the prospect of being responsible for blowing Logan.

"I see," Winterbourne said after a long silence.

And Fowler knew he had won yet again.

Logan could scarcely contain her feelings of relief and anticipation. The word "apples" on the message meant rescue would be forthcoming; but it meant something else too. "Apples" was the Department codename for Pross's file. It didn't matter how Fowler had managed it. Perhaps there were some "tourists" out there, after all.

She knew how Fowler had managed to get the message to her, though. It had been risky, because there could have been no guarantee that she would be given it to look at; but sent in clear so that anyone could have made an intercept – she was certain that was how it had been done – like a stone cast into a pond, its ripple had eventually reached her. She wondered how many unfortunates throughout the world were being asked about that same message, in an attempt by their interrogators to tease out what it meant.

She wondered too, whether her card had been sent, and whether Fowler had intercepted it, as she'd expected. It didn't matter now. None of it did. Pross was coming and that was all that truly mattered.

She wrapped the rough blankets about her in the cold and dark little room, and for the first time since her capture, felt warm inside.

He'll be surprised to see me, she thought. *I've grown a bit thin.*

How were they going to do it? she wondered. She tried to think of possible ways, then gave up.

All she could do was wait.

TWELVE

Pross felt a touch on his right shoulder, opened his eyes slowly, and turned his head to see who had done the touching — then almost wished he hadn't.

Sanders was occupying the seat that Wendy had sat in during take-off. The BAe 125 was flying high, jets spooled up to maximum cruise. With only five people aboard instead of its normal capacity of·ten, it would make good time. Outside the windows, the sky was bright with a warm sun.

Before he could say anything to Sanders, there was a gentle change in the aircraft's attitude.

"Kuwait," Sanders informed him. "We'll be going down for our refuelling stop."

"Where's Wendy?"

"Dozing up front. You've got me for company."

"What a cheerful thought."

"Look, Pross. Let's just accept we don't like each other . . ."

Does anyone *like you?* Pross didn't say.

"So?" he queried aloud.

"Let's handle the part of the job we're supposed to, and leave personalities out of it."

"It's amazing how people always say that," Pross remarked, "never seeming to realise the simple fact that it *is* the personality that affects anything to do with teamwork. But don't worry, Sanders. I'm interested in one thing only . . . getting Logan out."

"Then we both have the same goal."

Sanders spoke so pompously, Pross wanted to sigh with frustration, but he let it pass. Everything seemed to be a matter of striking the right pose for a given situation. There were a lot of people like Sanders about. Pross merely wished he hadn't been saddled with one of them.

But the first five hours of the flight had so far passed pleasantly enough. He'd had entertaining conversations with Wendy who had told him quite funny stories about herself — mainly about young men whose inflated egos she'd dented — but very little about her job with Fowler. He had not pressed her on that particular subject, neither had he talked about his own part in the scheme of things.

Sanders had kept much to himself, for which Pross had been grateful. Between dozes, Pross had been given the VIP treatment and served excellent food by Wendy. The fare was so good, he decided, that most airline catering managers would have been bashing their heads against a convenient wall in shame, had they the conscience for it. He only wished all this wonderful treatment didn't make him feel like a condemned man.

Now, as the descent began, Sanders said, "We shan't be leaving the aircraft. The fuel truck will come up to us, and the pilots will direct the refuelling. No one will board, and we'll be off again as soon as we're tanked up."

"How much is the next hop?"

"About four hours. We'll be down at Tribhuvan around midnight, local time. Suits our purposes perfectly."

"Do you expect people to be waiting?"

"Ours only, I hope. Kathmandu, Pross," Sanders went on, as if beginning a lecture and causing Pross to close his eyes briefly in despair, "is not all trekkers, hippies and Durbar Square. There's a sizeable diplomatic community, some of whom would be very interested in our arrival. This aircraft will be taking off again before the night's out, once it's picked up its fuel. It must not be there in the morning."

"What about the crew? They can't make that trip back without a rest."

"New crew, Pross, waiting when we get there. Our present lot will have a day in Kathmandu, then take a scheduled flight out."

"Fowler's thought of everything."

"Naturally. By the way, if it becomes necessary . . . for whatever reason . . . your name is James Lyle, and you carry a diplomatic passport. I'll give it to you if the need arises. However, we don't foresee that kind of problem."

"That makes me breathe easier."

Sanders nodded curtly, and went back to his own seat.

It was 16.00, local time, when they landed at Kuwait.

Logan stood by the window and stared out at the darkness. In the clear air, the lights from neighbouring buildings seemed much further than they were. She smiled to herself. It was the opposite in the daytime at these heights. Mountain peaks several miles away could give the appearance of being almost close enough to touch. She had experienced this apparent contraction of distance many times in the Himalayas themselves.

She drew her blanket tightly about her. Tonight had been treat night. The friendly young female soldier who had been assigned to her since her arrival, had brought her a Chinese meal, and had also accompanied her on the second of her twice-daily allowable visits to the very basic lavatory hut in a small courtyard at the back of the building in which she was held captive.

The lavatory didn't worry her. She had grown accustomed to it. There had been a new change in the routine, however. Fresh clothes had been brought: outdoor clothes. Padded trousers with pegged bottoms, padded jacket with a hood, a thick green sweater, and a scarf for facial protection against cold and wind. A pair of warm mittens had also been left. She had not yet put any of it on.

They were obviously going to move her on again. Why? And where to? She did not like to think it would be further north, into China itself. The friendly girl soldier had told her in Hong Kong-accented English that she was being held in a place called Yang-pachen, but there had been no further information, the girl clearly feeling she had already said too much.

Logan didn't know what to think. It was a blow, coming so soon after having become aware that moves were being made to rescue her. Did Fowler also have people in Yangpachen? And if so, when would they move?

The light came on suddenly, temporarily blinding her, Visitors.

In a few moments, there came the sound of bolts being drawn, and the door opened. Wu and Schuler entered.

Then Wu spoke directly to her for the very first time, in perfect English, "You are not dressed, Miss Stewart."

"Why should I be dressed? Am I going somewhere?"

Wu said, pleasantly, "But of course. We are deeply sorry for the inconvenience you have been caused. You are being returned to Nepal."

She stared at him. *"Tonight?"*

"It is a long journey. The sooner you're on your way, the sooner you will be there."

Logan regarded him warily, just as a real Janet Stewart would have, but it was not all play-acting. She was very worried indeed, though she succeeded in keeping it well hidden.

"Why tonight, all of a sudden?"

Did they know of Fowler's intentions? And if so, how had they found out?

Wu smiled. It chilled her.

"We have been thinking about it for some time, Miss Stewart."

"Then why not simply inform the British authorities and let them sort it out? Why sneak me out in the middle of the night and take me across a wild plateau –"

"Miss Stewart, Miss Stewart. I understand your anxiety, but I assure you you have nothing to worry about. Your presence here is . . . shall we say . . . a somewhat delicate matter, as was the method of your arrival in Xizang – Tibet, to you. We would prefer to solve our small problem with as little fuss as possible."

"Your small 'problem', as you want to call it, is a kidnap, from another country's territory. That's a serious offence, as well you know. You're trying to slide out from under."

Don't push it, Logan! she warned herself.

It was the sort of reaction that would be expected from an imprudent and innocent biologist, but it could also backfire spectacularly.

As if to confirm her own feelings, Schuler said, "Do not reject the Comrade Colonel's offer, Miss Stewart. It might not be wise. I shall be accompanying you, with an escort, to ensure your safety."

Deliberately showing caution, she said, "And how do I continue when we get to the border?"

"Trustworthy Tibetans will be found to take you on to Kathmandu."

"And when I do eventually get there? How do I explain my long absence, and the death of my guide?"

"Legitimate questions, Miss Stewart," Wu said, returning to the conversation. "It will all be arranged to the satisfaction of all concerned."

"And what about the guide's family? He was their sole breadwinner."

"Miss Stewart, we are a country of vast borders. From time to time, there are incidents in which lives are sometimes lost. This has occurred on our borders with Vietnam, Laos, Burma, India, and on that of our Soviet Comrades in the north. Each side has suffered loss of life. Despite that, such casualties are far less than those suffered each day on the roads of the countries of the world. I deeply regret the death of your guide. We paid more severely than he did, as we have already told you. The Gurkhas are sturdy warriors and we have not had a formal border conflict with them since 1791, when they were pushed out of this territory after their invasion a year earlier. I do not intend to be responsible for a new one. Your guide's family will be recompensed. Now, Miss Stewart, if you please, we shall leave you to get on with your dressing. Comrade Schuler will return in fifteen minutes. Goodnight, and a safe journey. Once more, I offer my sincere apologies."

He went out, followed by Schuler. The light was switched off almost immediately.

Logan listened as they walked away. She was under no illusions. Colonel Wu's pleasantries were merely a front for the singularly unpleasant fate he had planned for her. What had they decided to do? Take her out to some desolate place and leave her there with a bullet in the head? Bury her? Throw her into one of Tibet's beautiful turquoise lakes? Imagine drowning at 15,000 feet!

"I can't just stand here and take this," she said to herself.

But what could she do? She could hardly go very far without being noticed, even if she did manage to get away from this complex of buildings. From what little she had been able to observe, there were more soldiers around than Tibetans: so far, she had seen none. Perhaps there really weren't any in the area.

There must be a few, she decided after a while. Someone had to make the Tibetan food she'd been given. The Chinese, who viewed most things Tibetan with distaste, would certainly not have lowered themselves to prepare it.

"I hope you've got some good ideas, Fowler," she muttered grimly as she began to get into the clothes the girl soldier had brought. "I don't intend to die out here."

She wished she had a gun, though. She'd at least have been able to take a few of the bastards with her, instead of waiting like a resigned sheep for the end.

Don't wind yourself up, she thought firmly. *Wait for Fowler.*

But what if Fowler was already too late? She found she didn't want to think about that.

*

As they walked away, Wu said to Schuler, "You can see we have no choice. She would tell the entire world, so outraged is she. I do not blame her, of course. I would be as outraged. Unfortunately for her, she is expendable. If her body is ever found, it must be in Nepal."

Schuler said nothing. He knew that for all Wu's talk of being pleased to liaise with a member of the SSD, he was also speaking in a code that was none the less very clear.

Schuler had brought the woman in, and Schuler must take her out. The responsibility was Schuler's.

It was as plain as that.

When Schuler returned, Logan was ready. She had wrapped the scarf about her face in such a way that it formed a makeshift balaclava, exposing only her eyes and the upper part of her nose. She had then put the hooded jacket on, fastening it up to her chin; then she had drawn on her mittens.

Schuler, dressed for the journey, looked at her expressionlessly. He carried an AK-74 assault rifle, slung across his back. A holstered pistol hung from his belt.

"Well, Miss Stewart," he said. "Time to go. The trucks are waiting." He stood aside for her to pass.

As they went out, she noticed that the light had been left on. She hoped it was a good omen.

The BAe 125 was high above the Arabian Sea. Soon it would be curving left to overfly northern India, on its way to Kathmandu. Pross had enjoyed a splendid dinner in Wendy's company and was feeling reasonably at peace with the world, even though he was worried about Logan.

Then Wendy had gone forward, and Sanders had returned to spoil it all.

"Just under two hours from now, Pross, and we'll be there."

"That's good news."

Sanders was not sure how to take that, and stared straight ahead. Pross decided to relent. There was hardly anywhere else to go aboard the aircraft. He had been invited up to the cockpit, but after one visit for an hour or so when the co-pilot had gone into the cabin to chat Wendy up, he had declined a second.

"How did you get the Hammerhead in?" he now said to Sanders conversationally.

Sanders seemed keen to talk. The poor sod was probably bored with his own company, Pross thought, only mildly sympathetic. No point overdoing it. Neither Wendy nor the pilot had seemed particularly eager to engage Sanders in general talk. As a result, he had spent the greater part of the flight reading, or simply staring out of the window.

Sanders said, "It just happened that certain activities coincided with our interests. There's a minor Royal visit on, and someone thought it a good idea to hold an exercise in deployment to the region. 'Bold Knight', I think they decided to call it. Among the hardware used were five Hercules . . ."

"How very convenient."

"One had its cabin stripped as bare as was possible without affecting its structural integrity and its performance, then the Hammerhead was stripped as far down as was necessary to make it fit, again without affecting *its* structural integrity, its avionics and targeting systems, and so on. The Herk landed at a strip up-country, the Hammerhead was wheeled out, the minor reassembly was completed, and it was flown to the site. It was then checked out —"

"Who flew it in?"

"Captain Rees."

"Cado? Well, well," Pross said softly.

"Today was the last day of the Royal visit," Sanders continued, "but Bold Knight's still going on."

"I'll bet it is," Pross commented. Trust a master of schemes like Fowler to get an exercise laid on to cover the mission. "Will Rees be at the site when I get there?"

"Possibly. Possibly not."

"It's an answer, I suppose. Is the exercise common knowledge?"

"Of course not."

They landed at exactly midnight, Kathmandu time. Entry formalities were conspicuous by a swiftness that left Pross wondering whether there had been any, then it was into a waiting car to be whisked into the warm spring night. Both Sanders and Wendy accompanied him.

There was no sign either of the pilots who had flown the aircraft in, or of those due to fly it back. Sanders had climbed into the front with the Nepalese driver, while Wendy was ensconced in the back with Pross.

The car was speeding south along the ring road from Tribhuvan, when Wendy said, "I like coming to Nepal. Much of it is still unspoiled, although each year I think visitors are trying to turn it into a dustbin. A pity, really. If people could really appreciate it, there's no reason why it couldn't be enjoyed without ruining life for the people who've actually got to live here."

"You've got strong feelings about this place, then?"

She nodded in the gloom of the car.

"Been here a few times before?" Pross queried, wondering about her reasons for coming.

"Twice before. I—"

Sanders craned his head round long enough to interrupt, "Mr Lyle's rather tired, Miss Jones. I don't think he needs to be bothered by tales of your travels."

In the speeding car, a hostile silence descended. From the new stiffness with which Wendy Jones sat, Pross could tell that if her eyes could, they would have drilled two neat holes into Sanders' stupid head.

Pross reached across surreptitiously to briefly give her hand a conspiratorial squeeze, and said to the back of the head, "You must have been a very popular boy at school, Sanders."

Wendy Jones made a noise that sounded like a hastily-stifled snort, and the back of Sanders' head gave a little jerk, but Sanders did not turn round. It just wasn't his day.

The car followed the ring road over the Hanumanti River, then took the wide sweep westwards before again curving north. A left-hand bend took it across another bridge, this time over the Bagmati. Almost immediately, the driver turned right, off the ring road and onto one that was much narrower. Soon after that, he turned left and into a short bumpy drive. He pulled up before a brick-built building that seemed a mixture of Western and Nepalese architectural styles.

It was, Pross thought, either a small hotel or a big private house. There were lights on within the building, and the porch was lit by a single shaded lamp. There was very little traffic to be heard, but there was the sluggish sound of flowing water.

Sanders had climbed out of the car, indicating that Pross should also get out. Wendy Jones was already opening her door.

Pross eased himself out, and stretched in the pleasantly warm night. He was trying to reconcile in his mind something that Wendy Jones had said, triggering a sudden flash of recognition.

In her comments about what she saw as the inevitable destruction of the indigenous life-style of the Nepalese, she had reminded him of another person who had put forward that very same view, if a little more forcefully.

Perhaps it was the actual fact of his arrival here in Kathmandu that had triggered the connection with his previous visit. Someone else had been his minder then, a man he had first met in Berlin: a man who had then called himself Hansen; a man who had recognised him in the breakfast room of the hotel in Wales; *a man who had twice got away from Sanders, even after having been carefully laid on the hook by Logan.*

Sanders was saying, "Miss Jones, show Mr Lyle to his room, if you please. I've got some things to attend to. Off you go, Lyle. Miss Jones has your passport, should it become necessary for you to make use of it before I return. I doubt the need will arise, but you never know."

He re-entered the car and its engine which had remained at idle revved up softly as the driver turned and went back the way he had come.

"Looks like we're alone," Pross said. Their bags had been removed from the car and left at their feet.

"There are people around," Wendy Jones said. "By the way, thanks for slapping Sanders down. You didn't have to."

"Of course I did. The pompous bastard."

"I can see you like him." The hint of laughter in the voice.

"Is he your boss?"

"Good Heavens, no. My Section is sometimes attached to the Department, but Sanders is my superior on this job . . ." A shrug. ". . . so I shut up when he says."

"And what's your job exactly?"

"Doing what I am right now . . . minding you. I used to do the Royal ones . . ."

"Then I'm privileged."

". . . but I asked for a transfer."

"I'd have thought that was the best of all."

"You've got to be joking! How would you like to be the one on *that* duty when something went badly wrong?"

The stuff of nightmares.

Pross could well understand. When he was in the Air Force, he knew of people who would do almost anything to avoid getting selected for service on the Queen's Flight, despite the prestige that

206

duty brought with it. As soon as wind would come of new vacancies they would suddenly find themselves volunteering for postings they would normally have run a mile from. As Wendy Jones had said, they did not want to be the ones to go down in history as having blown it with a Royal in their care.

"I admire the people who do it," she was saying. "I really do. They're either very brave, very daft, or –"

"They have no choice. Someone has to do it."

"Exactly. And we can go in now. They've decided we're okay."

Someone had appeared on the porch: a Nepalese who looked very familiar.

"That," Pross said, "looks as if it's Lal."

"Know him, do you?"

"I met him when I was here last."

Lal had come forward to meet them. "Good evening, Mr Lyle," Lal said. "I hope you had a good flight."

"I did, thank you. And how are you?"

"I am well, Mr Lyle. Good evening, Miss Jones."

"Good evening."

"I'll take your bags," Lal said. "Follow me, please."

They followed, and entered the two-storeyed building. Lal led them, up uncarpeted wooden stairs that seemed freshly lacquered, to a short corridor with two rooms opposite each other. He handed them each their bags.

"Your room, Miss Jones," he said, pointing to one. "The other is yours, Mr Lyle. If you'd like a snack before you wish to retire, I shall be happy to have it brought to you."

"I'm fine," Pross said. "Perhaps Miss . . ."

"No. I'm alright. Thank you."

"Very well. Then I'll say goodnight."

"Goodnight," they both said together, and watched as he walked away to go back down the stairs.

"Where is everybody?" Pross asked her.

"They're about."

"Is this really a hotel?"

She smiled. "You can say it's ours."

"Not like the one I was taken to, last time I was here."

"Perhaps they had a good reason."

"Perhaps," he said. "Wendy, do you know what I'm here for?"

She shook her head. "And I'd rather not."

He smiled knowingly. "I get the point. Well . . . goodnight."

"'Night. See you in the morning."

"Yes."

They both turned then, and entered their rooms. Pross found that there was a bathroom en suite. He luxuriated in a warm bath for about twenty minutes, then got ready for bed, intending to have an undisturbed sleep, so as to be ready for the next day's action. He thought of Wendy Jones. A very pleasant young woman whose company he enjoyed, and who was no doubt quite skilled at her job. But she wasn't Logan.

In all sorts of ways.

Pross found that he was missing Logan's banter, her sometimes quite frightening professionalism; but most of all, he simply missed having her around.

"Wherever you are, Logan," he said softly, "hang on. I'm coming to get you out."

He wondered where Sanders had gone to.

The soft knock came when he was on the edge of sleep. He waited, just to make sure he'd heard correctly the first time.

The knock came again. Wendy Jones? Lal? Sanders?

The questions ran through his mind as he sat up in bed, and stared at the red lacquered door with its green border.

The knock came a third time.

He got out of bed, drew on his trousers, and went to the door.

"Yes?" he queried softly.

"It is I, Mr Lyle." *Lal.*

"Just a minute." He opened the door quietly, and Lal entered.

"I am very sorry to disturb you," Lal said in his correct manner. "I wish to speak to you alone."

Pross shut the door equally quietly and went to sit on the bed. "Have a seat," he told Lal, indicating one of the two chairs in the room. The other was draped with his discarded clothes. "Last time I was here, you called me Milner."

Outside, a heavy vehicle passed along the road.

Lal looked at him seriously. "That was a different time."

Pross nodded. "And I had a different name."

Lal said, "I arrived from Tibet yesterday."

"*Tibet!* Have you seen Logan?"

Lal nodded. "I have seen her, though only once. She appeared to be in reasonably good health; but that was nearly a month ago . . .'

"A *month*? But you said –"

"Yes. I did say I had just come from Tibet, but I walked most of the way. I had to keep off the roads to avoid patrols, and of course, I could not use any form of transport. Sometimes, I was able to join a yak caravan . . ."

"My God! You *walked?*"

Lal permitted himself a brief smile. "It is the way of life in the Himalayas, even in these days of motor cars. It is either walking, or take an aeroplane, if it is possible or can be afforded. Most people cannot, but I know of those who have been in an aeroplane but have never been in a motor car, or a truck. Our terrain, as you know, is not the best for vehicles."

"Where did you see Logan?"

"In Xigaze. They move her from place to place."

"So it couldn't have been you who posted the card from Lhasa," Pross said thoughtfully.

Lal stared at him in surprise. "You received a postcard from Lhasa? Who could have sent it?"

"Your guess is as good as mine. But it was from Logan. Most definitely."

Lal said, "Perhaps there are some of Miss Logan's people out there."

"Perhaps," Pross agreed. "How did you find out about her?"

"There were friendly Tibetans I could talk to. They do not like the Chinese much and have never forgiven them for destroying their temples and monasteries. Their land is full of such ruins. But perhaps it would be better for me to tell you how Miss Logan was first taken."

Lal recounted what had happened that day in the mountains until he came to the part where he had reluctantly gone over the top, leaving her to the patrol.

"I came upon the second patrol," he continued, "and there was an exchange. Three were killed, and I wounded three more. I'm fairly certain two of them took mortal hits, but I am not sure."

Pross wanted to smile. Some exchange! Lal sounded annoyed that he had not killed the other three as well.

"Then," he went on, "I played a trick on them. I had been very unhappy about leaving Miss Logan, even though she had ordered me to. I decided I would have to find out what they would be doing with her. I would have to follow. I led the patrol – what remained of it – to a spot where I could make them believe they had shot me. It was a dangerous chance, but I had to take it. There are many tracks in Nepal which seem to hang on the edges of cliffs. I chose one that was above a deep pool. By now I had led the patrol for many miles. They should have given up, but they were angry about their comrades.

"At the right moment, I moved from cover. They shot at me, but missed." Lal spoke with a gentle contempt for the patrol's level of marksmanship. "However, I pretended to be hit, and fell over the side and into the water. It was a long way down, and I was afraid I had misjudged, or that perhaps I would hit a rock." Lal's face showed nothing of his fear, if indeed he had been afraid. "Luckily, I did not. The patrol did not look for me.

"I went to Tibet, to find out about Miss Logan, then returned. I realise I should have done as she had commanded. Her decision was the correct one. The time I have spent travelling could have been used to prepare a rescue mission."

Amazed and impressed by what he saw as Lal's astounding sense of loyalty, Pross said, "What you did was incredibly courageous. You have nothing to be ashamed of."

"I disobeyed an order, Mr Lyle. That is very serious. I also discovered," Lal went on before Pross could say anything, "two matters of interest during my journey. The Tibetans in one of the yak caravans I had joined told me of a Russian detachment somewhere on the plateau, well away from the normal routes, but close to some ancient ruins, long abandoned, perhaps in the last century. I do not know how accurate they were about that. They were not sure themselves. But they were quite positive about the Russians."

"A detachment?" Pross began. "Of what?"

"Aircraft and troops. Helicopters and fixed-wing."

"*Fixed-wing?* Are there new airfields up there?"

Lal shook his head. "No airfields. These aircraft do not need them. According to the Tibetans, these go straight up when taking off."

Pross knew exactly what Lal's Tibetans had been describing, and he didn't feel good about it at all.

Bloody hell, he thought. *Yakovlev Yak-38s*. Russia's version of the jump-jet. Bad news indeed, if that info were true. Jump-jets and choppers. Christ. What was he going into this time? The detachment was obviously there to cover the search for the Hellhound.

He asked Lal to describe, as best as was possible, the helicopters as gleaned from what the Tibetans had told him. When Lal had finished, Pross wished he hadn't asked. If their descriptions were correct, the Tibetans had seen the dreaded Mil Mi-24 Hinds, as well

210

as Mi-28 Havocs which were as deadly as the Hinds, with the exception that being two-seater tandems, they were lighter, and even more nimble. The Russians had really come out to play.

"Anything else?" Pross queried drily. "It couldn't be much worse."

"My informants were very sketchy about detail. They claim there were some Chinese troops at the camp. The people who spoke of this did not come originally from the same caravan, but from a smaller one which they claim was hunted down and almost totally destroyed. Helicopters were apparently used in the chase. Those who survived hid for days in the mountains, travelling only at night. If caught in the open, there is of course little cover for miles. There are no trees on the plateau at those heights."

"How many survived?"

"Two."

"My God. Did they tell the authorities?"

"Who would they tell, Mr Lyle? It would be to admit to what they had seen. People die all the time in the mountains."

Pross nodded slowly. "You said there were two things of particular interest that you discovered."

"I have seen the man who appears to be in charge of Miss Logan. He was frequently in the company of a Chinese Colonel whose name is Wu. The man is European. I know him. I have seen him here, with you. He accompanied you the first time you came here."

"What!" Hansen? Pross thought. Impossible. Lal must be wrong.

"I know what you are thinking," Lal said. "I thought the same. I saw him only twice, and he was wearing a kind of combat dress; but it was the same man."

Hansen with Logan?

"I would like to come with you, Mr Lyle," Lal was saying.

Pross looked at him, but said nothing.

"That is my true reason for coming here tonight," Lal went on. "It is a matter of honour. I must do what I can for Miss Logan, if she is still alive. I should not have disobeyed her orders."

This was a proud man, with the honour and devotion of a Gurkha warrior. Pross did not want to make him beg.

He said, "I'll see what I can do, Lal, but it may not be allowed. Have you told anyone else about all this?"

"I have reported everything, except about the man with Colonel Wu. I was not certain whether I should report it ... but I felt I should tell you, for Miss Logan's sake."

"I understand, but I'll have to pass it on." Not to Sanders, Pross didn't say. "It's a very important factor."

"Yes. I know."

"And another thing . . . *if* it is agreed that I take you and we do find her alive, there won't be room in my aircraft. I won't be able to bring you back."

Lal actually smiled as he stood up. "Then I shall have to prepare myself for another long walk, because we must find her. Goodnight, Mr Lyle. Thank you."

Pross got up off the bed, and held out his hand. "Thank *you*, for coming. I'm grateful. Goodnight, Lal."

They shook hands, and Lal went out of the room. Pross closed the door softly behind him, wondering if Wendy Jones had heard anything, then went back to bed.

But he didn't close his eyes. He could not stop thinking about Lal's incredible journey, and the way in which the little man had taken such good care of himself.

Then he kept seeing Logan's face, and knew he wasn't going to get the good night's sleep he'd hoped for.

Logan's world was one of noise, dust, discomfort, and darkness broken by the dust-filtered lights of the following vehicle. She had no idea how long they'd been travelling, but it seemed like years. She felt almost certain that it was now well past midnight. Surely, she thought, Schuler would call a halt soon?

They were travelling in a convoy of three. At Yangpachen, in the sparse artificial lighting of their embarkation point, she had been able to take a good look at their transport. Two were open-backed, all-wheel-drive lorries, and one an armoured personnel carrier, a Chinese-built version of the Russian BTR-152 with six-wheel drive. It had the added modification of a roof-mounted twin cannon in a shallow turret, capable of a 360-degree swivel.

Schuler had put her in one of the open lorries, to sit in the back in company of four silent armed soldiers who appeared so keen not to be thought of as desiring to molest her they sat as far away from her as was possible within the limited space available. Perhaps Wu, she thought grimly, acting through Schuler, had warned them of dire consequences. Wu and Schuler wanted to do their killing properly.

The second lorry brought up the rear, with the BTR leading. Even if she were desperate enough to throw herself out of her lorry,

212

and into the cold, rushing darkness, she doubted whether it would
be of much use to her. Assuming she survived the fall, where would
she go on this desolate plateau, without supplies, without knowing
of her whereabouts, and with perhaps a battalion searching for her,
commanded by an enraged Schuler, backed by an even more
ominous Colonel Wu?

Once, twice, the lorry had gone round a hairpin bend, and had
seemed to totter momentarily. That could only have meant that the
edge of the rough road was very close. What lay beyond? A pre-
cipice?

Jumping was out of the question. Those silent, scrupulous soldiers
would probably shoot her in mid-flight.

Forget it, Logan, she said in her mind. Fowler's working on something, and Pross is coming.

The thought of Pross made her smile in the cold, dusty dark.

SINKER

THIRTEEN

By 07.30 the next morning, Pross was down for breakfast in the room that had seemingly been reserved for him. There was just a pair of tables, each set for two. He had been directed there by a Nepalese member of the household staff and was sitting in solitary splendour, finishing off a glass of freshly squeezed orange juice, when Sanders walked in.

"'Morning," Sanders greeted. "Sleep well?"

"I took some time falling asleep, but in the end, my body decided to take over. What was left of the night was spent in a reasonably deep stupor." Pross had hoped Wendy Jones would be the one to share his table. He did not relish sharing breakfast with Sanders.

"Good," Sanders said brightly; then as if reading Pross' mind, went on, "Don't worry. That's my table over there. Jones will be joining you. I wanted to speak to you first . . . in private." He sat down, and continued: "I . . . believe you had a visitor last night. No. It wasn't Jones who told me. Ever since you two became bosom pals, I very much doubt she'd give me the time of day."

"It's too early in the morning, Sanders. Give your nasty little mind a rinse."

"In any case," Sanders said, as if Pross had not spoken, "you won't be seeing her after this morning. She'll be remaining here when we leave. Her part of this job is over." He looked smug.

"This is going to be a long day."

Sanders said, "Look, *Mister* Lyle, left to me —"

"But it isn't, so let's get on with what you were about to say when you first came in."

"I saw Lal, on his way back from your room," Sanders began after a brief, stony silence. "I suppose he told you about Logan."

"Yes."

"Silly little man should have obeyed his orders. Logan told him quite —"

"Don't call him a silly little man," Pross said tightly. "He put himself through an incredible experience. Or don't you value loyalty, Sanders? Or the intelligence he's brought back about that Russian detachment?"

"So he's told you about that too. Yes. I do value loyalty; but when it is misplaced, it becomes dangerous. Lal should have known better. And as for that information about the Russians . . . we already knew about it. So in a way his efforts, which have obviously impressed you with their derring-do, were quite unnecessary. Oh dear, I've offended you. One of those with the romantic vision of the sturdy little Gurkha warrior, are you? Well, in this line of work, Mister Lyle, we have no room for that. *Professionalism.* That's what counts. Lal did not behave professionally, for all his valour against that patrol."

"You can talk," Pross said bitterly, thinking of Hansen.

"And exactly what is that supposed to mean?"

"Work it out for yourself, and if you're finished —"

"No, I am not finished."

Pross sighed. "Suit yourself, then. You've already ruined my breakfast."

"Better eat up. We'll be leaving in forty-five minutes. A helicopter will land outside to take us to the site. Be ready." Sanders stood up.

Pross said, "That's it? I thought you had more to say."

"It can wait." Peevishly.

Not a word about Hansen.

Pross said, "Lal wants to come on the pick-up with me."

"Don't be ridiculous. There won't be room on the return journey, after you've picked Logan up."

"He doesn't mind the walk back. It's almost a stroll for him now."

"Out of the question."

Sanders went across to his own table, picked up the small, gleaming bell at its centre, and rang viciously for service.

Breakfast was over, and Pross was back in his room. Wendy Jones had come in to check that everything was ready. He had spent the rest of his ruined breakfast time in pleasant but silent company with her, Sanders' brooding presence having effectively killed any attempts at light conversation. Somewhere, bells tinkled faintly.

Pross looked out of a window at a body of water that vaguely reminded him of the Serpentine back in London. Beyond the water was a road.

"Exactly where are we?" he asked her without turning round.

"On the south-western outskirts of the city. That's the university campus on the other side of the road. To the east of this place is the Patan district. Do you know Kathmandu at all?"

Pross turned, shook his head with a rueful smile. "The insides of hotels only."

"Oh well. We must change that when you've got more time."

"That might take a while."

Wendy Jones said, "You're probably right. Besides, she would probably scratch my eyes out." She gave Pross a tiny, knowing smile.

" 'She'?" Pross repeated. "Who's 'she'?"

Wendy Jones said, "Come on now, Mr Lyle. Let's not be too innocent." She stopped to listen. A faint thrumming was growing rapidly louder. "I think I can hear your carriage arriving, so I'll save you further embarrassment. It's been a pleasure working with you." She held out her hand.

He shook it. "Thanks, Wendy. Thanks for everything. I think I'd have gone mad if I'd had to put up with Sanders all the way here."

"As I've said, it was a pleasure. Don't let Cheerful Charlie get you down. We call him the Monday Baby."

"The Monday Baby?"

She grinned suddenly. "His mother hated having her weekend disturbed to give birth. It shows."

"Ouch. Sometimes, I could almost feel sorry for the poor sod."

"Don't. Save your sympathy for something harmless like a crocodile."

The helicopter was practically over the building by now.

"If she ever decides on a change of scene," Wendy Jones said, "let me know." She gave him a wicked wink, and let herself out of the room.

Pross smiled at the closing door, decided he would tease Logan about Wendy Jones just to see her reaction; then he picked up his bag, gave the room a quick once-over to check that he'd forgotten nothing, and left. He heard the chopper come in for a landing.

Sanders was waiting downstairs. Lal was with him. Wendy Jones was nowhere to be seen.

"Right, Mr Lyle," Sanders said briskly. "Let's go. Yes. Lal is coming with us, but not on the mission." He made sure Lal heard the last part quite clearly.

Pross glanced at the Nepalese. No expression gave away what Lal might be thinking. The eyes were neutral.

"Fine," Pross said, and followed Sanders, who was already moving towards the entrance.

Lal quietly brought up the rear.

The helicopter's rotors were whipping softly at idle, keeping alive the small dust storm it had generated during its descent. Pross recognised it as the same one that had taken him to the site the last time he had come to Kathmandu: a white MBB BK117. The same European pilot was in command. Pross wondered what he'd been doing during the intervening time.

It was all academic, he thought ruefully. No one would ever tell him.

The pilot looked at his approaching passengers with a singular lack of interest, then nodded slightly at Pross. Recognition. Well, at least that was something.

"Come on, Mr Lyle!" Sanders urged impatiently. "In you get."

Deliberately, he paused to turn round and look up at the building. From an upper-storey window, Wendy Jones was looking down at him. She smiled and gave a brief wave. He waved back at her.

"Lyle!" Sanders said crossly.

Pross turned to him. "It's too early in the morning," he said mildly, and climbed into the twin-engined ten-seater aircraft, ignoring Sanders' glare.

Pross took one of the rear seats. Lal entered, and sat next to him. Sanders sat up front with the pilot. Pross was not sorry.

Then the BK 117 was lifting swiftly to head north-east. The site, Pross remembered, was somewhere in the Lapchi Kang range. At least, that was what Logan had told him the last time. Was it a permanent post, then? Something that was being turned into an advance base, just in case?

He wouldn't be particularly surprised to find that to be indeed so. The borders with Tibet were probably some of the most sensitive in the world. His mind went back to what Lal had told him about the pair of Yak-38 Forgers the Tibetans had supposedly seen.

Land-based Forgers were not such a surprise either, if looked at from a tactical point of view. The Harrier had been developed in both land- and sea-based versions. Inevitably, the Russians would do the same. Having first created the aircraft for use on small-deck carriers of the *Kiev* class, a land-based version was sure to follow in time. There were bound to be all sorts of places in the Union where it would make sense not to try and build airfields, yet still give good deployment capabilities to such aircraft. High mountain passes and plateaux, for example. And what if they were trying to pass a few on to their big Comrade in the south, as a sort of carrot to keep the sleeping giant happy? It would make sense.

But that doesn't help me, Pross thought.

Military organisations the world over were always using all sorts of exercises and missions to try out new equipment, if there wasn't a genuine declared war to go to. Hitler had blooded his pre-World War II air force in Spain, Sabres had decimated MiGs in Korea, the US had discovered the value of helicopters in Vietnam, the Israelis had learned how to dodge SAMs, the Russians had discovered just how potent the Hind really was in Afghanistan, and the Harriers had learned in the Falklands that VIFFing really worked.

And Fowler, Pross's mind said, had discovered that both the Hind and the Hellhound could be brought down.

And now, there were Yaks.

Pross cast his mind back to his service days, recalling what he'd been told about that particular VTOL aircraft. Unlike the Harrier, the Forger was decidedly VTOL. No short take-off and landing capability. The Harrier had many permutations at its disposal, including remarkable agility. Forger couldn't VIFF.

The Forger had three engines, two of which were mounted vertically, for take-off and landing. Failure of any of the three, and it was time to leave. Most vulnerable time: during take-off and landing, when the aircraft had to be manoeuvred absolutely steadily in the vertical plane. Transition took a dangerously long $1\frac{1}{2}$ minutes. A sitting duck. The Forger had another liability. During take-off and landing, it would leave a black plume of efflux that could be seen from nearly 20 miles.

Vectoring in forward flight, the Harrier's VIFF, which enabled it to dart sideways, upwards, cut into a turning circle and do things that aerodynamically it wasn't supposed to, would chew such a target up for breakfast, but would the Hammerhead?

Pross decided that if the Yak-38s were indeed up on the plateau, his best bet would be to take them either at transition or on the ground. According to that briefing years ago, they had limited radar, and a maximum infrared missile range of 15 kilometres. But that was then. Had the specifications changed all that much, despite the conversion to land-based operations?

He stared out at the awesome belt of mountains that virtually enclosed the Kathmandu valley and saw not Himalayan splendour, but a cold and lonely death against one of the gleaming and indifferent faces of these ice-sheathed titans.

Lal, misreading the expression on his face, said, "It will take many journeys before you become accustomed."

The helicopter had been streaking low over the ground. Suddenly, the terrain dropped away and a gaping chasm, that seemed to go on for miles, appeared in its place. The drop was several thousands of feet.

Pross said, "The first time I came, I found it hard to accept that although I was already many thousands of feet up in the air, it was quite normal to have the tops of the mountains, and even *houses*, more thousands of feet above my head."

"Nepal is always full of surprises."

Not to mention Tibet, Pross didn't say.

The little convoy had driven past Tachukha during the night and were about twenty miles out of Xigaze when Schuler called a halt.

It was, Logan judged, as her lorry came to a jerking halt and she wearily opened her eyes to the cold morning, somewhere between seven and eight o'clock: closer to seven, perhaps. She was feeling a desperate need.

The soldiers were already thankfully dismounting, relief on their faces. They had desperate needs, too.

She stayed where she was, not wanting to provoke any hostile actions towards her. There was the sound of clanking as things were hauled off all the vehicles. The lorry clanged and shook. Then she smelled petrol and realised what was going on.

Schuler appeared. "You may climb down. Stretch your legs . . ."

"I need to go to the toilet."

"I expected that, which is why I stopped at this spot to refuel." He smiled, somewhat grimly, she thought. "I think you will find it appropriate."

She climbed stiffly out. He did not help her, but instead, moved a few paces back. He tried not to wrinkle his nose.

"I know I smell," she told him coldly. "Perhaps if you had allowed me more washing facilities —"

"Yes, yes, Miss Stewart. I have heard all your complaints before."

"It didn't do any bloody good though, did it?"

Two soldiers paused in the act of refuelling the lorry to give her curious, but strangely lifeless glances. Their rifles were slung across their backs. Schuler had not brought his own rifle, but the pistol was at his belt. His face did not even show the beginnings of a stubble.

"You had a better night of it, I can see."

"I have already shaved," Schuler said emotionlessly.

"I'm sure you have."

Logan stared about her. The convoy had stopped some distance away from the road, which she could not see. They were in a high wide valley, covered by stunted grass no more than perhaps ten millimetres high. It felt crisp underfoot. The valley stretched into the distance, to be blocked by dark rounded hills, beyond which could be seen the more sharply defined contours of taller land masses. Beyond those, Logan thought she could see snow-capped mountains, but was not sure. They could not be the Himalayas, she thought, the natural barrier between Tibet and Nepal. Not yet. But if she were looking south, that's where they would be. The sky was a rich blue, with a single tuft of brilliant white cloud suspended within it. A light wind flapped at the canvas of the trucks.

"So where's this place I'm to use?" she asked Schuler.

"On the other side of the trucks. Come."

Logan followed, and saw, about 150 yards away, a structure that looked like a tiny house with a pointed hat. It looked much the worse for wear. Even so, Logan was reluctant to do anything which she felt might desecrate it.

"I can't go in there," she said. "It's a shrine."

"Not any more," Schuler said. "Not for a long time. If you are worried about desecrating it, you are too late. It was done during the Red Guards' over-zealous Cultural Revolution. These scenes of destruction are commonplace. The Tibetans will never touch it again. To them, it has been soiled forever. Some are being rebuilt. Others, like this one, will be left to the elements. You will not be the first to use it."

Logan resisted wrinkling her own nose, and began walking towards the ruined shrine. As she took her first steps, she heard the snap of a holster flap being undone. It sounded unnaturally loud. She paused, turned slowly to look.

223

Schuler had drawn his pistol. Logan recognised it for what it was: a big Stechkin APS 9mm automatic. Those things carried a full load of twenty rounds. No point running. He wouldn't miss. Imagine, she thought. Not drowned in some beautiful blue lake, but being shot down here on this wild and desolate plateau. In the unlikely event of his missing her, there were still the soldiers.

She glanced slowly round before turning again to look at Schuler. All the soldiers had paused, all looking at her with the same lifeless eyes before continuing with their work. Their rifles remained slung on their backs, but she knew they would be quick to use them if need be.

The green eyes stared unwaveringly at Schuler. "I see," she said quietly, and turned once more to continue walking towards the shrine. Behind her, she heard Schuler's measured steps. She did not quicken her pace. No point giving him the satisfaction.

As she walked, she fought to control her breathing, not because of the elevation of the plateau — her weeks in Tibet had fully acclimatised her — but because she expected at any moment to feel the slam of the first of the heavy bullets striking home.

It was the longest 150 yards she could remember. She made it to the shrine, and entered the vandalised structure. Schuler remained outside.

Logan found that most of the little building was open to the elements, but there was enough of it left standing to afford her some privacy.

"Can you hear me?" came Schuler's voice suddenly.

"Yes," she answered uncertainly, wondering what was coming next. What sort of depraved game was he playing?

"Stay where you are and listen." And into Logan's astonished silence, he continued, "You are to be picked up tomorrow. We are about 300 kilometres from the border and must make the rendezvous point in time. That is why I have been pressing on without stopping. When we resume our journey, there will be further stops until we arrive at the rendezvous. You will be fed on the journey. The point is in the ruins of a village. It is very small. A few houses only ... what is left of them. You will remain there until the helicopter arrives."

Logan felt her spirits soar. *Schuler!* Schuler was Fowler's man!

In that case, what had he been doing in Wales? What had been his rôle? There were so many questions that needed answers.

"Who are ..." she began.

"Do not waste time with questions!" he cut in sharply. "My back is to the soldiers and they believe I'm guarding you. We are not conversing. I shall talk and you will listen! In the ruins, I shall leave you a weapon and ammunition, and a little food. I shall also leave you a homing beacon. It must be kept transmitting at all times, or Pross will be unable to find you quickly."

Pross! He knew about Pross!

He seemed to be smiling when he continued, "Yes. I know him. I can sense your surprise. I accompanied him to Nepal once before. He knew me as Hansen. I recognised him, of course, at that hotel. I did not know who you were, and assumed you were his wife, but I could not quite understand why he had chosen to bring his wife with him. As the operation was working in autonomous sections to ensure total security, I did not at first recognise you on the mountain. Then you put 'Freckles' on the card." Again the hint of a smile in the voice.

Logan felt her thoughts tumble about, seeking clues to all that had transpired over the past months. The message had been directed at Schuler, who had known she was the ultimate recipient; which could only mean he had somehow managed to contact Fowler. As for the card, it had been an elaborate way of getting her to haul Pross in. She was not sure whether to be angry at the way she had been used to get him, or to be pleased that he was coming for her. What other things, she now wondered, had Fowler kept her ignorant of?

"The word 'Freckles'," Schuler was saying, "made me realise who you were. You will remember, I asked you why you had signed yourself that way. Your answer, of course, explained it all. The woman with Pross had a very distinctive pattern of freckles. No two women, given the circumstances of our two meetings, could have so similar a pattern. It was far too much for coincidence."

Logan smiled ruefully. She usually hid the freckles with carefully applied make-up, if the disguise called for it. It all went to show how the slightest miscalculation could eventually prove fatal. What if Schuler had *not* been Fowler's man? She dared not think about the consequences.

"I should be more careful in the future," Schuler advised.

"I usually am."

"Ah well. We all have our off moments; but in our line of business, they should be few and far between. You were responsible, I take it, for the people by that lake?"

225

"Yes."

"Very good work." He sounded impressed. "Good work also, with the homer I put on your car. I was well taken. And now, we are conversing too much. Are you finished?"

"Yes."

"Very well. One last matter. The ruins are about 20 kilometres from a Soviet detachment . . ."

"*What!*"

"Please do not interrupt! It is necessary to put you there. The Soviets are in a wide valley, while the ruins are in another, smaller one. When I leave you, I shall pretend to shoot you. The soldiers will believe I have executed you. Do not worry. I shall shoot at the walls. You will be quite safe."

Safe, Logan thought drily. With a full detachment of Russians, certainly mobile, a mere 12 or so miles away. No distance at all in a helicopter.

"If you will please come out now, and walk ahead of me."

Logan came out of the ruins, and began the short trek back to the vehicles. Schuler followed, his Stechkin trained upon her back.

The soldiers, refuelling completed, watched their return with the same apparently lifeless expressions.

Then everyone climbed aboard their respective transports and the convoy continued on its way.

The BK117 seemed to be clawing its way up the mountain and although Pross had made the trip before, he still could not rid himself of the anxiety that the aircraft would run out of breath before it reached its destination.

Pross stared down at the slope beneath him which appeared to be much too close, and saw the familiar path that seemed an impossibility upon that steeply climbing terrain. But this was Nepal, where paths could apparently cling to virtually perpendicular surfaces.

Then, almost with a heave of relief, the helicopter had arrived at the top. As it came in for the landing, Pross looked out at the mini-fortress he remembered. 14,000 feet above sea level, and looking no bigger than a football pitch, it was perched upon its eyrie in lonely splendour. On all sides, the ground appeared to plunge into space. On foot, it could only be approached by a path that began 10,000 feet below, to cross it and descend equally precariously on the opposite side. Any other route would terminate almost immediately in a very rapid descent, with no soft landing at the bottom.

The same curving rampart rose from the northern perimeter, though to Pross it appeared that man-made fortifications had now added to its sturdiness. The rampart also continued around the camp, where previously, as Pross remembered it, this had only been partially so. The mottled fawn and white tents were still there, as were the air-defence Blowpipe quad launchers; but they had been augmented by two Rapier units. The air-defence systems stood at each quarter of the camp.

The BK117 went into the hover prior to its descent, and Pross continued to refresh his memory. There were still six tents of different sizes and the largest, the ops tent, still had its array of antennae and dish aerials outside, to give a 360-degree scan. The Gurkhas in combat gear were still there, as were three taller Europeans. They were not the same people, Pross knew, but despite the slight modifications, it was as if he had never been away.

People were standing around, watching the helicopter land. Pross saw no one he recognised; but even the small sheets of ice, scattered in speckled abandon on brown grass made brittle by the unfiltered sun, were still there as if the seasons had never changed. He remembered being once told that the climatic systems of the Himalayas were so regular you could almost set your watch by them. Winds came at the same time each day. Hailstorms, deluges, snowfalls, almost right on time each year. Almost – but not always. Making that mistake could cost your life. The man who told him had also been playing a double game and had made his own mistakes, for which he had eventually paid very dearly.

The helicopter settled down, and they all climbed out, save for the pilot who was already lifting it off the ground as they ducked and walked away from its downwash.

As the BK117 rose, Pross turned to look at the one thing that claimed his total attention. The Hammerhead, in its quadruple main camouflage colours of pale blue, white, black, and brown, looked more like a marauding shark than ever. The paintwork had been most skilfully done so that all the colours appeared to begin in their primary state, before merging into each other with no defined crossover, and no set pattern. It was impossible to tell where one began or ended. From certain angles, the aircraft looked as if it possessed a single colour which was hard to define. From others, the various ingredients of its camouflage came into play, breaking up the outline, making it difficult to acquire visually. Against certain backgrounds, Pross thought, it would be rendered almost invisible.

Pross walked slowly round the helicopter, touching here, stroking it there, oblivious of all else that was going on about him. Despite the height, he did not feel particularly uncomfortable, though, mindful of the warnings about oxygen starvation he had been given on his previous visit, he initially took everything slowly.

The Hammerhead was fully tooled up for action. On the left stub wing, the outer weapons station carried a quad load of Stinger missiles for air-to-air. On the inner station were eight SURA 81mm rockets in twin rows of four, instead of the standard configuration of twelve in triple rows. Pross assumed the reason was to enable stores to be hung from the outer station. He liked the arrangement. It gave him a choice of weapons. On most helicopters, once the full complement of rockets was loaded, that was usually your lot.

He moved round the aircraft to check the other stub wing. Here, on the outer station was a quad load of Hellfire air-to-ground anti-tank missiles. They would do equally well against any other heat-emitting targets, he thought grimly; such as Yak-38s caught on the deck.

The inner station carried another twin row of eight SURAs, but that was not all. Fitted snugly to the flat belly, in their container, were four lightweight anti-radiation missiles to take out the radar guidance systems of any air-defence units. Finally, he came round to the nose and the multi-barrel monster cannon: fully loaded this time, he hoped.

"Satisfied?"

He turned at the sound of the familiar voice. Mabel.

"I wondered if you'd find your way out here," Pross said to her, pleased to see a familiar, friendly face. In combat warms, with no mark of rank, it again seemed to Pross as if she'd never left. "If it hadn't been for the fact that I saw you in Wales, I'd think you've been here since last year."

"Rude as ever, I see, young man," Mabel said in her own peculiar brand of welcome. "Well? Are you satisfied?"

"You've done me proud, Mabel," he said, turning to look at the Hammerhead. "The question is . . . will it all work?"

The eyes peered at him from behind the imperious glasses. "Of course it will work! If you do your job properly."

Pross smiled. "Mabel, I'm growing attached to you."

"Heaven forbid!" But she seemed pleased. "And how was your flight over? Had fun with Sanders, did you?"

"It shows, does it?"

"He went into the ops tent with a face like thunder. The rest was not so hard to work out."

Pross sighed. "It's not my place to tell Fowler how to pick his staff, but from where I'm standing, the less I see of Sanders, the more I'd like it."

"He is a pompous idiot, I'll grant you," Mabel said. "But he's good at what he has to do."

"I wish I could believe you."

"You can. I see you've brought Lal with you," she went on. "Do you know what happened to him?"

Pross nodded. "He came to my room last night. I know the whole story."

"Even about the Forgers?"

Again, Pross nodded.

"We weren't too happy about that news," Mabel said, "but . . ."

"Perhaps those Tibetans were mistaken. Perhaps they were confusing different types of helicopters."

Mabel looked slightly anxious. "I wish that were the case, but I'm afraid we already have quite solid confirmation from another, most professional source."

"Hansen," Pross said.

Mabel peered at him. "You *know*? But how?"

"Lal. He saw him with Logan, remembered him from the last time — although Hansen in uniform must have looked quite different."

Mabel said, "What a remarkable man Lal is. To have made that journey . . ." She let her words die, and shook her head slowly as she thought of what Lal had done.

"He wants to go back. He wants to come with me, and then make his own way on the return journey."

"Not a chance, young man."

"That's what Sanders said . . . or words to that effect."

"For once, I agree with him. Not only must nothing take priority over getting Logan back, we cannot risk Lal being taken."

"I would not like to see him taken either."

"He's an extra you can't afford. Further, if he is taken, he could be made to say things he'd deeply regret."

"Not Lal. He'd die first."

"They may not allow him that privilege until they were finished

229

with him. Hansen's present identity cannot be compromised. You realise that, I hope."

"Yes. I do. Someone will have to tell him, then. Sanders went about it this morning with as much diplomacy as a rhino in a rage."

"Leave it to me. I'll sort it out. Now how do you feel? Any problems with the height? There's oxygen in the medical tent."

"None at all. No mountain sickness."

"Good. In which case, I suppose you'd like to get kitted up and try the Hammerhead out."

Pross grinned at her. "I thought you'd never ask."

He held the Hammerhead steady at 17,000 feet and a mile out from the site. There was no cloud in his immediate vicinity and a magnificent world was spread out around and beneath him. Far below, the land was still dark where the morning sun had not yet reached it; but on the high peaks and gleaming slopes, the snowy flanks seemed to blaze with an extra brilliance. He could almost believe he could feel their reflected heat. He knew it was because it was warm and comfortable in the machine.

He had kitted up fully in the tent that had been pitched for him, and wore the full helmet, with oxygen. He had the visor down, a practice from his service days. All missions, then, had been flown thus. More than ever, he thought, working for Fowler made it an imperative.

He moved the Hammerhead sideways and watched amusedly as the digital altimeter flicked off a few thousand feet of height above the ground, as the land below rose steeply. Height above mean sea level was still at 17,000. The specially modified Lynx he'd flown in the same environment had a ceiling of 26,000 feet, higher than any other working chopper, except perhaps for a stripped-down record-breaker, but Mabel had told him the Hammerhead would go up to 27,000, a full 10,000 feet above his present height. Which would still leave plenty of ground to slam into if he made a mistake.

He did not intend to go that high. It was nice to know the capability was there, but the helicopter's environment was low down on the deck. With ground level seemingly growing in the sky, however, low down on the deck could mean anywhere from zero feet to the full 27,000, depending on where your combat dragged you.

He flew about for a while, getting to know the aircraft once more. It felt as finely balanced as when he'd last flown it, the weapon load seemingly having no effect on handling. It was a finely-tuned ship that seemed only too pleased to do his bidding. Sitting in the rear cockpit, relaxed in his reclined seat, he felt as if the Hammerhead had become part of him; or, more appropriately, as if he had become part of it. He was pleased to note that the directional thrusters he'd had on the Lynx had been incorporated into the Hammerhead, with the familiar yellow buttons appearing on both sidesticks. Everything required for combat was hands-on-stick, as Rees had said in Wales.

He had enquired about Rees, but had been told that Rees had left the site and would not be returning. Pross had been disappointed, having looked forward to seeing the mournful-voiced scourge again. It would have been an antidote to Sanders.

But there was serious work to be done across the gleaming, razor-backed frontier. No time to worry about Sanders. Logan was out there waiting, depending on him, and on the Hammerhead.

Pross decided to test the gun and found himself a high, glaciated valley. Dwellings tended to exist in the most unexpected places in the Nepalese mountains, but he made sure there were none within twenty miles of where he was. He selected an ice-tower that grew from the bare, lifeless valley and first flew past it. The vibration of his passage left it intact. He had flown at fifty feet above the valley floor, which was itself 13,000 feet above sea level. He turned and, from a mile away, went into the attack. From half a mile and closing, he fired the gun; a short, one-second squeeze. Although he had been expecting it, the effect of the gun still took him by surprise.

A powerful, but well-dampened tremor pulsed through the aircraft, through Pross's body, seeming to enfold him in its embrace. The gun gave a sharp, multiple belch that blended into a roar that could be heard even through the headphones. Tracers streaked towards the 100-foot crystalline pinnacle and the massive shells tore into it, sending a million glistening shards explosively hurtling in all directions, in a continually expanding white sunburst.

The sound of the gun, the soft snarl of the Hammerhead, echoed down the still valley and the ramparts of the abode of snow.

Then he pulled the Hammerhead into a tight turn and headed back towards the site. He went in low, hugging the darkness of the ground and gradually losing height. When he reached the mountain upon which the camp was perched, he was at 12,000 feet, 4,000 below the top. He gently hauled on collective and went straight up. A minute later, he popped up above the perimeter, giving a couple of soldiers a severe fright.

231

He smiled grimly. If he could do it, others could; but perhaps they had strung listening devices down the sides of the mountain.

He brought the Hammerhead down to a featherlight touchdown. He'd remembered the wheels too, and felt quite satisfied with his performance.

Mabel came to greet him as he left the aircraft. "Pleased?"

"Very," he said as he removed his helmet. "I tested the gun."

"My word not good enough?"

"Your word's always good, Mabel, but there's nothing like being sure, is there?"

"And?"

"One less ice tower. Great gun."

"Vandal," she said good-naturedly.

"You're vulnerable to a pop-up attack," he said, deflecting her.

"No we're not. We saw you all the way. Impressive climb."

"Alright, Mabel. Don't look so smug."

"Who's smug?" she queried and pulled out the inevitable, unsmoked cigar. She gave it a cautionary sniff.

Pross stared at it. "For a moment, I thought you'd left that weed at home."

"That," she said seriously, "would have been a very bad omen indeed."

FOURTEEN

The dawn had come with a cold presence and a clear sky and, even at this height, there had been no wind. Now, as he looked at the distant peaks, range upon range of them, the morning sun painted some of them a golden yellow. Beneath the camp, the valleys were still dark, hidden, secret worlds awaiting their turn for the light of day. The mountain winds had still not come: a good thing.

Despite the bright sun, the air was very cold; but fully kitted up, Pross felt warm. About him, the camp was alive with movement and noises as people went about their duties. There was the clink of metal as someone checked a rifle.

Snakka-snakka-snakka-snakka, the conscientious soldier went as the mechanism slammed backwards and forwards. The noise seemed wrong, somehow. Despite the purpose of the camp, it intruded.

The world, he thought, must have been like this on its peaceful days, before man came. He tried to close his mind to the noises about him and pretend he was all alone on this mountain top, but could not. He gave up the unequal struggle.

He had spent the previous day checking out everything about the Hammerhead and going over in his mind, several times, the information he'd been given. Most of his briefing had been done by Mabel. Sanders had kept well out of it, for which he was grateful. Then he'd had a peaceful night in his tent, cosily snug in the down sleeping-bag he'd been given. He had slept well.

But the worries he'd forced out of his mind had returned, not to taunt him, but to remind him of their presence.

The Russian detachment was encamped in a wide valley, not

dissimilar to the one he'd attacked the last time he was here; but there were differences. And what differences!

True, there were no Hellhounds to cope with; but there were Hinds, radars, SAMs, troops, and a nasty piece of work called a ZSU-23-4 quad self-propelled anti-aircraft gun. Four bloody barrels, each firing between 800 and 1000 rounds per minute. The wretched thing had its own target acquisition system too, and was lethal at up to 2200 yards. The ZSU was an old system, but it was still very effective, particularly in high terrain against aircraft with limited ceiling; like helicopters. Perhaps they were trying to sell ZSUs to China.

But this was the Hammerhead. It wasn't just any old chopper.

There were still those bloody Yak-38s, though.

Logan was meant to be waiting in some ruins about 16 miles from the detachment. She would have a homing beacon whose frequency was tuned to a special receiver in the Hammerhead, and a NAV display on the MFD would lead him right to her. Great stuff, in theory, but what if the transmission were intercepted? It was just possible that someone at the encampment might take it into his head to do a frequency hop, and bingo. All it took was a bored operator trying to amuse himself. People had been caught out before, by all sorts of routine things happening at the wrong moment.

He'd raised the question, only to be told by an irritable Sanders that the frequency was secure. He hadn't retorted that something was secure only until it was broken. Sanders might not have appreciated the point, and Pross had no desire to go out there thinking about Sanders' mental processes.

A special program had been prepared for the central computer and the cassette was already inserted. All the NAV and TACNAV updates were on it, with a full menu for him to select as needed. The positions of all the known threats were supposed to be on it; but what about the unknown ones? The aircraft could be anywhere, and the radars could have been shifted since the last batch of information had come in. He had asked for the timings of the intreps. The latest was a week old.

A bloody week. More than enough time to shift the whole shooting-match elsewhere. Hadn't they heard of INTSATs? Perhaps Fowler wanted this to remain so tightly wrapped up, he had no intention of sharing the information; which was what would have happened if he'd brought other agencies into the intelligence-gathering process.

Whatever the reasons, it added a degree of uncertainty, and left several blindspots. Pross decided he'd have to go by instinct, and use the Hammerhead according to his own on-the-spot updates.

As the sun rose higher, he turned left and westwards where, some five or so miles away, its rays began to light up the vast cirque whose rim of peaks averaged 16,000–17,000 feet, and whose depths plunged for 9,000 feet over a lateral distance of less than two miles in places. At the far bottom ran a mighty river, fed by a multitude of tributaries. On part of that rim was the Tibetan border, where it dug deep into Nepal. He would not be crossing there.

The cirque held a special significance. This was the arena in which he had fought and defeated the Hellhound; and this same arena was now the battleground for another combat. Somewhere down there, the all-important flight recorders lay. After months of searching, neither side had found them. Perhaps the river held the secrets.

"Nice day for it."

Pross turned. Mabel was looking at him quizzically, cigar in hand. She took a post-breakfast sniff of it.

"Are you alright?" she asked.

"I'm fine."

She looked out at the mountains. "This is so beautiful. It seems a sacrilege to disturb it."

"It *is* a sacrilege," Pross said.

"I suppose we could pack it all in, and leave the mountains to their peace."

"If you really meant that, you wouldn't be here."

"No. And you would not leave Logan out there."

"No," Pross said.

"Then it's hardly a matter of choice." Mabel took another sniff, rolling the cigar back and forth between thumb and fingers slowly. "You won't forget, will you?" she added.

He knew what she was getting at. On the left console in the pilot's cockpit was what she called the panic button; a red switch that first had to be uncaged before activating. He was to press that if he got into real trouble ... which meant immediate danger of being shot down. It would set off a beacon to mark his position, and rescue would be on its way.

Assuming it would not already be too late ...

The next item was that he should not engage the Russian detachment unless forced to. That was a joke: they'd try to tear him out of the sky the moment they knew of his presence.

"Just to keep you happy, Mabel," he said, "I'll try to follow your instructions."

She looked at him warily. "You're agreeing far too easily."

"Now who's not trusting whose word?"

She said nothing for a while, and he began his final walk-round of the Hammerhead. The gun had been replenished and all weapons systems checked. If they didn't work now, they never would.

Mabel followed him, trailing behind as if reluctant to let him go. The various people employed in caring for the aircraft had moved away, leaving just Pross and Mabel to carry out the last inspection.

They had done a complete circuit of the helicopter and had stopped by the pilot's door before she said, "Be careful, David."

He smiled at her. "Why, Mabel, if I didn't know better, I'd say you're going soft on me."

"Get out of here, young man. And if you don't bring her back, you can stay over there."

He pulled the cigar out of her shocked fingers, sniffed at it before handing it back.

"That's more like the Mabel I know," he said.

She looked down at the cigar, looked back at him. "Nobody's *ever* sniffed my cigar before."

"Nobody would dare," he said. "I'm giving myself a slice of good luck." He opened the cockpit canopy, took his helmet from the seat, put it on, then climbed in. "See you soon." He shut the canopy and began connecting himself to the aircraft.

Mabel was still staring at him, as if from the shock of having her cigar sniffed by someone else, then she began to move out of range of the blades. Pross thought he saw a tiny smile on her face.

He turned on the master switch. The Hammerhead began to come alive about him.

Early morning on the Tibetan Plateau.

Logan decided that not only would she never feel clean again, she'd never be able to feel warm either. Despite the padding of the clothes she'd been given to wear, she felt as if she had slept in a freezer. Her bones ached from the constant jolting the truck had given her body, and the ever-present dust of the road seemed to have taken up permanent residence in her throat, in spite of the scarf she had worn across her face. As for her escort, they had spent most of the journey huddled together, talking to each other in quick hushed bursts, punctuated by the occasional uninterested glance in her direction.

It might have given her some light relief, she thought grimly, if they had bawled at her once or twice.

The relief came soon after when the convoy, which had long been travelling off the main route, pulled off the barely-defined track and onto another track that led to the deserted village. Logan was unaware of the reasons for the changes of direction until the convoy came to a halt. The soldiers stared at her, but remained seated.

She heard orders being given, the tramp of footsteps. From her position she could see the last truck, with a short length of track in the intervening space. Beyond the truck was the expanse of a small plain, with the dark masses of low mountains closing in on it. There was no snow on these slopes. The sun's light had not yet come to play upon them, and they looked forbidding in their sombre cloaks.

Schuler appeared at the back of her truck. None of the soldiers in the last truck had dismounted.

"Out you come, Miss Stewart," Schuler commanded.

Logan stared at the soldiers in her truck puzzledly. They looked right back at her, with no animation in their faces. They did not move.

"Come on, Miss Stewart. *Out!*"

Hesitantly, she raised herself off the floor of the truck where she had sat, bracing herself against the cab in an effort to ease the discomfort of the long journey. She moved to the back and climbed stiffly out. The soldiers did not move to help her; not even their legs were drawn out of the way.

When she was on the ground, Schuler raised an arm above his head briefly to describe a circle with a skywards-pointing finger. Almost immediately, the trucks and the BTR began to turn round with much revvings of their engines. When they were pointing the way they had come, they again halted.

Logan looked about her. About 100 yards away she saw the ruins of the village. Perhaps ten square-sided dun-coloured houses with flat roofs and built into each other on different levels, so that they looked like extensions of one building. Behind the tallest was a bare, ravaged mound out of which the gaping walls of another building seemed to grow. The entire village was sparsely overgrown with the yellowish scrub of the plain.

Schuler drew his pistol and began walking her towards the village.

237

In the vehicles, the soldiers remained where they were. Logan could feel every eye upon her back. A stiffish breeze came off the mountains to whip across the plateau.

When they had reached the village, Schuler directed her towards one of the houses and pushed her through a doorway which, like all the others, had long been left open to the elements. The musty smell of dry earth mixed with those of ancient habitation came to her. There were other smells too.

Schuler said, "We are out of sight here. I must not stay long. This is meant to be your execution. Behind that wall, you will find a weapon, ammunition, and some food, in case you must remain here longer than we hope. There is plenty of natural fuel." A thin smile. "I have left you matches."

"How far from the border?"

"Perhaps thirty kilometres in a straight line."

"As I can't fly, that's not much use, is it? Could I make it on foot?"

"If you were Tibetan, I would say yes. You would have to cross the mountains, and also avoid the patrols."

"What you really mean to say is that my chances are slim."

"Let us hope it will not be necessary. Here is the beacon."

It was no bigger than a man's palm, was circular and ribbed, and looked like an anti-personnel mine. From its centre protruded a small black cone about ten millimetres high. The body of the beacon was sprayed in camouflage patterns. It would be very difficult to detect visually, when placed on the ground. It had fitted snugly into one of Schuler's pockets.

"It looks like an AP mine," Logan said.

"Do you still not trust me? You believe perhaps this is the way I am really going to execute you?"

"I didn't say that."

"It looks like an AP because that is exactly what it is meant to do, to discourage the curious under certain circumstances. To activate it, pull out the cone. This also extends the aerial. Now, I must go."

He raised the pistol, and pointed it at her.

"Schuler —!"

The Stechkin roared twice. The noise echoed through the ruined buildings and onto the plain.

Logan felt the sting of the discharge and her ears seemed to ring. The heavy bullets had expended themselves into the wall a couple of feet from her head.

She stared at Schuler. He gave her another thin smile, then went out, making a great show of putting the pistol back into its holster. She knew he was doing it for the benefit of the soldiers who would be awaiting his return interestedly.

"Mad bastard," she breathed, happy to be alive. She almost felt like shooting him for what he had just done. "Bastard," she said again. She remained where she was, listening for the noise that would tell her the convoy was continuing its journey. She wondered what excuse he would give to Wu. Or had Wu intended that he should execute her, anyway?

Probably. She would not have trusted Wu for a second.

Schuler walked briskly up to the BTR.

The Chinese lieutenant who accompanied him in the vehicle asked, in good English, "What happened?"

"She tried to run away. Stupid woman. When she started demanding privacy to go to the toilet, I suspected she would try something like that." Schuler looked about him. "Although how far she thought she could get in a place like this is beyond me. Desperate people will try anything."

The lieutenant looked at him speculatively. "At least it saves us the walk into Nepal. However, the Comrade Colonel might not be pleased."

"Let me worry about the Comrade Colonel."

The lieutenant was not about to argue with an SSD major who in any case, was not subject to PRC army discipline. The major was in command, and the major had the responsibility. It was obvious the major had not liked the idea of going into Nepal again.

The lieutenant decided to do what junior ranks in any army did when confronted with confusing actions from a superior officer. Not being a political fanatic, he decided to leave it all to Schuler.

Schuler said, "Let's go." And entered the BTR without a backward glance at the ruined village.

Cold fish, these Germans, the lieutenant thought.

Logan heard the vehicles move off and felt immense relief. She then began to study her surroundings. She did not intend to move into the open until she heard the approach of the Hammerhead, and even then she would first make quite sure it was safe to do so.

Out of the wind, the temperature within the structure was appreciably higher, and she felt, if not exactly warm, certainly no longer

239

chilled. There were plenty of openings of course for the wind to moan through, but it was not strong enough to be a problem. At least, not yet. She hoped Pross would arrive before long. She did not relish the idea of spending the night in this desolate place.

Cautiously, she moved along the wall where Schuler's bullets had gone until she came to another room, again open to the elements. There, at the base of the wall, in a cluster of shrubbery, she saw the weapon with a good supply of ammunition — five 30-round magazines — and the food. The gun and magazines lay on the ground, while the food was in a grey-green field bag. She wondered how he'd managed to put them there. Not that it mattered now.

She squatted on her heels, and laid the beacon gently next to the bag.

"Important things first," she murmured, and picked up the gun with the same caution she had used to enter the room. No point in being reckless.

The weapon had been carefully wrapped in strips of rough blanket. She removed her mittens and began to unwrap it. The gun was in perfect condition and looked almost new. It was a cut-down version of the AK-74, with a heavy-gauge wire stock folded into the body. A full magazine was loaded into it, making a total ammunition stock of 180 rounds.

"Well, Schuler," she said. "At least you're not mean with the ammo. I hope I won't need them."

She checked the weapon thoroughly, felt it for balance. Weight, fully loaded, she judged to be just under $3\frac{1}{2}$ kilos. Length with butt retracted was about 18 inches and with the butt extended, perhaps just under $2\frac{1}{2}$ feet. She opted to keep the butt retracted. That placed the hand-grip at the end of the weapon, turning it almost, into a machine pistol. It would also be easier to manoeuvre on the run. Such metal parts as she would need to touch were not too cold against her flesh and would not affect her handling of it.

Next, she checked the food. They looked like cans of soup, and could be opened by pulling off the sealing ring. Oh well, she thought. She also saw Schuler's "natural fuel".

She could hardly complain. The soup was probably good stuff — there were no labels — and besides, she didn't intend to stay in this place forever. She tried not to think of what it would like if Pross did not make it. Perhaps a yak caravan would pass this way. But she strongly doubted it. Despite the scattered lumps of dried yak dung the place didn't look as if anyone but Schuler had been near it for ages; which was why he had chosen it in the first place.

By now, the sound of the engines had faded to a very thin background noise, indicating that the convoy had moved well away. Logan found an outside wall within the building complex and placed the beacon next to it, hidden in one of the ubiquitous tufts of shrubbery; then she pulled the cone upwards with finger and thumb. The dull green aerial extended to eighteen inches. There was a click and a soft bleep that came simultaneously. No further sounds came out of it. She assumed it was now activated and working properly.

She went back to where she had left the food. She had taken the gun with her, and would never be without it until she was eventually picked up. She collected a few pats of the yak dung and put some into a low pile, then lit it with one of the matches from the small box Schuler had left. Yak dung was a most efficient fuel and the Tibetans had been using it for centuries.

The pile began to burn well and gave off remarkable heat. Logan picked up one of the cans, shook it to make sure it really was soup. The heavy sloshing told her it was. She pulled off the sealing ring and saw it was chicken noodle. To her, it looked as good as a four-course meal in any decent restaurant.

She had built a rough structure from the fallen lumps of the crumbled walls, upon which she now set the can. Soon it was warm enough. Too hot, and she'd be unable to eat out of it.

The soup was delicious. She kept the empty can to use as a decanter for hotter soups. Then she killed the fire. There had been little smoke, but there was no point in taking chances.

She checked the rifle once more, then settled down to wait.

Pross had taken the Hammerhead low. His average height above sea level was now 5,000 feet, but above ground level it was sometimes only 30 feet when the terrain rose steeply: at others, a falling-away of the ground would make it 3,000. He continued north, threading his way along deep chasms, giving him the surreal impression that he was flying within the bowels of the earth. Above him, rising almost out of sight, were the massive, snow-capped peaks.

The Hammerhead undulated slightly in the dense air of the lower levels; but it flew sweetly and unfussed, its sleek form sliding menacingly across the landscape.

Glancing down, Pross saw he was passing over a row of houses on a steep incline. Strung together, they looked like the serrations

241

of a giant backbone as they lay along the spine of the ridge, while spreading from them were the inevitable ranks of terraces cut into the slopes, and looking for all the world like the massive scales of some primeval, armoured beast. Then it was gone, and he was banking the Hammerhead hard to the left, following the route cut by a large river now far beneath him.

A stiffish wind came off the sides of the mountains, but the Hammerhead was well able to cope.

On the NAV MFD, a computer-generated image of the landscape was on display, with his route clearly marked out in glowing red. A pulse was travelling along it, indicating the aircraft's current position. He could change the scale either to give him an overall view which would cover the whole area up to Logan's expected position, or bring it right up his immediate vicinity. The display would then be constantly changing to keep up with the aircraft's passage along its own track. He had selected an intermediate display. He liked to see where he was going.

Logan's beacon would show up when he got within range and was high enough to pick it up. He could then couple the imager which in daylight would look almost like a TV picture. On either MFD, he could superimpose as much information as he could handle.

The ground ahead had begun to rise steeply into a high pass. He gave the collective a gentle back-pressure. The stick, adjusted to his choice of sensitivity, responded with the right amount of movement, and the Hammerhead rose swiftly as if on self-propelled blades. Less than three minutes later it was at 15,000 feet, with the ground now no more than fifty feet beneath its sleek belly. Then it was time to descend once more.

In an effort to avoid confrontation, Pross's planned route had first taken him eastwards from the site towards the Rolwaling range, before curving round in a wide sweep that took him some miles west of Namche as he eventually turned north. The landscape was beginning to change as he approached the Tibetan border. A barren face had come to it. Below the snow line, the land was bare and the overall impression was of great rock faces of brown, ochre and black, some studded with tenacious clumps of shrubbery lower down.

Pross took the Hammerhead along a winding gorge. Briefly to his right a group of buildings flashed past, seemingly planted into a shallow, dusty-looking bowl in the side of a steep slope. An image remained in his mind of several tracks straggling away from it like so many spindly tendrils.

And again the land was rising. The Hammerhead rose with it, keeping a distance of 50 feet between itself and the terrain. Another phenomenon greeted Pross's eyes. Spouting between the masses of black rock faces were row upon row of ice towers, some of which soared above the fleeting aircraft, reminding him again of a prehistoric animal – this time of the dorsal sails of a stegosaurus.

Then, almost without realising it, he was in Tibet. He should be picking up Logan's beacon soon.

He checked all his systems, both defensive and offensive, to ensure he was ready for what the immediate future might bring.

The immediate future was planning a surprise.

The Hind gunship, carrying a full load of weapons and six assault troopers, lifted off the barren plateau that was its base, on a routine sweep over the surrounding area. The ground was carpeted with a mixture of smallish stones and sand, and the rotor downwash raised a whirling cloud of fine morainic debris about the aircraft, to be eventually dispersed by the strong breeze that blew down the length of the high valley.

The Hind climbed above the easternmost of the two ridges that stood at an average height of 2,000 feet on either side of the dusty plain, which was itself 15,000 feet above sea level. The Hind, in standard configuration, had a ceiling of just under the elevation of the plateau; but the aircraft belonging to the detachment were powerful Hind E/Fs whose limit of climb had, with continuing development, been taken close to 19,000 feet. It meant, however, that they were operating on the boundaries of their flight envelope, which could make them vulnerable to an adversary choosing to sucker them into a high combat.

The full rotary complement of the detachment was six Hinds and two Mil Mi-28 Havocs, whose own ceilings had been raised to 20,000 feet: while not as fast as their bigger sister ships, they were infinitely more nimble, and carried the same powerful armaments. Three of the Hinds had been virtually gutted and utilised as load carriers. The remainder had been used to carry the troopers to the detachment base.

On the ridges, whose sides fell steeply to the plateau and whose tops were made up of craggy outcrops and buttresses, there were areas of level ground upon which radar-guided SAMs had been positioned. Two were on each ridge, guarding each end of the encampment in pairs. Every SAM was manned by two troopers whose pale brown tents, like those on the plateau below them, blended perfectly into the arid landscape. The tents were pitched close to the weapons.

On the plateau itself, at the northern end of the encampment and close to the base of the western ridge, was the cluster of HQ, mess, and two-man tents. Further along the ridge and moving southwards, was the huge shelter of the fuel dump. Beyond that, lined up in a neat row, were the remaining five Hinds and two Havocs. A spares tent was pitched some distance from them to avoid rotor wash.

Across the plain, and midway along the base of the eastern ridge, was the tracked ZSU whose turret and quad barrels were being given a check-out. The turret swung through 360 degrees, while the barrels elevated up to plus 80 degrees and went down to minus 7 while swivelling. It could shift its own lethal patch of sky.

North of the ZSU, about 500 metres away, were the two Yak-38s, standing in quiet repose, their canopies shut. There was a tent a short distance from them. On the stony floor of the plateau, wheeled vehicles churned up puffs of dust as they moved to and fro across it

On the western ridge, Fyodor Nikoviev watched the Hind recede in the distance with a sour expression.

"At least they get something to do," he said to his companion "All we do is sit by these things, in the wind. It never stops blowing here."

"Stop complaining. It's not so bad today. We haven't had a really strong wind for a few days. In any case, we're being relieved thi afternoon."

"Not before time. I'm fed up with this plateau. If I don't get to woman soon, I'll fall in love with the first yak I see."

"Look at it this way . . . this is better than being in Afghanistar No one shoots at you here."

"That's about all this hellhole has to recommend it."

In the ruined village, Logan thought she heard a sound above th moaning of the wind. Senses immediately alert, she listened ur moving, for a full minute, but could detect nothing. She decide that her anticipation was such she was pre-empting in her mind th sound of Pross's arrival. Smiling ruefully at her eagerness, she con tinued to wait, but did not relax fully.

*

the front cockpit of the Hind, the gunner heard a screech on his
eadphones.

"What hell was that?" the pilot asked from the rear seat. "What
e you doing, Storozhev?"

"That wasn't me," the gunner said, aggrieved. "I was chang-
g frequencies when this came through. Sounds like a random
m."

"Our Chinese friends chatting to each other and not wanting us
 know?"

"I am not sure, Comrade. It's just noise, but enough to hide the
al signal."

"From the camp, perhaps?"

"I'm trying to trace it, but it keeps hopping frequencies —"

"Forget the frequencies. Try a location. Let's see what our little
omrades are up to."

"If I may suggest, Comrade Captain, they may not take
ndly —"

"A little fun, Storozhev. Let's find out where that transmission's
ming from."

"I'm trying," the gunner said with some reluctance.

his time, she was sure. She had definitely heard engines. She
sisted the temptation to rush outside to wave as the sound gradu-
y rose in volume. It was still some distance away, but it was
finitely approaching.

"You beauty!" she said softly, thinking of the homing beacon.

She remained where she was as the sound grew increasingly
uder, until it dawned upon her that the noise was not reminiscent
 the Hammerhead. With a sense of foreboding, and cursing the
ck that had brought whatever it was out there, she checked to
ake sure the rifle was cocked and ready for instant action, then
gan a fast crawl along the ruined earthen floor to one of the
ping windows that looked out on the valley.

What she saw was a nightmare.

The bulbous, tandem cockpits were unmistakable; as were the
ooping stub wings with their full load of weapons; as was that
ing hump of the engines and rotor housing. The Hind hovered
me distance away, pointing nose-on, swaying a little, as if trying
 make up its mind.

"Oh my God!" Logan said slowly in horror.

She crept back to a wall that would keep her well hidden, sat

down on the floor to lean against it, and wondered what the h
she was going to do.

The convoy was a bare mile from the camp when Schuler saw
Hind go over.

The Chinese lieutenant said, "I know they're our guests, bu
still feel uneasy when I see these things in our airspace."

"If all goes well, the People's Republic will have some of
own," Schuler said. He was uneasy too, but for very differe
reasons.

He did not like the direction the Hind had taken, and co
only hope it had not picked up the homer's signal. As usual
the business, it was always the unforeseen little things t
brought all your plans down about your ears. Who could ha
guessed some Russian pilot would have taken it into his head
go on a routine flight? It was the first time for days that any
the Hinds had left the ground. It had not been expected. Everyo
had been taking it easy at the camp. If the beacon were fou
and, worse, the pick-up, the whole area would turn into a horne
nest.

And he would be compromised.

The one hope was that the Hammerhead would arrive in time
take out the Hind, before whoever was on board discovered th
was someone hiding in the ruins.

Perhaps I should have killed her, Schuler said in his mind.

"Are you sure this is the place, Storozhev?"

"Positive, Comrade."

"But there's nothing here except these ruins."

"This is the signal source." The gunner refrained from soundi
smug. It hadn't been a bad job of tracing.

"Alright. Let's see what they're hiding in there."

"Comrade ... if I may say something. We would not wan
diplomatic incident. Perhaps they're conducting a field exercise.
none of our business."

"We're not going to interfere. We're only checking to see wha
going on. After all, this is only a few kilometres from where we a
I think we should know, don't you?"

The gunner shut his eyes briefly in exasperation. They were b
Afghanistan veterans; but whereas the captain was still a helicop
warrior riding the skies, Storozhev was quite happy to have a qu

246

life, even in a desolate place like this. *Anywhere* was better than Afghanistan.

The pilot said, "I'll land, and send some of our passengers to investigate."

Thus overruled, the gunner said nothing. He knew it would have made no difference.

Logan had decided to risk another quick look, and saw the four soldiers moving away from the helicopter, to come towards the ruins.

"Oh *shit*," she said, at once angry and resigned to what would now inevitably happen. "*Shit!*" she repeated.

They did not approach in a tight bunch, but fanned out, to come from four directions, splitting attention.

Professionals: perhaps even veterans. It was not going to be easy, but it would have to be quick. She'd have to hope their presence was accidental, and that Pross was still on his way.

"Don't lose it, Logan," she told herself softly. "You can take them. You can!"

She decided to wait until they had entered the ruins proper. Better chance of scoring with every shot than in the open where they could split in all directions. None seemed to be carrying a radio. Perhaps they didn't know she was here, after all. Their approach was relaxed, not as if they expected hostile fire. Even so, she was certain they would move with practised swiftness at the first shot. There would be no second chances with these boys.

They were talking to each other, almost shouting. There was a faint air of humour in the voices.

What was going on?

Perhaps they would give the place only a cursory search and she wouldn't have to shoot them, after all. It was a forlorn hope.

The first of the soldiers had entered the nearest building, only one away from where Logan hid, pressed against a wall. He was talking loudly to his friends, almost laughing. She understood him.

"This is a nonsense," he was saying. "The Chinese are having a joke. There is nothing."

The *Chinese?*

Logan could make nothing of it. She waited, the rifle primed for instant action.

"Nothing here, either!" called another voice. "Let's have a quick look and go back. They can send —"

The voice died as the speaker entered the building where Logan

247

waited and his eyes widened with shock and utter confusion.

She had time to notice they were very blue and though his face was young, there was a hardness in them. A man who had seen combat and whose shock would not last for long, especially as the person facing him was armed.

She saw his assault rifle beginning to point towards her. She fired her own AK-74, a single shot that seemed to echo through the very world, so loud did it sound. The man was flung backwards through the doorway he had entered, his rifle falling from already lifeless hands as he went. She had shot to kill, having no illusions about what would be in store for her.

"Vladimir, you idiot!" came the first voice. "What do you think you're doing?"

The owner came running through, saw Logan, opened his mouth to shout while bringing his own weapon to bear. Her second shot rang through the ruins. Again, the bullet was fatal. Vladimir's comrade slammed against a crumbling wall to subside slowly to the ground. A trail of bright blood followed him down. He remained as he had collapsed, sitting with his head bowed, propped against the wall.

Then there was silence, save for the strangely gentle moan of the wind.

She knew what had happened. The other two would be infinitely more cautious. A jaunt had turned into something shockingly dangerous.

She waited. Had they noticed on the helicopter? Did they know two of their men had just died? She would have preferred it otherwise, but there was little point in going on about it. She had not asked them to come. They had blundered into a simple pick-up that should have gone smoothly. No chance of that now.

She saw movement. Outside. Out on the plain.

She risked a cautious look. One of the remaining soldiers was running back towards the helicopter. Well, that was it. Everything blown now.

Halfway to the machine, the soldier stopped and waved his arm in an urgent beckoning motion. Immediately, two more troopers leapt out, and the gunship began to rise.

Now it was going to be the real business: the classic Hind-and-assault-trooper combination to flush her out. Four enraged Comrades and the gunship to contend with. She would have preferred better odds.

*

248

Pross had the homer on his MFD, but the radar showed something else too, where it shouldn't be. He immediately brought on the attack MFD and zoomed in on the target. The Hind filled the display. There were also four heat sources among the ruins, moving fast.

Four? Which was Logan?

Another source. Five now. Logan?

Time to worry about that later. Get the Hind before they spot you.

The Hammerhead was low down on the deck; perhaps a mere ten feet above the rushing plain. He selected a Stinger, watched the weapons station confirm. A gentle haul on collective. Hammerhead leaping upwards. Lock-on. Fire. Range one mile, closing fast. Perhaps they're asleep.

Bingo.

The Stinger tore into the unsuspecting Hind and turned it into a violently-expanding ball of flame that seemed to shoot laterally across the plateau before curving downwards to slam into the ground, in an even greater blaze of vivid yellow that sent black plumes billowing upwards. The wind seized it, and whirled it even higher, spreading it thinly as it went.

"That ought to set the cat among the pigeons," Pross said into his mask, thinking about the Yak-38s.

But there were still those traces down there, one of which was Logan.

He hoped.

Logan saw the Hind explode and knew with soaring spirits what had happened. There was little need to hear the soft snarl of the approaching Hammerhead.

He had come! *He had come!*

But there were still the four remaining soldiers to sort out. Two of them, stunned by the sudden loss of their helicopter, were standing out in the open, disbelievingly. The other two were running pointlessly towards the wreck. Logan decided she would shoot at them only if threatened.

Then the Hammerhead was passing and they raised their rifles. Though she doubted whether they would have done much damage, she did not give them the chance. Two quick shots, aimed with the butt extended, dropped them like sawn logs.

Then she was running out of the ruins, to where Pross was

hovering in the Hammerhead, some distance from the wreckage of the Hind.

"Fyodor!" the soldier on the ridge called. He was listening to message on his headphones. His eyes grew round.

"What now?" irritably.

"Something's happening!"

"That's a nice change."

"We've . . . we've lost that helicopter!"

"*What?*"

"That's what they're saying down there."

"But how?"

"That faint noise we heard. That was an explosion. They're sure of it down there. We are to go on alert."

"*Here?* But —"

"We'd better do it, unless you like the idea of a penal battalion."

All along the ridges, the SAMs went on full alert. On the plateau the ZSU got ready for action, and the Yak-38s were being readied for their hurrying pilots. Crews were clambering into the helicopters and vehicles were scurrying about as the encampment began to make ready for a threat, unknown and as yet unseen.

Pross saw the shape dart out of the ruins, and knew it to be Logan. He moved the Hammerhead towards her to reduce the distance she had to travel.

He had seen two soldiers drop, to lie permanently still; but now the surviving two had spotted her and were racing towards her firing on the run. He saw her drop to the ground, giving him the burning memory of the last time he'd had to pick her up. It had been pouring with rain and soldiers had been chasing her then, just as now. On the Hong Kong border, she had been shot, and had nearly died. He didn't want that to happen today.

He swung the Hammerhead round and, keeping low on the deck, selected the gun and squeezed the trigger briefly. Thirty millimetre shells erupted for a terrible fraction of a second about the running men. One was lifted into the air to fall back to earth a broken doll, ravaged and still. His companion was completely unscathed.

Still lying on her stomach, Logan was quick to seize the opportunity. She was up on one knee and firing two snap shots before the last soldier had recovered his equilibrium. It had all happened so quickly he had not really stood a chance. From the time Pross had killed the Hind to the death of the last soldier, barely a minute had passed.

Pross lowered the wheels and brought the aircraft down as Logan hurried up to it. She threw the rifle away as he released the canopy to the front cockpit. She grinned happily at him, picked up the helmet waiting on the seat, put it on, then climbed in. She shut the canopy and was strapping herself in as he lifted the Hammerhead swiftly and sent it skimming along the plain.

Two minutes.

"What took you so long?" she queried when she had connected herself up.

"A little detour. Had to sort out a Hind first. You're always getting into trouble, Logan. You look thin, by the way."

"The hotels were a bit rough."

"Thought it might be something like that."

"Pross?"

"Mm hm."

"Thanks for coming."

"It's good to have you back. Only thing is, I think we might have to fight our way out. That singing you hear is not a lullaby."

The radar warning was going berserk. So was infrared. Three minutes. One of the bloody Forgers must have got off and launched from max range. Shit.

"Somebody's sent us a present, or a couple of presents. Close your eyes and think of . . . anything. Here we go."

He hauled the Hammerhead up into a cyclic climb, swung the tail round, went in nose down, hauled up again and rolled, hitting chaff and flares as he did so. A brief touch of a manoeuvring button and the helicopter darted in a flat displacement to the right. A touch of cyclic forward, nose down a shade, collective up, just a little, build power. Hurry, *hurry!* Speed building, leaping fast. There. That slope. Up and over. Keep down. *Down!*

The missiles consumed each other as the first, eating its way into the sunbursts, exploded and took the radar homer with it. The twin explosions rolled across the plateau, disturbing once more the peace of the once-silent ruins.

Four minutes.

FIFTEEN

"Have you any idea, Pross," she said, "how frightening your antics look from here? I could have touched that lump of rock." A huge outcrop seemed to flash past, inches from the nose of the Hammerhead.

Pross had brought up the tactical map on the MFD, and had superimposed it upon the NAV display. The full horror of the situation was neatly laid out for him, if the information was still correct. Given what had just happened, he assumed it to be. Four SAM positions; *eight* bloody choppers – seven now, scratching one Hind. Small mercies. Two Yak-38s. With one already up, where was the other? Assorted vehicles and that vicious ZSU: and God knew how many man-portable SAMs.

Christ.

"You ought to see it from my seat, chuck," he said to her in a fake Lancashire accent. "By God, it terrifies me," he added for good measure, parodying Wellington.

"You'll cope."

"Such faith. Is your mask secure?"

"Yes."

"Visor down?"

"It's down, Pross. Stop worrying."

"Stop worrying, she says. Warm enough?"

"I'm warm. Nice and cosy. Satisfied?"

"I won't be until we're safely back across that border. A lot of people are out to kill us."

He'd hit them from the north. The high ground would shield him until the last moment. The SAM radars should go first; but there was that bloody Forger on the prowl, and his pal would soon join him if not stopped first. Must have been slow to get off. Perhaps still on the ground. Nice to get a sitting duck in transition. What about those SAMs?

Forget them for now, or take them simultaneously. Forget the choppers that would be rising like angry dragonflies. Forget the ZSU. Forget . . .

He kept the Hammerhead low, skimming the terrain, switch-backing over rising and falling ground, tilting into dark canyons, following the tracks of long-dried river courses. Hiding from the Yak. It would not want to follow, but would be waiting: waiting for the right moment.

Pross armed two high-speed anti-radars, then a Stinger. They would fire in sequence; the HARMs first, the Stinger almost immediately after lock-on. The weapons station display told him arming was complete.

He popped over the northern range of hills and saw the black smoke. For some reason, the second Yak had been really slow. The attack radar grabbed for it eagerly and the Stinger achieved lock-on. He zoomed in on the imager. *Transition!* The poor sod was hanging in the air, unable to manoeuvre.

Pross squeezed the trigger: a long pressure.

The HARMs took off gleefully, diverging across the plateau as they sought out the two closest SAM radars. The Stinger followed in their wake, making a bee-line for the unfortunate Forger.

He didn't hang around to see the results. Besides, that ZSU had woken up. With a 360-degree traverse and a virtually 90-degree arc of travel, it could throw its movable barrage as far out as two kilometres, and the Hammerhead was well within range.

A Hellfire would sort it out, but the time was not now. Three almost simultaneous explosions told him that all the missiles had scored. No time to gloat. He swung the Hammerhead round and scuttled back for the safety of the dark range beyond the plateau.

The ZSU tracers seemed to be curving ahead of him. Bloody hell! Hit the ECM. Jam his radar. The ECM began to yowl.

Then it began to *fade*. Shit. They were countering! Hit ECCM. Counter the bastards. The yowl came back, strongly. The tracers began to go way off track. Safe. For now.

Then *ping!* and a pulsing tone. Missile launch, infrared. Air-launched? Yes. There it was on the screen and coming fast. Bloody Yak-38, wanting revenge. Hit IR pulse jammer. Hear the tone.

Bloody orchestra in the headphones. Drop a flare for luck. Get out of the way. Get *out!*

He sent the Hammerhead crabbing this way, then that, displacing flatly across the plateau. The ZSU had given up for now. The increasing volume of the warning tone told him the missile was still coming. What was happening? Could the missile ignore the jammer? That would not be good news. What about the sunburst?

Then the tone began to wind down, as if someone had suddenly pulled the plug out on an electronic organ. The missile went for the meal that had been left for it.

The shock-wave of the explosion clutched at the Hammerhead, tried to shake it, but the aircraft shrugged it off with a slight weave and kept going.

How many more did he have? Pross wondered. Think! *Think.* Forger armament fit: usually two IR Aphids or Apex. Range 7 to 15 km. Would he carry four? Probably not. Probably? "Probably" is no sodding use in combat. Ceiling. What was its ceiling? 40,000 feet. Not much use to him if he wanted to mix it close, but more than enough for him to stay out of reach if he was out of the hot stuff.

The Hammerhead hopped over a dark ridge and sank thankfully down the other side. Safe for the time being; but only from the Yak. The choppers were sure to follow. Answer?

Wait. Wait for a couple of minutes. See who comes in; but avoid the bracket. They could try to come from as many directions as the terrain allowed.

"Logan? Are you alright?" He held the aircraft at the hover, tucked into a dark cleft between two rising peaks. Height above sea level 16,430 feet. Height above ground level, 20 feet. Hold it. Hold it! Keep the main blades away from that overhang.

"I'm fine," she said. "Don't worry about me. Concentrate on what you have to do."

One thing about these cockpits. You couldn't see if your partner was okay. You'd hear soon enough though, one way or the other. Just like in Phantoms.

Nothing on radar. Screened by the terrain, except in one direction. All warning systems taking a break for the time being. But that wouldn't last for long.

It didn't.

He had backed into the cleft, nose pointing north. A deep trough ran from right to left, about half-a-mile ahead, disappearing on either side behind high bluffs. There was a triangular patch of open space, with the thinner end starting at the cleft where he now hid. Beyond the triangle, and straight ahead, the way was blocked by a rising wall of high ground that went up for nearly 2,000 feet. This was to be a killing ground.

From above, none of the searching helos would locate him visually, and it was doubtful whether even search radar or infrared would find him until too late. He was well screened by the towering masses of rock. He hoped Logan was alright, and refrained from asking her, although he wanted to. He couldn't begin to tell her how glad he was she was safe. Well, not exactly safe. Not yet, anyway.

He armed the remaining Stingers. Just the two left. He'd have to make them count. He waited.

And then, nosing along the trough, came a Hind and a Havoc, obviously working together, from opposite directions. They must have picked him up at the same instant because both aircraft, about to cross paths, jinked suddenly upwards. It was a chance too good to miss. Besides, they were already much too late.

He had achieved lock-on and had launched a Stinger even as they were beginning their desperate break. The slim missile streaked towards them and exploded against the Havoc, the target it had chosen. The exploding Havoc in turn consumed the Hind, wrapping itself about its sister aircraft in a fiery embrace that sent their remains twisting and rolling in the air to slam against the far side of the trough, then the fireball rolled down the slope, leaving a trail of dense smoke and flames in its wake. The bottom was a thousand feet down. From where they were, neither Pross nor Logan could see the bottom; but soon a billow of smoke, rising in the thin air, told them the story.

But the Hammerhead was already moving from its hiding-place, sliding out like its namesake, looking for more prey.

"No point remaining any longer," he said. "They'll know where we are now. Pity. I liked it in there."

"Bet you say that to all the girls."

"Be quiet, Logan. I'm busy."

He smiled. It really was good to have her back.

One Stinger left. He'd love to get the remaining Forger with it, but he wasn't going to waste time chasing unless attacked. The choppers were more dangerous — and the bloody SAMs. Five choppers still operating, plus the Yak, plus the two remaining SAMs, plus the ZSU, plus, plus, plus —

They'd be waiting for him to go for the border, so that was out of the question for the time being. Fuel was not critical. Plenty left. Take out the helos and the SAMs. The ZSU was only for point defence. It couldn't follow and could be ignored, as long as he didn't go near the plateau. The choice, however, might not be left to him.

He turned right along the trough, heading eastwards. He stayed at a thousand feet above the bottom. He wanted room to manoeuvre, in case something nasty was launched at them. The warning systems were suspiciously quiet. The Yak could be high up, co-ordinating an intended attack by the helos. His own radar, searching high, found nothing.

Ping! Yowl. Missile launch, radar-guided. From behind. So that was how it was going to be.

He hit the ECM and the counter-yowling began. It was not interrupted, but the incoming missile, slavering on his very low echo, held its course.

Ping! Pulse tone. Missile launch, IR homing. From ahead. A bracket. They'd been waiting for him. If he went straight up, would a third be launched at him as he appeared?

Both aircraft were on the radar and approaching, but their missiles were streaking ahead of them. Pross wondered why the IR had not been launched from the rear. Instead, it was coming towards his "cold" nose. The IR pulser was working at the missile, attacking its guidance system. Again, Pross heard the "orchestra" in his headphones.

He released more chaff and dropped another flare, then hauled back on collective. The Hammerhead flung itself upwards. A little back cyclic and it began to tip over onto its back. Pross rolled upright, now heading west and towards the approaching helicopter.

The missiles flew into the dinners left for them, beneath him. Again, it was the IR missile that started the reaction, exploding against the flare and taking the radar homer with it.

But Pross was no longer thinking about them. He had selected the gun, and was closing fast on his adversary, a fat Hind. Their approach speed was over 400 miles an hour and the Hind, not having the advantage of height, tried to gain some.

Pross saw an upward tilt of the distinctive nose as he half-rolled, then pulled the Hammerhead's own nose up. He was now directly astern of the Mi-24 and dropping below as the other continued to climb, banking left. He gave a touch of collective, killed the descent and the Hammerhead seemed to float upwards, matching the Hind's rate of climb. Soon the pilot would be kicking the tail round, and he would lose gun solution.

The HUD had the Hind framed. It was within range and holding. The red dot of the SHOOT cue came in within the glowing green reticle, and positioned itself exactly on the root of the left stub wing. The Hammerhead was slightly below and to Pross's eye, the Hind looked like a fat grouper seeking a way out.

He squeezed the trigger. One second. Pause. One second.

The gun spewed its 30-millimetre shells in two bursts with the smooth chain-saw rasp of a giant sewing machine. The Hammerhead seemed to vibrate in a manner that gave the impression it was doing so in a cocoon padded with cotton wool. There was no deviation from the point of aim.

The massive shells exploded against the target aircraft, ripping the stub wing completely off. It floated down almost gracefully, turning over and over, a metallic leaf heading for earth. The Hind tilted onto its wounded side. The tail swung up, then the whole aircraft seemed to pirouette on its nose before suddenly exploding with such force the Hammerhead was lifted upwards even as Pross was swinging it tightly away.

"How many left?" came Logan's voice, full of tension.

"Too bloody many. You alright?"

"Stop asking me, Pross. When I'm not, you'll know about it."

As long as it wasn't the sound of choking on the blood in her mask, he didn't say. What a nightmare that would be.

Seconds. That was all it had taken. How much did a Hind and its crew cost? How many families had he destroyed today?

It was pointless thinking about it. They were still looking for him, and would not think twice about securing his own destruction; and Logan's with it as a bonus.

He could not disengage. They would not let him.

On the ridge, the sex-starved Nikoviev and his partner were pleased to be one of the two still-surviving SAM teams. They were angry too. They had witnessed the devastation wrought upon their camp by the strange helicopter and although it had not been near them, they dearly wished for a chance to get a crack at it. They had no idea where it came from, why it had attacked. They did not care. Their response was a simple one. The camp had been attacked. Their job was to defend it.

"If he pops up again from the north, Fyodor," the first soldier said, "we should take him."

"Too far."

"Too *far?* What are you talking about? We've got eight missiles loaded in two canisters and we've got reloads. We've got a range of nearly ten kilometres and it's not half as far to the northern —"

"I don't want to give him the slightest chance of dodging out of the way."

"*Four* missiles at a time?"

"We wait till he comes up this way."

"Wait till he sends *his* missiles at us, you mean. You saw what he did to the other two."

"You wanted action, didn't you?"

"*You* were the one who wanted action. Remember?"

Nikoviev grinned. "Think of the medals, if we get him. Girls will fall at our feet . . ."

"You think of the medals. I'd rather have feet, for all those girls you dream about to fall at. If we can take that helicopter before he gets near us, I'll be a happy man."

Nikoviev grinned once more. "We wait."

Three Hinds and a Havoc gone, Pross was thinking, plus the Forger.

But that still left three more Hinds, another Havoc, the Yak that seemed keen, for the time being, to stay out of reach, the SAMs, and the bloody ZSU. Too many, as he'd told Logan; but the border might as well be halfway round the globe unless he could improve the odds still further.

The SAMs, he thought. I'll go for the SAMs.

He decided to attack from the south. They wouldn't be expecting it, and if he stayed low in transit it would force any pursuers to come down among the ridges and valleys to find him. Screw up their radar too. His own radar was just as vulnerable to being screened by high ground, but at least he could choose the battleground.

With a bit of luck.

Schuler had mixed feelings as the convoy rolled across the stony plateau and into the encampment. He wanted the helicopter to get away. It wouldn't do to find Fowler's agent, whether alive or dead, inside the aircraft if in the end it was brought down. Only through complete destruction in the air, with the pieces falling somewhere totally inaccessible, would the fact that she had not died in the ruins remain hidden from Wu. On the other hand, he would feel it a sort of failure if she did not get across to Nepal safely; or at least, in one piece. The entire operation could be placed in jeopardy.

Shooting her would have removed that chance.

His face was grim as he thought of it. He hated even partial failure.

His Chinese companion in the armoured BTR was viewing the activity in the camp with interest.

"It would seem," the Chinese lieutenant began calmly, "that the helicopter is giving our Soviet comrades a rough time of it. Was that wreckage we've just passed not one of the Yaks?"

"It looks like it," Schuler said.

The lieutenant peered upwards out of the vehicle. The armour-plating for the window space in the cab door had been removed. "Smoke. He hit something up there too. What shall we do?"

"The choice is yours," Schuler said. "You can stay out of it, or you can deploy your men."

The lieutenant smiled. "I think I should like to do something about that helicopter. With your permission, I shall have our cannon manned. After all, it is our air space that has been invaded, and the ZSU is also manned by our soldiers."

Schuler nodded. "Very well. Drop me off at the Headquarters tent. I must speak to the commander."

A short while later Schuler climbed down from the BTR, then paused to watch as the three vehicles set off down the plateau in a flurry of dust and spinning wheels.

"Good luck," he muttered drily, and went to find the Russian commander of the camp.

He had nothing specific to say to the man, but had used it as an excuse to leave the lieutenant and his men to their own devices.

Pross had travelled south on a course roughly parallel to the west ridge, five miles away. He used every available source of cover, keeping so low that at times it appeared he was about to belly-flop onto the unforgiving terrain. A few times, something had popped on the radar, but had blinked out almost immediately. No warnings had sounded; nothing launched his way.

He had half-expected the Forger to come sweeping down for a look, but the pilot was obviously not going to risk playing with the hungry, jagged ridges and peaks.

The Hammerhead made it safely to the southern end of the camp, and Pross armed the anti-radars and wheeled in for the attack. Almost immediately the radar showed him company. He ignored it for the time being. Still too far. No launch as yet.

There was a barrier of hills guarding that end of the plateau as well and he kept low as long as possible, then sent the Hammerhead skimming up the slope. Then he was over, in the open, and almost at the same height as the ridges. This was his most vulnerable moment. He was hanging naked.

Then he had launched the HARMs and was dropping heart-stoppingly, winging over to head east, seeing more company on the radar and hoping the ZSU was still looking for him down the other end.

"I have him on radar!" the soldier screamed, the direction taking him completely by surprise.

Nikoviev said nothing. But he saw the image and initiated the launch sequence.

But before lock-on, his comrade yelled, "He's launched! *He's launched!"*

With despairing weariness, Nikoviev knew it was already too late. He was thinking with irony how this empty and wild place had become more dangerous to him than Afghanistan when his world was engulfed in an explosive ball of fire.

Schuler was standing with the detachment commander, a colonel whose home was on the Black Sea coast in the North Caucasus, staring at the twin plumes of black smoke rising high from each ridge.

"He's tearing us to pieces," the colonel said, voice tight with anger.

"You've got aircraft up," Schuler remarked. He had seen the attack, and marvelled at Pross's skill. It had been beautifully done. But even more impressive was the Hammerhead, a darting, barely visible speck in the distance; a speck that was lethal. Fowler had a world-beating machine on his hands.

Schuler's mind admired Fowler's cold professionalism. He admired Pross too, in his own way, though he thought Pross to be flawed: too much emotion.

But the woman . . . she was good: very good, and just right for Pross. A perfect foil. Fowler had chosen well to pair them together.

The colonel was saying, "Two of my 24s, as you can see, are grounded. Repairs. They're working close to their operational ceilings, even for these special ones. We're trying to get one airworthy. We've lost three more, one 28, and a Yak. So all we've got up are one 24, the remaining 28, and the Yak, which I've ordered to stay out of trouble unless he has a certainty of hitting the target. If we lose him, we cannot persuade our Chinese comrades it's a good aircraft to deploy in such regions." The colonel sighed. "He's destroying me. I've taken all they could throw at me in Afghanistan and I come here on what should have been a simple operation. Sensitive, yes ... but not particularly dangerous. Just look at the mess! They'll have my head for it, Schuler." He stared at the twin palls of smoke that marked the end of his career.

Within his mind, Schuler smiled with satisfaction. The operation was progressing smoothly towards its intended termination.

Pross felt a mounting elation. When he had broken hard away from the attack, he was certain he had caught a fleeting glimpse of two Hinds, still on the ground. If that were indeed so, the odds had improved far better than he had dared hope. Whatever the reasons for the grounding, it was obviously not something that could be rectified in a hurry; otherwise, they'd be up in the air, pounding after him with the rest of the hounds.

"Logan," he began. "Could you verify something for me? When we broke away, I thought I saw two helos on the ground. Tell me it wasn't wishful thinking."

"It wasn't wishful thinking, Pross," she responded drily. "Just before the world tipped over on its side, I saw them. Is that good news?"

"Every little helps, given our present situation. They're still up there blocking our exit back across the border, so if some of their pals are deckbound, then it's hooray for us."

The radar was still showing company, but the warning systems were keeping quiet. The Hammerhead's very low radar signature, he knew, in conjunction with the many peaks rising out of the great Tibetan Plateau, was giving his pursuers severe problems and buying him precious time. He had to utilise that to the fullest advantage.

The radar showed him that company was still there, but no one was launching at him. Why?

They wanted a certain hit; and as long as he stayed this side of the border, they would leave him alone – temporarily – but try to keep him onscreen.

"Logan," he said, "here's a problem. We've got company upstairs, but they're not shooting. I realise that because we're flying north again, they may be prepared to bide their time, while they'll do everything they can to stop us if we make for the border. But there could be another reason."

"Reinforcements?"

"Exactly. But where from? We've covered a lot of ground and, so far, there's nothing. The long-range radar tells me both sky and ground are empty of movement, save for our friendly neighbourhood friends."

"That leaves the other two helicopters on the ground. Perhaps they're trying to repair them quickly . . ." Her voice faded into uncertainty.

"You're doing well," he encouraged. "It makes sense. They can keep us boxed in like a big fish in a net while they work like sods to get the other Hinds flying – and while our fuel runs out."

"Are we?" she asked quickly, voice again tense. "Are we about to run out?"

"No. We're still okay, but combat guzzles fuel and we can't play around here forever or this wonderful machine, lovely as it is, will fly like a home-sick stone. Well, not quite. I could do an autorotative landing . . . but that would be our lot. I don't fancy falling into their hands, and I don't think you'd want to renew the acquaintance."

He could almost see the shudder. "I certainly don't."

"In which case, it's once more unto the breach. Watch the pretty pictures on your screens, and lie back and enjoy it."

"Promises, promises."

"Remember where you are, Logan, and behave."

He heard a distinct giggle.

"By the way," she said. "We've got a mutual friend."

"I know. Hansen."

"How?" she queried in surprise.

"Lal. He saw him with you." Pross told her briefly about Lal's marathon walk. "There's loyalty for you," he finished.

She was silent for a few moments, then, "Trust Sanders to behave the way he did towards him. God. What a shit."

She was beginning to relate her own experiences when the warning systems went into their routines once more. The Hammerhead was

262

skimming along a narrow valley with great walls of rock towering on either side.

Pross said, "Here we go again. Brace yourself."

He began weaving the helicopter across the valley, going close to one rockwall, then the next. If they were hoping he'd come leaping out to give them a nice target, they were mistaken. The launch was to flush him out, rather than an attempt to score a hit.

Again, they had sent both IR and radar homers. Pross watched the missiles hurtle towards the Hammerhead. The radar showed no indication of where they had come from. It was as he had thought. A quick launch and duck out of sight to see what would be flushed.

He continued his weaving, watching as the missiles closed range swiftly. Then he hit both ECM and IR jammers, and moments later, released chaff and a flare. On the radar, the missiles began to veer off course, trying to follow him as well as the flare and the chaff. In the end, their seekers went loopy. The radar homer followed the chaff into a rockface, and started an avalanche that brought great chunks tumbling down into the valley. The heat seeker took the easy way out, and bit on the flare to light up the darker recesses of the valley with the sunburst of its demise.

Pross brought the Hammerhead back onto its steady heading, and continued north.

At the site in Lapchi Kang, Mabel and Sanders were standing by the radio in the communications tent. They had sent the operator out. Sanders was speaking into it.

"You are not to go, Captain Rees," he was saying. It was very much an order.

"He should have been well on his way back by now." Rees' mournful voice, sounding even more so on the ether, gave the impression of heavy patience being employed. "Something's gone wrong. I know it."

"We have no evidence of that fact and besides, he has not touched the panic button."

"He wouldn't, would he . . . unless they were both already dying out there. Is that what you want?"

"Don't you use that tone —"

Mabel, who had been listening with increasing irritation to Sanders' responses, interrupted. "Cado, what is your appreciation of the situation?"

"I think he's in trouble, and can't get out," Rees answered without hesitation. "Perhaps they've not yet caught him, but he's being prevented from breaking out. I think we should lend a hand..."

"*No!*" Sanders was almost shouting. "Just you listen to me, Rees! One unmarked aircraft going over for the pick-up and getting into a firefight with people who shouldn't even be there anyway, is one thing, but *eight* other helicopters, all unmarked, invading a sovereign country's airspace is another matter altogether, *whatever* the reason. We cannot give such provocation..."

"You bloody hypocrite! So why give him a panic button if there was no intention to help?"

Sanders dodged the question and went in for bluster. "Those aircraft are here for a specific purpose, Rees! Altitude trials –"

"Balls! Sorry, Mabel."

"Be my guest," Mabel said calmly and sniffed at her cigar. Her eyes glared at Sanders, who ignored her.

"Insubordination!" Sanders snarled at Rees, giving the impression that if the focus of his anger were physically available, he'd strangle him. "I'll have you broken for this, Rees. You're prepared to risk a full incident, just because –"

"Cado," Mabel interrupted once more, "use your discretion," she said, turning away from Sanders' own glaring eyes. "I'm not saying you should go. But if you feel you should, I'll back you. Whatever happens, better not leave any bits out there – people, or machines, that belong to us."

"Got it," Rees said, and terminated transmission.

Mable turned her eyes upon Sanders. "If you say one word to me," she told him coldly, "I'll light up this cigar and stub it out on your face!"

Then she left the tent without a backward glance.

Pross had left the valley, and was heading westwards. He had convinced himself he would have to take out the ZSU. The suspicion had been forming in his mind that the surviving helos and the Yak would perhaps acts as beaters, intending to flush him into its waiting quadruple maw. Solution? Kill the ZSU and do it quickly, before they could put their plan into action.

Logan in the front seat. If that thing started firing, she would probably die of fright. Warn her what it could be like. On second thoughts, perhaps not. Ignorance is bliss.

He armed all four Hellfires, in case he needed more than one. The Hammerhead's Hellfires were third-generation missiles, but with modifications specially devised for its particular use. They could achieve their own lock-on, without the need of an external designator, either ground-based or chopper-based. The Hammerhead could do its own killing, all by itself.

Pross went in fast, up and over the northern barrier of the plateau. The attack MFD showed him that the ZSU was two miles distant. He called up full zoom. As the image drew closer, he saw that the turret was pointing the other way, to the *south*.

Time. Time was all he needed. Don't let them wake up until too late.

He felt moisture on his face. Sweat. Heat of battle? Perhaps, perhaps. Don't think about it. Think about that monster up ahead. Range closing. The turret will be turning soon. Four mouths, spitting death. A wall of fire. Logan in the front, probably scared now. Forget Logan. Forget everything except the ZSU.

Kill it.

He brought the Hammerhead right down, almost touching the deck. Radar? Nothing. They were probably still looking for him somewhere else; but the camp would see him, and everybody would know where he was. They'd come swooping out of the sky . . .

Later, later. *The turret was turning!*

End of surprise. The time was *now*.

The reticle on the MFD was shifting towards the ZSU. Now it was pulsing. Lock-on. SHOOT, it said.

Pross squeezed the trigger just as it seemed as if he was looking down its jaws. The turret, thin-skinned and vulnerable, had swung completely and was zeroed on target.

The first Hellfire launched itself explosively and hurtled towards its target. The second followed. The ZSU was quick, but not quick enough. A stream of tracer was actually coming from it even as Pross hauled on collective and pushed cyclic to the left. The Hammerhead was jinking out of the way and winging over to return the way it had come, when the first Hellfire went straight in between the quad barrels to impact on the turret, blowing it right off. The second missile trailed in its wake and entered the hull, which seemed to expand under an enormous pressure before ripping apart in a bellow that spread shock-waves the length of the entire camp.

Back down behind a friendly screen of rising ground, Pross felt a great relief. After that, he thought, the rest should be easy.

He could not have been more wrong.

*

Rees looked about him, and saw the other seven Lynxes floating in the thin mountain air. They were strung out in two echelon groups of four, his own leading: and fully tooled up with rockets and Hellfires.

He permitted himself a brief smile within the oxygen mask necessary for all the high-flying Lynxes. As soon as he'd finished speaking to Mabel, he had ordered the aircraft to fly towards the border. Unknown to either Sanders or Mabel, they had already been warmed up and ready for flight, even as he was in conversation with them. It had merely been a matter of lifting off from their temporary Exercise base, and heading north.

Rees allowed himself another smile. Pross was in for a little surprise.

Pross received a surprise he did not want. A new sound. A new sound had come on his headphones. Immediately, he began throwing the Hammerhead into a series of avoidance manoeuvres that made Logan cry out.

"Pross!" she exclaimed. "What's happening?"

"Bad news. We're being illuminated."

"What ... what does that mean?"

Her helmet phones were coupled to the warning systems, so that she could hear everything he got on his phones. The new sound was not unlike a less strident, twin-tone police siren. He thought it the best arrangement if she knew what was going on.

"It means," he answered grimly, "they've got a laser designator on the ground. He's targeting us for either a man-portable SAM, or the helos, or even the Yak."

He should have expected it, of course. Apart from being a flying tank, the Hind is also an assault ship supreme. No reason why they should not have dropped some troops, complete with either designators and/or SAMs. No wonder they had not come down after him. They had been laying their little trap and had the Hammerhead not got a laser warning system, the first surprise would have been a missile knocking on the door. Then the ball of fire.

"If we don't break away from his nasty beam of light," Pross continued as he rolled the Hammerhead over, reversed then continued turning in the same direction, "they'll send a missile to home on it. What I've got to do is fool the operator into misreading my intended direction. Ah!"

The noise had stopped suddenly.

"Have we done it?"

"I think we have. And here's a nice friendly hill to hide behind for the moment." As the Hammerhead ducked behind the welcome screen, Pross went on, "I know the clever sod's position." It was there on the MFD, conveniently recorded by the warning system. "If he remains in place, that is. But he can't get very far on foot."

"What are you going to do?"

"Track him with infrared. He's dangerous. He can keep us occupied while his other friends sneak up to finish us off. We've got to find him. It doesn't mean he's the only one either."

"That's cheerful. How long is it since you picked me up?"

He called it up on the NAV MFD. He had started the timer at the instant she had climbed aboard.

"Twenty minutes, thirty point two five seconds, and counting. Look at the pretty picture on your left-hand screen, top left corner. See it?"

"Yes."

"We can't let them keep us here for much longer. We're going home. I'll take out our friend on that hilltop, then home, James."

"Which way?"

"Straight down the plateau."

"But Pross —"

"It's the one place they won't expect me to try again. I hope. They're waiting outside the ridges. We'll go through them. The plateau should be safe enough for a single fast pass. I've taken out the air defence."

He said nothing about possible hand-held SAMs; but the Hammerhead's 270mph absolute max gave him a full 70mph lead over the Hind and even more over the Havoc. Only the Yak-38 would be able to catch him, but would it want to fight? It was wait-and-see time.

Small-arms fire would not be a worry. The Hammerhead could handle that, Rees had said. Up to 23mm calibre. Not the best moment in the world to prove that wrong.

He brought the helicopter round to the heading indicated by the laser warning system and began a low approach, circling round the base of the low range and avoiding the valley where he'd first been caught out. The radar showed no hostiles. Perhaps they were low down too, looking for him. So much the better.

He arrived at the reverse slope, hugging the terrain, going slowly as he climbed, tail-down. The Hammerhead looked like a great piscine predator of the deep stalking its prey, as it went up the slope. The treeless terrain offered little cover for those on the ground, and when the helicopter suddenly breasted the rise 500 metres away, Pross knew he had them. There were four, and on the MFD he saw their images beginning to dart in all directions.

He had armed the rockets, selecting a salvo of eight, ripple fire from both stations. He squeezed the trigger. Starting from the bottom and counting themselves off from left to right, the salvo roared off in less than one second. He watched as the ground erupted about the running men, spreading out to engulf them until they were completely hidden and enveloped by the dark, rising clouds.

It was time to go.

SIXTEEN

The Hammerhead, keeping low, went hurtling across the plateau. Pross could see, directly ahead, the gleaming white rows of the massive peaks that formed the frontier barrier into Nepal. Fearsome yet beautiful dragons' teeth.

The stony floor of the plateau had lost definition, looking at speed like a smooth and vast motorway.

Then suddenly a sound like a shower of hail rattled briefly against the fuselage. Damage warning showed no hits to be worried about.

"You alright?" he called to Logan.

"Fine. Just don't put the nose down any further!"

Inside the mask, his lips pulled into a grin that was more a reaction to the stress of holding his course than in reply to her comment.

"If that's all they can throw at us, we're nearly home and dry."

Nothing was on the radar. Strange.

Urgent warnings on the headphones: IR SAMs. Perhaps that was why. How many? Two, from opposite directions, low down. Portable SAMs then. Give them flares. Keep going!

He gained some height abruptly then dropped again, releasing a batch of six flares as he did so. They formed an almost circular concentration of intense heat behind the fleeing aircraft. The SAMs went straight into them and roared out their rage in a spectacular starbust of flame and thunder.

More hail on the airframe. Ignore. No damage. Keep going.

"Logan?"

"I'm *still* fine. Just watch the bloody ground."

She was amazing. Wonderful woman.

Trucks ahead. The Hellfires were armed. Two remaining. Three trucks. No. Two soft-bodied, one armour. Christ. *Cannon on the top.* Where had they come from?

The lieutenant saw the sleek shape racing towards him, still some distance away and a very difficult target, but growing fast. The leanness of the head-on view made it difficult to track. But he was determined that his men would get it where others had failed. After all the devastation it had caused, his success would taste very sweet indeed. He had even more motivation now. The soldiers in the ZSU had been his countrymen.

He ordered his men to take up positions near the trucks with their rifles, to pour a concentrated volley of fire upon the target as it flashed past. He himself would man the cannon.

The men looked at him with a mixture of surprise and respect. They had seen what the strange helicopter could do. If he wanted to take the brunt of its attack, they were not about to argue.

Pross knew that once the Hellfires were launched, the gun would arm itself automatically. He would spray the trucks for good measure as he came up on them, if any were left standing.

As he launched the Hellfires, he saw the armoured truck move so that it was temporarily screened by the soft-bodies.

Logan was shouting, "That's the convoy that brought me!"

Then the Hellfires ripped into the trucks, flinging them and the hapless soldiers into the air on a sea of flame, scattering their remains across the dusty landscape. The BTR was intact.

Shit, Pross thought, and squeezed the trigger.

The gun chain-sawed its 30mm rounds at the BTR; but it was firing back too. Pross saw, in a flashing instant, a series of shells exploding at the base of the cannon, tearing the gunner apart; then it was gone, and the Hammerhead continued its ground-hugging rush.

But something had scythed its way through the cockpit window, and his right arm was not feeling quite –

He paused. What the hell had happened? There was a different sound in the cockpit, and a slight chill. Then he felt a warm wetness, and he knew what had happened. That gunner had known his stuff, after all.

The environmental system in the cockpit would compensate for the change in temperature, but oxygen was a different matter.

There was still no pain; that would come. His body was still in a kind of shock. The Hammerhead was still hurtling close to the racing ground. Not the best time to lose control.

"Logan!" he said. "Are you alright?"

"I'm fine, Pross. That was brilliant."

Brilliant.

He said nothing, pleased that she was unhurt. Time to gain height. He tried to test the efficiency of his right arm by moving the fingers. Nothing happened. Bloody hell. That meant he couldn't use cyclic.

He would have to couple the two control systems. He might need Logan. He activated the coupler switch, then gently gave the collective some pressure. The Hammerhead leapt upwards. At least, the ship was okay. Better tell her before the pain came.

"Logan . . ."

"Yes?"

"Is your oxygen working properly and have you got your mask well secured?"

"Yes." There was puzzlement in her voice. "What's up, Pross?"

"Nothing we can't handle . . ."

"*Pross.*" Anxiety now. "Your voice sounds funny."

Shit. The pain was coming. Not yet. Not yet, for God's sake. And as if things weren't bad enough, friends on the radar. Hordes of the bastards. Not in sight yet.

"My voice is not funny . . ."

"It's not right. Pross . . ."

"Stop arguing with me, Logan." A gasp was torn out of him. Christ! The *pain.*

"*Pross!*"

He could sense her trying to turn round.

"Sit bloody still, Logan. You can't turn round in one of these things."

"What happened?" She was regaining control of herself.

"We collected a little present. Came through my cockpit . . ."

"Oh, Pross —"

"*Listen.*"

"Alright, alright. I'm listening."

"I've just coupled us together . . ." He paused, as a wave of pain hit him.

She did not throw a saucy repartee back at him, indicating, more than anything else could, just how worried she now was.

"Don't worry about the Hammerhead. I've also got her on automode. When we touch the controls, she'll revert to manual . . ."

"I'm not worried about the aircraft, Pross."

"I'll be alright. It isn't serious."

She didn't reply to that either. Another indication. She didn't believe him.

"What do you want me to do?"

"When I need help with the flying, I'll ask you to control the cyclic . . . that's . . . the sidestick on your right."

"I see it . . ."

"Don't touch it!"

"I wasn't going to. What next?"

"These controls have differing levels of sensitivity. You'll have to cope with whatever feel you get from it. I don't think we should try messing about with adjustments at this moment. When I ask you to, move the cyclic in the direction I indicate, very gently. Unless you know how to fly one of these, for the time being you're going to be a sort of robot, I'm afraid. I'll need you to think of other things for me. Aah! Bloody hell, Logan. I think the bastard gave me a good one. I . . . I also have a piece of bad news. The radar's full of company. God knows where they've come from. Sorry." Funny thing was, he thought he could hear Handel's *Water Music*; but there was nothing on the phones. Strange.

"Don't say that, Pross," she said gently to him. "Don't say that. You're the best and . . . *Pross!* Pross, look!"

"Don't shout, Logan. You're . . . Bloody hell."

Directly ahead, a pack of Lynxes was rising, gleaming and looking for trouble.

"It's the bloody cavalry!" Pross said weakly. "They look beautiful. But how . . .?"

"Who knows? I'm just glad."

The Lynxes split neatly into two groups of four, making a corridor for the Hammerhead to pass through. As he approached, Pross saw a simultaneous blooming of fire from the side of each Lynx, and a seemingly continuous hail of rockets was streaming towards the ground. Then followed more blooms of fire, and sixteen missile trails etched their way groundwards.

As the Hammerhead passed through, Pross thought he could hear a rolling thunder.

The Lynxes closed ranks, forming a protective barrier between the plateau and the Hammerhead. Pross wondered whether they would join combat with the remaining helos and the Yak. It might get hairy out there.

Then a voice was on his headphones. "Thought you might need he help of a good pilot."

Cado bloody Rees! Bloody Handel. But there was still no music on the phones. I must be dying, he thought quite calmly. His body seemed to be floating.

"Cado!" Logan was saying urgently. "Pross is hurt! Badly, I hink."

"*What?*" A shocked pause, then, "Alright, everybody. You all heard that. Playtime's over. Come on, children. Time to go home. I don't think they'll follow. What do you think this is? A war? Alright, Alpha Four. I can see you. Come back. You've had enough."

A great fire was raging on the plateau. The fuel dump, and the remaining Hinds on the ground, had been hit. The Lynxes began urning, heading back.

"Slow down, David," Rees' voice came again. "We won't be able o catch up, otherwise."

Pross smiled weakly, and reduced speed to match the Lynxes which soon began to crowd protectively about Hammerhead. He wondered whether Rees had judged the situation correctly. The Yak might still rush over to try its hand.

But as they flew deeper into Nepal, nothing showed on the radar.

Pross began to relax, but with relaxation came a sudden weariness. Air howled through the jagged slit made by the incoming fragment of shell. He wondered, tiredly, whether his blood would flow out of him before they reached the site. At this altitude, blood tended to low freely.

The Hammerhead flew, mainly on automode, sometimes with a weak Pross directing Logan on cyclic while he operated the pedals and collective. But he was getting increasingly weaker.

"Pross!" Logan shouted suddenly. "Don't you bloody die on me!"

"Fat chance ... with you yelling loudly enough to wake the dead."

"Just letting you know. Besides, I can't fly this wonder-machine alone. And I have a thing about heights."

He smiled. He wanted to sleep. Good old Logan. So much he would like to tell her. So ...

"*Pross!* Wake up! Wake up! *Don't fall asleep.*"

"Bloody hell, Logan," he said weakly, crossly.

"We nearly fell out of the sky."

He saw that she was right. His instinctive corrective action had carried no thought with it. The survival imperative had taken over.

Handel, who had been serenading him intermittently, decided to call it a day. 'Bye Handel.

"Are you alright, over there?" came Rees' voice.

"We're fine," Logan said.

"David?"

"Yes, Cado."

"Not too long now. The site have been warned. They're ready for you. Can you land?"

"No problem."

"Right. Hang on, mate. Not long now."

"I'm hanging on."

Sleep. Wonderful sleep.

"*David!*"

"Logan, for God's sake. Have you turned into a fishwife in your old age?"

"It would help if I did grow old first. Not much chance of that if we hit that mountainside I can see right in front of my nose."

"Bit of collective, David," came Rees' voice calmly. "You need a bit of space under you."

Pross roused himself and eased the sidestick back. The Hammerhead raised itself skywards and cleared a low peak with its cluster of precariously attached houses, by mere feet. It kept rising.

"Don't do that for an encore, will you?" Logan said with relief.

Pross did not reply. He was still applying pressure on the collective. The helicopter continued to climb, leaving the escorting Lynxes far below.

"Pross?" Logan began cautiously. "We're all alone again. Pross? *Pross!*"

"Not you again, Logan. I never knew you could yell like that."

"We're climbing, Pross. We've left Cado and his chums. We're going too ..."

"David, old son," came Rees' calm, mournful voice again. "Now you're too high. We're not as powerful as you, you know. Think of us, poor mortals that we are. Come down, David."

"Wha ... what? Oh. Yes. Yes."

He was so weak. If only he could sleep. Just a little snooze, and he'd be alright.

Suddenly, Pross roused himself again. Too high. Lose height. *Lose height.*

Then the Lynxes were there again, comforting with their presence.

"Nearly there, David," Rees said. "Nearly there. Take a look."

It was true. He could see the site. Cut speed for the approach. Back on the cyclic now. Why wasn't the cyclic moving? Why . . .

Then he remembered.

"Logan." Weakly.

"Yes, David."

Funny. Her voice sounded strange.

"Back . . . back on the cyclic. Gently."

By the time the Hammerhead came over the site, it was at the hover.

Pross said, "Right. Hands off now. I'll take her down. Don't need cyclic. Thanks, Logan . . . and thanks for keeping me awake. You're a great co-pilot."

"Any time, David. Any time."

Her voice was still sounding funny.

Gingerly, Pross brought the Hammerhead down. He had even remembered the wheels. It settled with barely a shudder. He shut down, then relaxed.

There was sudden activity all round the aircraft. It sounded as if Logan was trying to break out of her cockpit. Then she was clawing at his. It opened and someone was saying, "It's alright. It's alright. We'll do it. We'll take care of him. Stand back, my dear. Let us do it."

Mabel.

"If . . . if anything happens to him . . ." Logan again. "If he dies . . I'll – I'll shoot you all. I will. I will . . ."

"Of course you will, my dear. Of course, you will. Now, David, let's get you out. Easy, easy . . . Come here, Peter. Take him by that arm . . . not this one . . . it's a bit . . ."

Voices fading. Weakness. Pain. Funny about Logan's voice. Logan *crying*, of all things.

Darkness.

EPILOGUE

A week later, Pross was sitting propped up in a bed in a comfortable room that overlooked Fowler's splendid garden in the Cotswolds. His wound had first been attended to at the site, then he had been taken swiftly down to the lower altitude of the Exercise base where he'd been operated upon in a fully-equipped small field hospital. A shell splinter had lodged in his shoulder, pinching a peripheral nerve. Then it had been on to Kathmandu airport, for the flight home. The BAe 125 had been there, waiting. Pross later found out it had never returned to the UK but instead had gone to Delhi on a "day" trip; whatever that meant. He'd been given a blood transfusion too.

But he'd had a narrow shave: just how narrow he had not appreciated until told about the other splinter; the large one that had done the real damage to the cockpit window, and had jammed itself into the back of the seat, between headrest and shoulder, millimetres from the back of his neck . . .

The seat was being modified, to give more neck protection.

Fowler had insisted that he be cared for in the small mano house, sometimes used by the Department for its returning wound ed. Fewer awkward questions to answer than if he'd gone home Fowler said. Dee had had to be pacified, and persuaded it wa for the best. No one else at Prossair was told, for the time being where he was. He doubted whether they ever would be. That wa not Fowler's way.

The door opened, and Logan entered. In a yellow lightweigh sweater and tight jeans, she looked good. "How's the invalid?" sh enquired brightly. "And how's the wounded wing?"

Pross waved his uninjured left arm at the window. "The sun

276

come out for me, the wing's going to be as good as new, I've been told, and you're looking your old self again."

"I've been on an eating binge. I never realised how hungry I really was." She sat on the edge of the bed. The green eyes looked full of mischief.

"What a pig," he said.

"Careful. You're vulnerable."

He stared at the bag she had brought with her. "Got your cannon in there?"

"Of course. Lal saved it."

The conversation died as they found themselves looking at each other awkwardly. Then Logan stood up, and went to the window.

"Thanks for giving me the blood." His eyes followed her. She had also visited him daily, he knew; but usually, he'd been seemingly immersed in a sea of pain and had barely been conscious. "And for coming to see me."

"What's some blood between friends? They shouldn't have told you ... either about the blood, or the visits."

"Why not?"

"I asked them not to."

"Why?"

"Do you always ask questions?"

"Only when I need answers."

She smiled, without looking at him. "Thanks for coming for me."

"As I said then, nothing would stop me."

"And nothing did," she said softly. She still wouldn't look at him. "Mabel says I went a little out of control at the site."

"I was out of it. I wouldn't know. What did you do?"

"Oh nothing much," she said lightly. "Nothing important. Well .. I can see you're doing fine, I've got to be going. I think your wife will be here soon. The chopper's due in."

Every day, Dee was picked up by helicopter from the airport. Not a Prossair ship, but one that Fowler had supplied.

"You ought to meet her," he said.

"In her place, I wouldn't want to."

"Why are you standing over there, Logan?"

"I feel safer."

"I've never heard such nonsense."

She turned, came back towards the bed. The green eyes looked down at him. She sat down once more.

"You're on edge, Logan. What is it?"

"Oh Pross," she said with a rueful smile. "Sometimes . . ." She leaned forward suddenly, and kissed him full on the lips. Then she stood up. "Now I really am going. I'll look in again tomorrow. I've got someone to sort out."

"Oh? Anyone I know?"

The sudden grin was now quite wicked. "A lady called Wendy Jones."

"Logan—"

"'Byee. Be good." And she was out the door before he could say more.

He thought he could hear her laughing, with somewhat indecent glee.

Fowler was in Winterbourne's office.

Winterbourne said, "I hope you've sorted out the mess, Fowler. I don't want any brickbats coming my way."

"Everything has been sorted out, Sir John," Fowler said, concealing the ever-present contempt he felt. "There will be no . . . official repercussions. Our man survived, and will by now have removed all evidence of Logan's presence in the ruins. His position with Wu has not been compromised. None of the troops he travelled with have survived."

"I do wish you had told me about all this before."

"You've got the report."

"Yes." Testily. "But *after* the event. I should be told when an operation, particularly one of such magnitude, is being initiated."

"You were kept informed, Sir John."

"Of the general picture, Fowler, but not of the details. The details, man. *I* am Head of this Department."

"The oversight was not intentional," Fowler lied smoothly. "More to the point no one except those involved knows we picked up the flight recorders months ago. The opposition still believes we're desperately searching; which is precisely the situation we desire. Equally no one knows we deliberately leaked the information on the Hammerhead night trials in Wales. We wanted to flush their teams out."

"I suppose," Winterbourne began grudgingly, "one must accept we have scored some bonus points." He paused, hating to admit that Fowler had again succeeded. He thought of something, decided to have a go at upsetting Fowler's seemingly unshakable self

278

control. "No one, did you say? Does that include Logan and ... er ... Pross?"

"Especially Logan and Pross," Fowler said calmly. He turned, and walked unhurriedly to the door.

"I'm not quite finished." The testiness was back in Winterbourne's voice.

Fowler paused, the epitome of patience.

"Who exactly is Hansen, or Schuler, or whatever he calls himself?" Winterbourne demanded.

"Who indeed," Fowler said mildly.

"Now look here, Fowler! Are you insinuating I cannot be trusted?"

But Fowler was gone.